Robin Hood's RETURN

Book III
THE ROBIN HOOD TRILOGY

OLIVIA LONGUEVILLE
J.C. PLUMMER

The Robin Hood Trilogy, Book 3: Robin Hood's Return
Copyright © 2021 Olivia Longueville and J. C. Plummer
ISBN-13: 978-1-947878-10-5 (Trade paper)
ISBN-13: 978-1-947878-11-2 (Kindle)
ISBN-13: 978-1-947878-12-9 (EPUB)
ISBN-13: 978-1-947878-13-6 (Audio)

This work includes both fictional and historical persons and events. The historical events follow the timeline of history. Our representations of real historical persons abide by the known facts of their lives. However, the passage of so many centuries has obscured much about these historical figures; therefore, the dialogue, opinions, and personalities of these long-dead people are the products of the authors' imagination.

Likewise, the fictional characters and events are the products of the authors' imagination, and any resemblance to actual persons, living or dead, or actual events, is purely coincidental.

The characters described in the Robin Hood ballads can be found in numerous fictional stories which have been written over the course of centuries. These characters are in the public domain. The authors have created their own original versions of these well-known characters, and any resemblance to actual persons, living or dead, is purely coincidental.

Cover design: Damonza.com
Interior design and formatting: Damonza.com

AngevinWorld.com

CONTENTS

For my parents, Nadezda and Viatcheslav,
who are always so supportive and interested
in the work I do as a writer.

– Olivia

For Kathleen and Lesley
in heartfelt appreciation
for their support and encouragement.

– J. C.

Acknowledgments:
Many thanks to our pre-readers and editors.

Special thanks to author and historian Sharon Bennett
Connolly, author of
**Defenders of the Norman Crown: Rise and
Fall of the Warenne Earls of Surrey.**

We are grateful for her invaluable help in our research on the
Earl and Countess of Surrey, Hamelin and Isabel de Warenne,
their children, and the fortresses of Conisbrough and Tickhill.
These important historical figures and places play crucial
roles in this book, and she provided wonderful details that
helped us bring this family and their impressive keep to life.

WILLIAM THE CONQUEROR'S DESCENDANTS

King William I (King of England, 1066-1087)
married Matilda of Flanders

Children (partial list):
Robert II (Duke of Normandy, 1087-1106)
William II "Rufus" (King of England, 1087-1100)
Henry I (King of England, 1100-1135)
Adela of Normandy

Henry I (King of England, 1100-1135)
married Matilda of Scotland

Children:
Matilda
William Adelin (d. 1120)

Adela of Normandy
married Stephen II, Count of Blois

Children (partial list):
Theobald (Count of Champagne & Blois)
* Stephen of Blois
(King of England, 1135-1154)

Matilda married
Geoffrey V, Count of Anjou

Children:
Henry II (King of England,
1154-1189)
Geoffrey, Count of Nantes
William FitzEmpress

---

* Stephen of Blois (King of
England, 1135-1154)
married Matilda of Boulogne

Children (partial list):
Eustace (d. 1153)
* William (Count of
Boulogne & Mortain,
Earl of Surrey, d. 1159)

Theobald (Count of Blois
& Champagne) married
Matilda of Carinthia

Children (partial list):
Henry I of Champagne
* Adela of Champagne

Henry II (King of England, 1154-1189)
married * Eleanor of Aquitaine

Children:
William (b. 1153 - d. 1156)
Henry the Young King (b. 1155 - d. 1183)
Matilda (b. 1156 - d. 1189)
* Richard (b. 1157 - d. 1199)
Geoffrey (b. 1158 - d. 1186)
Eleanor (b. 1162 - d. 1214)
Joan (b. 1165 - d. 1199)
* John (b. 1166 - d. 1216)

---

* Adela of Champagne
(Queen of France, 1164-1180, d. 1206)
married Louis VII, King of France

Child:
* Philippe II (King of France, 1180-1223)

---

* Historical figures who appear in
The Robin Hood Trilogy

FICTIONAL FAMILIES IN THE ROBIN HOOD TRILOGY

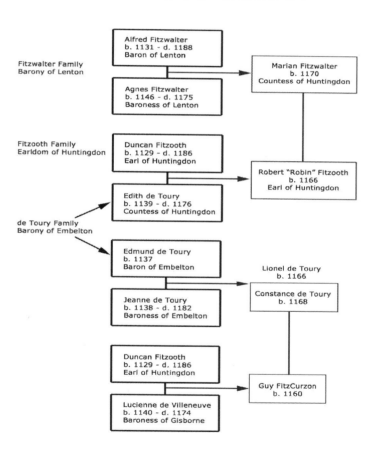

Fitzwalter Family
Barony of Lenton

Alfred Fitzwalter
b. 1131 - d. 1188
Baron of Lenton

Agnes Fitzwalter
b. 1146 - d. 1175
Baroness of Lenton

Marian Fitzwalter
b. 1170
Countess of Huntingdon

Fitzooth Family
Earldom of Huntingdon

Duncan Fitzooth
b. 1129 - d. 1186
Earl of Huntingdon

Edith de Toury
b. 1139 - d. 1176
Countess of Huntingdon

Robert "Robin" Fitzooth
b. 1166
Earl of Huntingdon

de Toury Family
Barony of Embelton

Edmund de Toury
b. 1137
Baron of Embelton

Jeanne de Toury
b. 1138 - d. 1182
Baroness of Embelton

Lionel de Toury
b. 1166

Constance de Toury
b. 1168

Duncan Fitzooth
b. 1129 - d. 1186
Earl of Huntingdon

Lucienne de Villeneuve
b. 1140 - d. 1174
Baroness of Gisborne

Guy FitzCurzon
b. 1160

CHAPTER 1
LIFE AFTER DEATH

25 January 1193, Embelton Castle, Northern England

"Marian, he's alive. Robin's alive."

Robin observed from the corridor outside the great hall of Embelton castle. He could barely restrain himself from rushing to Marian and telling her himself, but his experiences over the past few weeks had taught him that when people encounter a man who is supposed to be dead, they often either faint or drop to their knees. It was both distressing and oddly amusing, but he did not want Marian to swoon at his feet. He wanted to see her smiling and her eyes alight with joy and love.

His uncle Edmund and cousin Constance were standing in front of Marian as she sat near the roaring fire that warmed the great hall.

Edmund's brow creased in concern. "Marian, did you hear me? Robin is alive."

Marian stared up at him, frozen in place.

Constance placed a hand on Marian's shoulder. "It's true, Marian. I've seen him."

Robin stepped into the hall only to have Much pull him back.

"Lord Robin, wait. Let them talk to her first. She will faint if you go to her now," begged his loyal friend and servant.

1

Robin knew that Much was right, so he moved back into the corridor and watched the scene in the hall unfold.

Marian shakily rose to her feet and hoarsely replied, "No. I saw him die."

Edmund's expression softened in understanding. "He wasn't dead; he had fallen into a deep sleep, and he awoke the next day."

And then something happened that Robin had not expected.

His wife, the kind and well-mannered girl he had known since they were children, slapped Edmund's face and screamed, "Stop lying to me! Why are you doing this to me? Stop it!"

She raised her hand again, but Edmund caught her wrist before she could strike him a second time. With her other hand she hit him in the chest, and when he released his grip on her, she began to cry and pummel him with her fists.

"Marian, please stop! My father would never lie to you about something like this." Constance wrapped her arms around Marian's waist and tugged her away from Edmund.

Edmund pleaded with her, "Marian, he's not dead. He's here." He then looked at Robin in desperation.

At that point, no man could have stopped Robin as he strode across the hall towards his wife.

Marian's face was buried in her hands, and she was sobbing.

With Robin's approach, Edmund and Constance retreated.

"Marian." Robin spoke softly as he stood before her.

She stilled but did not look at him.

"Look at me, Marian."

Marian lowered her hands and stared at his boots. Her gaze slowly traveled up until she was finally looking into his eyes. In a reaction that Robin had seen again and again, she fell to her knees, as if she did not have the strength to remain standing.

At least she did not faint, he thought to himself. He dropped to his knees as well, facing her and cradling her hands.

"Marian, I've returned, and everything will be all right."

Her eyes had grown wide, and she was visibly trembling. She whispered, "I saw you die."

"No, Marian. I almost died, but I recovered. The truth of the matter is that you saved me." He let go of her hands and pulled off his tunic. He then loosened the neckline of his shirt to show her the scar at the center of his chest.

Her hand shook as she reached out and tentatively brushed her fingertips across the mark where Gisborne's dagger had pierced his skin.

"I don't understand." Her voice was still hushed.

"Your ring. Do you remember it? It was the ring that belonged to my mother before I gave it to you. When you broke our betrothal and returned it to me, I wore it on a chain around my neck and over my heart. Your ring stopped Gisborne's dagger from plunging too deeply into my chest. Your ring protected my heart."

Robin reached into a pouch tied to his belt and retrieved the ring. Marian was still staring at him in disbelief as he grasped her hand and restored the ring to its rightful place on her finger.

"Marian, promise me you will always wear my ring. As my wife, you are forever joined to me, and this ring is a symbol of our marriage." Robin stood and helped Marian to her feet.

At last, he drew her into his arms and held her. The anticipation of this moment had sustained him during the weeks of his recovery and the many long months that had followed. Robin silently vowed to never let her go. He would love and protect her for the rest of his life.

Marian stared in wonder at Robin as he laughed and joked with Edmund. His pale blue eyes twinkled with merriment. It was an expression she had often seen during those happy times before the arrival of Sheriff de Argentan and the murder of her father. His wheat-colored hair was longer than she recalled, and he still wore the short beard he had grown while crusading in the Holy Land. He looked as handsome as she remembered, except that he was thinner than she had ever seen him.

It had been several hours since his miraculous appearance in the great hall of Embelton's keep, and they were now enjoying a celebratory meal. She was seated between Robin and Constance while Edmund and Tuck were across the table.

She glanced at Brother Tuck, who had been invited to join them. Although the Knight Templar had been startled by Robin's unexpected arrival, he readily accepted the fact that Robin was alive. As a middle-aged knight who had spent most of his adult life in the Holy Land, he spoke reverently of the many miracles he had witnessed over the years, which he attributed to the holiness of the land where Jesus had once walked. To him, Robin's astonishing survival was further testimony to the sacred nature of Outremer.

Marian had to concede that Robin's amazing return from the land of the dead was beyond anything she could have dreamt, so it was undoubtedly a miracle. How many prayers had she offered to God over the past year, begging for Robin's return? They were beyond numbering. Night after night she had lain awake and imagined different scenarios where Robin did not die: where she had seen Gisborne creeping up behind Robin in time to warn him, where he turned sooner and successfully fought off Gisborne, and a hundred other alternatives that would have saved him.

She chastised herself ruthlessly: Why had she departed Acre so quickly? Why didn't she stay longer? She could have been there with him when he awoke the next day from his deep sleep.

Instead, she had run away and endured months of grief and torment.

Another thought occurred to her: she had nearly killed Gisborne for murdering Robin! And if she had slain him, not only would she be guilty of killing him for something he hadn't done, but Guy would not have been there to save her and Robbie from the sheriff's dungeons.

It had been a sennight since Gisborne had helped her, along with Robbie and Tuck, escape from Nottingham Castle. They had immediately left for Embelton, arriving after several days of difficult travel through cold and blustery weather.

Shaking her head, as if that would clear the jumbled thoughts crowding her mind, she focused on Robin's story.

"…Then I pulled back my hood, and Uncle Edmund collapsed on the floor in front of the queen mother. I think it's the first time I've ever seen Queen Eleanor speechless." Robin laughed. "But now that I've traveled to Huntingdon and Locksley, I've become accustomed to picking people up off the floor."

Marian watched as Robin gave a tidbit of food to a small reddish-brown dog that he had brought back with him from the Holy Land.

Her voice unsteady, she asked, "What happened when Sheriff de Argentan and Gisborne learned you had survived their attack?"

Robin grinned mischievously. "The sheriff doesn't know yet. I've sworn the people of Locksley to secrecy. As soon as we return to Nottingham, we will go visit the sheriff. I'm looking forward to seeing Argentan's face when I make my first appearance at the castle. Gisborne's too."

Marian eyed Constance and questioned, "Do they know about Lionel?"

Frowning at the thought of her treacherous brother, Constance acknowledged, "Father and Robin both know what happened."

"When we arrived in Locksley, we learned about Lionel's betrayal," Edmund growled. "We lured Constance away from the castle with a story of a sick servant at Locksley, and then we made haste to come here. Lionel doesn't know about Robin yet."

Robin interjected, "Nothing was more important than coming

here to find you, Marian." He smiled lovingly at her and clasped her hand as it rested on the table.

"We will deal with Lionel, Sheriff de Argentan, and Gisborne when we return to Nottingham," added Edmund.

"Perhaps we should stay here," suggested Marian. "It's not safe to go back to Nottingham." She swallowed nervously and moved her hand to her lap. Looking down at the table, she continued in a small voice. "I might be arrested."

"Nonsense," Robin dismissively replied. "Edmund told me what happened, and Queen Eleanor signed a proclamation declaring you innocent of murder since you acted in self-defense."

Edmund nodded. "I was there, and as an eyewitness, I assured the queen that the Earl of Bedford was running towards you with his sword drawn when your arrow struck him in the neck. You will not be held accountable for his death."

Marian was relieved to know that she was no longer an outlaw. Changing the subject, she inquired, "What about Lionel? What will you do?"

Edmund sighed. "I haven't decided. I have informed my steward and the guards that he is not allowed to enter Embelton's bailey or keep unless he is with me."

They resumed eating, and Constance tapped on Marian's arm, whispering, "When are you going to tell him about Robbie?"

Marian responded in an equally hushed voice, "I will tell him tomorrow. Please keep Robbie with you tonight."

Constance opened her mouth to object, but instead, she nodded in resignation and picked up a piece of bread.

25 January 1193, The Royal Palace, Paris, France

Ambroise de Limours, Count de Montlhéry, awaited the arrival of King Philippe as he stood in the monarch's sumptuous chambers. Increasingly impatient, he strolled to the vestibule that led to a balcony overlooking the Seine. Stepping out into the crisp, wintry air, he hoped it would cool his temper and calm his ever-increasing frustration with the course of his life.

For over thirty years, he had faithfully served the dowager queen, Adela, and her son, Philippe. During that time, he had worked many miracles for the French royal family. In return, he had been granted a lofty title, wealth, and immense power as the young king's closest advisor.

But now, when victory was within his grasp, it seemed to be slipping away. Just two sons of Henry Plantagenet remained. There was also a young grandson, but he posed no threat.

His scheme to eliminate the Plantagenets had seen great success in the early years. Henry the Younger, Prince Geoffrey, and King Henry had all met their fates according to the plans he had crafted so many years ago.

But every effort to kill Richard had been thwarted. There had been several attempts at poisoning, an ambush in the streets of Acre, and scores of mercenaries stationed along the ports of Toulouse, Provence, Genoa, and Pisa. Yet the wily Richard had avoided capture by the agents of King Philippe only to fall into the hands of the Holy Roman Emperor, Heinrich.

It was the only royal family in Europe over which neither Philippe nor Montlhéry had any control or connections.

It wasn't supposed to have happened like this. Philippe had been enraged that Montlhéry's plan had failed. The king had fully expected to take Richard prisoner in accordance with their elaborate kidnapping plot.

Leaning on the balustrade, Montlhéry gazed out into a black void. The moon and stars were hidden behind a heavy layer of clouds, and a few snowflakes drifted past him, as fleeting and fragile as the rapidly diminishing opportunities he would have to accomplish his life's purpose.

He briefly wondered whether all his planning and his years of work would come to nothing.

Angrily slapping the stone railing, he found the sting to his palm oddly comforting. He had experienced too much pain and disappointment in his life. Now was the time for him to triumph. For nearly forty years, he had waited. He was close. So close. This was *his* time. This was *his* moment. No one would stand in his way: not Prince John or King Richard, not even King Philippe.

He would take the throne of England as Philippe's vassal, or he would die trying. And if his fate was to die in the effort, then so be it. He vowed he would not go to hell alone; he would personally introduce to the devil all those who had failed him.

"Ambroise!"

The King of France was calling him, so he assumed his most pleasant expression and returned to the main chamber of Philippe's elaborate suite of rooms.

The French monarch was waiting for him, impatience clearly etched on his face. Philippe had celebrated the 27th anniversary of his birth the previous August, and he had recently begun the twelfth year of his rule. He was tall and thin with a prominent nose, pale complexion, and dark hair.

"Yes, Sire?" The count dutifully dropped to one knee and rose, striving to hide his discomfort as his aging joints protested.

"Now that John has returned to England, we must convince Emperor Heinrich to relinquish custody of Richard to me."

"Sire, as much as I tremble at the thought of disappointing you, we have nothing to offer Heinrich that will tempt him to surrender such a valuable prisoner. We have no influence over any of the German princes, and Richard is closely guarded."

Philippe became thoughtful. "Many of the princes are unhappy with Heinrich. Perhaps we can use this to our advantage."

Montlhéry sighed and reluctantly confessed, "Although many German princes despise Heinrich, I fear their antipathy towards

France would prevent them from helping you. Their dislike of you is, of course, due to jealously over your brilliant achievements and glorious person."

"True," agreed Philippe. "But at least we now have the youngest Plantagenet under our control. He has sworn fealty to me for all the Angevin lands and Normandy. John is in high spirits. He should arrive in England any day now, and he will demand that the English Great Council declare him king. With the uncertainty of Richard's future, perhaps they will do it."

"That's unlikely, but it would further our goals. I can easily arrange a fatal accident for John, but I cannot take the throne of England as your vassal as long as Richard is still alive. The Lionheart is beyond our reach for now."

"If I can wield enough power and influence over John, then putting you on the throne would serve no purpose." Philippe eyed him intently.

Montlhéry stiffened and fought to suppress the angry words that leapt into his mind. He had spent years advising Philippe and molding him into a cunning, successful king. He deserved his support. Yet, he was not surprised at the king's comment. Ever since their grand strategy to kill Henry Plantagenet and all of his sons had stalled after the crowning of Richard, he had worried that Philippe would abandon the plan to put him on the throne of England.

Affecting a calm he did not feel, he replied, "As always, your assessment of the situation is sensible and insightful, Sire. However, I will remind you that John will see himself as an independent king. His loyalty will be to himself, regardless of whether he has pledged fealty to you. He cannot be trusted. On the other hand, my loyalty to you is absolute. Do you doubt this?"

After a pause, Philippe pointedly changed the subject. "Are you ready to implement the next part of your strategy in England?"

"Yes, Sire. I will take your leave and proceed with our plans." Montlhéry genuflected and left.

26 January 1193, Embelton Castle

When Robin awoke early the next day, he was disappointed to find that Marian was gone, and his only companion in her large, comfortable bed was his dog. He quickly dressed and went searching for her.

He located her in the great hall where she was seated near the fire with Edmund at her side. They both had dour expressions on their faces, and it gave Robin pause. He would have hoped to see Marian's face aglow with the same happiness as the night before, when they had finally been alone and able to reunite as husband and wife. He took a moment to admire her beauty; perhaps she was thinner than he recollected, but her bewitching green eyes, pale blonde hair, and exquisite loveliness was just as he had remembered during their long separation.

"Good morning," Robin proclaimed with a smile as he entered the great hall and joined them.

There was a brief, awkward silence before Edmund and Marian both murmured a greeting.

Robin was growing increasingly alarmed, especially as Marian seemed unable to look him in the face.

Edmund stood and cleared his throat. "Robin, there is something very important that we have to tell you. Please, sit down."

"What is this about?" Robin inquired cautiously. "I think I would prefer to stand—unless someone else is about to rise from the grave." His attempt at humor fell flat.

"No, nothing like that," acknowledged Edmund. "Are you familiar with canon law regarding clandestine marriages?"

"If I remember correctly, that's when two peasants cannot afford to pay a priest, or their families object to their relationship, so they just declare themselves married."

Edmund replied, "That's not entirely accurate. A clandestine marriage is when two people announce their intention to marry in front of witnesses, and then they live together as man and wife.

And it doesn't matter whether you are a peasant or noble. All people abide by this teaching."

"I see," said Robin, although he didn't really understand the point of this particular lesson in church law.

Marian was still oddly silent and staring at her lap.

Edmund continued, "I'm not sure you appreciate what I'm trying to tell you. After you rescued Marian from the castle, do you remember where you went?"

"Of course. We went to Saint Mary's Church and waited for the other outlaws to join us."

Marian's head jerked up and irritation flashed in her eyes. Evidently, he had said something wrong.

She crossly demanded, "Don't you remember what happened? I would have thought it meant something to you!"

Robin rubbed the short bristles on his chin as he reflected on that night. He had definitely said the wrong thing. Suddenly, he realized something. "Of course I remember, we promised to marry after I was restored to my titles and lands. That's the night I gave you my mother's ring." His heart sank as he surmised that she must still be angry with him for breaking his promise to marry her as soon as Richard decreed his innocence in the matter of her father's murder. After he had been wounded in Acre, she had forgiven him, so why bring this up now?

Edmund then explained, "Don't you understand? You made a promise, a sacred vow, in the presence of the priest of Saint Mary's that you would marry her. And later that night, you and Marian..." Edmund's voice drifted off, and he glanced away as he was clearly too embarrassed to say more.

Robin was mortified that Edmund seemed to know about his indiscretion with Marian that night. Why would she tell him something so personal? He looked at her and noticed a steely intensity in her gaze.

"Robin," she said, "we promised to marry, and then we were

together as man and wife. We entered into a clandestine marriage on that night: the 8th of September, in the year of our Lord 1188. We've been married in the eyes of the church for over four years."

Robin countered, "But King Richard married us after Gisborne attacked me. That was our wedding."

Marian stood and faced him. "I only agreed to that ceremony because I thought you were dying, and there wasn't time to tell you about our clandestine marriage."

Robin spun around and paced back and forth in front of the grand hearth. He always found it easier to think when he was moving. Abruptly, he stopped. "What does it matter? Regardless of whether we married four years ago or one year ago, the important thing is that we are married now."

To Robin's surprise, Marian beckoned Constance, who entered the hall carrying a small boy. And then Robin realized that perhaps he should have sat down, as Edmund had suggested.

"This is why the date of our marriage matters," cried Marian.

"Mama!" The little boy squirmed energetically in Constance's arms, and she set him on the floor. He ran as fast as his legs would carry him to Marian, and she knelt to pick him up.

Robin felt the room shift, and he now had a better understanding of why people kept collapsing at his feet. He dropped heavily into the nearest chair and stared open-mouthed at Marian and the fair-haired toddler in her arms.

Marian beamed at him and announced, "This is our son. I named him Robin, but we all call him Robbie. He was born nine months after our clandestine marriage. For this reason, the date of our marriage is vitally important."

She then told their son, "Your papa is here."

The boy frowned. "Papa's in heaven."

"I was wrong, Robbie," Marian admitted. "He's here. This is your papa."

Robin watched in awe as Marian placed his son on his lap. As he held his son for the first time, his heart overflowed with emotion. Observing Robbie's pale blue eyes and light blonde hair, he could see traces of both him and Marian in the miracle of his son.

His son gazed up at him and declared, "Papa came back from heaven."

Several tears leaked from Robin's eyes, and he grinned with delight. Pressing his lips against the top of Robbie's head, he vowed, "I'm here now, and I will always take care of you and your mother."

Jack jumped onto Robin's lap, eager to sniff at the little stranger in his master's arms. Robbie squealed with delight at the sight of the dog.

"This is my dog, Jack," explained Robin.

"Can I have him, Papa? Please?"

Robin was so overwhelmed that he could no longer speak. Instead, he nodded and hugged the little boy tightly, closing his eyes to hold back the tears that were blurring his vision and rolling down his cheeks.

In his mind, a shadow loomed. He didn't want to think about his indiscretions in Poitou and his brief marriage to Blanche. He had unknowingly committed bigamy. How could he ever tell Marian the truth? He pushed such thoughts to the furthest, darkest part of his mind as he focused on the joy of the moment.

CHAPTER 2
SHROVE TUESDAY

9 February 1193, Nottingham Castle

Sir Guy of Gisborne stood with the sheriff on a small balcony overlooking the inner bailey of the great fortress of Nottingham. A large crowd had gathered for the celebration of Shrove Tuesday, the last opportunity for the people to engage in merriment before Ash Wednesday and the season of Lent.

Even the chilly morning air and overcast skies could not dampen the enthusiasm for this annual festival, which featured sports, games, and a grand feast. For the first time since his arrival in Nottingham four and a half years ago, the sheriff had agreed to host the festivities at the castle. In previous years, he had been loathe to spend the money on such frivolous endeavors. However, this year was different; Prince John was making a serious bid for the throne, and he needed the support of the public.

"People of Nottingham!" cried Argentan. He waited until the crowd quieted before resuming. "Today, Prince John has provided the funds to sponsor this day of merry-making."

Guy scoffed. More likely the day was funded by the excessive taxes the sheriff had diligently collected over the past few years. As it was, the sheriff was charging entry fees for many of the contests to recoup the expenses he had incurred.

Argentan continued, "This morning, in the outer bailey, teams from Carentune and Lenton will compete to see which village is best at camp ball." The people roared enthusiastically.

Guy mused that camp ball was little more than a mêlée without weapons, as the opposing teams attempted to move a ball into a goal while fighting off their opponents.

When the crowd settled, the sheriff announced, "At midday, there will be cockfighting, games of dice, and bowling in the inner bailey, while the outer bailey is cleared and prepared for the highlight of the day: the archery contest. Only nobles or men sponsored by their liege lord will be allowed to pay the entry fee and participate. And the winner will receive this silver arrow!" Argentan held up a small silver-plated arrow for everyone to see. It was much shorter than a standard arrow, but the silver shimmered impressively even in the dim light of an overcast day.

The throng of people, a mixture of peasants and local nobles from Nottinghamshire, reacted with astonishment at the sight of such a valuable and unique artifact.

"Finally, a grand feast will be held. Nobles and knights are welcome to join me in the great hall, while everyone else will be served here, in the bailey."

He emphasized, "Prince John is providing the prizes, the ale, and the feast. He has always championed the people of England, and especially the people of Nottinghamshire. While King Richard…"

The sheriff deliberately paused to allow a few of his paid men, who were mingling in the crowd, to boo and hiss at the name of the king. Unfortunately for the sheriff, the people seemed outraged that these men were not showing respect for the Lionheart. Guy contemplated the enduring popularity of the king. It was surprising considering the concerted efforts by the sheriff and King Philippe to spread rumors during the past year to besmirch Richard's reputation.

Frowning in disappointment, the sheriff insisted, "Prince John has been here, in England, protecting us from the dishonest men appointed by King Richard to rule England during his absence. King Richard has neglected England and spent his treasury to fund a foreign war. Perhaps if he had rescued Jerusalem, it would have been worth it. But he failed to win the war, he failed to liberate Jerusalem from the infidels, and now he has failed to return home."

Argentan subtly nodded at Guy, who dutifully stepped forward and shouted, "God Bless good Prince John!"

Only a few nobles echoed Guy's call, and Argentan scowled at the people's hesitancy to applaud John. He added, "I have received word that King Richard is likely dead, and that John will be crowned king soon."

Again he signaled to Guy, who called out, "God Bless King John!"

But now the people were distressed and anxiously talking to one another about the sheriff's stunning announcement.

At that moment, a familiar voice rang out, and Guy pivoted to see his wife, Constance, and her father join them on the balcony.

Holding his hand aloft to attract the attention of the crowd, Edmund proclaimed, "I am Edmund de Toury, the Baron of Embelton. I was in London when news of King Richard arrived. Our king is not dead. He is in Germany conducting important negotiations with the Holy Roman Emperor, Heinrich."

The people cheered.

Lowering his voice, Edmund faced Argentan and said, "Do not be so eager to announce John's coronation. I assure you that unless Richard's cold, dead body is delivered to the Great Council, they will never put John on the throne. As long as the hope of Richard's return endures, John's ambitions will be thwarted."

Argentan sketched a short bow to Edmund, as Guy briefly dropped to one knee.

Guy gazed at Constance, searching her face for clues as to her sudden, unexplained absence. He was relieved to see that her face was shining with joy, and that she smiled warmly at him. Her tall, thin form was elegantly dressed in an expensive blue bliaut with fur-lined trumpet sleeves—attire befitting her status as a wealthy heiress. Her long face was framed by hair as black as a raven's wing, and much of it was braided and coiled around her head like a crown. Over the months of their marriage, he had grown enchanted by her striking appearance.

The sheriff's gruff voice jolted him out of his reverie. "Gisborne, signal to the guards to send the crowd to the outer bailey for the camp ball match."

While Argentan stared sullenly at Edmund, Lionel arrived and smugly commented, "At last we are reunited, Father. Have you come to watch me win the archery contest?"

The arrival of his wife's duplicitous brother dismayed Guy. With his wavy blonde hair and blue eyes, he looked nothing like his sister. Instead, he appeared to be a younger, thinner version of his stout, middle-aged father.

Despite the flash of anger in his eyes, Edmund affected a calm demeanor as he replied, "I've entered my own man in the contest."

Lionel grinned. "I'm sorry you've wasted the entry fee; you know that few men can best me at archery."

"It's my money to waste," Edmund remarked. "I certainly wasted enough on ransom payments for a son who is a liar and a cheat."

"Oh, my!" exclaimed Argentan. "A family dispute! How entertaining. Can we continue this near the fire? Perhaps those dirty peasants in the bailey are unaffected by the cold, but I've had enough."

"Constance and I have only just arrived from Embelton. We plan to retire to our chambers to rest until the archery contest." With that, Edmund gestured for Constance to join him as they left the balcony.

Guy was disappointed that he had been unable to speak to Constance, and he wistfully watched them go. Nevertheless, he was gratified to see her glance back at him as she left.

꿍

Guy stood in the sheriff's tower room and endured the taunts of his master. He was alone with the sheriff following Edmund and Constance's departure to their chambers. Lionel had also conveniently disappeared. The wooden shutter on one of the tower's large windows was ajar, and he could hear distant, muted shouting from the camp ball match being held in the outer bailey.

The sheriff was in his mid-fifties, and his thinning hair had transitioned to mostly white over the past year. He was always clothed in somber black garb, as if he were perpetually in mourning. His wiry build gave him the appearance of a man of action, while his dark, piercing gaze was intense and unsettling.

"You're a fool," proclaimed Argentan. "A ridiculous, idiotic fool. I saw the look on your face when that woman appeared. What kind of spell has she cast upon you? This is worse than your infatuation with that viper, Marian."

"My lord—"

"Be quiet and listen to me, you pathetic excuse for a man. How many times have I told you that these women will poison your life? I've warned you over and over, yet you look at that horse-faced wife of yours as if she were a precious jewel."

Guy silently fumed. Although Constance's appearance was not beautiful in a traditional sense, there was something about her kind nature and intelligent conversation that he found unexpectedly alluring. He recalled their discussion in the chapel after he had mistakenly killed Osmund, the Locksley blacksmith...

"Are you listening to me?" yelled the sheriff.

"Of course, my lord. I always attend to your every word most diligently."

Argentan's eyes narrowed at the hint of sarcasm in his captain's voice. "Careful, Gisborne. I'm still not completely convinced of your innocence in Marian's escape. I know Lionel believes the Knight Templar orchestrated everything, but I'm not so easily persuaded." "My lord, if there is something you need from me, please ask. Otherwise, I should help oversee the activities in the bailey in case the crowd becomes unruly." He was desperate to leave and fearful that the wrong word or facial expression might reveal his complicity in Marian's escape. He hoped that Marian and her son were safely ensconced in Embelton's keep. Perhaps he could ask Constance at this evening's feast.

The sheriff continued his rant. "You need to face the truth: any day, Edmund might petition for an annulment of your marriage on behalf of his daughter. He only consented to the match to keep his son alive. He now knows the kidnapping was a ruse. You will lose Locksley, just as I have lost my access to the de Toury fortune. Our only hope is to claim that the marriage cannot be dissolved due to consummation, but with Edmund's resources, he could simply bribe a bishop to overlook that."

Guy sighed. Unbeknownst to the sheriff, the marriage had never been consummated in accordance with an agreement between Edmund and Guy. Even so, obtaining an annulment after eight months of marriage would not be easy, especially considering how Constance had provided an alibi for him on the night he helped Marian escape. He inwardly winced at the memory of Constance's mortification when her brother had burst into his bedchamber, seeking to blame him for Marian's escape, only to find his sister in Guy's bed. Despite her embarrassment, she bravely insisted that the two of them had shared a bed all night.

Lionel could prevent an annulment of the marriage, and Guy admitted to himself that he did not want the marriage to end.

"Again, you are not listening to me," thundered Argentan.

Guy realized that his thoughts had drifted, and he did not know what the sheriff had been saying. Eager to escape, he said, "My lord, my mind is filled with the pressing duties that await me. Please grant me leave." He genuflected to the sheriff and turned to go.

"Did I ever tell you about my wife?"

"My lord?" Guy was momentarily stunned at this unexpected revelation, and he again faced the sheriff. "Do you mean the daughter of the former Baron de Argentan?"

"Heavens, no," dismissed the sheriff. "That wasn't a real marriage; it was only a means to an end since I needed a Norman title as an entrée into the English court. I'm talking about the woman I married in my youth. Unlike most women, she is respectable and intelligent, a noblewoman without equal."

Guy's brow creased in confusion. "I've never heard you mention this wife. Where is she?"

"I will be reunited with her soon."

"Why have you kept this a secret?" Guy cautiously inquired.

"Soon everything will be made clear to you; you will meet her and understand why these other women, Marian and Constance, are vipers. Never forget that most women only care about their own whims and desires. They will betray you at the first opportunity if it benefits them. My wife is the exception, of course. She's the only woman I've ever met who was worth knowing."

Guy struggled to comprehend why the sheriff was revealing this to him, and he was intrigued by the mystery of this hitherto unknown wife.

"You are dismissed." The sheriff abruptly ended their conversation, and Guy wondered if his secretive master regretted his unusual moment of candor.

◈

The clouds had thinned, but the air was still brisk as everyone gathered in the outer bailey of Nottingham Castle for the highlight of the Shrove Tuesday festivities: the archery competition.

Constance and her father approached a hastily constructed platform located on one side of the wide expanse of the bailey. It was centered along the field and near the wall that separated the inner and outer baileys of the great fortress. The sheriff's throne-like chair had been brought from his tower room so that he could preside over the contest. On a small table adjacent to his chair, the silver arrow rested on a velvet cushion. Guy stood guard behind the table and next to Argentan's throne.

Edmund had arranged for additional chairs to be brought to the dais so they could join Argentan during the contest. After she was seated, Constance tried to catch Guy's attention, but he seemed distracted. She took a moment to admire her handsome husband. He was perhaps the tallest man she had ever met, which suited her just fine. She liked having to look up at him, since she had often towered over her suitors; obsequious men who were eager to marry the daughter of one of England's wealthiest barons.

Guy was not only tall, but his shoulder length, chestnut colored hair, angular features, and aquiline nose made him uniquely attractive. And his pale blue eyes were both distinctive and oddly familiar to her.

Disappointed that Guy seemed oblivious to her presence on the dais, she sighed and pulled her fur-lined cloak snugly around her shoulders. Lent was early this year, so the day was uncomfortably cold. She turned her attention to her father as he inspected the little silver arrow, which was the length of two hands.

"This is a generous prize, Sheriff de Argentan," commented Edmund. "I'm surprised that you are willing to give away such a valuable item."

Argentan responded, "I've seen your son with a bow. He's quite talented. I have no doubt that he will prevail over the other men who have been allowed to enter."

"Allowed to enter? What does that mean?" Constance questioned. She immediately regretted joining the conversation when the sheriff stared at her, his eyes glittering with undisguised hate.

Argentan elaborated, "We are here to raise the spirits of the people before the drudgery of Lent descends upon us all. More importantly, this entire spectacle has been staged to promote Prince John. The people will soon need to accept John as their king."

"But Lent is not drudgery, it's a solemn time of repentance and preparation for the sacrificial death and glorious resurrection of our Savior," countered Constance.

The sheriff had the temerity to laugh.

Edmund asked, "Don't you believe in the resurrection? Or, is it the repentance of sins that you disdain so casually?"

Constance noticed that Guy was now quietly attending to every word of the conversation.

Eyeing Edmund, Argentan sneered, "You are welcome to believe in dead men rising from the grave, but I will keep my opinion to myself. The last thing I need is for you to complain to the local bishop that I lack the piety to be sheriff."

"Look, Father!" cried Constance. "They're ready to begin the archery contest."

On the field before them, there were eighteen men. Most of them were wearing heavy, hooded cloaks against the bitter cold, and Constance readily recognized Lionel, as he was wearing the same style of fur-lined cloak as her own.

She despaired of ever understanding why her brother had staged his own kidnapping to extort money from their father to fund Prince John's schemes.

As the contest commenced, the men divided into three groups of six as they faced the three targets. The targets were made of white fabric anchored to small stacks of bundled straw. A red circle was painted near the center of each target, and hand carts were positioned behind the targets to prevent them from tipping. Each group moved forward, drew and released their arrows at the targets. The man with the poorest score from each group was eliminated.

Constance closely monitored Lionel and Robin as they advanced from one round to the next.

She leaned towards Edmund and whispered, "Father—"

"Yes?"

"I'm worried. Robin is not doing that well."

Edmund chuckled and responded in a hushed voice, "Would you have him raise suspicions by showing his true ability? He is doing just well enough to advance to the next round."

"That's clever. I had not thought of that." Relieved that all was going as planned, she searched the crowd for Marian, who was standing with a group of women from Locksley and wearing a hooded cloak to hide her identity.

❧

With his bow tucked under one arm, Robin puffed warm air into his cupped hands to ward off the chill of the day. He was struggling to keep his hood up to hide his face. A stiff wind could reveal his identity before he was ready. Fortunately, Edmund had instructed the judge to place the targets to the north of Argentan's platform. This would allow right-handed archers to stand with their backs to the sheriff as they endeavored to strike the targets.

He also needed to keep his back to Lionel whenever he had a turn at the targets. There was no way to draw his bow and take aim with his face completely hidden by a hood. Luckily, Lionel had insisted on using the target nearest the platform. Lionel's eagerness to be seen by Edmund and the sheriff had facilitated Robin's stealthy progression in the contest.

Many in the crowd had recognized him, but Marian and the outlaws were standing amongst the people and encouraging them to remain silent about his presence.

He watched Lionel take aim. His cousin was a talented archer, but he had never devoted himself to the rigorous training that would have taken him to the level of champion. Robin frowned as he considered that he had had few opportunities to practice over the past six months.

Finally, it was only the two of them remaining, and it was time for Robin to start winning more decisively.

Lionel's next attempt successfully found the center of his target, and he began to celebrate his win even before Robin had taken his turn.

Robin took aim, and his arrow also struck the center of his target. The judge called it a draw and ordered the archers to back up ten paces before trying again.

Once more, both Lionel and Robin's arrows found the center of their targets, and Lionel was becoming agitated that he hadn't yet won the contest.

When Robin realized that Lionel was straining to get a better look at him, he pulled his hood around his face.

"Who are you? What's your name?" shouted Lionel as they backed up another ten paces.

Altering his voice, he replied, "Robert is my name."

"Where did you train?" Lionel stepped closer, and Robin feared his ruse would be discovered.

"Archers," hollered the judge, "prepare your next attempt. Everyone is cold and hungry, and we are eager to begin the feast."

Huffing in irritation, Lionel aimed and released his arrow. It struck to the left of the red circle, and surprised murmuring rippled through the assembled crowd.

Lionel was stunned that his arrow had missed the center. "Wait!" he called to the judge. "I need to do that again." He indignantly pointed at Robin. "This man purposefully distracted me as I was taking aim."

Robin gazed at Lionel in disbelief. It was a bald faced lie.

"Ask him! If Robert is a man of good character, he will confess the truth and allow me to try again." Lionel stared at him expectantly, and Robin wondered if he truly believed that an opponent would meekly allow him another turn. He tugged the edges of his hood forward, anxious to maintain his anonymity.

The spectators were unimpressed with Lionel's demand to be given an unfair second chance, and they yelled at the judge.

"It's not true!"

"The other man is innocent!"

Robin grinned within the shadow of his hood. He decided he would take aim at Lionel's target while standing even further away. If his arrow struck the center of the red, there would be no argument over who had won.

The crowd grew silent as Robin notched his arrow and drew the bow string. The world around him faded away until the target in the distance was all he saw. A gust of wind rose from his left, and he hesitated, waiting for the air to settle. Then he held his breath, prayed that God would guide his arrow, and released it.

Robin observed the arrow as it flew across the ground, and he knew his aim had been true.

His arrow landed securely in the middle of the target, and the people roared with approval. He could hear Lionel shouting that it hadn't been fair, but the boisterous cheers of the crowd overwhelmed his voice.

Eyeing the platform, Robin could see that Argentan was on his feet, angrily gesturing and insisting that Lionel be allowed to try again.

The people gathered around Robin as he strode to the dais to collect his prize. Still hiding his face within his hood, he stood below the sheriff's perch.

The crowd quieted.

"Sheriff de Argentan, this man cheated by distracting me," whined Lionel, who was now standing near Robin and pointing at him. "I demand that I be allowed another try."

"Lionel, stop embarrassing yourself and your family," admonished Edmund. "I'm ashamed of you! You missed, and this man won fairly."

From within the shadow of his hood, Robin glanced up at Argentan, who was studying him intently.

"Is this your man, Embelton?" the sheriff asked.

"Yes," replied Edmund.

Argentan peered down at Robin. "I'm not sure this was a fair contest. Lionel says this man played a dirty trick in order to win."

Edmund scanned the crowd and questioned, "Did anyone see this man deliberately distract the other competitor? Step forward without fear. We only want the truth."

Silence reigned in the bailey.

"Sheriff, my man won fair and square. You must give him the prize," insisted Edmund.

A fuming Argentan watched as Robin circled to the rear of the platform and mounted the rickety stairs. After all this time, he was about to face his nemesis, but this time, he would have the upper hand.

The sheriff snatched the silver arrow from its velvet pillow, and he was clutching it so tightly that Robin was certain he was desperate to find some excuse to keep it instead of giving it to the winner of the contest.

Robin stood in front of Argentan and savored the moment. Recalling the engraved motto on Gisborne's sword, Robin announced, "From shadows to glory, I am immortal, and my kingdom awaits."

Argentan paled and sputtered, "What? What did you say?"

Robin pulled back his hood. "I have returned from the shadows, Sheriff de Argentan."

In a most gratifying reaction, Argentan gasped, dropped the silver arrow, placed his hand over his heart, and stumbled backwards.

Robin felt someone draw near to him, and he was pleased that Marian had joined him on the platform.

Argentan stared at him, wide-eyed, and his face drained of all color. He kept backing away from Robin until he collided with

Edmund, who grabbed his elbow and led him to his large chair, where the sheriff sat heavily, his mouth agape.

Robin chuckled. "It's been too long, Argentan. I won't pretend to be happy to see you, although I am enjoying your inability to speak."

He glanced at Gisborne. The tall knight was clutching the back of the sheriff's throne as if it were the only way he could keep from collapsing in a heap at Robin's feet.

"You...you." The sheriff stuttered.

"Yes, it's me. Alive and well, thank you for asking."

Argentan shook his head. "You're dead." He then leapt to his feet and yelled at the crowd, "This man is an imposter! The Earl of Huntingdon is dead."

Edmund responded in an equally loud voice, "This is my nephew, Robin Fitzooth, the Earl of Huntingdon, Lord of Locksley, and our beloved hero, Robin Hood. He was injured in the Holy Land but did not die. Look for yourself. You will recognize him."

Robin picked up the small silver arrow and faced the crowd, smiling and holding his prize aloft. In response, the people cheered and clapped.

It was good to be home.

CHAPTER 3
THE QUEEN'S WISDOM

28 February 1193, Oxford

The Great Council, led by Queen Eleanor and Walter de Coutances, the Archbishop of Rouen and chief justiciar, had summoned the nobility of England to Oxford in response to the crisis of King Richard's capture in Germany.

Robin had traveled with Edmund and a sullen, indignant Lionel to Oxford. They stood in the great hall and listened with growing alarm to the news of the increasingly dangerous state of the land. England was teetering on a knife's edge. Civil war loomed, and rumors that a fleet of Flemish mercenaries would soon invade led to a call to arms along the coast facing Flanders.

Upon his return from Paris, Prince John had demanded to be crowned king. He had insisted that Richard was dead. The council had flatly refused him, primarily due to Robin's report of the king's capture, which reassured them that Richard was alive. An enraged John took control of the castles at Windsor and Wallingford and garrisoned them with Welsh and Flemish mercenaries.

Queen Eleanor was adamant that her beloved Richard was still alive, and she insisted that all the nobility of England renew their oaths of fealty to him. Robin stood with the earls of the realm and solemnly vowed to serve Richard loyally. He then watched as Edmund and the other barons of England were called forward, followed by prominent heirs such as Lionel. At least Lionel had affected a suitable level of sincerity as he swore fealty to Richard.

Robin recalled how, before they left Nottinghamshire, he and Edmund had spent several hours arguing and debating with Lionel to convince him that he must accompany them to Oxford and participate in the ceremony. They reasoned with him that, if Richard died, Lionel could still be John's man. But if the Lionheart returned, his favor, once lost, could never be reclaimed. Robin emphasized that Richard never forgot a betrayal. Lionel's very life could be in jeopardy for his support of John, and neither Robin nor Edmund could save him from the wrath of the Lionheart.

Following the oaths, two Cistercian abbots were appointed as official representatives of the Great Council, and they were sent to Germany to find Richard and confirm that he was alive and well.

After leaving the council, Robin, Edmund, and Lionel found a local tavern. It had been a tiring day, and they were famished. They were enjoying a companionable meal as they recollected stories from long ago, studiously avoiding a serious discussion of either the dangers that faced England or the cruel betrayal that Lionel had perpetuated on his father.

"I don't envy you when we return to Huntingdon," commented Edmund. "Marian was so angry to be left behind that I half expected her to follow us by stealth. "

Robin chuckled. "I'm sure that after we left, she calmed down and realized the importance of remaining in Huntingdon with Robbie. The roads are dangerous, and we are traveling with only a small contingent of guards."

Lionel snorted derisively and said, "Perhaps we should have brought her. She and her outlaws tormented Argentan for months. Sir Marian thinks she's a knight."

The conversation came to an awkward end.

Edmund quietly admonished Lionel for mocking Marian, and Robin could see that his uncle was embarrassed by his son's poor manners.

Robin wanted to reconcile with his cousin. They had been close friends in the past. Many years ago, they had traveled together to Poitou: two young, fresh faced boys excited to train for knighthood. They had grown even closer during the two years they had studied there. But then Lionel had been called home because his mother was gravely ill with a wasting disease, and he had never returned to complete his training.

Before Robin could offer a light-hearted comment in hopes of recovering some semblance of friendly conversation, a royal guard tapped Edmund on the shoulder.

Robin, Edmund, and Lionel rose and faced the man who politely dropped to one knee before rising to announce, "I'm searching for the Earl of Huntingdon."

"I'm Huntingdon," responded Robin.

"The queen has summoned you to her chambers." The man gazed apologetically at Edmund and Lionel. "You're to come alone."

Robin was intrigued by the queen's demand that he meet with her at once. Perhaps she had more questions about Richard's capture. He didn't know the queen very well, and he wasn't sure what to expect. During his years of training in Poitou, she had been imprisoned by her husband for her schemes to place her oldest son, Henry the Younger, on the throne. Robin had first met her following Richard's coronation, and she had been with them in Aquitaine and Poitou when Richard was preparing for the Crusade. Later, she had traveled with Berengaria to Cypress, where Richard and the Princess of Navarre had married.

He was escorted to a well-guarded chamber devoted to various feminine pursuits—piles of fabric, balls of yarn, and tapestries were stacked on a table. Several torches lined the wall, and the roaring flames of the hearth provided both light and warmth on this frosty winter's night.

Near the hearth, Queen Eleanor stood waiting. She was dressed in the same elegant red bliaut embellished with gold embroidery that she had worn during the council meeting. In the privacy of her chambers, she had removed her wimple, and her long white hair flowed down her back. A circlet of gold rested on her head. The small crown was encrusted with precious gems, and they sparkled in the firelight.

Although the lines and creases that marred her face paid homage to her seven decades of life, Robin was struck by the fierce intelligence in her eyes. The depth of her gaze bespoke a wisdom of the ages, borne of a truly eventful and consequential life.

"Your Grace, I'm at your service." Robin went down on one knee and paused before standing, offering the elderly queen the utmost respect.

She moved to a chair next to the fire and sat, questioning Robin in detail about the journey that Richard had taken from Acre. She was especially focused on the king's reason for turning around at Sicily and sailing up the Adriatic Sea before hiking across the Alps towards Saxony. Robin explained how men loyal to Richard had warned them that all the ports in Toulouse and Provence were thick with mercenaries ready to capture the Lionheart for King Philippe. Even the ports of Genoa and Pisa had not been safe.

"Of all my sons, I know Philippe envies Richard the most."

Robin nodded. "I was there when King Richard captured Acre. I believe that King Philippe was embarrassed by his lack of success before your son's arrival."

He then realized that the queen needed to be apprised of the information he had gathered the previous year. "Last summer, King Richard sent me to Paris to investigate the attempted regicide in Acre; the attack where I was gravely wounded. We believe that

Sheriff de Argentan planned it, but he would not have had the resources to implement such a scheme."

Eleanor huffed in exasperation. "I requested that the justiciars remove Argentan from the post of sheriff, but Nottinghamshire is still under John's dominion, and John insists that it's all a misunderstanding, and that the sheriff was not part of the attack. He says the Genoese instigated the assault."

"It's true that the raid was carried out by Genoese men-at-arms, but someone had to pay them. And why would the Sheriff of Nottingham and his captain travel to the Holy Land? I assure you they were not making a pilgrimage to the Holy Sites."

The queen chuckled wryly. "Did your investigation bear fruit?"

"I discovered a connection between Argentan and King Philippe's chief advisor, Count de Montlhéry. The sheriff's captain, Sir Guy of Gisborne, is a high-ranking knight in Montlhéry's household."

"I have never met Montlhéry, but I've heard that he is fiercely loyal to Philippe and ruthless in his defense of his king. Every ruler needs men who are prepared to do anything and to sacrifice everything in service to their liege lord."

"Yes, Your Grace."

"Are you such a man, Huntingdon? I know Richard esteemed you highly. Are you worthy of my son's high opinion?"

Robin paused. He was troubled by the direction of the conversation, but he readily affirmed his loyalty. "Your Grace, I pray unceasingly that I will be worthy of your son's trust."

"And what of your uncle and cousin? Can the Baron of Embelton and his only heir, a son of questionable morals, be trusted?"

"I will vouch for Uncle Edmund without reservation. As for his son, I have known Lionel all my life. He has been manipulated by wicked men, especially the sheriff. He has now recognized the error of his ways, and he enthusiastically swore fealty to King Richard today. Lionel has seen little of the world beyond his home and the court in London. Edmund and I will help him make better choices in the future."

Eleanor fell into thoughtfulness. "I believe my youngest son is also under the influence of evil men, including Argentan and Philippe. Thankfully, I can manage him."

She gestured for Robin to sit, and he gratefully sank into the nearest chair.

"Over the years, I have carefully cultivated a network of men who provide me with information and keep me apprised of what is happening in the kingdom, including the lands on the continent. Ever since your return, I've been investigating Baron de Argentan."

Robin leaned forward, eager to hear what she had learned.

"I have come to one conclusion: Baron de Argentan is a ghost."

His brow creased in confusion, Robin asked, "What do you mean?"

"In the spring of 1188, Alaric de Montabard appeared in the Barony of Argentan and married the daughter of the baron, even though she was considered past the age of marriage. No one knew this man. The marriage was hastily arranged. A fortnight after the wedding, both father and daughter died of plague. A plague that sickened only those two people. The new baron installed his own men as castellan and steward of the barony before he departed. Income from the barony is sent to him here in England."

Robin was aghast. "Your Grace, this sounds like poison, not plague. I believe that Argentan has an affinity for poison. When he was in Acre, there was an attempt to poison King Richard. And I'm sure you remember the mysterious poisoning of Blanche and Clothilde in Poitiers before we left for the Crusade. The wine had been sent to your son. You know how he disdains English wine, so of course, he refused it. The sisters sampled it and died in agony."

"I agree, but we cannot make an accusation of murder against Argentan based on these vague suspicions. You must watch him closely. I want you to learn everything you can about this man without a past."

"Yes, Your Grace. May I ask your forbearance in another matter? It's about my marriage to Blanche."

"I remember attending your wedding. And then her funeral just a few months later. She was with child when she was poisoned, was she not?"

Robin nodded and then explained his clandestine marriage to Marian and the existence of his young son. "Is it possible for me to get an annulment of this other marriage? I realize now that it was not a legal marriage, but there were many people in attendance at the wedding. I've been searching my mind, trying to think of what to do and who to ask. Few people here in England know about this wedding."

Eleanor rose and moved closer to the hearth. Robin respectfully stood as well.

She spoke in a measured, even tone. "On one hand, you have a wedding attended by royalty and the highest ranks of the nobility, where you were joined in holy matrimony in the great cathedral of Poitiers to the noble daughter of a prominent family in Aquitaine—a family to whom I am related by blood. Her family's lands are strategically situated next to Angoulême, a rebellious county that requires constant monitoring. We need the loyalty of the de Châteauneuf family to maintain stability in that area."

Stretching her palms towards the fire, she continued. "On the other hand, you have a clandestine wedding, conducted by a priest with only one witness and held in a small church in the distant backwater of Nottingham. This was an unofficial joining between you and the daughter of a minor baron who was a stranger to me and rarely attended court."

Robin's heart sank as he realized the truth of her words.

"Huntingdon, your son will never be accepted as legitimate."

"But, Your Grace—"

She waved him off with a flick of her wrist. "Help me bring Richard home, and he will ensure that this boy has a bright future in the church. Geoffrey, Archbishop of York, is my husband's natural child, and he has had many fine opportunities. And I know you are on good terms with Hamelin, my husband's half brother. He is also illegitimate, but he became a wealthy earl by right of wife."

Robin tried again. "But the truth—"

"Let me tell you a story about the truth; it's a tale my dear father, God-rest-his-soul, was fond of telling. Truth has two younger brothers: Untruth and Near-truth. Untruth was the most handsome of the three. Near-truth was the most charismatic. These two brothers received all the attention and adulation.

"Meanwhile, Truth was as plain as a peasant's hovel. His personality was as dull as an old dagger. It was always difficult for him to emerge from the shadows of his attractive and personable brothers. No one wanted to listen to what Truth had to say—not when Untruth and Near-Truth could always be counted on to tell others what they wanted to hear. So, Truth was usually ignored.

"Sometimes when war, plague, or disaster descended upon the people, they would seek Truth, hoping to receive comfort. If they humbled themselves and sincerely listened, then they would find Truth. But even in difficult times, many preferred the seduction of Near-truth's honeyed words, or the fantasies of Untruth's fables."

She looked him squarely in the eye. "I am an old woman, but I have lived much of my life surrounded by men. I see in your face the earnest determination to fix this problem and control the course of your life. Such is the folly of young men." She barked a short laugh. "You want me to give you solace and reassurance that you will succeed. If you want to hear the words of Near-Truth and Untruth, you have come to the wrong queen. I am offering you Truth, and he is unyielding and merciless."

Robin's eyes narrowed in anger, and he quickly glanced away, unwilling to reveal how much she had unsettled him.

"I will think on your words, Your Grace," he declared.

She cackled loudly. "No, you won't. Unless you're thinking

about how to prove me wrong. You will not accept my words, even though they are wise."

"I promise to consider them, and I will learn everything I can about Sheriff de Argentan and pass my knowledge to you or your agents."

"There is one more thing, Huntingdon, and then you are excused. Earlier today, you renewed your oath of fealty to Richard. And now, I need your solemn vow that you will do anything to secure his safe return."

"Of course, Your Grace. I am impatient for King Richard's return."

"I don't think you understand what I'm saying. Nothing is more important than Richard's return. You must do everything that I require of you, up to and including sacrificing your life. Your loyalty to your king demands it. I demand it. Richard is more important than you. He's more important than your family, your wife, and your son. You must stand ready to sacrifice everything for your liege lord. He is counting on you, and so am I."

Robin knelt. "Your Grace, I humbly submit to your authority. I will not fail you, and I will not fail my king." In his mind, he silently swore that he would fulfill his duty to Richard without sacrificing either his life or his family. He would also find a way to establish Robbie's legitimacy, despite the queen's cynical assessment.

He swiftly rose and exited the chamber without a glance back at the aged queen.

2 March 1193, On the Road North of Oxford

Robin and Edmund rode in silence as they made their way north. They would first travel to Northampton, and from there, to Huntingdon where Marian, Robbie, and Constance were eagerly awaiting their return from the meeting of the Great Council.

March had arrived, but spring still seemed a distant hope as icy winds and occasional light snow had delayed their departure from Oxford.

Lionel was leading the group, followed by Much and half a dozen mounted men-at-arms from Huntingdon who were there to safeguard their journey. Robin and Edmund brought up the rear, and they remained alert to signs of danger, especially whenever the road narrowed or the distance between the road and the trees was too close for comfort. At least, traveling in winter was often safer because the bare trees and bitter cold reduced the risk of an attack by bandits.

Edmund broke their companionable silence. "You have said little about your meeting with the queen."

Robin replied, "There's not much to say. She wanted to hear, once again, all the details of Richard's travels from Acre to Vienna." He paused. "She also wants me to learn more about Sheriff de Argentan. I plan to stay at Locksley for a time with Marian and Robbie."

"Perhaps Lionel, Constance, and I could lodge at Lenton, since there is limited room at Locksley," proposed Edmund. "I would like to help."

"Can we trust Lionel to resist the influence of the sheriff? And what of your plans to annul Constance's marriage? I can't imagine the suffering she has endured after being forced into such an alliance."

"Constance has not suffered. Gisborne has treated her with kindness and respect. In truth, I fear she has grown fond of him. I confess that I've been impressed with his hard work in managing Locksley. You will find that Locksley is more prosperous than when you left to go on crusade."

Robin was briefly stunned into silence. This was not at all what he had expected to hear.

Edmund continued, "As for Lionel, I share your concern. It would be best to separate him from Sheriff de Argentan, yet I fear having him out of sight. It's my fault that he has failed to become a better man."

"You cannot believe that."

"Oh yes, I assure you, I firmly believe it. Now that you are a father, you will soon understand. I failed Lionel by holding him too closely to my heart."

"What do you mean?"

"You know that my beloved wife and I had many children."

"Yes, I remember that several died."

"Our first daughter was stillborn. And we had three sons who died of a plague when they were young. Lionel and Constance had the same sickness, but they survived. Six cherished children, yet only two grew to adulthood."

"I'm sorry, Uncle. As a father, the thought of losing my son is terrifying."

"I had been reluctant to send Lionel to Poitou for training, but I was glad he was going with you. And then Jeanne became sick..." His voice grew thick with emotion.

"Your wife was always very kind to me," Robin recalled.

Recovering his composure, Edmund resumed. "When she fell ill, she begged me to send for Lionel. She was weeping, saying that she only wanted to hold her son one more time before she died. I could not deny her."

"I was sorry to see Lionel leave Poitou, but having lost my own mother a few years prior, I encouraged him to go."

"She was so happy to see him. We thought she was near death, but she lingered for months. After she passed away, I was so heart-broken that I could not bear to send Lionel back to Poitou. I convinced myself that I could teach him the skills he needed."

"And so you did," suggested Robin. "He's gifted with a bow, and I'm sure he has many other talents."

"But he lacks the good judgment to understand how Argentan manipulated him. He lacked the moral courage to do the right thing when the sheriff lured him into this kidnapping scheme. And it's my fault for not sending him back to Poitou to complete his training."

"Uncle, you cannot take the blame—"

"Robin, I coddled him. I allowed him to escape punishments that he deserved. When a son misbehaves, it's the duty of his father to correct him. Never forget that with your own son. And now I must reap the poor harvest I have sown."

At that moment, Robin noticed dark shapes on the road ahead. Lionel and the other men continued, maneuvering around a group of peasants who had moved into the ditch to allow them to pass.

"Wait, Lionel," shouted Robin, as he swiftly dismounted and approached one of the men.

Lionel, Edmund, Much, and the men-at-arms stopped and watched.

In a friendly manner, Robin asked, "Good day to you. Where are you headed in the midst of winter?" He took note that there were four able-bodied men, four women, and an elderly man. There were also two young children and a babe who were carried by the women. Their threadbare cloaks were insufficient for the wintry weather, and they were haggard and nearly frozen.

But most noticeable about their appearance was the look of terror in their eyes. They backed away from Robin, and one man begged, "My lord, please have mercy! We mean you no harm, and we have nothing to surrender."

One man muttered to the others, "On my signal, run into the woods."

A young woman began to sob. "I can't run; I'm so cold that I can't feel my feet."

Robin's brow creased in concern. "Wait! Don't run away. These men are my guards, and they're under my command."

Beckoning to Much, Robin ordered, "Lead the men a short distance down the road and await me there. Keep your weapons sheathed."

The men dutifully obeyed, and then it was only Robin, Edmund, and Lionel with the vagabond peasants.

"Where is your village?" inquired Edmund.

"It's a small place close to Wallingford," answered the man who seemed to be the leader of the group.

Lionel echoed Robin's questions. "Why are you on the road, far from your homes, when it's winter? You will freeze to death tonight, as you will never make it on foot to the next village before nightfall."

Robin recognized the desperation and fear in their eyes. He had seen the same expressions countless times over the years, particularly in the war-torn villages of the Holy Land. He retrieved a loaf of bread from one of his saddlebags, and he handed it to the man, who immediately gave it to the nearest woman. At the sight of food, she burst into tears. She tore a piece from the loaf and passed the rest to another woman. It wasn't enough, so Edmund took a loaf from his saddlebag and offered it as well.

"You are too kind, my lords." The man's eyes shone with emotion; he was on the verge of tears as well.

"Tell me what happened," Robin gently insisted.

The older man stepped forward. "As he said, we come from a village near Wallingford. Prince John has taken the castle of Wallingford, and he brought many soldiers with him. These brutal men do not speak our language, and they have been killing men, raping women, and burning our villages. They took all the food, and we were starving."

The first man explained, "We heard there was food and work in Oxford, but no one would help us. Now we are going to Northampton."

Lionel exclaimed, "Northampton! Do you know how far you are from there?"

The man lowered his gaze. He was obviously ashamed to admit that he had not realized just how difficult the journey would be in winter.

Robin cautioned Lionel with a shake of his head.

Edmund addressed the older man. "Did their language sound something like this?" He then spoke a few words in Welsh.

Several of the peasants recognized the language as the one the men had spoken.

Looking at Robin, Edmund disclosed, "Welsh mercenaries. John has been assembling his own private army, and he has hired scores of these men."

Robin nodded in understanding. "We must reach the next village before dusk." He signaled for his men to return and said to the peasants, "There are enough horses for each of you to ride the rest of the way. These are sturdy horses, well fed, and perfectly capable of carrying two persons each and these small children."

Unexpectedly, the man who had been speaking for the others fell to his knees and wept. Robin, embarrassed to have brought the man to tears, encouraged him to stand.

"You must be a holy saint to take such pity on us!" cried one of the women. She also dropped to her knees, and then the others knelt as well.

Robin didn't want such recognition. He implored them to stand.

"We need to hurry," remarked Lionel. "If you insist that we take a bunch of dirty, smelly—"

"Hush, Lionel," demanded Edmund. "We can't leave these people to die along the road."

"Who are you, my lord?" the older man asked Robin.

"I am the Earl of Huntingdon. If you cannot find work in Northampton, then I urge you to come to Huntingdon. I will give you work. But my cousin is right, we cannot tarry here, we must make haste to the next village where we will warm our bones by the fire, and I will see that you are well fed."

CHAPTER 4
CONISBROUGH CASTLE

23 March 1193, On the Road North of Nottingham

"Papa, can your horse fly?"

Marian grinned as utter confusion washed over Robin's face at the unexpected question. They had left Locksley at dawn and were on their way to Conisbrough Castle in South Yorkshire. As usual, Robin had insisted that Robbie ride with him, and he had one arm wrapped around the little boy while his other hand held the reins. Robbie also had ahold of the reins, because he wanted to help his father steer the large destrier.

They were following a sizeable contingent of mounted men-at-arms. In the front, Lionel and Much were leading the way. Despite his humble origins, Much had more battle experience from his time in the Holy Land than any of the other men accompanying them, so Robin considered him his unofficial second in command.

Bringing up the rear was Constance. Marian glanced back at her friend and was amused by the sight of Robin's little dog in the canvas bag strapped to Constance's back. He was peeking over her shoulder. Constance had taken a liking to Jack, and she was using the carrier that Robin had brought from Outremer.

Marian returned her attention to Robin's sputtering attempt to answer Robbie.

"Son, horses don't fly. Birds fly."

"Cousin Lionel's horse can fly. He showed me."

In desperation, Robin looked to Marian for help, and she laughed out loud before mouthing the word 'jump' to him.

A relieved Robin promised, "The next time I see a log or rock along the road, I will show you that my horse is better at flying over it than Lionel's."

Marian tilted her head and enjoyed the warmth of the sun on her face. At times like this, she felt so much contentment that it worried her. Over the past two months, she had often feared that her heart might burst with happiness, or that she would awake to find that Robin's homecoming had been a vivid dream.

When he had left her to go to Oxford, she had awoken every morning, searching for proof that Robin was really alive and begging Constance to reassure her. Now he was going to leave her again. Her mood darkened.

"Robin, are you certain that I can't go to Tickhill with you? Constance can look after Robbie."

"Marian, we've already discussed this. I'm taking Lionel, Much, and these men to Tickhill to join the siege, where, by the grace of God, we will end John's ambitions for the throne. This is a battle, not a tournament. The men leading this siege are interested in learning about the siege of Acre."

"But a siege isn't like a battle."

"And how would you know?"

"Just common sense. You're outside the walls, and the other soldiers are inside the walls. Everyone is standing around watching each other."

Robin frowned. "That's not exactly how it works. There are times during a siege when each side is watching and waiting to see what their opponents will do next, but I assure you that an actual battle can start at any time. It's a volatile situation, and it's not safe for you to be there. Besides, you will enjoy spending time at Conisbrough with Countess de Warenne."

Marian fell silent, searching her mind for a suitable rebuttal. She wanted to scream that if it's not safe for her to go to Tickhill, then it's not safe for him! And she could not survive losing him again. But she knew it was pointless to argue further.

"Papa, can your horse fly over that?"

"Perhaps. Let me take a look." Robin reined in his horse and studied a log lying across the ditch.

Constance pulled up alongside them, and both of the women stopped to observe.

Abruptly, Robin stood in his stirrups and swiveled to scan the road behind them.

Marian stared at him curiously. "What—"

"Quiet," commanded Robin. Without another word, he lifted Robbie from his saddle and passed him to Marian, and the little boy began to cry.

"Hush," Robin harshly demanded, and Robbie was so startled by his father's unexpected rebuke that he grew silent.

Robin hopped off his horse and dropped to his hands and knees on the road.

Marian and Constance exchanged a confused glance before returning their gaze to Robin, who now had one ear pressed to the worn road, listening to something.

"Robin, what's the matter?" asked Marian.

Without answering her, he leapt back on his horse and whistled loudly at the men who had continued down the road and were pulling ahead of them. Everyone stopped, while Lionel and Much spurred their horses towards Robin.

"Robin?" Again Marian questioned him, and she was growing alarmed at the strange look on his face. He was scanning both sides of the road.

"Marian, take Constance and Robbie and ride into the woods there," he pointed to a specific spot. "Ride at least thirty yards into the forest. Then, tie the horses to a tree and continue on foot an additional thirty yards. Do you know how to cover your tracks?"

"Yes, of course. What's wrong?"

At this point Much rode up with Lionel and inquired, "My lord, is there trouble?"

"There's a large group of mounted men riding hard towards us. They will be upon us any moment. We will divide our men and move just inside the tree line. There's not enough foliage to hide us, but if they are peaceful, they will simply ride by without stopping."

Lionel regarded him skeptically. "How do you know this?"

Robin glared at Marian and roared, "I told you to go! We could be facing a battle, and you must hide in the woods, now!"

Marian was taken aback. He had never spoken to her like that before, and he was unmistakably furious. Then she felt a faint tremor along the ground. It must have been what had alerted Robin. She immediately turned her horse and led Constance into the trees.

Robbie was frightened and sobbing, and Constance's face was as white as the puffy clouds drifting overhead. Deeper and deeper they moved into the forest until they reached a small clearing. Tying their horses to the low branches of a tree, they made their way through the ever-thickening woods. Constance carried Robbie, and Marian broke off a short leafy branch, walking backwards and sweeping it side to side, hoping to obscure their tracks.

"Be quiet!" she ordered Robbie, who was still crying.

Marian realized that not only was Robbie sobbing, but Constance was whimpering and on the verge of losing her composure completely.

"Constance, you need to be strong. If you are afraid, then Robbie will never settle. He's making too much noise," insisted Marian.

Constance took several deep breaths, recovering somewhat.

They arrived at a second clearing, and Marian instructed

Constance to set Robbie down on an old tree trunk lying on the ground.

Marian knelt in front of him. "Robbie, remember when we left the bad place? And we all had to be quiet?"

"With Brother Tuck and the tall man?" Robbie asked.

"Yes! You must be quiet now, just like you were that night. And your papa will be so proud when I tell him how brave you were."

Robbie calmed a bit. "Papa will be proud? Will you tell him I was brave?"

"I promise. Now, I want you to wait here with Cousin Constance and Jack." She retrieved the dog from his carrier on Constance's back and handed him to the boy. "Robbie, I think Jack is scared. Can you help him? I'm going to go help your papa, and I'll return soon."

Robbie hugged Jack tightly and started talking to the dog, reassuring him that everything would be all right.

With Robbie suitably distracted, she turned to leave.

"Marian!" cried Constance. "You can't go back! You might get hurt or killed!"

"No, I need to see what's happening. I will not sit here when I could help. You will stay here and keep Robbie safe."

"Please don't go," begged Constance.

"Wait here, and I'll be return shortly." Marian pivoted and left before Constance or Robbie could say another word.

⁓

Marian ran through the woods, leaping over fallen limbs, ducking under low branches, and navigating around patches of thick underbrush. She stumbled and fell several times as the skirt of her bliaut kept getting in her way. If only she had the chausses she had worn during her outlaw days! Her heart was thudding, and as she neared the road, she heard shouting. Her heart beat even faster, and her chest grew tight from her exertions.

Approaching the road, she slowed and moved behind a tree. She peeked around it, and the battle she witnessed reminded her of the one she had survived on the streets of Acre.

The road was littered with at least half a dozen bodies with protruding arrows, and she surmised that Robin and his men's positions at the tree line had given them the upper hand at first. But apparently the mounted attackers had surged into the ditches to strike at Robin's men, and they had switched from bows to swords.

A few men, including Lionel, were still using their bows as they remained near the trees, efficiently eliminating as many men as they could, but some marauders were wearing chain mail. When she located Robin and Much, they were engaged in sword fights with their opponents.

She briefly recalled Robin's insistence that all the men-at-arms accompanying them be mounted, and she could see the wisdom of it now, although she had originally felt it was an extravagance. A man without a horse would have had no hope of survival, and any man who fell from his horse was doomed.

Nearby, she spotted a riderless horse with a bow and quiver strapped to its saddlebags, and she swore that never again would she travel without her bow. Creeping to the horse, she grabbed the bow and quiver of arrows and darted back to the tree line.

She notched an arrow, took aim, and released it at one of the attackers. The arrow struck the hauberk around his neck and fell away. When he rode out of her range, another man appeared. She aimed for the man's leg, which was not protected. He was likely a lower ranking soldier who could not afford to be fully armored. Her arrow struck his thigh, and he howled in pain, turning his horse to search for the archer targeting him.

Marian notched another arrow and released it, but this time it lodged in the man's saddle. Just as he pulled the arrow out, the strangers retreated, and he joined them, riding south in the direction from whence they had come. They swiftly disappeared around a bend in the road.

She was relieved that Robin was all right, and she listened as he commanded his men, sending Much to examine the injured and directing several other men to drag the dead to the side of the road.

Robin gestured to his cousin. "Lionel, follow their retreat. We must determine if they've truly withdrawn, or if they're regrouping and planning to attack again."

To her surprise, Lionel obeyed without complaint.

It was then that Robin noticed her behind the tree, and he quickly drew his bow and aimed at her. "Alert! They've left a man!"

An embarrassed Marian dropped her bow and stepped into full view with her palms raised.

All the color drained from Robin's face.

A smirking Lionel rode past her and announced in a sing-song voice, "Sir Marian is in trouble." His obnoxious laughter was loud along the otherwise quiet roadway.

She already disliked Lionel, but at that moment, she truly hated him.

"Robin, let me explain," she suggested as she smiled sweetly.

He marched towards her with an implacable expression.

The other men were attending to the wounded and dead, and Lionel was riding away. It was only the two of them, and she trembled at the look on his face.

"What in God's Holy Name are you doing here?" he bellowed. "I told you to hide in the woods. You could've been killed. I almost killed you myself just now, when I realized there was an archer hiding behind a tree." He glanced over her shoulder. Returning his glare to her, he roared, "Where's my son?"

And with that, Marian's temper ignited. "*Our* son is hiding with Constance in the woods. I followed your directions exactly. But you never said I had to stay hiding. I came back to help."

"Help?" Robin's voice rose incredulously. "You're lucky to be alive. Those men weren't forest bandits. They were trained soldiers."

He picked up the bow she had dropped and shouted, "Where did you get this? Why is your face bleeding?"

Much and the other men had stopped their work to observe their argument.

Marian touched her face, and there was a trickle of blood on her cheek. She defiantly lifted her chin. "I was running through the woods, and a branch scratched my face. I stole the bow from that horse over there," she pointed at the nearby beast. "And I *did* help because I wounded one of those men. I may not be a champion archer like Robin Hood, but I have some skill with a bow."

Robin angrily tossed the bow on the ground. He then realized that the other men were listening, and he yelled, "Back to work! See to the dead and wounded."

They grudgingly refocused on their tasks.

"Marian, never, ever do anything so foolish again. Do you understand me? I need to hear your solemn promise at once."

Her anger boiled up inside of her, and she hissed, "Don't you dare call me stupid. I make no such promise. If I need to protect myself, or our son, or you, then I will do it." To her dismay, tears were now blurring her vision and rolling down her cheeks.

Robin's face softened at the sight of her tears. He reached for her and drew her into his arms, and even though she initially pulled away, she could not resist being close to him, and she relaxed into his embrace.

His voice gentled. "I didn't call you stupid. I would never say that. But what you did was incredibly dangerous. Please, don't risk your life; I need you, and our son needs you."

She nodded against his shoulder.

"Show me where you left Robbie and Constance. We must hurry to the closest village. It's a small hamlet, but it's situated on a hill where we can keep watch for another attack."

Just then, Lionel returned and spurred his horse towards them.

Dismounting, he reported, "I went about a mile down the road, and I didn't see them. But that doesn't mean they won't strike again."

"Lionel, ride as fast as you can to Conisbrough," Robin instructed. "Tell Earl de Warenne what has happened and request that he dispatch a company of men-at-arms to escort us to his castle. We've lost too many men, and if we're attacked on the road a second time, we will be defeated. We will await you in the next village where we'll be able to better defend ourselves until reinforcements arrive."

Lionel nodded, but as he was preparing to mount his horse, he froze when he saw the dead lined up in the ditch.

Robin asked, "Do you recognize any of these men? They aren't wearing heraldry."

"Several of those men are familiar to me. They are mercenaries employed by Sheriff de Argentan."

26 March 1193, Near Conisbrough Castle, South Yorkshire

They had left Sherwood Forest and were now traversing rolling hills and pastures, but Marian could not appreciate the lovely scenery. The closer they were to Conisbrough, the more nervous she felt.

She was riding next to Constance, and they were protected by an escort of twenty of Earl de Warenne's mounted men-at-arms. At the front, Robin rode with Lionel and the earl's son, Guillaume. All three were the same age, and Marian observed them as they enjoyed a friendly, animated conversation.

Robbie, as usual, was riding with his father.

Although Marian was apprehensive about staying at Conisbrough, Constance was elated. She was enthusiastically telling Marian what she knew about the de Warenne family.

Once again, Marian was lamenting her lack of interest in politics during her youth. She had never paid much attention to stories about the royal family or the elaborate familial web of royals, near royals, and distant relations to the king's family.

In contrast, Constance was very knowledgeable. Marian knew her friend had traveled to London with her father and brother every year to attend court and celebrate Midsummer.

Marian's father had never taken her to court, or even to London. Perhaps it was his own aversion to politics and big cities. And it's likely that he considered it unnecessary, since it was always understood that Marian would wed Robin, so there had been no need to search for a suitable husband among the nobility of England.

"Constance, I'm confused," she reluctantly confessed.

"About what?"

"Didn't you say that Earl Hamelin was illegitimate? How did he inherit his title?"

Constance smiled indulgently. "Every time I've tried to explain this, I can see your mind wandering. Please concentrate on what I'm saying."

"My mind is wandering because so much of this seems like pointless court intrigue. I just want to go back home and stay there."

"You're the wife of an earl. I think you can learn a lot by spending time with Countess de Warenne. You can't hide at Locksley and Lenton. You have duties to perform at Huntingdon."

Marian released a noisy sigh of defeat. "Tell me again."

"Hamelin is the illegitimate son of Geoffrey, Count of Anjou. He's the older half-brother of the late King Henry, God-rest-his-soul, and he's King Richard's uncle. Of course, he's Prince John's uncle, too."

"But instead of Count of Anjou, he's the Earl of Surrey?"

"Now I'm certain that you weren't listening," Constance chided. "He married Isabel de Warenne, the Countess of Surrey, who was the only child of her father. So, she inherited the earldom. When Hamelin married her, he took her family name and became earl by right of wife."

"Oh. But isn't that unusual? I mean for a man to take his wife's name."

"Yes. However, it can happen if the man has no family name or a name without noble connections," replied Constance. "Since Hamelin was illegitimate, it was the best choice for him."

Constance reminded her, "Like Isabel de Warenne, you were an only child, and you inherited the Barony of Lenton, so Robin is now Baron of Lenton by right of wife, as well as Earl of Huntingdon."

"That's true. I often helped my father by performing the duties of a baroness. Perhaps I don't really need to learn anything new to be a countess."

"Marian, there is a difference. What's the matter, my dear friend? You don't seem yourself."

Marian rode silently for a while, pondering how to answer. At last, she confessed, "Constance, I've never been to court. I'm afraid I'll do or say the wrong thing and embarrass Robin."

Constance pulled her horse closer, and stretched her hand out to Marian, who grasped it, seeking some reassurance.

"I've never met the de Warennes," said Constance, "but I've heard both Robin and Lionel speak of them with admiration and affection. Remember, Robin and Lionel spent time with Earl Hamelin at the beginning of their training, before they went to Poitou."

"I remember. Robin says the family is very welcoming."

"We'll find out soon enough. Look!" cried Constance as they crested a hill.

In the distance, the great fortress of Conisbrough Castle stood proudly overlooking the surrounding lands.

Constance eagerly explained, "According to Father, Earl Hamelin completely rebuilt the keep as a six-sided tower. No other castle in England is like it. Father was so disappointed that he couldn't come with us to see it for himself."

"I wish he could have come too," admitted Marian, "but I'm glad that he stayed behind to watch over Locksley and Lenton during our absence. We don't know what the sheriff might do while we're away."

⤚

A short time later, Marian and Constance were ascending the wide stairway leading into the keep as they walked behind Robin, Robbie, and Jack. Glancing over her shoulder, she noticed Lionel had gone with Guillaume to the stables. She returned her gaze to the tower as it seemed to soar towards the clouds above her; it was truly impressive, and she took a deep breath as they entered the keep.

"Robin!" a pair of joyous voices rang out.

An older couple crowded around Robin, hugging him and exclaiming that it had been too long since his last visit.

The earl was a tall, muscular man whose auburn hair was streaked with grey. Marian speculated that he would have been quite handsome in his youth. He exuded vitality, which reminded her of Robin's energetic nature.

The woman next to him was elegantly dressed in a green bliaut. Her hair was hidden beneath a wimple, and even though Constance had said that Isabel was similar in age to her husband, her face was smooth, with only a hint of lines at the corners of her mouth. She was lovely, and her expression was kind.

Countess Isabel declared, "This handsome boy must be your son." She smiled and reached for Robbie, taking him from Robin's arms. Marian was pleased that Robbie willingly went to her.

Robin made the introductions. "This is my son, Robbie, my wife, Marian, and my cousin, Lady Constance de Toury of Embelton."

Marian and Constance curtsied.

He continued, "This is Hamelin and Isabel de Warenne, Earl and Countess of Surrey."

Robbie then announced, "That's Jack." He pointed to the little dog that had followed them into the keep.

Earl Hamelin chortled. "That's a dog? A full-grown dog?"

"Papa brought him all the way from heaven."

"The Holy Land," Robin corrected.

"Ah," the older man grinned. "That makes him special, doesn't it?"

To Marian's surprise, Isabel set Robbie on the floor and embraced her, stating, "I'm very happy you are here. We've been looking forward to meeting you."

The Countess then hugged Constance.

Turning once more to Marian, she excitedly proclaimed, "I want to hear all about your adventures in Sherwood Forest as Marian Hood!"

27 March 1193, Nottingham Castle

Sheriff de Argentan listened as the knight he had sent to ambush Huntingdon delivered his report.

"They had more men than us, and all of them were mounted. We took out a few of Huntingdon's men, but we were losing too many, so we retreated to regroup. By the time we returned, Huntingdon had assumed a defensive position in a nearby village."

"And you just gave up?" Argentan's annoyance was steadily building. With all the money he had spent to hire these men, he had expected Huntingdon to have been thoroughly defeated. He had given explicit directions to his mercenaries to leave no survivors.

"No, my lord. We did attack, but they were well situated on a hill. We laid siege to the village, but before we could prevail, reinforcements arrived to help Huntingdon."

The sheriff leapt to his feet. "From where? I control all of Nottinghamshire. They were still within my domain, and I know of no force of arms that would dare interfere with my plans!"

At the sight of the sheriff's legendary temper, the knight nervously replied, "My lord, it was the blue and yellow checkered heraldry."

The sheriff blanched. "There is only one shield like that," he remarked, almost in a whisper.

"Yes, my lord, the men were from the Earl of Surrey, Hamelin de Warenne."

"NO!" howled Argentan. "Never speak that name." He stalked towards the other man, who backed away.

"My lord, I'm sorry—"

With the speed of a hawk swooping down on a small rodent, the sheriff drew his dagger and plunged it into the unsuspecting knight.

The man fell to the floor and begged for his life. "My lord, no! Please—"

Argentan dropped to his knees next to the man and thrust his knife into him over and over again. The knight attempted to draw his own dagger, but the sheriff's persistent assault thwarted him. He then tried to block the sheriff's relentless blows, and soon his hands and forearms were bleeding profusely, and he grew weaker. Even after he stopped crying out, and long after his soul had departed, the sheriff continued to stab him.

Finally, Argentan had exhausted his fury. He tossed his dagger across the room.

"Never say that name," he panted.

Shakily rising to his feet, he noticed that his hands and the heavy ring that he wore were covered in blood. He stared at the blood for a long time, and he fantasized it was the blood of his enemies and not some random, low-ranking knight.

"My lord! What has happened?"

The sound of Gisborne's voice stirred him from his trance, and he realized his captain was trying to wipe the blood from his hands with a cloth.

Guy said, "You've cut your hand. If Constance were here, she could tend to your wounds. Do you want me to call for another healer?"

Slowly returning to the moment, Argentan squinted at Guy. "Bring me water to clean my hands, and remove that fool from my presence," he commanded as he gestured towards the bloodied man on the floor.

"May I ask what this man did?" Guy inquired cautiously.

"He failed me, Gisborne."

"I will need to get help to carry him down the winding stairs, and I'll summon a cleaning woman."

Argentan waved him away. "Just do what is needed to clean up this mess."

"Yes, my lord."

As the sound of Gisborne's heavy footsteps faded, Argentan walked to the north-facing window and gazed out. It was too dark to see much, but he raised his blood-stained fist and swore, "Soon it will be your turn, Hamelin, you loathsome bastard."

CHAPTER 5
ALMOST A QUEEN

27 March 1193, Conisbrough Castle

"The battle raged from dawn to the middle of the afternoon," Robin explained. "By that time, so many horses had fallen that their bodies had become a barrier to the Saracens as they charged our defensive line."

"It's always a shame to lose good horses like that," remarked Hamelin.

Robin, Hamelin, Guillaume, and Lionel were walking along the tall wooden palisade that surrounded Conisbrough Castle, and the other men were hanging on Robin's every word as he described various battles from the Crusade.

"Ultimately, the Saracens refused to mount another charge, and Sultan Saladin had no choice but to retreat. But before they left, Richard rode out from behind the line—"

"Was he still bare-legged?" asked Guillaume.

Robin replied, "Yes, he was wearing a long chain mail shirt over the clothes in which he had been sleeping. We only had an hour to prepare for the dawn attack."

"What happened next?" Hamelin's brow was creased with worry; Richard was his favorite nephew.

Robin finished his story about the Battle of Jaffa. "Richard seized his lance and boldly paraded along the entire Saracen line, challenging any man there to come out and fight him. But so fearsome was Richard's reputation among the Saracens that not one man dared come forth."

The other men chuckled with admiration.

Hamelin shook his head in wonder. "Richard has no sense of his own mortality. It worries me, but I guess that's a sign that I'm getting old. These tales remind me of my father during the battles he fought to gain control of Normandy while his wife was fighting King Stephen for the crown of England. My father was bold, and sometimes he was reckless, but he was always a brilliant commander, God-rest-his-soul."

Everyone crossed themselves, and the other men murmured reverent prayers for the soul of the late Count Geoffrey of Anjou; the man whose habit of wearing a sprig of yellow broom blossom in his hair had given birth to the name "Plantagenet."

Changing the subject, Lionel inquired, "When will you replace this wooden palisade with a proper stone wall?"

"Exactly!" cried Guillaume. "Father, I've told you we need a stone wall. Our keep is the best in England, but what good is it if we don't have a secure wall?"

An exasperated Hamelin countered, "All in good time. We can't spend money we don't have. The expense of building the keep exceeded the estimates I received from the engineer and his stone masons. We mustn't go into debt; one poor harvest could ruin all I've worked so hard to build over the years."

Guillaume grumbled under his breath.

They were approaching the stables, so Lionel and Guillaume left to see a new foal that had been born the previous day.

Robin and Hamelin walked in amiable silence for a while until Robin asked, "Are you coming to Tickhill with us?"

"No, I'll send Guillaume, some men and supplies, but the siege is under the leadership of Hugh de Puiset, Bishop of Durham. You might recall that he was one of King Stephen's nephews." Hamelin paused as if he were searching for the right words. "I avoid him whenever possible."

"I've never met Bishop Hugh. Does he have military experience?"

Hamelin snorted in amusement. "He's not a military man, which is probably why he's so eager for your arrival. His life is centered on his mistress and their extravagant way of life."

Robin refrained from offering his opinion of high-ranking churchmen who lived like lords of the manor instead of humble servants of God. He questioned, "Is he a reliable supporter of Richard?"

"As long as Richard is alive and expected to return, Hugh will defend him. But he will quickly throw his support behind John, if Richard's fate becomes uncertain. I would not consider him a steadfast advocate for anyone except himself."

"I will keep that in mind."

"Don't judge him too harshly. We must all be prepared for the possibility of a King John."

Robin became subdued.

"I support Richard whole heartedly," Hamelin stressed. "He has the talent and temperament to rule. Nevertheless, it's my duty to defend my king, whether it's Richard or John."

"Do you think John would be a good king?"

They were nearing the keep when Hamelin finally responded. "You've been gone for several years, so I might as well tell you this before you hear it from someone else. My daughter, Ela, has recently remarried."

"I remember attending her first wedding when I returned to England after my father's death. I can't believe that was seven years ago."

"Her first husband was not of noble blood, but he and Ela had strong feelings for one another, and my wife convinced me to allow them to marry."

"Was he a good husband?"

"Oh, yes. He was very good to my daughter. But he died in an accident, and she fell into a deep melancholy."

They paused at the base of the stairs leading into the keep, and Robin remarked, "She seems happy with her second husband."

"He's also a good man; I hired him as constable of Conisbrough. But you should know the truth about her son, and I would rather you hear it from me instead of some gossipy courtier in London."

"Her son is close in age to Robbie; I saw them playing together earlier today. I'm sure that her son was a great comfort to her during her time of mourning. Was she carrying him when her husband died?"

Hamelin sighed. "Her husband died two years before that boy was born."

Robin gazed at the other man in surprise.

"Just as Ela was emerging from her grief and becoming the lovely, charming girl we had always known, her cousin, John, came for a visit."

"John? You mean Prince John?"

His voice taut with anger, Hamelin replied, "Yes, *that* John. Unbeknownst to us, at the time of his visit, he beguiled her with honeyed words and empty promises and seduced her into his bed."

A stunned Robin asked, "Does Prince John know about his son?"

"Of course. He's quite pleased with his bastard son by his first cousin." Hamelin's hand balled into a fist, as if he were wishing he could strike his nephew. With a long exhalation, he calmed himself. Grinning wryly, he disclosed, "We insisted Ela name the boy Richard, in honor of our king."

Hamelin continued, "You asked me if John has the competence to rule." He shrugged. "Perhaps he does. He is clever, especially as an administrator. But my question is whether he has the character to be a good king. He cares nothing about Ela. This scheme to seduce my daughter had one purpose, and he knows I am aware of his true motives."

Robin frowned in confusion and admitted, "I don't understand."

"He is seeking to bind me to his cause, along with the wealth and prestige of the de Warenne name and the Earldom of Surrey. It is widely known that he is the father of my grandson, a boy I am raising in my keep. My loyalty to Richard will now be in question among some people."

"Have you been accused of disloyalty to Richard?"

"Not directly, but I can see the doubts on the faces of some at court. Many still resent that I've risen to the status and wealth I have achieved. I believe that John's wicked plan to beget an illegitimate child with my daughter was also intended to remind everyone of my illegitimacy. It's a stain upon the family."

"What of Eleanor and the members of the Great Council? Do you have their support?" queried Robin.

"I've never been close to Eleanor, but since Richard's coronation, I think she's come to appreciate my affection for her favorite son. For now, I have her trust, and with her trust comes the support of the council. I won't do anything to threaten my relationship with her."

There was no need to say more, and the two men entered the keep.

⁓

Staring out the window, Marian saw Robin and Hamelin below her as they stood on the wide stairs leading into the keep. They were obviously deep into a conversation, but since she was three levels above them, she could not hear their voices.

The day was sunny and beautiful, and she longed to be outside. She thought about taking Robbie to play in the bailey, but then she recalled that he was napping. He had enjoyed a busy morning playing with Jack and Ela's son, Rich. She could imagine Robbie as an older brother, and she briefly prayed to God for another child.

"Marian?"

Constance was calling to her, and she reluctantly turned away from the window. She was in a chamber filled with women. Besides Constance, there was Isabel de Warenne, her daughter Ela, and her son's wife, Maud. The other women were busy with their embroidery while Marian's small piece was sitting neglected on a table.

At the moment, Countess Isabel was lamenting the absence of her two other daughters who were away from home, living with their husbands.

Marian had spent most of the day talking about her time living in the woods, and the other women had asked many questions. They had been very attentive, even excited, to hear her stories. It reminded her of how the outlaws would gather around the fire and listen to Brother Tuck's stories about the Crusade. She then realized how much she missed her adventures in the woods as leader of the outlaws. She had spent months helping the people of Lenton and Locksley, and she had accomplished truly important things.

And now she was expected to stitch flowers on fabric and feel satisfied. She sighed.

"What's the matter, dear?" Isabel inquired. As an accomplished hostess, she was concerned by Marian's glum expression.

Although Isabel was older than Marian's mother would have been had she survived, Marian believed that her mother had been kindhearted like Isabel. She had been so young when her mother died in childbirth that her memories were like gazing across a meadow on a foggy morning. She could just see the outline of a person, but the details of her mother's appearance were long lost to her.

"I'm all right, Lady Isabel," Marian replied.

"Marian loves the outdoors," Constance helpfully divulged. "I'm sure she would prefer practicing archery instead of embroidery."

Maud and Ela tittered in amusement, but Isabel admitted, "I wish I knew archery. In all my many years, I never considered that it was something I could learn. But you have inspired me. After the men leave for the siege, will you teach me?"

Isabel's words surprised the two younger women, and they excitedly announced that they also wanted to learn.

Marian was pleased, and she said, "We need bows that are smaller than the ones the men use. Maybe the captain of the guard can find a few for us. And bracers! Everyone must use a bracer."

"What's a bracer?" asked Ela.

"It's a piece of leather that you tie around your forearm to protect it from the bow string."

The other women looked confused, so Marian pulled up her sleeve and showed them the red mark on her forearm. "When we were attacked on the road, I didn't have a bracer, and you can see what happens if your arm is unprotected."

The women chatted for a while about archery, until Isabel remarked, "When I heard about Robin's death, I wanted to comfort you, but by that time, you were an outlaw in the woods, and Hamelin wouldn't let me go to you. Besides, the Sheriff of Nottingham had specifically sent word that we would not be welcome in his town."

Constance and Marian were both surprised by this news. "How could he prevent you from visiting Nottingham?" questioned Constance.

Isabel explained, "Hamelin had planned to confront John about it, since Nottinghamshire is under John's dominion, but he's been busy with all the disputes between John and the chancellor that Richard appointed before he left for the Crusade."

"Thank you for thinking of me, even though you could not visit me. That was kind of you," said Marian.

Isabel reminisced, "I became a widow at a young age, and it was devastating."

"You were a widow when you married Earl Hamelin?" asked Marian.

Maud and Ela groaned noisily.

"Not this story again," moaned Maud.

Marian frowned, irritated by what she considered their disrespectful response.

Ela proclaimed, "Mother was almost the Queen of England!"

Marian glanced at Constance, but evidently she didn't know the story either.

Ela and Maud stood and stretched; they had both been sitting with their embroidery for a long time.

"Mother, please excuse us," requested Ela. "We will go check on Robbie and Rich to see if they are still napping, and you can tell Marian and Constance your story."

Isabel graciously granted them leave, while Marian and Constance stared at her expectantly.

"Would you like to hear my story?" the older woman inquired, and when they nodded, she continued, "My first husband was William of Blois."

Again, Marian and Constance glanced at each other in confusion.

Isabel sighed. "Oh, my. He would be horrified to learn that he's been forgotten so soon. William was the second son of King Stephen, and after the death of his brother, he was heir to the throne."

Even though Marian was usually bored by such tales of royal intrigue, she found herself eager to hear more.

Constance's face brightened. "I'm sorry, Lady Isabel. Now I remember his name. My father has told me many stories from that time; I believe he was born the same year as William of Blois."

Isabel recalled, "We were children when we were married, so at first we were more like brother and sister. William was very smart, perhaps the most clever person I have ever known. His intelligence often intimidated me, but he was always kind to me and never made me feel like a silly girl."

Smiling wistfully, Isabel gazed into the distance, reminiscences of her youth filling her mind. She added, "He was proud to be the son of a king, and he was a good husband. I was very fond of him."

"I'm sorry," offered Marian with sincerity. The raw anguish of widowhood was still fresh in her memory.

"We were so happy together. But when his older brother died, all William could think about was inheriting the throne. I didn't understand his desire to be king, especially since I did not want to be queen, and we were already so blessed. In addition to my family's Earldom of Surrey, he was also Count of Boulogne and Mortain. We were young, and I hoped we would soon start a family."

Constance's brow knitted in concentration as she tried to recollect the stories she had heard about that time. "But didn't King Stephen sign a treaty that removed William from the succession?"

"Yes. A year before King Stephen died, he named Henry Plantagenet as his heir, effectively ending twenty years of civil war, and ending William's hopes of becoming king. Truthfully, I had never felt such relief."

"Did he accept his father's treaty?" Constance asked.

Isabel grew silent, and just as they wondered whether she would answer, she admitted, "I think William and his father were scheming to take the throne from Henry. During the last year of his father's reign, William was often away from home."

"My father told me that Henry's ascension to the throne after Stephen's death was blessedly peaceful. Did anything come of these schemes?" questioned Constance.

Leaning forward and lowering her voice, Isabel revealed, "Something happened, but it was hidden from everyone, including me. I know William was at his father's deathbed, and he once referred to men who had betrayed him. He was not the same person after his father's death. He became secretive and bitter."

Isabel set aside her embroidery. "I encouraged William to find contentment with our lives, and I begged him to share his troubles with me, but he refused. Men are like that; they are loath to talk about problems or their feelings with their wives."

Marian recognized that Robin was like that too, and she was comforted by the idea that this was simply the way of men and not a sign of problems in their marriage.

Isabel concluded her story, "William died of plague during the siege of Toulouse. Such a waste of his life!"

"My father was at the siege of Toulouse and so was Robin's father," Marian suddenly recalled. "I wish he were still alive so I could ask him about it. I wonder if they knew your husband."

Isabel observed, "It's likely that William knew Earl Duncan; after all, it was King Stephen who bestowed the Earldom of Huntingdon on Duncan's father."

"My father was not at the siege, but he once told me that Duncan saved King Henry's life at Toulouse," commented Constance.

"I heard that story years ago, but I don't remember the details," Marian confessed.

"I should ask Hamelin about it. He was also at the siege," remarked Isabel. "I was so distraught after receiving word of William's death that I never wanted to hear any stories about Toulouse. But I would like to know how Robin's father saved the king."

Several tears wet Isabel's cheeks. "The only thing I know for certain about the siege is that it had to be abandoned because so many men were dying of plague. So, William died for nothing."

Marian heard the grief in Isabel's voice, and overcome by compassion, she knelt in front of the older woman, gently grasping her hands to comfort her.

With a trembling smile, Isabel declared, "But God has blessed me. A few years later, I married Hamelin, and I've realized that Hamelin and I are much better suited for each other. Over the years, we have become like two sides of the same coin. We have four wonderful children, and now we are grandparents."

29 March 1193, Conisbrough Castle

It was mid-morning, and Robin was frustrated by the delays in leaving for Tickhill Castle. Hamelin's men were dutifully loading wagons with supplies, and Robin had already said goodbye to Marian and Robbie.

He hated the look of dread in her eyes, and he recognized her fear that something would happen to him, and he would not return. He was confident that this would be a short separation with little danger that he would be injured or killed. But yet, there were no guarantees in life, and he would never again promise her that he would not die as he recalled the reckless vows he had once made to her.

Standing by his horse, he tapped his fingers against the side of his saddle, fidgeting and struggling to be patient as someone announced a problem with one of the wagons, and a second man left to find the wheelwright.

Robin wondered if he could leave at once with a few men. He waved at Hamelin, who soon joined him.

"Tickhill is only eight miles away; perhaps a group of us could go ahead," suggested Robin.

Hamelin squinted at the sun and advised, "It's such a short distance that even if you left at noon, you'd still arrive before sunset. Besides, I'm worried about the marauders who attacked you on your way here. It'll be safer for everyone to travel as one large group."

Robin knew he was right, and he took a calming breath.

"Robin, there's something I need to say before you leave," declared Hamelin.

"Is there a problem?"

"No, but I want to assure you that no one will say anything to Marian about your marriage to Blanche."

"I appreciate your discretion."

"However, Isabel is adamant that, if Marian asks about it, we will not lie to her."

"I understand. I'm not asking you to lie, but since she knows nothing about it, I'm certain it won't come up in conversation."

"Agreed," said Hamelin. "I need to warn you about one more thing. Hugh de Puiset will probably corner you and ask about Isabel. It's none of his damn business, but he's always sticking his nose into our affairs."

"What do you want me to say to him? And what is his interest in her, if I may ask?"

"He considers her part of his family because William of Blois was his cousin. Just tell him she is happy and in the best of health."

"That's easily done. I'm trying to remember; that was her first husband, right? The one who died at the siege of Toulouse?"

"Did your father tell you what happened there?"

"Was that the siege where my father saved King Henry's life?"

"I was there, and I remember it well. Your father learned that William was plotting to murder Henry. Duncan saved the king, but William died before we could arrest him. We believe he committed suicide to avoid facing the consequences of his attempt to kill Henry."

Robin considered Hamelin's words. "It must be difficult for Lady Isabel to be reminded of such dark deeds. Is that why you keep Hugh de Puiset away from her?"

Hamelin nervously cleared his throat. "This is why you must tell Marian the truth about Blanche as soon as possible. The longer you keep a secret from your wife, the harder it is to tell her the truth. And eventually, it will be impossible to reveal it. Isabel was fond of her first husband. She has good memories of him, and I didn't want to distress her by telling her what had happened."

"Are you saying that she doesn't know how her husband died?" questioned Robin.

"She thinks he died of plague. Many men were dying of a mysterious illness, and that was one reason for Henry's withdrawal from the siege. But it wasn't plague; your father discovered that the ale had been poisoned. It was part of William's plot to kill Henry."

An increasingly alarmed Robin asked, "The men were poisoned? Although my father told me about the siege and the attempt to murder Henry, he never mentioned poison." Robin was briefly overcome by memories of Blanche writhing on the floor and foaming at the mouth, as the poisoned wine she had tasted took her life and that of their unborn child.

"Your father found the poison in William's tent after his death. Isabel doesn't know how evil this man was or how he really died. And now, after all these years, I'm not sure how she would respond if she knew that I've hidden the truth from her."

Just then, there was a commotion at the front of the keep. Hamelin and Robin turned to watch as Marian led Isabel, Ela, Maud, and Constance out of the keep and towards the other end of the bailey. To Robin's surprise, they were all carrying small bows, the type that young boys used in training, and they had bracers wrapped around their arms.

Marian glanced in his direction, lifting her chin with a stubborn expression he had seen far too often. She was daring him to forbid whatever scheme she had planned.

Hamelin chortled. "I was hoping you'd be gone before this. Don't worry; I'll go and supervise."

"Supervise what?" asked Robin.

"Marian is going to teach archery to the other women. They've organized an area on the other side of the bailey with targets and such."

Robin grinned. "She has some skills, but I would feel better if you were there to prevent them from accidentally killing each other."

Laughing, Hamelin walked away.

At that moment, Guillaume rode up and informed Robin that everything was ready.

It was time to set off for Tickhill Castle.

CHAPTER 6
THE SIEGE OF TICKHILL

8 April 1193, Tickhill Castle, South Yorkshire

Robin was so focused on making some final adjustments to his siege machine that he was startled by Lionel tapping on his shoulder.

"He's coming. I thought you'd like to know."

"Thanks for the warning," replied a resigned Robin.

"Here," Lionel thrust a rag into his hand, "you better clean up a bit. You know how he feels about proper decorum."

Robin rolled his eyes and took the cloth, wiping the sweat from his brow and the dirt from his hands. A side wise glance told him that the elderly Hugh de Puiset, Bishop of Durham, Earl of Northumbria, and Sheriff of Northumberland, was gingerly stepping across the muddy field in his fine robes. The pained look on his face was unmistakable: this was a man who had spent most of his life within the comfort of his well-furnished home.

Bishop Hugh was approaching his seventh decade, and he had never served as a military commander. He had a keen interest in architecture and the art of construction, and he also owned an extensive library, but he seemed more interested in collecting books rather than reading them. He lived with his long-term mistress, the mother of his four grown sons, all of whom had remained in Durham instead of assisting with the siege.

His life in the church and his royal connections as a nephew of King Stephen had led to an impressive accumulation of wealth and prestige, which he had enhanced by purchasing the Earldom of Northumbria and the post of sheriff shortly after King Richard's coronation, when the king had been raising funds for the Crusade.

It had been ten days since Robin's arrival at the siege of Tickhill. He had been tasked with building a siege machine and taking command of the men-at-arms and knights who had assembled to wrest control of Tickhill from Prince John's supporters. Although the area around Tickhill was under John's dominion, the castle itself belonged to the crown.

Prince John was currently lodged in Windsor Castle, where Walter de Coutances, the Archbishop of Rouen, was leading the siege against him. In Tickhill, many of John's northern liegemen were defending the castle in his name. Because Bishop Hugh was one of the highest ranking men in the north, he had been given the responsibility of taking Tickhill Castle from John's men.

Unlike Conisbrough, Tickhill was not set upon a natural hill, but it was built on a motte surrounded by a wall and a moat. King Henry had rebuilt Tickhill's keep and wall in stone. Bishop Hugh's camp was just beyond the range of the castle's archers as they stood on the wall.

In the time since Robin's arrival, rainy weather and a lack of supplies had hindered him in his construction of the siege machine. Robin had hoped to build a trebuchet with the same design as the ones King Richard had used to end the siege of Acre, but with the lack of materials, the finished machine was much smaller than the mighty siege engines deployed at Acre. He hoped that Bishop Hugh would not be disappointed.

Guillaume joined Robin and Lionel. "Is it ready?" he asked, a note of optimism in his voice.

"I've no way to test it, so we'll just have to hope for the best," responded Robin.

Lionel said, "Finally, we can start this siege in earnest. I'm tired of waiting."

"I'm tired of the rain," whined Guillaume as he gazed at Tickhill.

Just then, Bishop Hugh arrived, and he was slightly winded from his walk across the camp.

Lionel and Guillaume genuflected, while Robin bowed and announced, "Your Grace, I'm ready to use this trebuchet against the walls of Tickhill. I've not been able to test it, but with your approval, we can begin the attack."

The bishop frowned. "Very well, I grant you permission. But you must avoid damaging the bridge and the chapel in the bailey; Queen Eleanor commissioned the construction of both, and they were completed last year."

Lionel asked, "Your Grace, we can only see the roofs of the buildings from here. Is the chapel adjacent to the keep?"

"Yes," answered Hugh. "It would be terrible if I had to report to Queen Eleanor that it was damaged."

"The wall is also new," commented Guillaume. "Even though King Henry ordered it built many years ago, it was recently completed as well."

Hugh proclaimed, "This is an excellent wall; I doubt we will have much success in defeating these fortifications."

"We will find out soon enough," Robin declared. "Your Grace, please stand back; there is a dry patch of ground over there. Although the wheels of the machine are blocked to keep it in place, I fear that the movement of the trebuchet as it throws the rock might splash mud on you if you're standing too close."

As the bishop moved to a safe place, Guillaume and Lionel set a large stone in the sling and moved the counterweight into place. Once everything was set, Robin again checked the aim, knowing that the bridge was to be avoided. The chapel was out of range, so he wasn't worried about damaging it.

Everyone backed away as Robin released the counterweight. The wood creaked under the strain, and there was a whoosh of movement as the arm swung. The stone was released from its sling and hurtled towards the wall. With a crash, it knocked down the upper three feet from a small section. Robin was pleased that it had functioned correctly, but he was dissatisfied with the aim. He would have to adjust it lower to take out a complete section of the wall.

His men were whooping with excitement at the direct hit to the wall, and Robin turned, beaming with pride, to see Bishop Hugh's reaction.

Hugh cried out in distress, and his expression could only be described as horrified.

Robin rushed over to the bishop, along with Guillaume and Lionel.

"Your Grace, this was only our first attempt. With any new machine, small adjustments are required. I will correct the aim lower, and the next strike will demolish the remaining portion of that part of the wall," explained Robin.

Shouting in the distance distracted him, and Robin glanced over his shoulder to see the men in Tickhill working to refortify the area of damage.

Lionel motioned to their men to retrieve another large stone and work to reset the trebuchet.

"But, but," stammered Hugh, "it knocked down part of the wall!"

"Please don't be disheartened," replied Robin. "As soon as we reload, we can take the rest of that section out. Then we'll take down the next section. When enough wall has been demolished, then we can mount an attack. Hopefully, they'll surrender first."

"Demolished?" Hugh's voice went up an octave, and all the color drained from his face.

Robin looked at him curiously.

Recovering his wits, the bishop cried, "No! Stop! Tell your men to cease at once!"

Lionel promptly signaled to the nearby men to wait.

At that moment, Robin realized Hugh was not lamenting the trebuchet's failure to take down the entire section; he was upset that the wall had been damaged at all. Struggling to contain his rising aggravation, Robin inquired, "What did you think my machine would do to the wall? Don't you understand the purpose of such a device?"

"I thought it would frighten the defenders, but I didn't think it would damage such a sturdy, well-built wall. It's very important that the defenders surrender with a minimum amount of damage to Tickhill's fortifications," disclosed Hugh.

Robin silently fumed. Breathing deeply through his nose, he regained his composure and asked, "If we can't knock down the wall, how do you propose we win this siege?"

Hugh harrumphed in irritation. "You're the military genius; you tell me. That's why you're here."

Still reining in his emotions, Robin tightly gripped the hilt of his sheathed sword as he described another option for ending the siege. "Sometimes sieges are ended by tunneling under a wall and undermining it, which would cause it to collapse. But you don't want to harm the walls, and with this wet weather, digging is out of the question. I will point out that most sieges involve destroying walls so the attackers can enter the city or fortress and fight the defenders."

"Heavens, no! I told you we cannot destroy the wall," insisted Hugh.

Guillaume offered, "We could build a siege tower and roll it up to the side of the wall. We could even build it to fit within the width of that new bridge."

Robin nodded in agreement. "King Richard often affixed small catapults to the top of his siege towers. But siege towers are typically deployed after a portion of the wall has been destroyed. The defenders are then forced to divide their men between the breach in the wall and the approaching siege towers. If we had a multitude of men and towers, we could overwhelm the archers on the wall. But we don't have enough men, and I refuse to send my men on a hopeless assault that is tantamount to suicide."

Lionel added, "And siege towers are susceptible to flaming arrows. I've heard of men who were burned alive in these towers."

"God forbid!" Hugh exclaimed, crossing himself at the thought of such a horrible death. He demanded, "We must come up with another option. I don't want to lose too many men, but most importantly, we can't damage a royal castle."

"Don't you think that King Richard would want *his* castle cleared of men who are opposed to his rule?" Robin suggested. "Their support of Prince John is an act of treason."

Hugh's face brightened with an idea. "Let's starve them. That way the wall will not be damaged, and King Richard will not have to spend money to repair it."

Robin, Guillaume, and Lionel looked at each other with matching expressions of dismay on their faces.

As the highest ranking man of the three, Robin tried to reason with the bishop. "Depending on their supplies, it could take months to force their surrender. And what if there are women and children within the walls?"

"Perhaps we could cut off their access to water too." Lionel proposed.

"They might have good stores of water," Guillaume countered, "and with this rain, it will be replenished."

Hugh made his decision. "We will starve them. Earl Robin, you have the most military experience of all the men here. You must devise a strategy that will encourage them to surrender without damaging the wall or losing too many of our men." He then eyed

Robin's trebuchet with disgust, and lifting the edges of his robes to avoid the mud, he returned to his large, richly appointed tent on the other side of the camp.

When he was far enough away to give them privacy, the men moaned in frustration.

Robin questioned, "Doesn't he *want* to prevail in this siege?"

Lionel barked a short laugh. "Robin, surely you are not this naïve. Bishop Hugh doesn't want to treat John's supporters too harshly. If Richard doesn't return, then John will be king, and no one wants to incur the wrath of their future king."

"He is trying to play both sides," surmised Guillaume. He then remarked, "I'm well acquainted with John; after all, he's my cousin. His temper is fearsome to behold."

Robin knew they were right, and he admitted, "I've never fought in such a war—where my side was afraid to win."

Calling over several of the more senior men-at-arms, Robin explained the need to encircle the fortress to prevent anyone from entering or leaving Tickhill. He then instructed them to implement a system of staggered shifts to avoid the problem of men sleeping during their watch. They would also need to maintain positions either behind cover or beyond the range of the archers stationed on the wall.

27 April 1193, Tickhill Castle

It had been nearly three weeks since Bishop Hugh had decided to starve the defenders into surrender. Robin and his companions had spent the time practicing archery and sword fighting, and whenever the rains forced them into their tent, they played games of Nine Men's Morris and backgammon.

Robin had become increasingly restless, and he was reminded of Marian's description of a siege as two sides 'standing around and watching each other.' After ten days of wasting time, Robin could not bear the continued monotony of the stalemate. Working with Guillaume and Lionel, he devised a new strategy.

First, they built a shell that surrounded the main body of the trebuchet where the mechanisms to set and release the arm with the counterweight were located. Then they constructed a small siege tower.

Their idea was to position the trebuchet closer to the fortress, so they could launch their missiles *over* the wall. The protective shell around the workings of the trebuchet would shield the men who were arming it from the archers along the wall. The small siege tower would move forward and backward between the trebuchet and the supply of large rocks that served as the machine's ammunition.

Their goal would be to target the kitchens and storerooms near the keep, hoping to destroy Tickhill's food supplies while, of course, avoiding the chapel and the keep itself.

Fortunately, Guillaume was familiar with Tickhill, as he had grown up only a few miles from it. He knew the layout of the buildings in the bailey, and although the keep and the chapel were constructed with stone, the remaining structures were mostly wood, and they would be easily demolished.

They just needed a series of sunny, rain-free days to dry the ground over which the trebuchet and tower would be rolled, and at last, the sun had cooperated.

Bishop Hugh spent most of his time in his tent, and he had shown little interest in Robin's activities.

Two days after the Feast of Saint Mark the Evangelist, Robin visited Hugh and explained the new strategy. The bishop was still worried about Queen Eleanor's chapel, but he grudgingly gave permission for Robin to proceed.

Robin, Guillaume, and Lionel were in high spirits as they rolled the trebuchet to the foot of the bridge. Shouts along the walls of Tickhill indicated that the defenders had seen their approach and were suitably alarmed. A hail of arrows descended on Robin and the others, but they remained protected within the new shell shielding the trebuchet.

While the other men under Robin's command provided cover and distracted the archers on the wall by releasing arrows at them, Guillaume and Lionel loaded a large rock into the sling, and Robin adjusted the aim.

Their first attempt sailed safely over the wall and landed with a thud in the bailey.

A disappointed Robin knew he had missed the target, and he signaled for the men in the small siege tower to advance with another rock. They delivered their cargo and promptly backed away beyond the range of the archers defending Tickhill.

Once more they armed the trebuchet, and Robin corrected its aim. He was launching his projectiles blind, relying on Guillaume's descriptions of the distance and location of the kitchens and adjoining storerooms.

Again he released the trebuchet's load, and this time, everyone heard a satisfying crash as the rock landed on a building. Robin prayed it wasn't the chapel.

He signaled to the men behind him, and they delivered a torch and a rock covered with tar.

Robin had taught both Lionel and Guillaume how to operate the trebuchet. Leaving the aim as it was, Lionel launched the next rock while Robin ignited an arrow. He aimed at the tar-covered rock as it sailed above the wall. His arrow skimmed along the side of the rock before falling away, but it was enough to ignite the tar. When the flaming rock landed, there was a whoosh of flames greedily attacking the wooden structure damaged by the previous rock.

Robin and his men repeated this sequence again, and they successfully targeted a second building, crushing it and then sending a flaming projectile to set it alight.

At that point, the archers on the wall commenced releasing flaming arrows at both the trebuchet and the siege tower. Not wanting to lose his siege machine, Robin signaled for everyone to withdraw from the bridge to the safety of the camp.

When they arrived at the camp, he could see that they had inflicted serious damage to the buildings Guillaume had identified as the kitchens and food storerooms. Eleanor's chapel was untouched.

Bishop Hugh seemed pleased by the result.

The sun was setting, and bright flames from Tickhill's bailey continued to light up the darkening sky.

Robin hoped that enough of their food supplies had been destroyed to end the siege sooner rather than later.

⨎

After a second day of destruction within the bailey, the commander of Tickhill sent word that he wished to have a parley to discuss terms. It was agreed that at noon on the following day, Prince John's supporters would surrender to Bishop Hugh.

Robin was elated. Other than the small amount of damage to the wall from his initial use of the trebuchet, the wall was intact, and the all-important chapel and bridge were unscathed. He would soon be on his way home to Locksley with Marian and Robbie.

29 April 1193, Tickhill Castle

The sun was approaching its zenith as Tickhill's gate opened, and three unarmed men emerged. They made their way on foot over the bridge and into the camp. Bishop Hugh greeted them cordially and offered them food and wine before officially accepting their surrender.

Robin was content to defer to Hugh for the formalities, and he excused himself.

Walking across the camp, he had to maneuver through a chaotic scene as men were taking down tents and packing their belongings.

Everyone was in a jubilant mood; they were victorious, and they were going home.

When he found Guillaume, Robin inquired, "Is everything prepared for our departure? If we leave soon, we could be back at Conisbrough before dark."

"The siege machine has been dismantled, and my father's men are eager to depart," Guillaume replied.

Robin realized that Lionel was missing. "Where's Lionel?"

"He was standing over there." Guillaume scanned the immediate area.

Suddenly, Lionel rushed up, breathless. "Someone's just arrived from London; come quick!"

"Who?" chorused Robin and Guillaume.

"It's Hubert Walter. He has word of Richard!"

∽

A short time later, Robin was listening to his old crusading companion, Hubert Walter, the Bishop of Salisbury and a close friend of the king. He was describing how he had arrived in England on April 20th, after visiting Richard in Germany, and he had traveled to Tickhill to apprise Bishop Hugh of the latest developments.

"On April 22nd, the Great Council and Queen Eleanor entered into a truce with Prince John. He has surrendered control of Windsor and Wallingford to the queen mother while retaining Tickhill and Nottingham. This truce will be in effect for six months beginning on May 1st."

Hubert addressed the men from Tickhill, "Please return to your keep. You are in no danger of further attack."

Robin watched the men, who moments ago were surrendering under duress, leap to their feet, grinning and thanking the Bishop of Durham for his hospitality and praising Prince John for successfully negotiating such a generous truce.

Hubert Walter dismissed everyone from the tent except for Bishop Hugh and Robin.

"Is King Richard in good health?" asked Robin.

"He is in good health and high spirits," responded Hubert.

Hugh was noticeably relieved, even exuberant. "This is wonderful news! Please grant me leave; I must make sure that my people will be ready to depart for Durham at first light tomorrow. At last, I can go home!"

Hubert graciously dismissed the older man, and as soon as they were alone, he briefly embraced Robin. "My friend! I am so happy to find you here. King Richard commanded me to search for you. Your king needs you."

Robin did not hesitate to reply, "I am honored by Richard's confidence in me, and I stand ready to serve him. What is the situation in Germany?"

Hubert's face fell into dismay. "Robin, the situation is dire. Last month, on Easter Sunday of all days, Richard was placed on trial—"

"For what?" cried Robin. "He's a returning Crusader under the protection of the Truce of God."

"The accusations were absurd. They were based on gossip I've heard since my return from the Holy Land. I was in Rome when word of Richard's capture reached me."

"I was in Paris last year, and I heard these outlandish rumors as well," recalled Robin.

"Richard brilliantly defended himself, and he convinced Heinrich and the German princes to dismiss the charges."

"When will he be allowed to leave?"

Hubert touched the large gold cross that hung from his neck as he contemplated his reply. "They will not release him without a payment."

"A ransom?"

"Of course it's a ransom, but they are careful to avoid using that word. They claim it is a dowry for Richard's niece to marry the son of the Duke of Austria."

"How much?" questioned Robin. He was growing alarmed at the fretful look on Hubert's face.

"One-hundred thousand silver marks and hostages from the noble families of Richard's lands."

Robin was speechless, and he gaped at the other man. Recovering some, he blurted out, "Does any land have such wealth to give away? It will be impossible to deliver such a ransom."

Hubert laid his hand on Robin's shoulder. "Be at ease, my son. By the grace of God, King Richard's lands will find a way to gather this vast sum. This was one reason for giving John such a lenient truce. Everyone must be focused on raising the ransom, including Prince John. Already, Queen Eleanor and the Great Council are laying plans for the collection of this payment."

"I'm ready and willing to contribute to this ransom, but is there something else that Richard needs me to do?"

"Richard is counting on you. He knows there are men who will need to be watched; men who will not willingly help raise the ransom."

"John's supporters," surmised Robin.

"Certainly. But Richard is also concerned about men who are loyal to King Philippe. One of our goals in granting John this truce was to drive a wedge between him and Philippe."

"Did he name anyone?" Robin asked, although he was convinced he knew their names.

"Richard's exact words were, 'Robin must watch those who dwell in the shadows.' Does that make sense to you? The king did not reveal any names to me; we could not speak with any privacy as his jailers were nearby," divulged Hubert.

"I am well acquainted with these men in the shadows, and I know what needs to be done," Robin replied, his face set with a grim determination.

❦

A glum Robin approached Guillaume and Lionel and delivered the shocking news of Richard's ransom to them.

"Richard will never return," Lionel adamantly proclaimed. "We should prepare for John's coronation instead of giving the wealth of England to the Holy Roman Emperor."

"We can't abandon Richard," insisted Guillaume. "I'm willing to swear fealty to John as my king, but only if Richard is dead. As long as Richard lives, he is our king, and it's our duty to raise this ransom."

Robin silently listened to their argument. He was still reeling from the news of the ransom, and he was daunted at the prospect of raising such a staggering sum. But Robin also feared that if John ascended to the throne, a vengeful King John would destroy him and his family.

Just then, a familiar figure rode past them, heading south along the main thoroughfare.

Robin was alarmed to see Tancred de Payen, Argentan's loyal lieutenant, leaving Tickhill. He knew Argentan was not at Tickhill, but seeing one of the sheriff's most senior knights was proof that Argentan was still actively supporting John.

Payen was an odd looking young man; his pallid complexion, grey eyes, and white hair gave him a ghostly appearance, and his reputation for mixing poisons was widely acknowledged. Robin knew that one of Payen's poisons had killed all but a few of his band of merry men following his departure for the Crusade, and he couldn't help but wonder if Payen had played a role in the poisoning of Blanche and her sister.

"Payen!" Robin angrily shouted as he drew his sword.

The other man's eyes widened in alarm when he saw Robin, but he rapidly recovered his composure and replied in his thick French accent, "You have no authority over me. The truce gives me free passage to return to Nottingham."

Robin fumed, knowing that he was right, and he watched the other man as he spurred his horse into a trot. He shoved his sword back in its sheath with a force that nearly split the aging leather.

"Who was that man?" asked Guillaume.

"He's one of Sheriff de Argentan's knights," responded Robin through gritted teeth.

Guillaume squinted at the retreating figure. "Isn't Argentan the man who sent those mercenaries to attack you on the road?"

"We have no proof of that," countered Lionel.

Still attempting to calm himself, Robin solemnly vowed, "When I return to Locksley with Marian and Robbie, I will bring Sheriff de Argentan out of the shadows and into the sunlight."

CHAPTER 7
OUT OF THE SHADOWS

4 May 1193, Nottingham Castle

An exhausted Guy of Gisborne trudged along the deserted, dark corridors of Nottingham Castle, thankful that he had grabbed a torch to light his way. Although it was nearing midnight, he was certain that the sheriff would still be awake and working in his tower room.

When he arrived at the tower's winding staircase, he was surprised to find that there was no guard on duty. The stairway was lit with evenly spaced torches, so he left his torch in a bracket on the wall, and he somehow mustered the strength to mount the steep stairs. He had been riding hard for several days to deliver the sealed message he carried from King Philippe.

At the top of the stairs, there was an antechamber that led to a pair of large wooden doors. Beyond the doors was the chamber where the sheriff sat behind his big, messy desk and conducted his business. The tower room was brightly lit, and his master was apparently awaiting his arrival and the delivery of the king's dispatch.

Guy entered and briefly dropped to one knee before rising.

The sheriff frowned. "What's your excuse for arriving at this late hour?"

"The ship was delayed, so I disembarked at Dover later than expected. I rode here with all haste."

Standing and moving to the front of his desk, the sheriff held out his hand with an air of impatience, and Guy gave him the letter. After examining the seal for signs of tampering, he opened it and silently read.

Gisborne remarked, "My lord, I'm troubled that there is no guard at the foot of the stairs."

His master refolded the missive and casually tossed it on his desk. Dismissing Guy's concerns, he declared, "This late at night, I see no reason to pay for men to stand around listening as I conduct important business. I moved the guards to the far end of the corridor that leads here."

"But, my lord, we always speak in French. The guards will not understand what we're saying."

"Are you so sure, Gisborne? Did you know that your charming wife is fluent in French?"

His brow creased in confusion, Guy countered, "I'm sure she would have—"

"That she would have told you?" The sheriff laughed. "Your idiocy is a constant source of amusement. After speaking to Lionel, I learned that their mother was French. They both speak it, and so does Baron Embelton."

Guy was alarmed at this news and incensed that she would keep such a secret. How many conversations had he conducted in French with the sheriff or Payen in her presence? It occurred to him that Marian's uncanny ability to find nobles along the road and her success in thwarting so many of the sheriff's schemes might have been his fault. Even though he knew Constance's loyalty would be with her family and Marian, there was a twist in the pit of his stomach at her betrayal.

The sheriff interrupted his dark musings. "We must be more

careful, particularly at this critical juncture in the implementation of my plan."

"What is the plan, my lord?" Guy wearily asked, knowing that he had asked this countless times before, only to be repeatedly rebuffed and informed that he was too stupid to understand it.

"We are supporting John's claim to the throne. John has already pledged fealty to King Philippe, and when you were in Paris, I'm sure you heard about our king's many triumphs in capturing important castles along the frontier between Normandy and France. Some of these fortresses surrendered to our glorious king without a fight."

Guy attempted to feign the proper level of enthusiasm. "I saw several grand celebrations in Paris. Many believe the king will soon conquer all of Normandy and perhaps even the Angevin lands." Changing the subject, he inquired, "Has Payen returned from Tickhill? I suppose he will resume his role of messenger, and I can return to my duties as your captain."

The sheriff's eyes narrowed in annoyance, and Guy immediately regretted his words; they had probably sounded like a complaint to his master.

"The siege of Tickhill ended with a truce that allowed Prince John to retain control of Nottingham. Again, events are turning in our favor. Payen should appear at any moment; I was expecting him when you arrived. For now, you will continue to carry dispatches between Paris and Nottingham. I have other plans for Payen."

Knowing he was dismissed, Guy departed. At the bottom of the stairs, he found himself face to face with the pale poisoner. The two men eyed each other with suspicion.

"Is the sheriff alone?" asked Payen.

"Yes. He's expecting you."

Without another word, Payen swiftly mounted the stairs and was soon out of sight.

Guy lingered by the stairs, deep in thought. He was tired of always playing the role of a puppet dwelling helplessly in the dark.

One thing he had learned from the sheriff was that knowledge was power. An idea formed in his mind.

Removing his scabbard and sword, he then slipped off his boots and left everything at the foot of the stairs. His heart pounding in his chest, he quietly climbed towards the tower room. Near the top of the stairs, he paused when he could gaze across the floor of the antechamber. To his relief, only one door was closed completely, and the other was ajar. Noiselessly gliding through the antechamber, he stood behind the closed door and listened through the narrow space of the partially open door.

"…Huntingdon was at the siege of Tickhill. Lionel was with him," Payen reported.

The sheriff remarked, "I will persist in my cultivation of Lionel. He may be under his father's authority for now, but I have hope that he will rejoin our cause."

"My lord, what is your plan for me?"

"You will be my liaison with John. He's currently sulking in Dorset after losing control of Windsor and Wallingford. Keep in mind that agents of the Great Council will read all his correspondence, so the dispatches you carry will be innocent, banal missives."

"Will the messages be in code?" questioned Payen.

"Heavens, no," responded the sheriff. "That's much too complicated. You will memorize the actual messages, and when you and John are alone, you will recite my words and receive his response. Can you handle that, Payen?"

"Yes, my lord, of course."

"This first letter is an accounting of spring planting in Nottinghamshire, but the message you will give him is to explain how we will exchange information in the future, and you will also tell him I'm very worried for his safety. Just as I once sent you to protect him, I'm sending you again."

Payen laughed. "I remember that time so well. I was with John and his father at Christmas and Easter. The feasts were magnificent."

"Perhaps not so tasty for King Henry, I suppose."

Again, Payen chortled. "I was well-placed to season his food with the same poison we used on Henry the Younger. Unfortunately, the old man kept recovering, so I doubled the dosage and mixed it in his favorite wine."

"I hope he suffered," growled the sheriff.

"I assure you he died a miserable death."

Guy was initially aghast, but then, he recollected many clues over the years that he had foolishly ignored. He had suspected that King Henry and his oldest son might have been poisoned, but he hadn't spent any time thinking about it because he didn't really want to know the truth.

And then he recalled the tournament in Paris and Prince Geoffrey's fatal accident. A few days later, Duncan Fitzooth had been murdered, and for the first time, he fully understood that he served the man who had murdered his real father.

Guy's hatred and resentment nearly overwhelmed him. Murderous thoughts caused him to strike the stone wall with a clenched fist. Fearful that he had made too much noise, he forced himself to refocus on the conversation within the tower room. He needed to leave before he was discovered, and just when he started moving away from the door, he heard the sheriff speaking.

"You will spend most of your time with John. Stay with him, even if he leaves Dorset. And especially if he departs England. Keep me informed of your location whenever it's safe to send word."

"My lord, how will I know when to serve John our special seasoned wine?"

The two men chuckled, and the sheriff explained, "King Philippe has invited Emperor Heinrich to Paris for the Feast of Midsummer. His strategy is to convince him to hand over Richard. If Philippe takes custody of Richard, then I will send you the message, 'Serve my favorite wine.' After you've poisoned John, return to Paris, and we will begin the process of slowly poisoning Richard…"

Guy had heard enough. He cautiously backed away and hurriedly descended the stairs.

As he pulled on his boots and picked up his scabbard and sword, he was struck by the realization that the sheriff's plot was to kill both Richard *and* John. But then who would rule England? Did King Philippe believe he could conquer the island? That seemed unlikely. Guy would need to keep listening to learn as much as possible.

8 May 1193, On the Road Near Lenton

Guy spurred his horse into a trot. After receiving a note from Constance, he had experienced conflicting emotions. He enjoyed her company and had missed her greatly over the past four months, so he was eager to see her again. He wondered if her opinion of him had improved now that he was no longer guilty of murdering Robin.

But he was also dismayed by the revelation that she had deceived him by purposefully hiding her knowledge of French while listening to his conversations with the sheriff and Payen.

As he rounded a bend, he saw her standing next to her horse, waiting for him at the fork in the road that led to Lenton. He knew she was staying at Lenton with her father and brother while Locksley housed Robin, Marian, and their son.

Thinking of Locksley filled him with a sense of loss. After living in the small manor these past few years, he had grown very fond of it. It had become a home to him; his first real home since the death of his mother nearly twenty years ago.

Guy hopped off his horse and approached her, admonishing, "You should not be alone on the road like this. Does Lord Edmund know you are here without a guard?"

She smiled at him and insisted, "I'm in no danger here. And yes, my father knows I've come to meet you."

Although he was still uncomfortable with the idea that she was alone on the road, he decided to put her to the test. He boldly embraced her, and she did not resist. Addressing her in French, he softly declared, "I've missed you, my wife. Will you allow me to greet you with a kiss?"

Constance blushed and nodded.

Guy recognized that, not only did she understand French, but she was so comfortable with the language that she did not notice what he had done. Despite the disappointment he felt over her deception, he lowered his face to hers and gave her a kiss that she would not soon forget.

∽

A startled Robin observed from within the tree line. He had been told by Edmund that this marriage was merely a ruse, and that it had not been consummated. Yet, the kiss he was watching was undeniably passionate.

Deciding that he needed to put an end to this display of affection, he signaled to his men.

Led by Little John, who was carrying a length of rope, Much, Allan-a-dale, and Will Scarlet emerged from the trees. Robin tapped Gisborne on the shoulder, chagrined that the man was so engrossed in kissing Constance that he was oblivious to their presence.

Guy jerked to attention and instinctively moved Constance behind him. "You!" he cried.

"Unhand my cousin, Gisborne."

Guy released Constance, and the surprised look on his face morphed into an expression of disgust. Glaring at Constance, he hissed, "You've betrayed me to my enemies!"

Constance paled. "No, Guy! It's not like that at all. Robin just wants to talk to you, and he couldn't send you a message."

Gisborne turned his back on her. Facing Robin, he crossed his arms. "All right. Talk."

"You're coming with us," Robin announced.

Gisborne abruptly charged towards his horse and attempted to mount it, but John grabbed him by the collar of his tunic and tossed him on the ground. The remaining outlaws piled on him until Gisborne was pinned. John secured his hands by tying the rope around his wrists, while Much took his sword and dagger.

Constance was shrieking, "Robin, stop them! You promised you wouldn't hurt him!"

"Settle yourself, Constance," Robin scolded. "They aren't hurting him. They're simply persuading him to cooperate."

Will and Allan retrieved everyone's horses from their hiding place in the trees, and John handed the end of the rope to Robin. Then, they began their journey to Lenton Manor, which was less than a mile away.

Gisborne was forced to walk behind Robin's horse, and he had to jog to avoid falling to the ground and being dragged along the road.

Constance implored, "Please let him ride his horse."

"It's too risky. He might escape if he's on his horse." Robin glanced at Guy. "Unless he would like to be draped over the saddle with his arse in the air."

The other men laughed, but Gisborne remained silent as he focused on staying upright.

✍

Robin watched as Little John roughly shoved Gisborne to one end of Lenton Manor's great hall and, after retying his hands so they were secured behind his back, John forced him to kneel.

"Much, I want you, Allan, Will, and John to go outside and keep watch," ordered Robin.

After the former outlaws had left, only Edmund, Marian, Constance, and Brother Tuck remained with Robin and Guy.

Robin stood in front of Guy and interrogated him. "Did Argentan hire mercenaries to kill me and my family on the road to Conisbrough?"

"I know nothing about that," Guy replied.

Robin was inclined to believe him, as the look of surprise on his face had been spontaneous and unguarded. "What is Argentan's plan? Is he supporting John's bid for the throne?"

"I don't know."

This was clearly a lie, as Gisborne's eyes had shifted to the left. Robin applied a bit more pressure. "Do you realize that the Great Council will execute you for your attempt to murder Richard in Acre? Treason is a hanging offense."

Constance cried out, "No! You promised he wouldn't be hurt."

Robin glanced over his shoulder and observed as Edmund impatiently tugged her arm and whispered into her ear. She instantly sobered.

He returned his attention to his prisoner. "What do you have to say for yourself?"

Guy responded, "It's within their power to take vengeance on behalf of Richard, or even retaliate for my attack on you, but I've never committed treason."

Robin dismissively countered, "Attacking your king is treason. You are speaking nonsense."

Edmund stepped forward. "Wait, Robin. Let me ask him something. Guy, who is your king? Whom do you serve?"

"I am a vassal of King Philippe," announced Guy. "I've never betrayed him. I have always served my king faithfully."

Finally understanding his meaning, Robin stated, "Then you are a spy sent by a foreign power to interfere in the affairs of England. The penalty for that is also death."

Guy nodded in agreement. "You speak the truth. At least I will die knowing that you are alive, and that gives me hope for God's mercy."

Robin studied Guy and noticed that he had changed since their last meeting on that fateful day in Acre. His pale blue eyes, so much like their father's, were not as hard and cruel as he remembered.

Instead, they were shaded with sorrow and regret. At that moment, Robin believed Guy could be redeemed.

"Lord Robin, Gisborne bravely rescued your wife and son from the dungeons of Nottingham Castle," asserted Brother Tuck.

Marian grudgingly agreed. "It's true; at great risk to his own life, he saved us."

"Robin," Constance interjected, "Argentan was going to kill Robbie and auction Marian's hand in marriage to one of John's supporters in order to take control of your earldom."

There was a brief silence.

"Gisborne, is this true?" questioned Robin.

A subdued Guy answered, "Yes, it's all true."

Turning his back to Gisborne, Robin divulged, "There's another reason why I'm hesitant to send this man to be executed. Gisborne is my father's bastard son."

For a moment, Constance and Marian gazed at each other in confusion until understanding dawned on their faces.

"That can't be true," insisted Marian.

Edmund acknowledged, "I can confirm that it's true. Duncan sent Baroness Gisborne to Embelton to hide the truth from my sister, Edith. Guy was born in Embelton."

"Why didn't you tell me?" Constance exclaimed.

"When we thought Robin was dead, I didn't think it mattered. To be honest, it wasn't my story to tell. But if Robin wants to reveal it to you, then he is within his rights," explained Edmund.

Robin emphasized, "I don't want Lionel to know the truth about Gisborne. Until we can trust him completely, we must be cautious."

Just then, Marian walked up to Guy and peered down at him. He tilted his face to meet her scrutiny, and she gasped. "Your eyes, they look like Robin's. Now I understand why I kept thinking of Robin when I looked at you, and that's why I couldn't kill you."

Guy did not respond; he had suspected as much when he saw the expression on her face as she raised her dagger over his head.

Refocusing on Guy, Robin remarked, "You are not a member of the nobility, so I doubt you paid homage directly to King Philippe. Give me the name of your master."

"Baron de Argentan, of course."

"How do you expect me to show you mercy when you are lying to me? Last summer, I traveled to Paris and learned the truth about Count de Montlhéry."

The shock on Guy's face was unmistakable.

Encouraged by this reaction, Robin asked, "That's his crest and creed on your sword, isn't it?"

Guy's shoulders sagged, and in quiet resignation, he admitted, "Yes, I serve Count de Montlhéry, and he gave me that sword at my knighting ceremony."

Robin proclaimed, "As an earl of the realm and a faithful subject of King Richard, I should hand you over to the Great Council as a spy now—"

"Robin! Please—" begged Constance.

Edmund shushed her again, his agitation growing along with his alarm over her obvious attachment to this man who, in his opinion, was unworthy of her affections.

Ignoring his cousin's outburst, Robin offered, "However, we are family. I'm willing to grant you mercy, but it comes at a price. What price are you willing to pay?"

Guy gazed into Robin's eyes and vowed, "I will pay any price."

"You must be prepared to risk your life in service to me and my liege lord, King Richard."

There was a slight pause, as if Guy were weighing his options, and then he stated, "I risk my life every day in service to Montlhéry and King Philippe. I know nothing about your king, but I believe you would treat me fairly. Montlhéry will kill me as soon as I'm no longer useful to him."

"As long as you are faithful to me, I will be faithful to you." Robin gathered his thoughts. "But I cannot guarantee that King

Richard will show you mercy. Even if you serve Richard well, it's likely that he will still execute you as a spy."

The others murmured at this revelation, and Robin gestured for them to be silent. He continued, "I loyally serve my king, but I'm not blind to his faults. Richard is capricious; he can be magnanimous on one day, but pitiless and spiteful the next. He rarely forgives a betrayal. Can you accept this?"

For a few moments, Guy became thoughtful. At last, he affirmed, "For an opportunity to live, I'm willing to take my chances with your king. Over the past year, I've realized that I have no future with Montlhéry."

His brother's wise assessment pleased Robin, and he disclosed his demands. "You will renounce Montlhéry and King Philippe and take a new oath of fealty to me and King Richard. You will become my vassal and live under my authority. Do you agree to these terms?"

"Those are generous terms," remarked Guy. "But what services could I offer you?"

Robin explained, "You are an experienced spy, and my enemy trusts you. You will now become my spy and return to Argentan to gather information for me."

Robin requested that Brother Tuck bring the other men into the manor as witnesses.

When everyone was crowded into the hall, Robin announced, "Guy of Gisborne has agreed to become my vassal—"

The surviving members of his band of outlaws started talking over one another, arguing against the idea.

Much's voice rose above the others. "You can't trust this man! He's a murderer who'll betray you."

Robin tried to calm them, and to his utter amazement, Marian stepped in front of him and lifted her hand. The men immediately hushed and stared at her attentively.

She declared, "Robin has interrogated him, and we must trust

Robin's judgment. Also, you should know that Gisborne risked his life to rescue me and my son from the dungeons of Nottingham."

Brother Tuck added, "When he saved our lives, he asked for nothing in return."

There was a bit of grumbling, and John contended, "But he killed Kenric and the others after you left for the Crusade."

Guy indignantly asserted, "I did not kill those men! When I arrived in the dungeons to interrogate them, Payen and the sheriff had already poisoned them."

Robin concurred. "From my questioning of the staff at the castle, I was told the same story." He then addressed Brother Tuck. "Will you oversee the ceremony? We can use your cross; I assume the king blessed it."

Tuck retrieved a gold cross from under his tunic and removed it from the leather cord around his neck. It was a modest cross without decoration, and it was the length of his palm. He stated, "Both King Richard and the Grand Master of the Templars have blessed this cross."

Edmund untied the rope from Gisborne's wrists, and Guy approached Robin and knelt.

Robin addressed the assembled group. "You are here to witness a Commendation Ceremony. But first, Gisborne will renounce his allegiance to King Philippe, Count de Montlhéry, and any other man to whom he owes fealty. We don't have a sacred relic or a Bible, so we will use this cross."

Tuck stepped forward and held the cross in front of Guy, who crossed himself and briefly pressed his lips against it. "I renounce all ties of fealty to King Philippe and Ambroise de Limours, Count de Montlhéry," he swore.

"Now you will perform an act of homage to me," Robin instructed.

Guy raised his hands to carry out the traditional act of homage by placing his hands between the hands of his brother.

Robin clasped Guy's hands and said, "You have all witnessed

Gisborne's act of homage. Tuck will again bring forth the king's cross, and Gisborne will take an oath of fealty to me."

With their hands still joined, Guy pressed his lips to the cross again as Tuck held it in front of him. He then recited, "I take this oath of fealty to Robin Fitzooth, Earl of Huntingdon. I pledge my loyalty to him and submit myself to him wholly and without reservation. I vow to protect and obey my liege lord, the Earl of Huntingdon. I swear upon this holy cross, and in front of these witnesses, that my oath is true."

"I accept your homage and fealty, Sir Guy of Gisborne. You are now my vassal, bound to me by your sacred oath upon this cross and in front of these witnesses. I claim authority over you, but I make no provision of land as part of your vassalage. As long as you remain loyal and faithfully fulfill your duties, I will protect you. I only offer my protection until King Richard's return. Ultimately, your fate will be decided by the king." Robin then released Guy's hands.

Guy stood, and the others began talking to each other about what they had just seen.

Robin bade them to be quiet. "One of Gisborne's duties will be to act as my spy in the castle of Nottingham," he divulged. Then he faced Guy and demanded, "Now that you are my vassal, you must reveal to me the truth about Argentan and his ties to King Philippe and Montlhéry."

A bewildered Guy replied, "But you said you went to Paris and learned the truth about Montlhéry."

"That's right," acknowledged Robin, "and now you will tell us the truth about Argentan."

The great hall grew silent as everyone was eager to hear what Gisborne would say next. But to everyone's shock, Gisborne grinned and then laughed loudly. They all looked at each other in confusion.

Edmund harshly rebuked Guy. "Gisborne, you must answer your liege lord truthfully or we will doubt your sincerity. Robin could still send you to the Great Council."

Guy calmed and proclaimed, "Argentan is a shadow; he does not exist."

Robin rolled his eyes in exasperation. "Now you sound like him. Enough with the absurd riddles. Tell us how Argentan is tied to Montlhéry. How does he serve him? As a vassal?"

Guy revealed, "Sheriff de Argentan does not serve Count de Montlhéry. Sheriff de Argentan *is* Count de Montlhéry."

The silence in the room was deafening.

At last, Robin sputtered, "That's impossible! How can they be the same man?"

Guy explained, "I've known Count de Montlhéry all my life. Whenever he undertakes a service for the royal family that requires discretion, he assumes this alternate identity, Alaric de Montabard, to shield the reputation of King Philippe. Using this name, he secured the Barony of Argentan, and then he presented himself at the English court as a Norman baron."

⁓

Constance was reeling from everything that had happened. Standing next to the corridor that led from the great hall to the kitchen, she watched as Guy and Robin sat near the hearth with their heads inclined towards one another. Robin was speaking quietly, and Guy was attentively nodding and occasionally asking a question.

When Guy stood, stretched, and walked to the front door of Lenton Manor, Constance backed into the corridor, and as soon as she was out of her father's sight, she fled through the kitchen and out the side door. Rounding the corner of the house, she saw Guy unwinding the reins of his horse from a post and preparing to leave.

"Guy," she breathlessly called to him.

To her dismay, he stiffened at the sound of her voice and without looking at her, he declared, "Constance, I need to leave. I don't want the sheriff to realize that I've been gone all day. Such an absence will be difficult to justify now that I no longer live at Locksley."

"But, I just wanted to explain—"

"There's nothing to explain." He swiftly mounted his horse and spurred it into a fast trot as he headed towards Nottingham.

Constance was taken aback that he hadn't even looked at her. Ever since Robin's miraculous return, she had been forced to acknowledge the depth of her feelings for this man who was her husband in name only. She believed he cared for her as well, but what if her ruse to lure him out of the castle had destroyed any affection he felt for her?

Her face warmed as she remembered the passionate kiss he had bestowed upon her when they met on the road. She absent-mindedly touched her lips as she recalled his tender words. And then she froze with the awareness that he had spoken to her in French. She had been so pleased to see him after their long separation that she hadn't noticed.

Regret pierced her heart.

CHAPTER 8
THE PAPER TRAIL

16 June 1193, Locksley Village

As Robin neared the crest of the hill overlooking Locksley, he was elated to be home at last. He eagerly anticipated reuniting with his wife, not to mention Elvina's excellent cooking. Regrettably, he had missed Robbie's fourth birthday, but to make amends for his absence, he carried a small gift in his saddlebag for his son.

He was returning from a long trip that had taken him to Saint Albans for another meeting of the Great Council, and then to Huntingdon, where he had made arrangements for his steward and the Sheriff of Huntingdonshire to begin the collection of all the taxes that had been levied to fund the newly created Exchequer of Ransom. One-hundred thousand silver marks was still an unimaginable sum, but now that there was a plan in place to raise it, he had a new level of confidence that it could be done.

He reined in his horse, and Much pulled up beside him.

The two friends gazed down at Locksley, expecting to survey the village's bucolic, tranquil scenery, only to see a crowd of people gathered in front of the manor. They could hear indistinct shouting.

In alarm, they spurred their horses down the gentle slope of the hill, hopping off their mounts at the rear of the crowd. Robin reckoned that every villager in Locksley was there, as well as a handful of the sheriff's men-at-arms. Gisborne was there too. The man was well over six feet tall, and he was always easy to spot in a crowd.

Everyone was so engrossed in whatever was happening, that few noticed his arrival.

Leofric, the elderly steward of Locksley, made his way through the throng of people to him. "Lord Robin, thank God you've returned. You must do something!" he cried.

"What's happened?" asked Robin.

"Lady Marian—"

Without waiting for another word, Robin pushed through the people, with Much close on his heels. When he reached the front of the assembled group, he froze.

Payen, the sheriff's lieutenant, was lying on his back, his nose bloodied and a dagger in one hand.

Looming over the man was Marian, her bow drawn, and an arrow mere inches from Payen's chest.

Robin paused; Marian was focused so intently on Payen that he feared to distract her. She might inadvertently release her arrow, or if her attention was diverted, Payen might stab her.

Payen screeched, "Gisborne, get her away from me!"

Guy was enjoying Payen's predicament. Robin observed him grinning as he remarked, "Payen, you insulted Lady Marian's servant and threatened to kill the girl's husband. What did you think would happen?"

At that moment, Guy realized that Robin had arrived, and he sobered, dipping his head in an acknowledgment.

Again, Payen was hollering, "Gisborne, help me, or I'll tell the sheriff that you're stealing the tax money for yourself!"

Robin cautiously moved forward and spoke softly. "Marian, I'm here; please back away and then lower your bow."

At first, Marian remained in place, glaring fiercely at Payen.

Finally, she took two steps back before lowering her bow and looking at Robin.

Robin was impressed with her control. Before he could dwell on that thought, Payen sat up and slashed at her with his dagger. Gisborne kicked him in the shoulder, causing him to drop his weapon.

"Get up," ordered Guy as he seized the other man's knife.

Payen obeyed, standing and brushing the dirt from his clothes.

"What's going on here?" demanded Robin.

A dozen people started talking to him at once. Briefly closing his eyes in frustration, Robin raised his hand and shouted, "Quiet!"

When the noise had subsided, he scanned the courtyard. A small table was resting on its side, and a few coins and the tax rolls were scattered on the ground. Alongside the table was a cart with a locked strong box. The sheriff's men were evidently collecting taxes from the villagers. Near the table, Odella was sobbing, her face buried in Allan-a-dale's chest, and her arms wound tightly around him.

Robin knew that Allan and Odella had been married the previous Christmastide, and Odella was now carrying a child. What immediately struck Robin was the fury in Allan's eyes. The minstrel was typically unflappable and merry, but today, he looked lethal as he glowered at Payen.

Marian's eyes were filled with rage and anguish, while Gisborne's expression was guarded. He had grabbed Payen's collar and was firmly in control of the much smaller man.

"Marian, tell me what happened," requested Robin.

She pointed at Payen. "That monster came here to take everyone's money, and he had the audacity to insult Odella. I've told Gisborne that Payen is not allowed to set foot in Locksley, yet he is here. *Again.*"

Payen sneered, "I don't answer to you or Gisborne. I only serve the sheriff."

Robin gestured at the far side of the crowd and instructed Guy, "Take him over there and wait for me with your men."

"We can't leave the money box," responded Guy, but when Robin leveled a withering glare at him. Guy reluctantly did as he had been told, taking Payen and the sheriff's men to where their horses were tied.

When they had left, Robin ordered the crowd to disperse. Soon, it was only Allan, Odella, Marian, and the rest of the former outlaws.

Odella was weeping uncontrollably, and Elvina, an elderly servant who had served Robin's mother, came forward and took Odella by the arm, carefully prying her away from Allan. "Come, Odella," she cooed, "Let's go to the kitchen. Now that Lord Robin has returned, I need your help with the meal."

Odella initially went with her, but after a few steps, she pulled away and hastened to Robin, where she fell at his feet and wailed, "Please, Lord Robin, please don't let them arrest Allan." Her sobs drowned the rest of her words.

Robin knelt and spoke soothingly. "Odella, do you trust me?"

Allan had hurried to her side, and he assisted Robin as the two men helped the distraught woman to her feet.

Robin insisted, "Go with Elvina, and let me handle this, all right?"

Odella, still crying and shaking with fear, allowed Elvina to guide her into the manor.

Robin turned to Allan expectantly.

Allan was obviously struggling to contain himself, and through gritted teeth, he explained, "We had come to pay our taxes. I didn't realize that Payen was here with Gisborne, and when we arrived at the front of the queue, he…he said…something, and then I punched him in the face."

An alarmed Robin questioned, "You struck the sheriff's man in front of witnesses? While he was collecting taxes? What the devil is the matter with you? The sheriff will hang you."

"But Allan was provoked," Little John elaborated. "The poisoner asked Allan how he would ever know if the child was his, since his wife was a whore."

Will Scarlet added, "Payen then made a crude remark about…" The young man's voice faded; he was reluctant to repeat the exact words that had been spoken.

Marian concluded the story. "He made a vulgar reference about the time he *raped* Odella."

Robin was shocked. No one had bothered to tell him that this had happened. "When?" was all he could say, fearful that Odella might be carrying Payen's child.

Marian must have deciphered the expression on his face; she clarified, "It was last October, more than two months before they wed. The babe will not arrive until October of this year."

A thankful Robin commanded, "Allan, go to Odella and stay with her. John, keep guard over the sheriff's taxes. Marian, where is Robbie? Go check on him."

"Robbie is inside, and he's fine. What are you going to do?"

"I'm going to talk to Gisborne. I want you to go inside and stay with Robbie."

"No, I'll go with you."

"Marian, do as you're told and go inside," Robin harshly demanded.

Marian's eyes narrowed, and Robin sighed, adding, "Please."

"I'm not a child," she countered.

"I know; I just need to talk to Gisborne alone."

Marian made no move to go into the manor, and with resignation, Robin pivoted and strode over to Guy and his men. He half expected Marian to follow him, and he was relieved when he realized she had remained with the others.

Payen whined, "I want that man arrested now! He attacked me."

Robin beheld Payen with disgust. "You will stay here with the other men while I discuss the matter with the sheriff's captain."

Payen opened his mouth to object, but Gisborne gave him a menacing stare before he accompanied Robin to a spot where they could speak privately. Guy confirmed the story that Robin had already heard, although he candidly quoted all the vile things Payen had said to Allan.

Robin was appalled, especially since he had not known that Payen had attacked Odella the previous autumn. "Gisborne, I don't want Payen here in Locksley. You must keep him away."

Guy admitted, "I've been trying to keep him from Locksley, but today he asked the sheriff if he could join me, and so it was out of my hands. He's fixated on Odella, and I believe he came here to visit her. I don't think he knew that she's a married woman now."

"I don't want him here; do you understand?" repeated Robin.

"Yes, my lord, I understand," sighed Guy. "I don't think it will be a problem. Payen is passing messages between the sheriff and Prince John. He won't be around much as he will be traveling frequently."

"Are you able to intercept any of these messages?"

"They are not written messages; Payen is memorizing them."

"That's a shame," lamented Robin. "When is your next trip to Paris?"

"Not for some time. Montlhéry is leaving for Paris tomorrow. Emperor Heinrich will arrive soon to celebrate the Feast of Midsummer with Philippe, and they will negotiate Richard's custody. I will remain here as acting sheriff and continue with the collection of the taxes."

"Damn!" Robin exclaimed. "Richard cannot be given over to Philippe."

"It would be a death sentence," observed Guy. "However, I believe it is unlikely that Heinrich will surrender such a valuable hostage."

"We can't continue talking like this; it will raise suspicions. Are you done here? Were you collecting the quarter tax on income or the quarter tax on moveable property?"

"A quarter?" Gisborne questioned. "I was told to collect a tax of one-third on income today and return in a fortnight to collect a one-third tax on moveable property."

Robin scrubbed his face in an attempt to calm his anger. "The tax levied by the Great Council is one-quarter, not one-third."

A corner of Guy's mouth lifted in an amused smirk. "I'm sure that the sheriff is just demonstrating his zeal for ransoming the king by collecting additional taxes." He then asked, "What about your minstrel? Payen wants him arrested."

"That will not happen. He was provoked. Do you blame Allan?"

"No. Payen's lucky that he was goading a minstrel and not a soldier. If he had insulted my wife in such a way, he'd be dead. As it was, Lady Marian nearly finished him. "

"You should have done a better job of managing the situation so that Marian hadn't felt the need to get involved," Robin chided him.

Guy scoffed. "I have no control over your wife. She has the heart of a warrior."

Robin was taken aback by Gisborne's assessment of Marian, but returning to the matter at hand, he reached into a pouch tied to his belt and retrieved a few coins. "Here, give this to Payen as compensation for Allan's assault on him. Convince him it's in his best interest to take the money to soothe his injured pride."

Guy took the coins and went to Payen.

Robin watched as the two men argued. Ultimately, Payen relented, and Gisborne sent his men to retrieve the cart with the locked chest and the tax rolls. Soon, they departed and disappeared over the hill.

"Papa!"

Robin pivoted to see Robbie running towards him with his arms outstretched, and every care and worry that had been weighing him down lifted, fading like smoke wafting above a campfire.

Robbie jumped into his arms, and Robin spun in a circle before tossing the little boy up in the air as he squealed with delight.

Robin caught him and hugged him close.

"Again! Again!" Robbie insisted.

Robin dutifully tossed him overhead a few times, and then he noticed that Marian had joined them.

Thankfully, the angry storm that had clouded her eyes earlier was gone, and she was smiling at him. In relief, Robin wrapped his free arm around her waist and pulled her close, kissing her with all the passion of a man who had been away from his wife for several weeks.

She blushed. "Robin, people are watching."

"I'm sure this isn't the first time they've seen a husband kiss his wife." He gazed at her ardently.

"Papa, did you go to heaven again? You were gone a long time. I had a birthday."

Robin chuckled, "It was more like hell—"

Marian cleared her throat disapprovingly.

Changing the subject, he said, "I heard about your birthday. Are you two years old?"

Robbie giggled. "No, I'm four."

"Four!" gasped Robin in mock surprise. "You are almost big enough to be a knight and serve the king."

Robbie beamed with pride.

"Robin, don't talk like that," scolded Marian.

"I'm sorry I was not here for your birthday," Robin said, "but the queen needed me. I brought you something—"

Just then, Jack trotted up, and Robin fondly greeted the little dog.

"What did you bring me?" demanded Robbie.

Robin was still holding him, and the three of them walked over to his horse. Setting the little boy on the ground, Robin queried Marian, "Has he been a good boy? Does he deserve a gift?"

Robbie hopped up and down in anticipation, readily answering Robin's questions, even though they had not been directed at him. "Yes! Yes! I've been good!"

Marian and Robin laughed. Reaching into his saddlebag, Robin retrieved a miniature bow, a bracer, and a quiver with small, blunt-end arrows.

"Robin, he's too young for that."

"A boy is never too young to start learning the finer points of archery from his father," proclaimed Robin.

18 June 1193, Nottingham Castle

As Robin climbed the winding stairs to the tower room, he reminisced about his first encounter with the sheriff almost five years ago. So much had changed since that fateful day; he was not the same young, naïve man who had been ensnared by the sheriff's verbal traps and lies.

For that reason, Robin was determined to have the upper hand in his future dealings with Montlhéry. He had decided that no one would disclose the truth about the sheriff's identity; instead, everyone would maintain the fiction that he was Baron de Argentan.

Robin glanced over his shoulder and paused as he waited for Edmund to catch up with him.

Wheezing from his exertions, Edmund asked, "Are you certain that the sheriff has gone to Paris?"

"We'll find out soon enough. Hopefully, Gisborne is alone. If the sheriff is there, we'll make this a brief visit and leave."

When they reached the antechamber at the top of the stairs, the doors to the tower room were closed, and the guard, who was leaning against the wall with his eyes shut, snapped to attention.

After genuflecting, the man said, "My lord, the sheriff ain't here."

Robin announced, "I have urgent business that cannot wait until he returns. Is the sheriff's captain here?"

Without another word, the man opened one of the double doors and let them enter. At the far end of the chamber, Gisborne was standing at a window and contemplating the bright, beautiful day. At the sound of their entrance, he startled, but then he promptly approached them and went down on one knee before rising.

"Lord Huntingdon, Lord Embelton, how might I serve you today? Sheriff de Argentan is away, and I am acting in his stead."

"Gisborne, we have matters to discuss with you," replied Robin. "Private matters."

Guy nodded in understanding, and he instructed the guard, "Go to the foot of the staircase, and if anyone arrives to meet with me, they must remain there until Earl Robin departs."

They watched as the man left and descended the stairs.

Guy shut and latched the double doors before turning to the others and inquiring, "What has happened?"

Robin grinned. "It's not what *has* happened. It's what is *going* to happen now."

At Gisborne's confused frown, Edmund elaborated, "We're going to search through Montlhéry's desk and read his papers."

All the color drained from Guy's face, and he stepped between them and the large, cluttered desk, spreading his arms wide as if to block their access to it. "You can't do that," he asserted.

"Have you forgotten whom you serve? Do your vows of allegiance mean anything to you?" an irritated Robin demanded.

Guy huffed in annoyance. "My lord, I'm acutely aware that you are my master, and that I serve you. But we can't just rifle through his papers."

"What's the problem, Gisborne?" asked Edmund.

"It only looks as though the papers are randomly strewn across the desk. I assure you that Montlhéry knows exactly where every piece of paper is and how it is positioned relative to the others."

"That's preposterous," Robin argued. "His papers are a mess."

Guy contended, "They might seem like a mess to us, but Montlhéry has an ability to look at something once and memorize it. It's amazing. If a single page is even slightly askew, he will notice it."

"Have you witnessed this?" Robin questioned.

"Many times. Once, I took a few scraps of paper from the bottom of a pile; they were old notices. The next time he was at his desk, he flew into a rage because the stack was disturbed, and there were missing items. I told him a servant had accidentally shifted them while cleaning, but I did not account for the missing items. He spent days searching for them and torturing the servant."

Robin and Edmund exchanged a knowing glance. They were certain that those pieces of paper had been locked in Edmund's desk in Embelton for nearly five years. The scraps had love poetry that Guy had written for Marian on one side, while the reverse sides had snippets of official dispatches that had been their first clue that the Sheriff of Nottingham had a connection to the King of France.

"Very well," Robin conceded. "We will move around the desk, without touching anything, and see what we can learn."

"Did Montlhéry take any papers with him when he left?" Edmund inquired.

"Unfortunately, he took the last few missives he had received from King Philippe," Guy admitted.

The three men circled the desk, each starting at a different section as they craned their necks at various angles while leaning from side to side to read the observable sections of a wide range of dispatches, letters, and official documents.

Edmund hummed and leaned closer to get a better view. "Robin, what do you think of this?" he asked.

Robin and Guy crowded around Edmund; the document was only partially visible.

"It appears to be a list of names," commented Robin.

"I recognize that," claimed Guy. "It's an old list from when we first arrived in England. These men are not allowed to enter Nottingham or meet with the sheriff."

"Who's on this list, and why is it needed?" Robin demanded.

"No one on this list has ever tried to enter Nottingham, so I doubt that it's important."

"You didn't answer Robin," countered Edmund. "Who is on the list and why does it exist?"

Guy recalled the names from memory. "There is Walter de Coutances, Archbishop of Rouen, Hugh de Puiset, Bishop of Durham, Hamelin de Warenne, Earl of Surrey—"

"Those men are some of the most prominent nobles of the realm. Why are they banned from Nottingham?" questioned Robin.

Shrugging, Guy suggested, "Perhaps these men can identify him as Montlhéry and not Baron de Argentan."

"That seems reasonable," acknowledged Robin. "I'm well acquainted with Earl Hamelin, and I'll ask him if he has ever met Montlhéry."

They resumed circling the desk, occasionally pausing to scrutinize and discuss what they could see.

"This isn't good enough," declared Robin. "We must look under some of these papers. Gisborne, you will hold down one edge of a message while we lift the other side to read what is underneath."

Guy nervously advised, "My lord, please, it's too risky—"

"Grow a backbone, Gisborne. This is too important for us to allow fear to dictate our actions. Besides, even with his magical powers of memory, Montlhéry will be gone for at least a fortnight. A blast of wind through that open window could easily alter the positioning of the papers. Now, do as you're told," admonished Robin.

He then pointed to a paper, and Guy grudgingly anchored a corner.

Robin and Edmund scanned several pages that were mostly hidden, finding nothing. They continued to walk around the desk, and Robin knew they should leave soon. Already they had been there much too long.

"This one." He pointed, and Guy dutifully placed his fingers along its side.

Robin lifted the top page and found an invoice. He was about to move on, when Edmund said, "Wait a moment. This is a large amount of money."

"Gisborne, are you familiar with this?" Robin inquired.

Guy squinted at the invoice. "That is a bill for a group of mercenaries that he hired."

Robin nodded, assuming it was the group that had assailed him on the road to Conisbrough. Just as he lowered the document that had been on top, something struck him. Again, he lifted one side of the page and examined the invoice. And that's when the date leapt from the page into his notice.

14 June 1193.

The attack had occurred at the end of March.

"Gisborne, what is the purpose of these mercenaries?" asked Robin. "He hired these men only a few days ago."

Guy frowned. "I'm not sure. I suppose he hired them to help guard the taxes we are collecting for the ransom."

"The cost of these mercenaries exceeds the difference between collecting one-quarter and one-third of the people's income," remarked Edmund.

"Perhaps they are needed in case the people refuse to pay their taxes," suggested Guy.

Edmund asserted, "Guy, that doesn't make much sense. There are plenty of men-at-arms here at the castle to intimidate the people. How many men were hired? And where are they?"

"There are several dozen men, and Montlhéry has put them in a camp in the forest because there aren't enough beds in the barracks to accommodate them. The kitchens regularly send carts of food and barrels of ale to them."

Robin began pacing, deep in thought, and the other men silently observed him. At last, he paused and spoke, "Edmund, I need you to take Marian and Robbie to Conisbrough; they'll be safe there. Do you know if Constance would prefer to stay with them or return to Embelton?"

Edmund reluctantly disclosed, "Constance wants to return to the castle and become the liaison between us and Gisborne. She's the only one of us with a reason to be in Nottingham Castle, because of her marriage to *him*." Edmund gestured towards Guy.

Ignoring the bitterness in Edmund's voice, Guy pledged, "If Constance comes here, I will protect her. I agree that the sheriff would give her presence little thought, unlike visits from either of you."

"Robin, what are you thinking? Are you expecting trouble?" queried Edmund.

Robin replied, "Montlhéry is building an army. I'm not expecting trouble; I'm anticipating a war."

CHAPTER 9
RIVERS OF SILVER

26 June 1193, Sherwood Forest, The Meadow

obin leaned against the great oak, looking up at its tangled branches as they gracefully reached across one side of the meadow near Locksley, providing welcome shade on this warm summer's day.

Marian and Robbie had been gone for six days, and he missed them terribly. They had left for Conisbrough with Edmund, and Robin expected Edmund to return any day. He was impatient to hear from his uncle whether Marian had calmed down after their argument on the eve of her departure.

He hadn't been surprised when she refused to leave, and he regretted that he had been forced to claim his prerogative as husband and head of the family to command her to go. To make matters worse, he had thought it would be a good time to confess his sins in Poitou to her; after all, she would be gone for weeks, perhaps a couple of months, and by her return, he hoped her anger would have passed.

When he had cautiously revealed that he had been unfaithful to her after *she* broke their betrothal, he had anticipated an explosive reaction. He had even braced himself for the expected slap to his face. Instead, she had covered her face with her hands and wept. In what had seemed to be an unending deluge of tears, she had sobbed as if her heart had been shattered.

Nothing he had previously experienced in his life compared to the sense of utter failure and worthlessness that he had felt at that moment. Watching Marian's sorrow over his betrayal was agonizing to the point of physical pain.

And now he was also guilty of cowardice. After witnessing Marian's heartbreak over his indiscretions, he could not bear to admit that he had committed bigamy by marrying one of his many conquests during that period of immoral living.

He absentmindedly punched the side of the tree, and the sting to his knuckles couldn't begin to match the punishment he deserved.

How was he ever going to tell her about Blanche? Would Marian believe that Blanche had gotten him drunk and seduced him? Would she understand that some women will do anything to ensnare a wealthy earl as a husband? Even though Blanche was a distant cousin of King Richard through her family's ties to Queen Eleanor, their domain, Châteauneuf, was not particularly prosperous, and they were members of the lowest ranks of the nobility.

"Lord Robin!"

He observed Brother Tuck making his way across the meadow towards him. Schooling his features into a more pleasant expression, Robin greeted the Knight Templar amiably and invited him to sit in the shade of the great oak.

"How did you find me?" he asked.

Tuck smiled and disclosed, "Lady Marian often came here when she needed time to herself. I suspected you might favor this spot as well."

Robin chuckled at Tuck's perceptive wisdom. "Have you just returned from London? Tell me of your journey."

"The great city is receiving rivers of silver flowing from across Richard's lands into the vaults below Saint Paul's Cathedral."

"How are they securing such a cache of wealth?"

"It is heavily guarded and under the seals of Queen Eleanor and Walter de Coutances."

"Did you have an audience with the queen?" Robin inquired.

Tuck replied, "Yes; thank you for allowing me to go to her. Last year, when she commissioned me to be her eyes and ears in my travels, I'm sure she expected me to report back sooner than this. She was quite displeased with me."

"Brother Tuck, I'm certain that you were able to charm her into forgiving you."

"You are too kind, my lord. The queen was eager to hear about Lady Marian's adventures as leader of the outlaws. I told her many stories, but I promise that I have not betrayed any confidences."

Eleanor's interest in Marian's life as an outlaw troubled Robin. It was usually best to avoid inviting the notice of the royal family.

Deciding to shift the focus of their conversation, he noted, "Two of the men entrusted with raising the ransom are well known to me, Hubert Walter, the new Archbishop of Canterbury, and Earl Hamelin de Warenne. Did you meet either of them in London?"

Tuck nodded. "When I arrived for my audience, they were both with the queen, giving her an accounting of the latest deliveries of silver. I also heard many discussions about the need for hostages from among the children of the nobility. People are very anxious about sending their sons to Germany."

"I'm thankful that Robbie is too young to go."

"Do you think the ransom will be raised?" asked Tuck.

"I don't know. It's hard to imagine 100,000 silver marks. But when I've talked to the people of Huntingdon, Locksley, and Lenton, I'm humbled by their willingness to sacrifice in order to ransom Richard. As king, he only spent a couple of months in England before leaving for the Crusade, while John has been here nearly the entire time that Richard has been gone, trying to win the hearts of the people."

Tuck suggested, "Richard is a warrior, and people respect that. They want a king who can defend his kingdom. Perhaps they have seen enough of John to doubt his abilities. But there is also the Pope's latest edict."

"I have not heard about that," Robin remarked.

"The Pope has threatened to lay England under an interdict if Richard's subjects fail to raise his ransom," explained Tuck.

Robin frowned. "That's not fair. The people are doing all they can. Their only complaint has been that some nobles are not paying their share. Many question whether Prince John has made any contributions to the ransom. Because of Richard's generosity, John is the wealthiest man in England."

"Passing along gossip is a sin, so I will need to atone for this later, but I heard a rumor that John has yet to make any contribution."

"I suspect the rumor is true." Robin gazed at the sky to gauge the time of day. "It's getting late; let's return to Locksley to see what Elvina and Odella have cooked for us."

When Robin entered Locksley Manor, the first face he saw was Edmund's. The second face was Marian's.

Initially, he was too stunned to say anything, but he soon recovered his voice and thundered, "What are you doing here? I told you to stay at Conisbrough until it's safe for you to return. Is Robbie here too?"

Marian calmly replied, "He's at Conisbrough."

"Alone?" an alarmed Robin questioned.

"Not alone!" Marian exclaimed. "Countess Isabel and her family are there. Her little grandson, Rich, is there, and so is Jack. Robbie's excited to spend time with them while I help you."

"Help me?" Robin's voice rose in alarm. "Marian, I don't need your help. You're going back to Conisbrough."

"No."

Robin glanced around the room. Edmund, Tuck, Much, and Allan were all there, studiously avoiding eye contact with him, and he realized this was a conversation that required privacy.

"Come outside, and we'll discuss this," he demanded. Before she could answer, he seized her by the wrist and towed her from the great hall, through the kitchen, past Elvina and Odella, and out the back door. He marched through the garden to the small clearing between the manor and Sherwood Forest.

Although Marian kept trying to pull out of his grasp, he did not release her until they were at the tree line. They stared at each other as Robin strove to find the words to convince her to go back to Conisbrough.

"I *can* help you," she insisted, her chin lifting slightly in that determined expression that always put him on guard.

"You can help by obeying me. I'm only trying to protect you," he countered.

"Why are you sending me away? We have already been apart for such a long time. You are my husband; I should be with you."

"Wives do not accompany their husbands into battle."

Her brow lifted in surprise. "Are you expecting a battle?"

"Montlhéry has hired trained soldiers. This is a dangerous situation."

"Perhaps you want the freedom to do as you please without the burden of a wife."

"What are you talking about?"

"Maybe I'm worried that wine and other women will distract you." Her eyes narrowed suspiciously.

"That's ridiculous!" he shouted. Modulating his voice, he contended, "*You* broke our betrothal. I didn't know we were married. By the way, if you thought we were married, why did you send a letter breaking our betrothal? That doesn't make any sense."

"Well...*you* sent me a letter first. A letter where you instructed me to wait while you went to the Holy Land to achieve, what did you call it? Oh, yes, 'glory on the battlefield.'"

Robin fumed. He couldn't argue with her on that point; he now recognized that his letter had been a dreadful mistake. He should have kept his promise to her. Shifting the debate, he demanded, "Why didn't you tell me you were having a babe, or that we were married?"

"You told us not to contact you. You didn't want the sheriff to know I was in Embelton. Don't you remember?"

She was right, and it only increased his irritation. He reminded her, "And then, after King Richard's coronation, you still didn't tell me."

"I thought if I sent you that letter, you would immediately come to me to make amends."

He indignantly recollected, "You told me you were ending our betrothal. You returned my mother's ring to me. Why would I doubt your word?"

Marian sighed loudly. "All right, I was wrong. I admit it. That letter was a mistake, and I wish I had never written it."

Robin conceded, "My indiscretions were a mistake. I wish they had never happened. I only wanted to be with you, and when you pushed me away, I did things that I would have never otherwise done."

Her eyes flashed as her temper rose again. "Is it my fault that you bedded all those women?"

Robin rubbed his face in frustration, realizing that his words had been poorly chosen. He acknowledged, "No, of course not. I take responsibility for my mistakes. I just wish you had told me about the clandestine marriage and Robbie's birth instead of sending that letter ending the betrothal."

Several tears rolled down her cheek. "I wanted to tell you in person. I wanted to see the joy on your face when I handed our infant son to you. I had everything planned out in my mind." She dried the dampness on her face with the sleeve of her bliaut. "It sounds silly now, and I regret my foolish actions. I'm sorry."

He pulled her into an embrace. The thought that perhaps he should tell her about Blanche flitted through his mind, but he decided it was more important to convince her to return to the safety of Conisbrough.

Speaking softly into her ear, he said, "Marian, I understand because I regret my actions too. I'm sorry."

He led her over to a weathered log lying across the tree line, and they sat together. Observing her closely, his mind drifted to the past. When he had taken her to Embelton four and a half years ago, his love for her was focused on her exquisite beauty, genteel manners, and witty conversation.

When they were briefly reunited in Acre, he had been struck by her audacious disregard for her own safety in traveling so far to warn him of an impending danger. He would have never expected his Marian to do something so reckless, yet so brave. In the months since his return, the stories of her exploits in leading his men against Gisborne and the sheriff had amazed him.

In that moment, he recognized that she was not the same girl with whom he had become betrothed during a sunny, joyful May Day celebration five years ago.

And he was not the same man who had foolishly broken his promises to her in order to seek glory on the battlefields of the Crusade.

In some respects, they were strangers.

Marian frowned at him. "Why are you looking at me like that?"

Robin cradled both her hands and gazed into her eyes, knowing that he must discard his outdated notions of Marian. He needed to understand her better.

"Marian, tell me about the future you envision for us."

"I would like more children."

He beamed. "I would like that too. When Richard returns, we

can settle into a normal life; you can take up your duties as Countess of Huntingdon, managing our home and our children."

To his surprise, her face fell in disappointment. He asked, "Isn't that what you want?"

She looked away, scowling and worrying her bottom lip.

Becoming alarmed, he queried, "Marian? What's the matter?"

"I was thinking about the plans I had made when I thought Richard was returning."

"I would like to hear them." He squeezed her hands to reassure her.

Marian nervously cleared her throat. "Well, I was going to take control of Huntingdon, Lenton, and Locksley. Edmund was going to teach me about estate management."

"And this is something you find interesting? Accounts and record keeping?"

She laughed, and the tension in her face relaxed. "Not really. I was thinking of ways to help the people of Huntingdon, Lenton, and Locksley. I wanted to improve their lives, especially widows like myself and children without fathers like Robbie."

He glanced away to hide his reaction from her. Never had he suspected that such things interested her, and then it occurred to him that this was the Marian of today, and not the Marian he had known five years ago. He met her gaze once more, and smiling, he encouraged her to continue. "Tell me more."

The lengthening shadows of twilight crept across the clearing between the tree line and Locksley Manor as Robin listened to Marian. She spoke passionately about her ideas to help the poor, and the joy she felt whenever she gave food to hungry people during her time as leader of the outlaws. She also confessed to relishing the excitement of outwitting Gisborne and the sheriff, and her sense of accomplishment as she learned how to lead his men.

Robin not only listened, he also observed. The fiery glow of the setting sun was nothing compared to the way Marian's face lit up as she talked about leading the outlaws and helping the people. Her eyes sparkled with enthusiasm.

Perhaps Marian was not interested in the feminine arts of embroidery or planning feast day celebrations, but in every way that mattered, she was perfect for him, and Robin fell in love with her all over again. Only now, he was in love with the flesh and blood woman at his side, and not the idealized memory of a girl who no longer existed.

Her voice faded, and she eyed him anxiously. "I'm probably boring you with my rambling talk."

"I'm not bored. I like your ideas," he emphasized, "and after Richard returns, we will work together on them. But for now, I want you to stay at Conisbrough; I fear we are facing dangerous times."

Her expression darkened, and she grew quiet.

Robin patiently waited, certain that he had finally convinced her to leave.

When she spoke again, her words were measured and thoughtful. "I don't have the strength of a man. I'll never be able to hit a man hard enough to hurt him."

Robin chuckled. "It might depend on *where* you hit him."

She smiled knowingly and resumed, "I don't have your skill with a bow, and I can barely lift your sword. But I want to help ensure the king's return. If Prince John ascends to the throne, we will be in terrible danger."

"I fear John's wrath as well. He will never forgive us for the trouble we've caused him and his supporters."

"Robin, I want to *do* something. I want to protect the people of Locksley and Lenton, and I want to give our son a better future."

"After Richard returns, you will have many opportunities to do those things. There is nothing you can do now."

"When I was living at Embelton, Edmund told me stories about King Henry's parents, and how they fought for the crown against King Stephen. Although their marriage lacked affection, they still had many victories. But we love each other, so if we work together, we will surely have even more success in our efforts to defeat the sheriff and Prince John."

"If King Henry's parents had a marriage built solely on political ambition, then it might have been easier for them to work together," Robin remarked. "But our devotion to each other will put us in peril because we will be vulnerable if one of us is attacked."

When her brow furrowed in confusion, he explained, "Worrying about you is a distraction that could be fatal, particularly in a fight. Do you remember the battle in the streets of Acre?" At her nod, he continued, "I kept looking for you, fearing for your safety. My lack of focus almost resulted in me losing my life. Thank God, my friend André was there to save me."

Robin added, "It's not just the risks of battle. If the sheriff captured you, I would be at his mercy because I cannot bear the thought of losing you. Robbie needs you; I need you. The challenges that we face are more dangerous than anything you confronted last year as leader of the outlaws."

"I will never forget the anguish I felt when I thought you were dead, so I understand what you're saying," Marian conceded. "But a plague could take my life, just like the one that took your mother. Or I could die in childbirth, like my mother. I can't live my life in fear of losing it—that's not living."

"Marian," he admonished, "this is very different from a plague or childbirth. You are asking to put yourself in the midst of battles."

Marian countered, "No, I'm not. I know I can't fight against soldiers in combat. But I could help with the type of disruptive tactics that were so successful last year. And I could be a lookout, or I could spy on our enemies, just like Guy and Constance are your spies at Nottingham Castle."

She proposed, "I'm asking to be with you and to be part of what you're doing. I don't want to accompany you into battle. But in all other things, I want to be your partner."

"There can be only one leader. We cannot argue in front of the men or give them conflicting commands," Robin stressed.

"You will make the final decisions and lead the men," acknowledged Marian. "All I ask is that you consider my ideas."

"I will always give your ideas serious consideration," Robin pledged. "Nevertheless, there will be times when I can't explain my reasoning to you until later. You must trust my judgment."

She promptly agreed to his terms.

Dusk had fallen, and they stood to return to the manor. Just then, Robin realized she had somehow convinced him to allow her to stay. He chastised himself for succumbing to her pleas, but she had a way of beguiling him that he could not resist.

30 June 1193, Ernehale, Nottinghamshire

Allan-a-dale smiled affably and nodded at the people he passed as he rode into Ernehale. It was the feast day commemorating Saint Paul the Apostle, and he hoped to earn a few coins by singing songs and telling stories to entertain the crowd.

A couple of middle-aged ladies who were strolling towards the market paused to stare at him. They were dressed in expensive clothing with bright white wimples covering their hair, and he winked playfully at them, announcing, "I'll be performing in the square! I hope you'll come, because I need beautiful women in my audience to inspire me as I sing love songs!"

They giggled in response, and one of them replied, "We'll be there, Allan-a-dale!"

He was always pleased to be recognized; returning admirers of his songs were often the most generous. And even though his heart was wholly owned by his wife, it never hurt to use his good looks and charm to earn additional coins.

Allan was well-known throughout Nottinghamshire for his songs about Robin Hood and his theatrical retellings of King Richard's voyage from Acre to his capture in Vienna. Thanks to his friendship with Robin, Allan had learned all the exciting details, from negotiating with pirates, to a shipwreck, to a dangerous trek across frozen, mountainous lands far from the shores of England. It was all very exotic and dramatic, and people were eager to pay to hear the tales.

He hopped off his mount at the stables and left a coin for the stable hand to look after the old mare. The horse belonged to Lord Robin, of course, and although Allan was grateful for Robin's generous nature, he was also aggravated by his inability to provide for himself. After all, he was a married man with a wife and a babe due in a few months. He should be able to support his family without charity from his lord.

His sweet wife, Odella, worked hard every day in the Locksley kitchen, and Robin had promised that she would be in charge of the kitchen after Elvina retired. Robin paid Odella well, but since Allan had no steady source of income, her ability to earn money made him feel like a failure as a man and a husband. He couldn't read or write, so he couldn't hope to become the Locksley steward once Leofric retired. Besides, it was likely that Much, who could read and write a little, would eventually step into Leofric's shoes.

When he first started earning his living as a traveling minstrel, he had been happy performing and collecting enough coins to live from day to day. But as a husband and father, that wasn't sufficient.

Already this month, he had been forced to hand over a third of his and Odella's income to the sheriff for the king's ransom. And then he discovered that the amount should have been a quarter.

He would never get ahead at this rate. The previous Thursday, he had been in Nottingham entertaining people during the Feast of Midsummer, but he had only collected half of his normal earnings despite it being such an important feast.

To his regret, he had to acknowledge that, with all the taxes people were required to pay, they had very little left to spend on entertainment, even for a popular minstrel such as himself.

As he made his way towards the town square with his lute tied to his back, a subdued parade of mounted men-at-arms rode past him, heading out of town. Moving to the side of the road, Allan could see that the men were guarding a wagon weighed down with several chests.

He asked the man next to him, "What's that all about?"

The man somberly answered, "That's the town's payment for the quarter tax on income and our church's plate. Those men are escorting it to Nottingham, and from there, it will go to London."

Allan observed with heightened interest. In addition to taxes on the people's income and property, all churches had been compelled to surrender their silver plate, including candlesticks and communion goblets. Even the small church at Locksley, the site of his wedding to Odella, had been stripped bare.

As the wagon passed, Allan and the other bystanders reverently crossed themselves in acknowledgment of the sacred items that were going to London to be melted and shaped into silver marks.

It seemed sacrilegious, but Allan reasoned that the king had been put on his throne by God, so perhaps it was only fitting that these items be surrendered to bring Richard home.

He wondered if it would be a waste of his time to try to earn anything in Ernehale, when the people had just handed over so much to the tax collectors. Since he was already in the town, he decided that there was no harm in trying. Whatever he earned, it would be worth having during these hard times.

⚜

The feast was winding down, and Allan was counting the coins he had earned, taking them from the tin cup he had placed on the ground at his feet and dropping them into a pouch tied to his belt.

It was summer, and the days were long, but tonight would be a new moon. As soon as the last rays of sunlight yielded to the shadows of dusk, it would be too dark to travel, so he would not return home tonight. There was a cemetery on the outskirts of town, and he decided to save money by bedding down amongst the tombstones. He briefly recalled that he had been sleeping in a cemetery on the night he had met Robin and Marian.

First, he needed to make sure that his, or rather, Robin's horse could stay in the town's stables over night.

He was almost to the stables, when a man entered Ernehale's gate, galloping towards the center of town. His curiosity getting the better of him, Allan pivoted and jogged behind the rider.

He watched as Lord Ernehale and his son rushed to the man. There were still many people in the town square, and Allan joined the crowd to listen.

"They took everything," gasped the man.

Lord Ernehale paled, and his son demanded, "You mean all the silver? And the church's plate? It's all been stolen?"

"Yes, we were surprised on the road by bandits who attacked without mercy, killing all our men except for me. I barely escaped with my life."

The assembled people began talking all at once, and Lord Ernehale signaled for quiet.

When the noise had subsided, Lord Ernehale asked, "Would you recognize these men if you saw them again? Is there anything you can tell the Sheriff of Nottingham to help him catch these bandits and recover our silver?"

The man loudly proclaimed, "These forest bandits have no fear of the sheriff. Their leader proudly announced that he was taking our silver and giving it to the poor."

The lord's son questioned, "Are you trying to tell us you were robbed by—"

"That's right; Robin Hood and his men stole our silver. He's probably going to give it to the people of Locksley. We should ride there and demand it be returned to us."

Lord Ernehale disagreed. "Lord Huntingdon has many men at

his disposal who are trained to fight, and we've just lost all of my best men-at-arms. We will go to the sheriff and seek justice from him."

Allan opened his mouth to argue that Robin had not taken their silver and killed their men; the idea was ludicrous. But he realized that no one else was standing up for Robin. The other people were discussing the wealth of Locksley and Lenton, and the unfairness of Robin Hood taking their silver.

Suddenly, a man on the far side of the gathering hollered, "One of Robin Hood's men was just here singing songs."

The mood of the people had grown ugly, and a cry arose to find the man.

Allan backed away from the crowd and ducked into the nearest alley. The moment he was out of sight, he ran to the stables.

The sun was just touching the horizon, so the sky was still bright. He would try to get as close to Locksley as he could before the total darkness of a new moon blanketed the land.

He had to warn Robin.

CHAPTER 10
CHARADES

1 July 1193, On the Road to Locksley

he old mare that Allan was riding refused to move any faster than a slow trot, no matter what he did to prod her. Lacking a whip, he was resigned to the horse's pace, and he wondered if he could reach Locksley sooner if he ran instead.

The incident in Ernehale had just happened the previous day, and Allan assumed it would take time for the sheriff to mobilize against Robin. Even so, he felt a sense of urgency that he couldn't explain. He was convinced that he needed to warn Robin immediately.

Shouting and the rumble of galloping horses caused him to glance over his shoulder. Observing a large group of mounted men-at-arms, Allan moved off the road to allow them to pass.

Although he was initially dismayed to see Gisborne at the head of the group, he became alarmed when the sheriff's captain stopped on the road in front of him and ordered his men to surround him.

"Get off your horse and come here," demanded Gisborne. His stony expression caused a stirring in the pit of Allan's stomach as he meekly slid off his horse and walked to stand near Guy's mount.

"We've captured one of Robin Hood's men," Gisborne announced to the group. "He's the spy who pretends to be a minstrel."

Allan was speechless. He had been there when Gisborne had sworn fealty to Robin. His shock quickly morphed into outrage. Not only was he betraying Robin, but Guy was also the man who had murdered Odella's beloved father.

Guy must have recognized the resentment on Allan's face, because he was smirking when he dismounted.

Without warning, Allan's head exploded in pain, and he found himself on his back in the middle of the road. He tasted blood and woozily staggered to his feet. He then swung at Gisborne with all his strength.

Guy simply stepped to the side as Allan stumbled from the momentum and fell to his knees.

"He fights like a woman!" Gisborne declared, and all the men laughed loudly.

Allan had never felt so embarrassed in his life. He was thankful that his wife and friends weren't there to witness his humiliation.

Gisborne began barking orders to his men. "The other outlaws might be nearby. I want four of you to advance to a forward position about twenty yards down the road. Four of you retreat twenty yards to the rear. The rest of you divide into groups and look for the outlaws along the tree line and within the first ten feet of the forest."

The soldiers promptly dispersed, and Gisborne grabbed Allan by the front of his tunic and pulled him to his feet.

"Listen to me; I'm only going to say this once," he growled in a low voice. "Do you understand?"

Although his head was spinning, Allan nodded.

"Go to Locksley and tell Robin and Marian to hide in the forest. I'll be there soon to arrest them." Raising his voice, he shouted, "Where is Robin Hood?"

Allan tried to speak, but Gisborne slapped him, and he tasted more blood. But he also recognized that it hadn't been as forceful as Guy's first strike.

Once again, Guy pulled him close and muttered, "When I

arrive in Locksley, I don't want to see you or that nag you're riding. If my men see you, I'll have to kill you."

Allan moaned, "All right."

Gisborne shook him roughly. Quietly ending their conversation, he commanded, "Next time I hit you, fall to the ground and stay there. Don't get up until we've left."

Just as the words 'next time I hit you' seeped into Allan's consciousness, Guy back-handed him across the face. Allan fell into the ditch and realized that he would have no problem lying still until the men were gone.

Gisborne whistled loudly to recall his men, and they promptly returned.

Allan listened as Guy alleged, "This worthless excuse for a man kept trying to tell me that Robin Hood is not at Lenton. He's a poor liar, so we'll search there first before we go to Locksley."

One man asked, "What about this outlaw? Shouldn't we arrest him?"

There was a brief silence, and then Allan heard Gisborne's icy reply. "He's been beaten senseless. Are you willing to carry him until we return to the castle?" Guy then proclaimed, "The next man who dares to question me will join the minstrel in the ditch."

Soon, the ground under Allan trembled as the men spurred their horses down the road. Because they were near the fork that led to Lenton, he knew it wouldn't take long for them to learn that Robin wasn't there.

Allan struggled to stand. His head swam, and darkness crept along the edges of his vision. He willed himself to stay conscious. His horse was happily grazing on the tall grass in the ditch, and it took him three attempts to mount her. As he settled himself into the saddle, he looked down and saw that the front of his tunic was covered with blood. Touching his lips, he discovered he was bleeding from his nose and mouth.

There was no time to waste; his head cleared a bit as his stomach lurched from a mix of fear and pain, and he kicked the old mare in the side as hard as he could as he headed towards Locksley.

1 July 1193, Nottingham Castle

It was market day, and Constance was strolling amongst the tables, admiring the variety of wares offered. She enjoyed shopping, and she was grateful that her father was so generous in giving her spending money. Spying a table filled with skeins of yarn, she approached it and examined the impressive assortment of colors. Her time at the castle would pass more pleasantly if she distracted herself with embroidery.

Selecting a lovely light blue, she said to the elderly woman selling the yarn, "This reminds me of a robin's egg." In truth, it reminded her of Guy's eyes. After choosing several other colors, she paid the woman and placed the skeins in a pouch hanging from her belt.

She had been in Nottingham for nearly a fortnight and had helped Guy organize the Feast of Midsummer at the castle, since he had been acting sheriff at the time. He had been polite, but noticeably reserved with her, and she was distressed that he was avoiding anything that resembled a real conversation.

Then the sheriff had returned two days ago. Even though she had only seen him from a distance, her heart had been seized with loathing for this man who had beaten and abused Guy's mother.

She knew Guy had loved his mother and had been close to her. So, why would he stay with this man, Montlhéry? She also recalled many incidents where the sheriff had treated Guy with cruelty and contempt. Again, she wondered, why would Guy tolerate such treatment?

More than anything, she wanted to ask him, yet she was hesitant. As long as he remained so formal and aloof, she could not bring herself to pose such personal questions.

She was absentmindedly walking to the castle, when the noise of riders passing through the bailey caught her attention. Looking up, she saw Guy, and their eyes met.

Reining in his horse, Guy ordered one of his men to take it to the stables as he dismounted and strode towards her.

She smiled at him, hoping he would smile back. Instead, he scowled.

"What are you doing here?" he demanded.

"I'm shopping."

"Shopping?" His brow creased. "Do you have money? Are you requesting credit? I have very little money—"

"Please don't worry. I have money."

She observed the realization dawning on his face. He gruffly stated, "Your father's money."

"Yes." She tilted her head and gazed at him. For some reason, this upset him, and she wondered why.

He changed the subject abruptly. "It might be too dangerous for you to remain at the castle."

"What's happened?"

"As you know, the sheriff has returned. Things did not go well in Paris." Guy scanned the area to determine whether anyone was listening. He grasped her by the elbow and led her from the busy market to a spot near the wall that divided the inner and outer baileys.

He continued, "Emperor Heinrich never arrived in Paris for the Feast of Midsummer. Somehow, King Richard persuaded him to stay in Germany."

"Thank God," breathed Constance. She had understood the danger if Richard had been given to King Philippe.

"I've learned that Richard's ransom has been renegotiated. It's now 150,000 silver—"

Constance gasped, "Oh, no!"

"However, the king will be released after delivery of 100,000 marks and 67 hostages as a guarantee for the remaining 50,000."

"Does Robin know about this?"

"No. Also, Prince John has fled to Paris, and Payen is with him. Montlhéry is concerned that John will lose control of his lands in England, because he was told not to leave. If that happens, Montlhéry and I might have to flee as well."

"Do you want me to go to Locksley to tell Robin?"

"No—"

There was a commotion in the market, and Constance heard the familiar voice of the sheriff.

"Where is he? I want the outer bailey searched—"

To Constance's surprise, Guy pulled her into an embrace and kissed her passionately.

"Gisborne!" yelled the sheriff. He was now only a few feet away.

Guy released her and faced Montlhéry, dropping to one knee before rising and inquiring, "My lord, were you looking for me?"

The sheriff glowered at her, disgust and disdain clearly etched on his countenance. Returning his attention to Guy, he asked, "Did you deliver Huntingdon to the dungeons, or have you failed me again?" He took a menacing step towards Guy.

"My lord, I was on my way to explain everything to you when I saw my wife in the market. I was just greeting her when you arrived."

"Gisborne, I am your priority. You should be focused on me and my needs. You're fortunate that I tolerate you, considering your repeated failures and idiocy. Where is Robin Hood?"

"My lord, I searched for him at Lenton and Locksley. He wasn't there, and neither was Lady Marian."

"Well? Where is he?"

Guy responded, "The servants weren't sure if he had left for Huntingdon or Conisbrough. But since he's not here, he could not have robbed the men from Ernehale."

"Robbed?" Constance interjected. She immediately regretted attracting the notice of the sheriff.

"Where is your father, Lady Constance?" the sheriff questioned.

"He has gone to Embelton to supervise the collection of the taxes for King Richard's ransom. Lionel is with him."

"And you remained here, alone?"

"I'm not alone. I'm with my husband," she replied.

For a moment, the sheriff studied them. To her relief, Guy wrapped his arm around her waist, pulling her close and giving every appearance of happy matrimony.

The sheriff resumed his interrogation. "What is the relationship between Robin Hood and the de Warenne family?"

Constance hesitated, reluctant to give him any information about Robin, but she couldn't think of a reason not to share the truth. "Robin and Lionel both trained with Earl Hamelin when they were boys, before they went to Poitou. Robin is on friendly terms with Earl Hamelin and Countess Isabel. Why do you ask?"

Montlhéry's eyes narrowed. "Are you acquainted with them?"

"Yes, I've met them and their children."

Guy re-entered the conversation. "My lord, as I said, if Huntingdon is not here, then he could not have—"

"Gisborne, you are not paid to think. You are not here to offer opinions. You will accompany me to my tower room where we can discuss our next steps. That is, if you can separate yourself from this vision of...*loveliness*." His mocking tone was unmistakable, and Constance cringed in mortification.

The sheriff started marching to the keep, and Guy followed, offering only an apologetic glance at her as he left.

6 July 1193, Ernehale, Nottinghamshire

The noise and smells in the tavern nearly overwhelmed Marian, and she was so nervous that her hands were trembling. Nevertheless, she was determined to prove to Robin that she could do this. From within the shadow of her hooded cloak, she scanned the crowd until she found Little John standing behind a table. Their eyes met, and he subtly gestured at the man sitting in front of him.

After three nights of searching, Allan had located the soldier who had accused Robin Hood of stealing Ernehale's tax money. It was late in the evening, and the man was drinking alone. Allan had briefly spoken to him, learning his name, and then pointing him out to John before Marian's entrance into the tavern.

Nearing the man's table, she cried, "Garin!" She pulled back the hood of her cloak to show her face. Marian was counting on her beauty to charm this man.

He startled and stared at her in open-mouthed surprise.

"I've missed you," Marian sweetly announced as she sat on the bench next to him and boldly put her hand on top of his as it rested on the table.

Stunned, he stuttered, "Do I know you?"

"Don't you remember me?" her face fell dramatically, and she lowered her eyes. "Garin, I thought the time we spent together meant something. I know I could never forget you." She wiped a non-existent tear from her cheek.

Recovering from the shock of having a beautiful woman approach him in such a familiar manner, Garin replied, "Forgive me, my dear. I, uh, of course, I remember you. How could any man forget such a pretty face?"

He leered at her, and to her distress, he wrapped his arm around her shoulders, pulling her closer.

Marian's skin crawled with revulsion, but she forced herself to smile, lowering her eyelids in what she hoped was a seductive gaze.

Garin whispered in her ear, "I'm eager to renew our acquaintance, but I live in the barracks. Do you have a place nearby? It's too noisy to talk here."

The hand resting on her shoulder drifted down her arm, and when his fingertips brushed against the side of her breast, Marian leapt to her feet.

He also stood, swaying slightly as he had been drinking heavily. Still ogling her, he said, "Impatient, are you? I like that in a woman."

He tried to kiss her, but because of his unsteadiness, she slipped out of his embrace, taking him by the hand and making her way towards the door. Glancing back, she spotted John following the man, and Marian relaxed, knowing that the big, burly former outlaw would protect her.

As soon as they exited the tavern, Marian inhaled the fresh air. Once again, the man attempted to hug her, but she squirmed out of his grasp and ducked down the nearest alley where Robin was anxiously waiting for her. When she recognized his form in the shadows, she drew near to him, reveling in the sense of safety she felt when she was at his side.

Garin stumbled into the alley, and he exclaimed, "Hey! Where are you going?"

"I'm here, Garin," she beckoned in a sing-song voice, despite Robin's hushed plea for her to be quiet.

"I can't see you, girl," he declared. "Come closer."

Marian watched as Little John walked up behind the man and tapped him on the shoulder.

Garin pivoted and irately demanded, "What do you want? I saw her first. Get out of here."

With that, John punched him, and he collapsed in an unconscious heap. After draping Garin over the back of a horse, Allan covered him with a blanket. Then they nonchalantly passed through the town gate and returned to their camp in the forest.

Marian stood at the edge of the camp and observed as Robin searched the unconscious Garin, retrieving something shiny that was around his neck and hidden under his tunic. Much then bound his wrists and ankles.

Little John and Much worked together to drag the man over to a large tree where they propped him against the trunk. Will

Scarlet splashed water on his face, and he sputtered and cursed as he regained consciousness.

"Where am I?" he shouted. "Where's that little bitch? If you've stolen my money, I promise you'll regret it!"

Alarmed by Garin's angry words, Marian moved behind a tree, even though he was not looking in her direction.

Robin stood in front of Garin, while Little John and Much flanked him, John with his staff and Much with a sword.

"It's good to see you again, Garin," Robin calmly stated.

"I don't know you. What do you want from me?" Garin's eyes narrowed. "I'm the captain of Lord Ernehale's guard. I will find you and the rest of your forest bandits, and then you'll be at my mercy."

Robin grinned. "I thought you knew me. Are you saying you don't?"

"You're a forest rat. You and your type are as common as any other vermin."

"It's odd that you don't recognize me. After all, you told Lord Ernehale and his son that I robbed you on the road to Nottingham."

"What?"

"I am Robin Hood." He bowed theatrically. "And these are my men. We would like to know why you are accusing us of robbery and murder."

Garin blanched, but then he recovered his wits and professed, "I recognize you now; you robbed me of Ernehale's taxes and our church's plate."

"Garin, we don't like liars." Robin gestured towards John. "My friend here is very upset that you've besmirched his name. I think you should tell me what really happened on the road between Ernehale and Nottingham."

John tapped his staff against his open palm, suggesting what he might do to Garin.

"You can beat me or torture me; I won't tell you anything," Garin declared, although his anxious expression belied his brave words.

Marian noticed that Robin was no longer smiling, and his demeanor had grown somber. "Are you refusing to cooperate? I can't be held responsible for what might happen to you."

For all his bluster, Garin hesitated. But then a resolve settled over him. "You're bluffing," he asserted.

Robin motioned towards the shadows at the opposite side of their camp, and to Marian's surprise, Brother Tuck stepped forward. He was dressed in his Knight Templar garb, and his white mantle with its red cross gleamed eerily in the fire's light.

Robin announced, "He's all yours, Brother Tuck."

"What's this?" cried a distressed Garin. "Who is this man?"

Tuck sat on a log very close to Garin and began speaking quietly to him.

All the other outlaws backed away, while Robin came and stood next to her.

"What's Tuck doing?" questioned Marian.

With a twinkle in his eye, Robin replied, "Just watch."

Marian observed Tuck and Garin, although she could not hear what they were saying.

At first, Garin looked angry, but his expression gradually transitioned from defiant to contrite.

Tuck fished something out of the pouch at his belt. It was an elaborate silver cross on a chain.

"Robin, I don't understand," Marian whispered.

"Garin was wearing that cross. Do you think it belongs to him?"

"It looks like the crosses that priests wear during Mass."

"Exactly. I'm sure that cross belonged to Ernehale's church, and that it had been surrendered for the ransom."

"But, why would he have it?"

"I think we'll find out soon."

Marian gazed at Tuck and Garin again, only to see that Tuck was patiently nodding, and Garin's face was wet with tears. This continued for a while, as Garin was telling Tuck a long story.

Finally, Tuck placed his left hand on the other man's shoulder in a comforting gesture. He then made the sign of the cross, and Marian recognized that Tuck was praying over the man.

Tuck stood, and Marian could hear him inform Garin that when he returned, he would be allowed to leave. He then signaled for John to stand watch over the prisoner.

Brother Tuck approached Marian and Robin, and the other outlaws joined them. Leading them a short distance away from the camp, Tuck proclaimed, "I can tell you what happened."

Everyone crowded around, eager to hear what Tuck had learned.

"The beginning of his story is true; they were on the road to Nottingham when they were surrounded by a large group of men-at-arms. These men were soldiers, not forest bandits. The Ernehale men surrendered in the face of this overwhelming force."

"They did not resist?" asked Robin.

"They thought the men would just steal the silver and release them. They were forced to disarm and kneel along the road. Without warning, the marauders attacked and killed most of the men."

"While they were kneeling and unarmed?" an alarmed Will questioned.

Tuck nodded. "The surviving Ernehale men jumped to their feet and tried to flee, but they were quickly apprehended, and every man was killed except for Garin."

"There is only one reason they would allow a single man to survive their attack," commented Robin.

"What do you mean?" Marian asked.

Robin disclosed, "They wanted a witness to accuse me of this foul deed."

"That's correct," replied Tuck. "They let Garin fill his pouch with silver, and they allowed him to keep the cross as well. He had seen that cross in his church all his life, and he was outraged that it would be confiscated and melted for Richard's ransom."

"But once the men let him go, why did he continue to lie?" inquired Allan.

Robin answered, "With a pouch full of silver, and that cross in his possession, he became complicit in what they had done. It's a very clever way of preventing someone from betraying you. If Garin had failed to follow their instructions, I'm sure an anonymous note accusing him of being part of the plan would've been delivered to Lord Ernehale, and a search of Garin's belongings would have confirmed it."

"Greed has caused many men to stumble," observed Much.

Tuck nodded. "In scripture, it says that 'the love of money is the root of all evil.'"

Marian proposed, "Can we force him to identify the real robbers in order to clear Robin's name?"

"He would probably recognize the men if he saw them again," remarked Tuck, "but we can't expect him to change his story at this point. If he confesses that he lied, he will be hanged."

"I believe those men were the sheriff's mercenaries," Robin declared. "We must determine where they will strike next. I'm sure they will focus on stealing the taxes from small towns and villages, as the silver from larger cities is guarded by the queen's men-at-arms."

"Can't the queen's soldiers guard all the silver?" suggested Will.

"There are too many villages and too few soldiers," Robin explained.

"Garin has agreed to surrender the cross and the silver he took," Tuck said. "I assured him we will add it to the king's ransom. He knows that Lord Robin is the king's man. I also instructed him to do penance, and I offered him the peace of God."

Robin nodded in satisfaction. "His silver is in the bag tied to his belt. I suspected it was more than his wages from Lord Ernehale. Blindfold him and tell John to take him to the edge of the forest near the gates of the town and let him go."

❦

Later, when Marian was alone with Robin, she asked, "How did you know Garin would talk to Brother Tuck?"

"Two reasons: first, despite his bluster and his refusal to talk to me, I could see the fear in his eyes. However, I surmised that he wasn't afraid of us. He's not stupid, and he knew that if we were going to steal his silver, we would have done it in that alley when he was unconscious."

"And the second reason?"

"When I found that he was wearing that cross, there could be only one motivation for him to have it."

"Which was?"

Robin grinned at her persistence. "It was reckless for him to keep it. If anyone had discovered that he had the cross that belonged to his church, he would have been hanged for theft. As I said, I don't think Garin is foolish; I believe he has a fervent connection to his church. A man with such abiding faith can be persuaded to confess to a man of God who is wise, compassionate, and has the authority of a respected order like the Templars."

"You're describing Tuck, of course. What will we do next?"

"I plan to apply more pressure on Gisborne. We have to find these mercenaries before they kill more men."

"And steal more of the king's ransom," Marian added.

CHAPTER 11
GAMES OF HIDE AND SEEK

8 July 1193, Sherwood Forest

Robin and Much crawled on their stomachs as they moved into position behind a fallen tree at the edge of the camp. It had been easy to locate, as the sheriff regularly sent supplies to the mercenaries, and Robin had simply followed the wheel ruts that veered from the main road and into the forest where the sheriff's men had cleared a path just wide enough for the wagons to pass.

Gisborne had alerted Robin that a shipment of food and ale would be delivered today.

It was a large encampment, consistent with Guy's estimate that three dozen men lived there. But since it was midday, only six men were there to guard the silver, and Robin assumed the others had already left to rob towns of their ransom payments. In the center of the camp, there was a stack of small wooden chests and leather bags—the stolen taxes and church plate.

As they were watching, a loud whistle and a rumbling along the ground under their bellies heralded the arrival of provisions from Nottingham. They observed as two wagons entered the camp, and the men worked to unload crates of food and barrels of ale.

The men loaded empty barrels onto the wagons, pried them

open, and put the bags of church plate into them. The chests of silver were also placed in the wagons, and they were covered with threadbare blankets secured at the corners by rocks.

Since the men were talking and joking noisily with one another, Much felt it was safe to whisper to Robin, "Those men driving the wagons aren't servants from the kitchens or brew houses. I think they're soldiers."

In an equally hushed voice, Robin remarked, "It's a bold tactic to transport all that silver without an additional guard. But then, if 'empty' barrels arrived at the castle surrounded by men-at-arms, it would attract unwanted attention."

Robin and Much carefully backed away, still hugging the ground. The moment they were safely out of sight, they stood and jogged to where they had left John, Will, Allan, and their horses.

Robin announced, "We have an opportunity to recover some of the stolen silver as there are only four men with the wagons returning to the castle."

"It almost seems too easy," Much commented.

"If there are only four men, then they're not expecting trouble," surmised John.

Robin agreed. "When the sheriff realizes what has happened, then all future wagons will be heavily guarded, regardless of whether it attracts the notice of others."

The men quickly mounted and rode to the path which the wagons would follow as they traveled to the castle.

Robin knew they had to be far enough from the camp so that the soldiers in the wagons could not cry for help, yet he had to stop them before they left the forest and returned to the main road.

Along the path, there was a massive tree that had toppled to the ground, probably during the previous winter. The mercenaries had been too lazy to move it out of their way, and instead, they had cleared a path around it, creating a sharp curve that Robin could use to his advantage.

Leading his men past the curve, he instructed them, "John, Will, and Allan, you will wait on the other side of the road. As soon as they round the bend, we will confront them with our bows drawn. The three of you will target the second wagon while Much and I will take the first."

Much always had a knack for knowing what needed to be done, and he hopped off his horse, darting through the trees along the worn path to make sure that the same four men who had brought the wagons were guiding them back.

Just as Robin heard the wagons, Much returned, mounted his horse, and nodded. No additional men were coming.

The sheriff's men were loudly conversing without a care in the world. As they steered around the bend, they were so inattentive that none of them saw Robin until he and Much rode out onto the path with their bows drawn.

"Halt!" cried Robin.

The men were briefly stunned, and by the time they realized what was happening, they also understood that they were at a distinct disadvantage, since their swords were in their scabbards, and they weren't carrying bows.

Three of the men raised their hands in surrender, but the fourth, a large soldier who was closest to Will, lunged towards the slightly built young man. He grabbed Will, knocking his bow out of his hands and attempting to pull him off his horse.

Robin promptly took aim and released his arrow, striking the soldier under his upraised arm. He fell to the ground, and the other men raised their hands even higher in the air, hoping to emphasize their willingness to surrender.

At Robin's signal, Allan and a shaken Will dismounted and took the soldiers' swords, including the weapon of the injured man.

Robin commanded, "Come down from the wagons. If you do as you're told, no one else will be hurt."

One man questioned, "What do you want from us? We've no

money, and these barrels are empty. Open their spigots, and you'll see that I'm telling you the truth."

Robin did not answer him; he watched as John and Much led the men to the side of the path and bound them at their ankles and wrists.

"You're taking the wagons?" asked one man incredulously. "Do you have a death wish? These wagons belong to the Sheriff of Nottingham, and he will hunt you down and kill you."

Once the men were secured, Robin lowered his bow and dismounted. He went to the injured man and was dismayed to realize that it had been a fatal wound. The arrow must have pierced his heart.

Robin walked over to a wagon and lifted the corner of a blanket, exposing the chests of silver. He opened one, much to the chagrin of the soldiers, and demanded, "Tell the Sheriff of Nottingham that Robin Hood has collected this shipment of taxes for the king's ransom."

John and Much each climbed aboard a wagon and urged the draft horses forward. The wagons, weighed down with silver, rocked back and forth but did not advance.

Robin, Allan, and Will got off their horses and hurried to the rear of John's wagon, pushing with all their strength to help the horses get a start. After that wagon began to travel forward, they repeated the exercise with Much's wagon. As soon as the wagons were lumbering down the path, Robin and his men followed on horseback.

The pace of the horses pulling the heavy wagons was much too slow for Robin's comfort, but eventually they reached the main road where they turned north towards Locksley.

❧

By late afternoon, Robin and his men had unloaded the silver into his family's hunting lodge, a small structure that was hidden deep in the forest. His father, Duncan, had built it many years ago, and following his return from the Crusade, Robin had arranged for a new roof and various repairs to the aging structure. Although he had not anticipated needing to use the lodge as an outlaw hideout, he was thankful to have a safe place for Marian to stay when it was too dangerous for her to accompany them.

He was inspecting one of the wagons they had taken earlier. Both were well-built and sturdy, so decided to keep them at the lodge as well, in case a situation arose that required moving the taxes to a different location. He was still considering what to do with the extra horses.

Marian walked up to him as he tugged on a floorboard that wasn't quite flush with the others to see if it was loose.

She sighed loudly. "The inside of the lodge smells like the tavern in Ernehale," she complained. "Even though the bags were in the barrels for short time, they have absorbed a strong odor of ale."

Robin absentmindedly nodded. Examining a wheel, he said, "That can't be helped. We should leave the door ajar and open the window's shutter."

"You seem distracted," observed Marian. "Aren't you happy about recovering these taxes?"

"Of course," he replied. He straightened, leaned against the wagon and faced her. "But next time, the sheriff will be more careful to guard his wagons. And we know the mercenaries are still attacking and killing the men who are escorting shipments of silver from the smaller towns to Nottingham."

"What can we do?"

"I've sent Allan to Nottingham with a message for Gisborne."

Her brow creased in confusion, Marian noted, "But he still has bruises on his face from the last time he met with Guy. Are you sure that was wise?"

Robin shrugged. "It's likely that he will try to find Constance first, and only if she is unavailable will he approach Gisborne. Allan will be all right."

10 July 1193, On the Road North of Nottingham

Robin and Marian were concealed within the tree line as they watched the road and waited. At last, John whistled that someone was coming.

Cresting a nearby hill, Guy and Constance appeared; Guy was mounted on a fine destrier, and Constance was riding a staid palfrey. They slowed and scanned the trees, recognizing that they were close to the rendezvous point.

After a second whistle from John indicating that no one was following Gisborne, Robin and Marian emerged from the forest.

Constance's face lit up at the sight of them, and she pulled her horse alongside Marian's. They both dismounted and began to chat, so Robin focused his attention on Guy.

"You are alone? Just the two of you?" Robin inquired, dispensing with any pretense of a friendly greeting.

Guy answered, "The mercenaries know that I'm the sheriff's captain, so they won't bother us."

Robin nodded. "Did you find it?"

Guy twisted in his saddle and retrieved a folded piece of paper from his saddlebag. "Constance and I worked together to create a copy of the original." He handed it to Robin.

Robin took it and silently reviewed the list of when the towns and villages of Nottinghamshire were scheduled to send their tax payments to Nottingham for the Exchequer of Ransom. He asked, "Do you know which shipments will be raided?"

Guy offered, "I can only assume they will focus on the villages and towns that lack a large force of men to guard the shipments."

Robin refolded the list and tucked it into his saddlebag.

"Earl Robin," Gisborne formally addressed him, and Robin was wary of this newfound respect coming from his brother. "You should know that, after your raid—"

"Recovery," Robin corrected him.

With a wry grin, Guy acknowledged, "After your recovery of the taxes from the camp, Montlhéry has demanded that the mercenaries bring the stolen treasure directly to Nottingham, and they are smuggling it into the castle in empty ale barrels that are delivered to the kitchens."

"The kitchens?" questioned Robin. "How are they securing the taxes? How are they explaining all these barrels?" He noticed Guy hesitate, and Robin was instantly suspicious. Gisborne seemed to be formulating an answer instead of responding honestly.

"There is a large pantry with a lock. It's used to secure valuable spices."

"Do you have access to this pantry?" Again, Robin observed as Guy struggled to answer a simple question.

"Yes, I have a key, but—"

Marian and Constance walked up, interrupting their conversation. The two men dismounted, and Robin greeted Constance with a brief hug, inquiring, "Why are you here? Were you bored in the castle and wanting a diversion?"

She was momentarily confused, but then she looked at Guy and asked, "Did you tell him?"

Robin gazed expectantly at Gisborne, who explained, "Montlhéry has instructed me to deliver a message to Earl Hamelin at Conisbrough, and he insisted I take Constance with me so that she could visit her friends."

A perplexed Robin questioned, "Since when has the sheriff ever been concerned about Constance? And what is in this message?"

"Unfortunately, it's sealed," replied Guy.

"It's widely known that Earl Hamelin is in London managing the collection and storage of the ransom, so sending a message to Conisbrough makes no sense," remarked Robin.

"Perhaps the sheriff received word that Earl Hamelin is traveling home," suggested Gisborne.

Robin countered, "There's an important meeting of the Great

Council that will be held in Ely in seven days, and I'm certain that Hamelin will remain in London until then."

"Will you be going to Ely?" asked Marian. She frowned at the thought of Robin leaving for another of these gatherings.

"Edmund and Lionel are attending the meeting, and I've requested that they represent me there. I must try to thwart these mercenaries, and if I'm away for any length of time, I fear they will inflict more carnage here."

Guy added, "Now that you have that list, you'll know where they are likely to strike next."

Constance reached out and took Marian's hand. "Come with us to Conisbrough, Marian. We won't be gone long, and you can visit Robbie."

Robin watched closely as a myriad of emotions passed over Marian's face: excitement, yearning, anxiety, despair. He could see that she was conflicted over whether to go to Robbie or stay with him.

"Marian, I would like you to go check on Robbie. I want him to know that we haven't abandoned him, and that we're thinking about him all the time," declared Robin.

Marian continued to dither, averting her eyes as she contemplated her response.

"Please come with us, Marian," Constance begged.

She finally spoke, "I want to go, but I feel my place is here with Robin." She glanced down at the male attire that she was wearing. "Besides, I don't have any clothes to wear that would be appropriate."

Constance smiled. "I sent Allan to Locksley to retrieve a bag of clothing for you." She pointed at the two bulging bags hanging from either side of her saddle. "One of those is filled with your favorites."

Marian still hesitated.

Robin caught Gisborne's attention, and the other man nodded in understanding. Guy led Constance back to their horses so that Robin and Marian could talk.

"Marian, I'm not trying to send you away again. I'm just worried about Robbie."

She admitted, "I'm worried about him, too. I don't like being separated from him for so long. When I traveled to Outremer, I was gone for six months, and he had grown and changed so much…and I wasn't there to see it. Then last summer, I could only see him once a month when I was leading the outlaws."

"So, why are you hesitating?" Robin asked.

"I worry more about you than Robbie. I know Robbie is safe at Conisbrough, but I don't think you are ever safe enough."

Robin gathered her into his arms, not caring if Gisborne and Constance were observing them. He insisted, "I can't promise you that nothing will happen to me. But I want you to know that you and Robbie are more important to me than anything or anyone—"

"Or any king?" she interjected.

He leaned away from her to gaze into her eyes. "Of course. I promise I won't take any unnecessary risks." Cupping her face with his hands, he assured her, "We won't be apart for long. Go to Conisbrough. Tell Robbie that I miss him, and that we'll all be together soon."

He kissed her tenderly before watching her ride off with Constance and Gisborne.

12 July 1193, Carentune, Nottinghamshire

Robin and Brother Tuck stood in the great hall of Lord Carentune's manor. He was a heavyset, middle-aged man, and Robin wondered if he was always so agitated. The man was wringing his hands and sweating profusely, although the mid-July heat might have contributed to that.

"I don't know," he moaned. "This sounds risky."

"Compared to losing your men-at-arms and your taxes to these mercenaries? They rarely leave any survivors," Robin asserted.

"Are you certain they will attack my men? We're not as large or wealthy as Ernehale."

Robin could see skepticism in the other man's eyes. He tried to assure him, "Carentune is the only town scheduled to transport taxes to Nottingham tomorrow. I'm certain that you will be targeted."

Brother Tuck inquired, "Why do you doubt us?"

At last, Lord Carentune admitted, "Look, I know you've been at odds with the sheriff for a long time; ever since that mix-up after the death of Baron Lenton. But I've always had a friendly relationship with Baron de Argentan. We get along well. If these mercenaries are truly under the sheriff's control, then he would never attack me."

"Mix-up?" Robin's voice rose in anger. "Are you referring to the time that Sheriff de Argentan tried to hang me for a murder he knew I hadn't committed? The murder of Baron Lenton?" Robin indignantly stepped towards the other man, and Brother Tuck discreetly took his arm and pulled him back.

Hoping to give Robin a moment to calm down, Brother Tuck spoke. "Lord Carentune, what is most important to you? What is your priority?"

The other man paused to think. "Well, I want to ensure that our taxes are safely delivered to London. I don't want them to be stolen, and I don't want my men killed. The people of Ernehale lost their first payment, and now they've been told it must be replaced. We are a small town, and we can barely afford to pay these taxes once. We can't pay them twice."

Robin's temper had cooled, and he tried to reason with Lord Carentune. "The help I'm offering will guarantee that your taxes are safe. Do you want to take a chance with the mercenaries? Regardless of whether they are tied to Sheriff de Argentan, they exist. You've heard the stories. These men aren't bandits; they're trained soldiers, and they're ruthless."

Lord Carentune wiped the sweat from his brow and sighed. "Tell me your plan again."

Robin explained, "My men and I will take your tax payment today. We will hide it in a safe place. Brother Tuck and I will sign a receipt stating that we have received your taxes, the amount we've received, and the date. I will arrange to send your taxes to London as soon as I can secure a large group of men-at-arms from Earl Hamelin de Warenne to protect them. He is one of two men in charge of the Exchequer of Ransom."

Nodding, Lord Carentune remarked, "I know Earl Hamelin. He's an honorable man, and I trust him."

Brother Tuck commented, "The queen holds him in the highest regard as well."

"I'm only asking you to do one thing in return for my guaranteed delivery of your taxes," Robin stressed. "I want you to send word to the Sheriff of Nottingham that the mercenaries stole your taxes."

"But that would be a lie," countered Lord Carentune.

"Think of it more like a test, a way to find the truth," suggested Tuck. "If the sheriff is directing these men, and they deny that they have your taxes, who will he believe? He will believe you; you've already said you're on good terms with him. This could cause a schism between the sheriff and the mercenaries. "

Robin added, "And if the sheriff is innocent, then later you can send word that there was," he paused for emphasis, "*a mix-up.*"

Finally, Lord Carentune agreed, and after giving him a receipt, Robin and Tuck made plans to remove the taxes in secret later that night, under the light of a nearly full moon.

15 July 1193, Nottingham Castle

Although the Feast of Saint Swithun was not a major feast day, this year it coincided with Nottingham's usual market day, making it the perfect opportunity for Robin and Allan to slip into the inner bailey of the fortress unnoticed.

They entered the castle's open gate and nonchalantly meandered among the vendors selling their wares in the outer bailey. They were wearing plain hooded cloaks that shadowed their faces, and they hoped to blend into the crowd.

Allan sighed. "I wish I had my lute. The people are in high spirits, and I could have earned some coins."

Robin slapped him good-naturedly on the back. "There's always another feast day just around the corner. In the next fortnight, there will be two major feasts. As soon as my uncle Edmund returns from Ely, we will resume our normal lives."

"Are you sure he'll be able to sort out everything with the Great Council?" inquired Allan.

Robin replied, "He'll explain to them that these accusations against me are lies invented by the sheriff. Queen Eleanor knows that I'm loyal to Richard. And my old crusading companion, Hubert Walter, will vouch for me. Did I mention he is now the Archbishop of Canterbury? And Earl Hamelin will be there too. By this time next week, it will all be resolved."

"I'm glad to hear that. I don't like being away from Odella," admitted Allan.

Robin nodded in understanding, and proposed, "Let's find out where the sheriff is storing all the silver he's stolen."

"How much silver do you reckon he has?" Allan asked.

"I'm not certain of the exact amount, but it should be a big enough hoard that hiding and securing it would be a challenge," responded Robin.

They wandered amongst the market stalls, gradually making their way to the gate that divided the inner and outer baileys. A group of men carrying supplies walked past them, and an older man at the rear of the group stumbled. Robin and Allan hurried to him and offered to carry his bundle. He gratefully handed it to Robin, while Allan began chatting with him about the weather. Joining the larger group allowed them to stroll casually past the guards.

As luck would have it, the men were delivering provisions to the kitchens, so Robin and Allan continued to walk with them.

The main kitchen was inside the keep, and most of the cooking was done there. But some food preparation was performed in auxiliary buildings just outside the door that led to the main kitchen. This area was commonly called 'the kitchens,' and it included a bakery, a butcher's stall, an array of pantries, and two open spits, which were used when the sheriff was hosting large parties in the great hall.

After they separated from the other men, Robin noticed a pantry unlike the others. It was obviously locked, and its impressive oak door appeared to be relatively new. He tapped on Allan's shoulder and gestured towards it.

In a low voice, Allan disclosed, "I remember seeing that pantry last year when I was here during the Feast of Midsummer. It was locked then too. I'm not sure it's the one."

"It's the only locked pantry," countered Robin, "and it matches Gisborne's description."

At that moment, several kitchen workers strode by them, so Robin and Allan backed into the narrow gap between the bakery and another building. Realizing that the spot was a good location for them to remain hidden while they waited, they settled into position and observed the locked pantry.

Robin's stomach rumbled as he inhaled the fragrant bread baking near them. He looked forward to returning to Locksley and resuming normal life; he especially missed Elvina and Odella's fine cooking.

The unmistakable sound of an approaching wagon brought both men to full attention. A soldier marched into the center of the kitchens and ordered everyone into the keep. The kitchen workers grumbled, but they didn't seem surprised as they left. Robin and Allan dropped to their hands and knees and hid behind several large bags of flour.

Just then, the sheriff appeared, and a wagon filled with barrels pulled up to the locked pantry. Montlhéry unlocked the door, and the men began unloading the barrels and moving them into the pantry. From the strain on their faces, it was obvious that these were not empty barrels.

Robin watched with interest, finding it odd that the sheriff would rely on this pantry as a secure location for the stolen taxes, regardless of the strength of its oak door and heavy lock. It was smaller than his hunting lodge, and it was impossible that all the money that had been stolen was stored within it. He would demand that Gisborne find the primary cache of treasure and report back to him.

It occurred to him that the silver he had recovered from the mercenaries, combined with the tax payments he had personally collected, had nearly filled his hunting lodge, and he would have to find another place to store all of it, if there were any delays in organizing its shipment to London.

Allan whispered, "What's taking them so long? They go into that pantry, but they're not coming out right away. What do you think they're doing?"

"I'm not sure," admitted Robin. "When Gisborne returns from Conisbrough, I will insist that he give me access to that pantry. He claims to have a key."

Montlhéry marched towards their hiding place, and they stilled, fearing that he had overheard their conversation.

A man joined the sheriff and announced, "That's all we have for today."

Montlhéry snorted derisively. "So you claim, Gaspard. Towns are reporting that bandits have stolen their tax payments, yet the amounts you're delivering are far smaller than I would expect."

The other man bristled at the sheriff's words. "My lord, these men are lying. Lord Carentune didn't send a tax payment on the appointed day. And it's the same with these other villages. They didn't transport their taxes according to the schedule you gave me."

Robin shifted closer; he wanted to hear this.

The sheriff retorted, "These men have no reason to lie. It's not like they can keep their tax payment if they claim it has been stolen. They'll have to replace any missing taxes. So you tell me: where are these payments?"

Gaspard argued, "I don't know why they're lying. But I tell you, we did not steal those payments. Maybe other bandits stole their taxes. Maybe the real Robin Hood took them."

Montlhéry scoffed. "You need to find these other bandits, whether it's Robin Hood or someone else. I want those taxes. I'm not paying you for silver that isn't delivered to me. If you want more for yourself, you'll have to earn it."

The two men moved away, and their voices faded. Then Montlhéry locked the pantry, and the other men turned the wagon, mounted their horses, and left. After the sheriff waved at someone they couldn't see, the kitchen workers resumed their duties, still muttering about the interruption.

Waiting until they were certain that Montlhéry was gone, Robin and Allan stood and made their way through the baileys. Exiting the fortress was always easier than gaining entrance, and soon they found themselves back in the city of Nottingham.

Passing the Church of Saint Nicholas where they had first met almost five years ago, Robin and Allan strolled in silence for a while.

"Lord Robin, what did you think of the sheriff's suggestion that the mercenaries search for us to find the rest of the silver?" questioned an apprehensive Allan.

The implications of the sheriff's words troubled Robin, but he affected an air of confidence as he declared, "Don't be concerned. The Great Council is meeting in Ely in two days. Edmund should return a couple of days after that, and then everything will be resolved. I will coordinate with Earl Hamelin, and all those taxes in the hunting lodge will be on their way to London."

A relieved Allan said, "That's good to know. Now that I'm a married man, I worry a lot more than I did when I was just a wandering minstrel without a care in the world."

"And soon you'll be a father," Robin reminded him.

"Some days, I'm excited about that, but most days, I'm terrified," Allan confessed.

They laughed amiably as they neared the outskirts of town.

"It's imperative that I recover those taxes from the sheriff," Robin remarked. "I must get inside that pantry."

CHAPTER 12
THE COUNCIL AT ELY

17 July 1193, Ely

Edmund and Lionel stood amongst the nobility of England and listened as Hubert Walter, the Archbishop of Canterbury, announced the terms of the Treaty of Mantes, which had recently been finalized between King Philippe, Prince John, and representatives of King Richard. Edmund was appalled that, yet again, Prince John was being rewarded for his treasonous behavior.

Contrary to explicit orders from his mother and the Great Council, John had left England and fled to Paris at the end of June. The Council had confiscated his lands in England, but just a few days later, this treaty had restored John's properties and titles on both sides of the Channel.

Even more shocking, the treaty allowed Philippe to retain control of all the castles he had taken in Normandy during the past three months. Richard had also agreed to pay Philippe 20,000 marks to secure peace in the borderlands between Normandy and the French king's domains.

This was on top of the 150,000 silver marks demanded by Emperor Heinrich. The new agreement with Heinrich stipulated that Richard would be released upon payment of 100,000 marks and delivery of 67 hostages as a guarantee for the remaining 50,000.

Edmund wiped the sweat from his brow. It was a warm July day, and the great hall was crowded. As he mulled over the terms of the treaty, he speculated that the settlement with Philippe was likely a stalling tactic; once Richard was freed, he would immediately fight to recover these castles. And he admitted that the agreement would also keep John from making a direct play for the throne.

Edmund studied the impressive array of powerful people sitting on an elevated dais at the front of the assembly. Queen Eleanor sat in the center, and at her right was Walter de Coutances, Archbishop of Rouen, while Hubert Walter was on her left. Next to Hubert Walter was Earl Hamelin de Warenne. The remainder of the men seated on the dais were members of the Great Council. Unquestionably, Eleanor was in charge; she dominated every discussion and resolved each dispute.

At the moment, Archbishop Hubert was explaining to everyone how King Richard was ruling England from afar, regularly sending dispatches to the Great Council and receiving their reports. Several of these messages from the king were read out loud, and they encouraged the noble attendees to redouble their efforts in collecting the ransom.

The council voted on additional taxes to be levied, and Edmund sighed in resignation. It was vitally important that Richard come home; otherwise, Robin would be in terrible jeopardy from a triumphant King John. But the cost of Richard's freedom was crushing the economy of England.

Edmund's mind had wondered, so he startled to attention when Eleanor beckoned the Earl of Huntingdon to come forth.

Edmund pushed through the crowd, approached the dais, and genuflected. Eleanor, Hamelin, and Hubert all knew Robin, and Edmund felt confident that he could resolve the accusations against his nephew.

"I did not call you, Baron Embelton. Where is Earl Robin?" Eleanor's voice quavered with age, but there remained a sharp edge to her words that gave Edmund pause.

He cleared his throat nervously. "Your Grace, Robin could not attend this meeting, and he requested that I represent him today."

"Are you here to answer for these reports I'm receiving from Nottinghamshire that he is stealing the taxes intended to ransom my son?"

Her expression was implacable, and Edmund felt confused. "Your Grace, Robin is not stealing your taxes. That is a lie invented by the Sheriff of Nottingham. It is the sheriff who is stealing the missing money."

"What is your proof?" challenged Eleanor.

"Proof? Robin is wholly devoted to the king. He has always served the king faithfully, and he saved the king's life on more than one occasion." Edmund gazed at Hubert Walter. He had been in the Holy Land with Robin; surely he would defend him.

But Hubert Walter stared back at him, his face unreadable.

"Baron Embelton, the reports I'm receiving are not from the Sheriff of Nottingham," the queen chided. "Minor lords and officials from numerous small towns and villages across Nottinghamshire report that Robin Hood has stolen their taxes."

"That's not true!" cried Edmund, and at the queen's raised brow, he implored, "Forgive my outburst, Your Grace. But Robin is innocent of these charges."

"Prove his innocence," she demanded.

An astounded Edmund again sought help from the powerful men seated next to the queen. They stared at him stonily. "How can I prove his innocence?" a bewildered Edmund asked.

"Only Earl Robin can prove his innocence, yet he has ignored my summons to this council meeting. I can only surmise that his cowardice in hiding from me is conclusive proof of his guilt."

"Cowardice?" Edmund's temper began to rise. "My nephew is

the bravest man I know." He looked at Hubert Walter. "Archbishop Hubert, you served with Robin in the Holy Land. Tell everyone about his bravery and honor. He saved King Richard's life several times."

Hubert acknowledged, "It's true that Earl Robin served Richard courageously in the Holy Land. But that has no bearing on today."

Edmund sputtered in confusion. This conversation was becoming absurd, yet he had to control his temper. Behind him, he could hear the buzz of the other men in the hall talking.

An attendant standing at the side of the dais loudly commanded everyone to be quiet, and the noise faded into a hushed silence.

Trying once more to reason with the queen, Edmund repeated, "Robin is not stealing the people's taxes. He wants King Richard to return. The men who have accused him are mistaken, or they're lying."

"The reports say that Robin Hood is stealing the taxes needed for the ransom and giving the money to the poor. Five years ago, there were many such stories about Robin Hood taking money from the nobility and giving it to peasants. Are you telling me that this never happened? Are the people who told those stories liars too?"

"No, those stories are true, Robin was trying to help the poor who were suffering under Sheriff de Argentan's unfair taxes." As soon as the words left his mouth, he wanted to take them back.

The queen's eyes narrowed. "So Earl Robin is opposed to taxes, is he? I suppose he believes that the taxes for the ransom are unfair as well."

"Your Grace, please, that's not what I meant. Robin supports the taxes needed to bring Richard home." Sweat was pouring down the side of Edmund's face, and he hastily wiped his brow with his sleeve.

The queen rose from her throne, and all the men on the dais stood as well. Edmund's heart sped to a dizzying tempo.

Eleanor revealed, "I've already discussed this with the council. We had hoped that Earl Robin would have the courage to face us and defend himself. But because he is not here, he leaves me no choice."

She raised her voice to address the crowd. "Robin Fitzooth is guilty of theft and treason for stealing the silver needed for Richard's ransom. I am declaring him an outlaw with a bounty of 100 silver coins on his head. His titles are forfeit, and all his property has been seized by the crown."

She then emphasized, "I hereby proclaim that the Earldom of Huntingdon is now under the control of the Great Council. His properties in Nottinghamshire, Locksley and the Barony of Lenton, are under the jurisdiction of Prince John, and he is granted dominion over them."

Edmund swayed on his feet, overcome by the sheer gravity of what the queen was doing to Robin. He sputtered, "Your Grace, this is an injustice—"

"Baron Embelton, do you support the crown or your nephew? Are you prepared to surrender your barony to the Great Council?" proposed the queen.

Collapsing onto one knee, Edmund bowed his head and beseeched, "Your Grace, please, I meant no disrespect. I will abide by all rulings of the council."

"I'm glad to hear it," crowed a triumphant Queen Eleanor. "You will be pleased to learn that I've selected your son, Lionel, as one of the hostages who will be sent to Germany with the ransom. This is a great honor, of course. Wouldn't you agree, Baron Embelton?"

The outrage and fear whirling in his mind subsided just long enough for him to murmur, "Yes, Your Grace."

Somehow, he found the strength to stand and stumble away from the dais and towards the back of the great hall. Lionel joined him, and he commanded in a low voice. "Don't say one word, Lionel. Not here."

When they exited the hall, Edmund staggered a short distance from the building to the trunk of a sturdy oak. He leaned against it, gasping for air as he fought the nausea stirring his stomach and the dizziness that threatened to render him unconscious.

⌒

Edmund sat on the edge of the bed with his elbows perched on his knees and his face buried in his hands.

He was in the shabby chamber he had rented upon his arrival in Ely the previous day. The better inns were already filled because so many people had traveled to Ely to attend the council meeting. This inn was at the outskirts of town, and it was the only accommodation he could find. Thankfully, he and Lionel did not have to share the room, or its bed, with strangers.

Just then, it occurred to him that, if there had been a stranger sharing the room, perhaps he would not have to endure Lionel's bitter recriminations and fuming harangues as he paced back and forth across the small space between the bed and the door.

Lionel mocked him, echoing in an exaggerated tone, "My nephew is the bravest man I know." Switching to his normal manner of speaking, he cried, "What about me? I'm your son, your heir, but you would stand there before all those people, including *my friends* at court, and boldly champion Robin while you meekly allow them to send me away."

Edmund sighed. He was so tired, yet how would he ever be able to sleep tonight?

"If you hadn't been defending Robin, they wouldn't have punished *you* by sending *me* to Germany. This is your fault!" Lionel asserted.

Edmund lifted his head. "Son, I believe they had already chosen you as a hostage, and not because of anything I've done or said."

Lionel's eyes narrowed. "Are you blaming *me* for this? I wasn't the one who uttered the words 'unfair taxes' in front of the queen and the Great Council. What were you thinking?"

"Lionel, do I have to remind you that you faked your own kidnapping to extort money from me and give it to Prince John?

170

The queen is likely putting you to the test because of your actions, not my words."

"How would the queen even know about—" He paused, and comprehension dawned. "You told her!" he shouted. "How could you betray me like that?"

Edmund wearily rubbed his face and wondered how Lionel could sustain such emotional energy for this length of time. He replied, "The queen has a network of spies. She knew I was giving money to the sheriff, and we had to explain the reason why I seemed to have thrown my support to John."

"We? To whom are you referring?"

"Me and Robin, of course. When he returned with news of Richard's capture, I was in London, and I met with him and the queen."

If possible, Lionel became even more shrill in his denunciations. "Robin! Again, you're always so eager to help him, even when it's at my expense. And now, you've ruined my reputation at court by telling everyone about this one trifling mistake I made. What kind of father are you?"

Edmund observed his son. Lionel looked very much like a younger version of himself, but he had to admit that, beyond their appearance, they had little else in common. His heart was weighed down by guilt; of four sons, only Lionel had survived childhood, and yet, Edmund had always felt closer to Robin.

A despondent Edmund confessed, "I guess I'm the worst kind of father. I've known for a long time that I've failed you, and I'm sorry."

"Sorry? That doesn't help me now. How are you going to get me out of this? I'm not going to Germany as a hostage. You need to fix this. Pay off someone to go in my place."

"Lionel, last year I paid a significant amount of money to your 'kidnappers.' This year, I'm paying all these taxes for the ransom in addition to my usual tax obligations. I don't have any extra money to bribe someone to take your place. And frankly, I don't think the queen would allow it."

There was a knock at the door, and Lionel answered it. Edmund was vaguely aware of him saying something, but he was lost in his despair until his son thrust a sealed dispatch under his nose.

"A boy just delivered this," he announced.

Edmund took the letter and examined it. It was sealed, and there was no mark to identify the sender. He opened it and read:

Tell your son you need to settle your account with the innkeeper. Leave him in your chamber and meet me in the alley behind the inn. Bring this message with you.

The lack of a signature troubled Edmund, but he felt compelled to follow the note's directions.

He stood and insisted, "Lionel, wait here and try to calm yourself. Nothing can be resolved tonight. The innkeeper has a question for me. I'll return soon."

Without waiting for Lionel to respond, Edmund left the chamber and made his way down the rickety stairs and into the kitchen, which was at the rear of the inn. It was late enough that the kitchen was dark and empty, but the embers of the hearth facilitated his search for the door. When he exited, he was in an alleyway that reeked of rotting food and urine. His stomach roiled again.

At first he wondered if he was alone, but as his eyes adjusted to the dim moonlight, he made out the shape of a man in a hooded cloak. For a moment, he thought it was Robin, but when the man moved closer and lowered his hood, Edmund recognized Earl Hamelin.

"My lord," Edmund exclaimed as he briefly dropped to one knee and rose.

"Give me the message I sent you," Hamelin curtly demanded.

Edmund obediently handed it to the other man.

Tucking it inside his tunic, Hamelin declared, "Agents of the queen are watching you."

His brow creased in confusion, Edmund asked, "Why? Does she suspect me of disloyalty? Earl Hamelin, I don't understand how she could think that Robin is stealing the ransom. You know he's innocent." In the low light, he could barely make out Hamelin's features, and so he could not decipher his expression.

"They are hoping that you will lead them to Robin," Hamelin explained. "You must return to Embelton without contacting Robin and stay there with your son."

"But I need to get word to Robin, to warn him about what has happened. And you didn't answer my question: do you believe Robin has betrayed Richard?"

"I've known Robin since he was a boy. He's an honorable man, and I trust him. But appearances matter, and the reports the queen received look very bad."

"Did you try to defend Robin?" Edmund winced as he realized his words sounded more accusatory than he had intended.

"I said as much as I could, but some members of the council question my devotion to Richard, and I must be careful not to feed their suspicions."

Edmund considered Hamelin's words before replying, "Thank you for trying to help. But I must talk to Robin."

"No, you must avoid him at all costs. Eleanor would happily seize your prosperous barony if you were found to be in contact with Robin." Hamelin then disclosed, "I received a letter from my wife, and she told me that your daughter and Lady Marian are visiting Conisbrough. I will leave first thing in the morning to return home. If you have a message for Robin, tell me, and I will relay it to Marian."

Edmund quickly composed a short message for Robin, and Hamelin pulled his hood up to obscure his face before he strode away, disappearing in the darkness.

20 July 1193, Conisbrough

In the bailey, Constance was standing with Marian and Countess Isabel as they enjoyed the lively entertainment a few feet in front of them.

Guy was on his knees and defending himself with a child's wooden shield as two small boys wielding miniature wooden swords relentlessly swung at him. In between his comical animal-like roars at his attackers, he was laughing.

Constance marveled at the sight. She had never heard him laugh so freely; in fact, she had rarely seen Guy smile. But to see him playing with Robbie and Rich made her ache for children of her own. His children. She finally confessed to herself that her attachment to Guy had blossomed into love. She had become the moth to his flame.

Countess Isabel linked arms with her. In a hushed voice, she advised, "Be patient, my dear. Sometimes it takes a while before a marriage is blessed with children. Don't despair."

Blushing at Isabel's kind words and amazed by her ability to mind-read, Constance mumbled a polite reply. Silently, she considered how it would require them to consummate their marriage before they could be blessed with a child. Unbeknownst to Isabel, Constance had been sleeping with Marian and Robbie in their chamber, and not with her husband.

Marian had moved away to admonish Robbie to take care not to hit Rich by accident, and Isabel added, "Your husband looks at you as if you had hung the moon. Is he always so attentive and kind to you?"

"Yes, my lady," Constance answered. "He has always treated me well, and I'm thankful for that."

Just then, Robbie landed a solid strike on Guy's head, and Guy toppled over, lying still on the ground. Robbie began jumping up and down, shouting that he had killed the monster.

Constance's heart sped in fear, and she rushed to Guy's side, dropping to her knees next to him. "Guy?" she beckoned as he lay motionless with his eyes closed. She reached out and ran her fingers through his hair to search for blood or any other noticeable head injury. Increasingly anxious, she called to him. "Guy? Are you all right?"

She continued to examine his head, and to her shock, he opened his eyes and burst into laughter. She realized he had been pretending, and her temper rose.

He grasped her hand and proclaimed, "Your miraculous touch has healed me. I am forever indebted to you, my lady wife." He then pressed his lips to the back of her hand, and her heart leapt with joy.

✎

The boys had been put down for a nap, and Constance was sitting with Marian and Isabel as they chatted about raising children. The pleasant morning had become an uncomfortably hot afternoon, but it was cool inside the keep. A light breeze blew through the window and threatened to disturb the piles of embroidery yarn stacked on a nearby table.

There was a loud tapping on the door, and Isabel summoned the person to enter. To Constance's delight, it was Guy, but she sobered when she saw his solemn expression.

"My lady, forgive the interruption, but Earl Hamelin has just entered the main gate. He should arrive at the keep shortly," disclosed Guy.

The three of them rose, and Isabel fretted, "I wasn't expecting him today. I hope everything is all right."

Soon, they had gathered in the great hall, and Guy was holding the dispatch from the sheriff. Constance reflected that they had been in Conisbrough for a sennight, and the days had passed swiftly. After Guy delivered that message, they would have to leave. This saddened her, as life at Conisbrough was so agreeable and normal, in contrast to the drama and uncertainty of life in Nottingham.

Earl Hamelin marched into the hall, and his gaze initially focused on Isabel. The joy that lit his face at the sight of his wife abruptly morphed into a scowl the moment he noticed Guy.

Unexpectedly, he drew his sword and approached Guy, demanding, "Who are you, and why are you here?"

Guy respectfully went down on one knee, remaining in that position as he replied, "My lord, I am Sir Guy of Gisborne, and I'm delivering a message addressed to you from the Sheriff of Nottingham."

Constance became alarmed as Hamelin glowered at her husband. She opened her mouth to speak, but Isabel gently squeezed her arm to discourage her.

Isabel cautiously interjected, "My dear, Sir Guy is also Constance's husband. You remember Constance, don't you? She's Baron Embelton's daughter."

Hamelin did not take his eyes off of Guy. He questioned, "Gisborne? You are Baron Gisborne's son?"

"Yes."

"You're lying."

Isabel gasped, but Marian and Constance remained calm.

A befuddled Guy responded, "My lord?"

"I knew Baron Gisborne. He was at the siege of Toulouse in '59. He died there. You look nothing like him. And you're not old enough to have been born before his death."

Guy was still kneeling, and when he started to rise, Hamelin stepped closer, his sword mere inches from Guy's chest. Guy dropped back to one knee, and he tried to explain, "I was born in the spring of 1160, not that long after the siege, and I've been told that I look like my mother."

Hamelin scoffed. "Was your mother over six feet tall? Look at me."

Guy stared at the other man, and Hamelin studied him closely, until recognition flashed in his eyes.

"Drop the message on the floor and stand up. Lace your fingers together and place your palms on the top of your head," commanded Hamelin.

Guy obeyed, and Hamelin continued to brandish his drawn sword as he directed Marian to take Gisborne's weapons and put them on a table at the far side of the hall.

While Marian followed his instructions, Isabel and Constance quietly watched, unsure of what was happening and hesitant to interfere.

Hamelin sheathed his sword once Guy was disarmed. He ordered, "Give me the message from the sheriff."

Guy lowered his hands and picked up the dispatch. He gave it to Hamelin, who broke the seal and read it silently.

Isabel inquired, "What does it say?"

"It says very little," he admitted. "Sheriff de Argentan is warning me that Robin Hood might start robbing ransom payments collected in my domains, particularly those near Sherwood Forest."

Marian boldly asserted, "That's ridiculous. Those thieves are mercenaries hired by the sheriff."

Hamelin's gaze swung between Marian and Guy. He challenged, "Aren't you going to defend your master, Gisborne? Are you going to allow Lady Marian to accuse him of this?"

"Earl Hamelin, Gisborne has sworn fealty to Robin," revealed Marian. "He's Robin's spy at Nottingham Castle, and he will confirm that the sheriff controls these mercenaries."

"Lady Marian speaks the truth," declared Guy. "I'm the Earl of Huntingdon's vassal, and I've been helping him in his efforts to thwart these mercenaries who are robbing the towns and villages of Nottinghamshire."

Again, suspicion shaded Hamelin's eyes. "How were you able to earn Robin's trust?"

Guy audaciously suggested, "I think that you have recognized the connection I have with Earl Robin."

"Who else knows?" the earl asked cryptically.

Marian divulged, "Constance and I know everything."

Hamelin nodded in satisfaction. "You are Duncan's son. You

might have your mother's dark hair, but your height, your eyes; they are unmistakable. I knew Duncan well, God-rest-his-soul."

Everyone reverently crossed themselves.

A surprised Isabel questioned, "Is this true?"

Guy dipped his head and acknowledged, "Yes, my lady."

For the first time since his arrival, Hamelin relaxed. "Tell me the real motive behind the sheriff sending this message to me."

"My lord, his purpose in sending us while you were away was to give me time to gather intelligence about Conisbrough, the lay of the land, your defenses, the number of men-at-arms, and so forth."

Hamelin began pacing, deep in thought, as everyone observed him.

At last, he paused and decreed, "You will leave first thing tomorrow morning, and this afternoon, I will tell you exactly what I want the Sheriff of Nottingham to know about my defenses and my keep."

"Yes, my lord," agreed Guy.

Hamelin declared, "I don't know you, but Robin trusts you, and considering Robin's disastrous trial in Ely, I have to trust you as well."

Marian exclaimed, "Trial? What trial?"

Hamelin took hold of Marian's elbow and led her to a bench next to one of the trestle tables in the great hall. He insisted she sit down, and then he gestured for Constance and Isabel to sit on either side of her.

"Robin's in trouble, and we're going to help him."

CHAPTER 13
A SENSE OF DUTY

21 July 1193, Carentune, Nottinghamshire

"𝕴t speaks well of Lord Carentune that he is so diligent in paying his taxes for the Exchequer of Ransom," observed Tuck.

Robin hummed his agreement as he stood with Tuck and the rest of his men at the edge of the forest on a low ridge overlooking the town of Carentune. Their horses were tethered nearby.

"What's the plan?" asked Much.

Robin explained, "The note that Lord Carentune sent to Locksley said that he had underpaid his taxes, and that he wished for us to collect the additional money that he owed today. He said that the sheriff had men watching him, and he's afraid, so we're to slip into town at dusk and go directly to his manor."

"So why are we standing here at midday?" questioned Will.

Allan interjected, "I thought you said that Lord Carentune was friends with the sheriff."

Robin rubbed the back of his neck and was thoughtful for a few moments. "I find his sudden change of heart to be odd, but the important thing is to make sure that the taxes for the ransom do not fall into Montlhéry's hands."

Looking at a taciturn Little John, Robin inquired, "What do you think, John? You're even more quiet than usual."

John squinted at the town as it shimmered under the hot July sun. He then leaned to the side and spat on the ground. "I never met Lord Carentune, but I don't trust him. He's just another rich lord who loves his money more than his people."

"You might be right, John," allowed Tuck, "but he is probably worried about falling out of favor with the queen if he doesn't contribute his share to the ransom."

Robin countered, "Except that Nottinghamshire is under Prince John's control. It's likely that he would be more concerned about striking a balance between supporting the queen and Prince John."

"So, what's the plan?" repeated Much.

"We're going to divide up and move through the town to determine if he's being monitored and the number and location of these men," responded Robin. "I'm not going into this situation blind."

The men walked into the town in pairs, each group waiting until the previous two men had disappeared from sight. Lord Carentune's manor was situated on the highest point of the town, and it was surrounded on three sides by a small church, a market, and the abodes of various craftsmen such as the blacksmith, wheelwright, baker, and so forth. The town had no wall, so the buildings gradually transitioned to the humble homes of the peasants who worked the fields between the town and Sherwood Forest. There was only one road that led into Carentune, and the river snaked along the north side of the town.

The outlaws surveyed the town, and then they made their way to an agreed upon spot behind the tavern. As soon as everyone was gathered, Robin took their reports.

"Lord Carentune is definitely being watched," Tuck stated. "Allan and I went to the east side of his manor, and we saw three men-at-arms standing in the shadows."

"Little John and I went to the south side, and we saw four armed men there," remarked Will.

Robin added, "Much and I saw several men to the west of the manor. The north side, which faces the river, is the only area that is unguarded."

"I'm surprised," admitted Tuck. "After our earlier meeting with Lord Carentune, I would have characterized him as a man who is prone to exaggerating danger, but it's obvious that the sheriff is monitoring him."

"Maybe the sheriff discovered you were coming to collect his taxes today," suggested Allan.

"Perhaps," Robin replied. "Hopefully, Gisborne will return from Conisbrough soon; I need his eyes and ears in the castle."

"What's the plan?" asked Much. Again.

The men chuckled at Much's focus on the plan, and Robin declared, "We're going to retrieve Lord Carentune's tax payment, but we're not going to wait until dusk."

᠅

"Are you ready for your performance, Allan?" Robin asked with a grin.

"I'm always ready to perform," he answered with a wink.

They were at the east side of the manor where the fewest number of men were on watch.

Taking a skein of cheap ale he had purchased at the tavern, Allan splashed some on the front of his tunic and grumbled, "I hate to waste ale like this." He then took a large swig, grimacing at the ale's sour taste.

Little John, Much, and Tuck stood nearby, and Robin glanced at them. John nodded; they were also ready.

In the shade of a building, three armed men were listlessly leaning against a wall. Between boredom and the oppressive heat, they appeared to be half asleep, but they snapped to attention when Robin and Allan stumbled towards them.

Allan loudly complained, "It's a hot day, and I need another drink." He fell to his knees and staggered back to his feet.

Slurring his words, Robin whined, "But we ain't got any more coins."

The three soldiers laughed at them, and one demanded, "Go home. You've no business here."

A tottering Allan shuffled to stand in front of the men. He offered, "If I sang a song for you, would you give me a coin?"

Another soldier chortled and pushed Allan away. Allan fell down and lay still on the ground.

"Hey!" yelled Robin, "you've killed my friend!"

The soldiers guffawed, and one said, "He's just passed out, you daft fool. Get him out of here."

Robin knelt next to Allan and roughly shook his shoulder. "He's dead!" he exclaimed. "I tell you, he's dead! Come look! He ain't breathing."

One soldier rolled his eyes, but they crowded around Allan as John, Much, and Tuck rushed up behind them and threw burlap bags over their heads. As the startled men fought, Allan, Robin, and Will took the men's swords while the other men struggled to hold them.

Their muffled cries were too loud, so the outlaws worked together to drag them into a narrow alley at the rear of the building. One at a time, the men were secured with rope that Much had stolen from the town's stables and gagged with cloth torn from their own tunics.

Robin decreed, "John, Allan, and Will, put on their capes and stand in the shadow of that building where they were on watch. Much, stay with these men to ensure that they don't free themselves from their bindings. Tuck, let's go visit Lord Carentune."

Tuck and Robin crept carefully along the side of the manor, tugging on the shutters covering the two windows that faced east. They were both locked. Rounding the corner, they found an open window facing the river. Peering inside, they observed that it led to a relatively dark corner on the far side of the great hall.

They slipped into the manor and crouched behind a trestle table. In contrast to their hiding place, the other end of the hall, near the hearth, was brightly lit with candles. They saw Lord Carentune sitting in a large, cushioned chair and sipping wine from an ornate goblet. He was staring into the distance, lost in his thoughts.

Robin and Tuck approached him, and when he spotted them, he sputtered and choked on his wine, spilling some of it down the front of his expensive silk bliaut.

"You!" he cried. "How did you get in here? You're too early!"

Robin frowned. "Why does that matter? I'm here now, and I was able to avoid the men-at-arms surveilling you and your manor."

A frightened Lord Carentune questioned, "How did you get past them?"

"That's not important," remarked Tuck. "Why is the sheriff watching you so closely?"

Before the other man could respond, Robin insisted, "Never mind that; we can't waste time. Give us your tax payment now. Don't worry; we'll be able to leave without alerting the men surrounding your manor."

Lord Carentune paused, and Robin was startled by the pale and anxious expression on his face. Without warning, Carentune screamed, "Help! Help! Robin Hood is here!"

Tuck and Robin briefly froze in shock and confusion. But then several guards rushed into the hall, their swords drawn. Tuck drew his sword, and Robin slid his bow off his shoulder and nocked an arrow.

"Arrest them!" shouted Carentune.

As the men ran towards them, Robin rapidly released arrows with deadly accuracy. Those men fell, but more guards appeared.

Tuck grabbed a candelabra with three lit candles and threw it at the men, igniting the rushes that littered the floor.

Robin and Tuck hastened to the open window, exiting the manor and sprinting towards the other outlaws. Behind them, they could hear Lord Carentune screeching for someone to extinguish the fire.

They quickly reached the location where they had left John, Much, Allan, and Will.

With no time to explain, Robin instructed, "Split up and meet back where we left our horses."

The outlaws scattered, and Robin saw men-at-arms running from the manor to search for him and Tuck.

"The river?" proposed Tuck.

Robin nodded. Thankfully, it was summer, and the river was at its lowest point of the year. The two men waded across the swiftly flowing, waist deep water and dashed into the cover of the forest.

Robin and Tuck hurried away from Carentune, jogging along the tree line until the town was out of sight, and then crossing the river again using a small foot bridge. Eventually, they made their way back to where the others were waiting.

"Thank the Lord," Much exclaimed.

The others also welcomed Robin and Tuck, relieved to see them safe and sound.

Allan asked, "What happened? All we know is that the alarm was raised, and then you appeared."

"We approached Lord Carentune, and he called for his guards," Robin replied. "I don't understand it."

Much revealed, "While you were gone, I talked to one of the soldiers we captured. I asked him if he knew why the sheriff was spying on Lord Carentune, and he laughed."

Robin looked at him curiously.

"Those men who were watching the manor all serve Lord Carentune," Much explained. "It was a trap to arrest you and collect the bounty."

"Bounty?" echoed Robin. "The sheriff is willing to part with some of his silver for me? That's quite an honor." Robin snickered.

A somber Much shook his head. "No, Lord Robin. Queen Eleanor has put a bounty on your head."

23 July 1193, Nottingham Castle

"You were gone long enough," chided Montlhéry, as he greeted Gisborne in his tower room.

Gisborne genuflected and replied, "My lord, you told me to stay until Earl Hamelin returned, and that's what I did."

"Did you and that plain faced wife of yours enjoy your time at Conisbrough?"

Guy knew the sheriff was trying to goad him into defending Constance, so he calmly answered, "Conisbrough is an impressive keep, and Countess Isabel is a gracious hostess."

"First, I want you to tell me about the de Warenne family."

Guy diligently described Countess Isabel, Earl Hamelin, their two married children who lived with them, and their young grandson. He added that two other daughters were married and living with their husbands.

"I've heard of this grandson. Did you know that he's Prince John's bastard? Illegitimacy is a tradition in the family." Montlhéry snorted in amusement. "You have that in common with Hamelin; both of you are first-born sons, unable to inherit because you're bastards. Oh, the sins of the fathers." He continued to chuckle.

Constance had explained Hamelin's complicated relationship to the royal family to him, but Guy was surprised to hear about the little boy.

Montlhéry pointed at the rolled paper in Guy's hand. "Is that the layout of Conisbrough and a description of its defenses?"

"Yes, my lord." Guy moved to the sheriff's desk, carefully unrolled the diagram, and described the fortress just as Earl Hamelin had instructed him.

Rubbing his chin, Montlhéry seemed disappointed. "It's more formidable than I had been led to believe. Once again, my brilliance in sending you as a spy has saved the day."

Guy swallowed nervously, but bolstering his courage, he questioned, "Why do you need to know about Conisbrough? I remember that Earl Hamelin was on the list of men who could not come to Nottingham. Would he recognize you as Montlhéry?"

Silence stretched ominously in the chamber as Montlhéry's dark eyes studied Guy. At last, he said, "You are excessively curious about matters that have no relevance to you."

Guy shifted nervously on his feet. "My lord, why not tell me about your plan? Perhaps I could be of better assistance to you if I knew more."

"I'm planning to put John on the throne, of course."

Gisborne glanced away. He knew that was a lie, but he didn't want to confront the sheriff about it, at least not yet. Instead he asked, "How does Earl Hamelin fit into your plan? Is it because he is a supporter of King Richard?"

"My business with Hamelin is not part of the plan to crown John," Montlhéry admitted. "Tell me, was the friendship that your wife has with the de Warennes extended to you?"

Guy's mind drifted to his memories of his visit to Conisbrough. The familial love between members of the de Warenne family was something that he had never experienced in his life. He recalled the prior summer, when he had been living with Constance and Edmund at Locksley. He wondered what it would have been like to grow up with Edmund as a father.

"Gisborne!"

Guy snapped to attention. "Yes, my lord?"

"Stop wool-gathering and focus. Do you believe that you've gained the trust of Hamelin and Isabel?"

"Yes, of course." Guy knew the de Warenne family would trust him as Robin's vassal, and a sense of dread settled over him.

"Excellent," exclaimed Montlhéry, who rubbed his hands together in glee. "I have a score to settle with Hamelin, and the trust they have in you will make it possible."

Guy's heart sank. Whatever the sheriff was planning, Hamelin and Isabel surely didn't deserve it. He strolled to the window. It was the middle of the day, and not a single cloud shadowed the great forest that stretched to the horizon under a cerulean sky. He was lost in thought and only vaguely aware of the sheriff walking to the double doors and speaking to a guard.

❧

Constance cautiously entered the sheriff's tower room. When she saw Guy standing in his usual spot, she couldn't help but smile. She longed to ask him what he saw when he looked out that window.

"Gisborne, your beautiful wife has arrived," declared Montlhéry.

Guy startled and turned from the window.

"Sheriff de *Argentan*," she emphasized, "I'm here because you summoned me." She was pleased to note that her slightly sarcastic tone had gone unnoticed by Montlhéry.

"Quite right," agreed the sheriff.

Guy joined them next to the messy desk.

Montlhéry inquired, "Did Hamelin apprise you of the decisions made at the Council of Ely?"

"Are you referring to Lionel's selection as a hostage, or the unfair prosecution of Robin?" Constance bitterly responded.

The sheriff laughed in her face. Recovering his demeanor, he proposed, "Perhaps we would all be better off if John were king. Don't you agree, Lady Constance?"

Refusing to answer such a question, she countered, "Did you invite me here to discuss politics?"

"I have a proposition for you and your husband."

Guy and Constance eyed each other, their brows creased in identical lines of worry.

"Robin Hood's properties have been seized. While the crown will take control of Huntingdon, Prince John has granted me both Locksley and the Barony of Lenton."

Constance had feared this would happen. The previous day, she had been with Guy when he escorted Marian to Locksley after their return from Conisbrough. Marian had immediately ridden into the forest to find Robin and deliver the devastating news from Ely to him.

Montlhéry continued, "Locksley is full of traitors who are loyal to Robin Hood. I need someone there to keep him away from Locksley and discourage the people from helping him."

To her surprise, the sheriff walked up to her and tenderly cupped her cheek with his hand. She took a step back, only to feel the iron grip of his other hand on her arm. From the corner of her eye, she saw Guy take a step towards them.

Montlhéry slid his hand down the side of her face until his fingers were firmly wrapped around her neck. She gasped in fear.

"My lord!" cried Guy in alarm. He took another step closer.

"Not one more step, Gisborne," Montlhéry warned, his eyes never leaving hers. He then sneered, "He might be your husband, but he's my pet. Do you see how he obeys me? Never forget that I own him, body and soul."

He squeezed her neck, and her lungs constricted painfully as tears pooled in her eyes.

Abruptly, he released her, and she recoiled, wheezing and coughing, her eyes watery, and her face damp with tears.

"I trust Gisborne, but I don't trust *you*, my dear," the sheriff announced. "Always remember that I am in command of everything that happens here."

Constance rubbed her neck and watched as Montlhéry pivoted towards Guy. Her husband was pale, and his eyes were wide with fear.

"Gisborne, would you like to return to Locksley? Can you rule those people without mercy and ensure that they are not colluding with Robin Hood?"

Finally taking his gaze from Constance, Guy looked at the sheriff and affirmed, "Yes, my lord."

"What are you willing to do to gain Locksley?"

After a brief pause, Guy admitted, "Anything, my lord."

Montlhéry demanded, "Get on your knees and beg."

Guy dropped to his knees, and implored, "Please, my lord, allow me to serve you at Locksley."

"Hmmm," hummed the sheriff. "You don't seem humble enough. Locksley is not a large fief, but it's prosperous." He stepped closer to Guy. "Kiss my boot, and perhaps you can have Locksley."

Constance watched in horror as the emotion on Guy's face morphed from stunned to resentment to resignation. Still on his knees, he leaned over and pressed his lips against the sheriff's boot.

Montlhéry cackled triumphantly, and Guy sat back on his heels, staring up at the sheriff with an expression that Constance interpreted as an echo of his childhood experiences in submitting to this monstrous man.

The sheriff looked at Constance and gleefully proclaimed, "I'm granting Gisborne control of Locksley. He will divide his time between Locksley and serving me here at the castle. I have one stipulation. You will accompany Gisborne wherever he goes, and you will be required to sleep under the same roof as your husband. Agreed?"

Constance shakily nodded her assent. She glanced at Guy, but he was still kneeling while studiously observing the floor in front of him.

Once more, Montlhéry walked up to her. Standing much too close, he declared in a quiet, menacing voice, "Never forget that he belongs to me. Whatever affection he might feel for you is nothing compared to my power over him. He will always choose me over you. Go back to your chamber and pack for Locksley."

With tears rolling down her cheeks, Constance spun on her feet and ran to the door.

1 August 1193, Sherwood Forest

Marian nervously watched Robin and his men tugging on ropes tied to a tree as Little John swung an axe at its trunk. A loud cracking noise echoed throughout the forest, and the tree shuddered and began to lean. John then delivered several more blows to its base.

Robin glanced over his shoulder and yelled, "Marian, back away. You're too close."

She obediently stepped back as the men pulled the ropes in unison. John set down his axe and joined them.

After more unbearably loud and ominous groans from the tree, it leaned further and further towards the men, and Marian realized it was falling.

Robin and the other men scattered, and the tree toppled with a thud, raising a cloud of dust and debris that caused Marian to cough and wipe her eyes. It landed near the caves where the outlaws spent their winters, and the men retrieved the ends of their ropes and worked to shift it even closer to the caves' entrances.

When she had returned from Conisbrough, the hunting lodge had been overflowing with coins, church plate, and silver, all intended for the king's ransom. Robin had apologized that there was no longer room for her to sleep in the lodge, and she had suggested they move it to the caves.

It had been gratifying to observe Robin's reaction to her idea; he had beamed and then grabbed her and kissed her. Knowing how upset he must be at the queen's condemnation of him at Ely, Marian was pleased to see him smile. Unfortunately, he refused to discuss how he felt about what had happened, and Marian now understood that he would talk to her only when he was ready.

The caves were on the opposite side of Locksley from the hunting lodge, and the path that led to them could barely accommodate a wagon. The final twenty yards descending to the mouths of the caves was too steep for horses, so over the past few days, the outlaws had been forced to carry the bags and boxes of the people's taxes down to the caves. It had been exhausting work, but finally, it was done.

Pulling down the tree to hide the entrance to the caves had been necessary since they could not keep the area under guard. Besides, if an enemy ever followed their tracks, it would be best not to set up camp next to such riches.

As soon as they had dragged the fallen tree as close to the mouth of the caves as possible, they gathered their ropes and trudged up the steep hill to where their horses were waiting. Little John was the last to leave as he walked backwards and obscured their tracks.

As they passed Locksley on their way to the camp next to the hunting lodge, Robin left the safety of the trees and rode towards his home. Leofric must have seen him coming; he exited the manor and walked towards Robin.

Marian watched Robin dismount, and the two men spoke briefly.

When Robin returned to them, he explained, "Leofric tells me that men have arrived from Embelton and Lenton. Along with a number of Locksley men, he sent them all to the meadow to await my return. We'll go there now."

⊰

Robin surveyed the men who were standing in the meadow; they were staring at him and waiting for him to speak. All the adult men from the villages of Locksley and Lenten were there. Additionally, six trained soldiers from Embelton had arrived. Edmund had given his men the option of volunteering to help Robin, provided that they kept their affiliation with Embelton a secret.

He was both pleased and humbled that these men were willing to join him in his quest to defeat the sheriff's mercenaries and recover the stolen taxes for the king's ransom. These were peasants and tradesmen who had labored long and hard to pay their share of the crushing taxes levied by the queen and the Great Council. Yet, they all felt a sense of duty towards their king; a man placed on the throne of England by God.

And perhaps, after living under the sheriff's tyranny for five years, they were convinced that Richard was preferable to Prince John.

Robin had spent some time speaking to these men, and he had divided them into two groups: older men with families and younger, unmarried men.

Raising his hand to get everyone's attention, Robin declared, "The Great Council has disavowed me, yet my duty to my king remains. With or without the support of the queen and her council, it's my intention to send our taxes to London for the Exchequer of Ransom. My mission is to recover the taxes stolen by the sheriff's mercenaries."

The men murmured their agreement.

Robin asked, "Who is willing to join me?"

All the men raised their fists and swore that they were with Robin.

Addressing the older men, Robin requested, "I need the men in this group to return to your homes. Be my eyes and ears in your villages. Be ever vigilant to what is happening around you. Will you do that for me?"

The men pledged their willingness to serve, and Robin was certain that he saw looks of relief on more than one face.

To the younger men, he announced, "If you are willing to join my band of men, then you must understand that we are facing professional soldiers who sell their lethal services to the highest bidder.

Five years ago, when I first became Robin Hood, my men and I avoided taking lives. The guards employed by the sheriff were local men, and we had no wish to kill them."

He paused for emphasis. "If you join me, you must be prepared to fight and to kill. We cannot show these ruthless men mercy; I assure you they will slaughter you in a heartbeat."

After surveying the faces of the men, Robin shouted, "Will you stand with me against the sheriff and his men?"

The men yelled their eagerness to stand with Robin.

"Are you ready to fight to recover the stolen ransom needed to rescue our king from his captors in Germany?"

The men whooped and hollered.

Robin sent the older men back to their families, and with Brother Tuck's help, he had the men from Embelton swear fealty to him, even though Robin was no longer an earl.

In the end, there were six men from Embelton, five from Locksley, and six from Lenton. Robin now had almost two dozen men, and he instructed Little John to lead everyone to the outlaw camp. Tomorrow, he would ask Much and Tuck, his two most experienced military men, to evaluate the new recruits, and to train them as needed.

∽

Only Robin and Marian remained in the meadow. Robin took her by the hand and led her to the great oak where their initials still proclaimed their love. He drew her into his arms and reveled in the joy he felt whenever he held her close.

To his consternation, Marian seemed distracted. She questioned, "How will we recover the taxes? Do we know where the sheriff is hiding them?"

Nuzzling her neck, he mumbled, "I'll figure that out later."

When she stepped away from him, he nearly groaned in frustration.

"Robin, be serious. Do you think the mercenaries are hiding the stolen taxes in the forest?"

He recognized that she wouldn't relent until he answered her. "Gisborne told me that the taxes are somewhere in the fortress of Nottingham. Allan and I gained access to the inner bailey, and we saw men unloading heavy barrels and taking them into a pantry. I'm certain that those barrels were filled with taxes, not ale." Hoping that he had satisfied her curiosity, he embraced her once more.

She pulled away again, frowning in concentration. "The locked pantry?"

This gave him pause. "Yes; have you seen this pantry?"

She beamed, her face shining with excitement. "Montlhéry must be hiding the taxes in the tunnel!" she exclaimed.

"Tunnel?" asked a befuddled Robin. "What tunnel?"

To his surprise, she laughed. "Well, the tunnel that the sheriff dug after he first arrived in Nottingham; the tunnel that Gisborne used to help me and Tuck escape. Didn't Tuck ever mention it?"

Robin was flabbergasted. "Well, no. But you never mentioned it either. Why am I just learning about this now?"

Marian shrugged. "I guess Tuck thought that I had told you, and I thought that Tuck had told you. But now we know where the taxes are, and we just need to devise a plan to get them."

She then threw her arms around him and kissed him passionately. Robin decided he'd think about the tunnel later.

CHAPTER 14
ROBIN AND MARIAN HOOD

3 August 1193, Nottingham

Robin and Marian lay in the wagon, grimly enduring every bump and jostle as they traveled to the brew houses at the foot of the cliffs under the fortress of Nottingham. They were nestled between several empty barrels and covered by a rough burlap cloth, while Little John was driving the team. Tuck was sitting next to him.

Fearing that someone might recognize him, or that wearing a hooded cloak in the summer heat might attract undue attention, Robin had opted to hide in the back of the wagon, but seeing Marian's pained expression made him regretful that he had allowed her to come. Then again, he wasn't sure that he could have dissuaded her. Robin reflected on his uncle's description of Marian as strong-willed, and he had to concede the truth of it.

A clattering sound under the wheels heralded their arrival at the bridge that crossed the moat and led to the row of brew houses. Before long, the wagon shuddered to a stop.

"Finally," Marian moaned.

They heard Tuck declare, "We're alone. It's safe for you to come out."

Robin hastily exited the wagon so that he could help Marian down, and the four of them approached a brew house. It was one of several shabby buildings along a row of similar structures, and Tuck paused.

"I think this is the right one, do you agree, my lady?" he asked.

"Yes, that's the one," replied Marian.

Just then, Gisborne appeared, walking between two other brew houses with a lit torch in one hand and his horse's reins in the other. An unlit torch was tucked under his arm. He tied his mount to their wagon.

Robin's brow arched. "It's the middle of the day, Gisborne. Don't you think that someone observing you would wonder why you're carrying a lit torch?"

Guy countered, "I had no choice. It's a tunnel. It's dark."

They entered the brew house, and Guy showed everyone how to open the trapdoor in the floor. Soon, they were all standing in the tunnel at the bottom of a small ladder, and Guy lit the other torch and gave it to Tuck.

Robin had visited underground vaults beneath various citadels and cathedrals, but he had never been in such a tunnel. The ceiling was so low that Gisborne could not stand straight. Crudely hewn wooden planks braced the walls and spanned the ceiling. The dirt floor was bare. Gazing into the tunnel, he saw an abyss beyond the weak light of their torches. The void was darker than any unlit room and blacker than any moonless night. Above ground, a wagon trundled along the road in front of the brew house, and the tunnel vibrated. Puffs of dirt fell from the gaps between the ceiling boards.

At that moment, Robin began to sweat. The walls appeared to be leaning towards him, and in the flickering light of the torches, he was convinced that they were slowly collapsing. A roaring sound in his ears pulsated with the same rhythm as his heart. The stale, cool air seemed too thin to breathe, and his chest tightened painfully.

He had to get Marian to safety. He kept trying to step forward, but his feet wouldn't move.

In the distance, he heard Marian call his name. Other voices joined hers, but he couldn't comprehend them.

He felt someone grasp his arm, and he heard Tuck speaking into his ear in a soothing, quiet tone. "Let's go back up into the brew house and devise a plan of action."

Robin wasn't sure how he managed to climb the ladder, but he found himself sitting on a crate in the brew house, wiping the copious sweat from his brow, and gasping for breath. A strange exhaustion weighed him down.

He looked up and was annoyed to see everyone staring at him with concerned faces. Well, except for Gisborne, who was smirking at him. Robin glared at Guy, who had the good sense to assume a more neutral expression.

Marian knelt in front of him. "Robin, what's the matter? What happened?"

Now Robin was even more irritated. He abruptly stood. To his mortification, he swayed unsteadily and dropped heavily back onto the crate.

The worry on Marian's face intensified, but Tuck encouraged her to stand and step away from Robin, counseling, "My lady, Robin is fine. Give him a few moments."

Little John, who was usually a man of few words, announced, "That tunnel was like a grave. It ain't natural to be underground like that. I'm not going back down there."

Tuck acknowledged, "Many men are uncomfortable in such a place. There's no shame in that." He turned to Guy. "Gisborne, I want you to take me through the tunnel, and we can search for the taxes."

Gisborne nodded and walked back to the trapdoor.

"I remember the tunnel has a steep slope, since the keep and the kitchens are well above us," Marian remarked.

Robin stood and proclaimed, "I feel fine now; let's go."

Tuck advised, "Robin, if you go down again, it won't be any

easier. Gisborne and I will go through the tunnel and report back to you."

"I'm going too," Marian insisted.

"No, Marian, it's not safe," cautioned Robin. "You will stay here."

"I will not. You seem to forget that I carried our son through this tunnel. It's dark and dirty, but it's sufficiently safe. I will go with Tuck and Gisborne, and then we can develop a plan for removing the taxes from the tunnel."

"Removing the taxes?" Guy's voice rose in alarm. "We can't do that without the sheriff realizing what we've done."

"Enough, Gisborne," barked an exasperated Robin. "Your fear of Montlhéry grows tiresome. Have faith that I'm aware of your precarious situation, and I will take it into account as I formulate my plan. You're my vassal and my responsibility. I'm not trying to get you killed."

Standing at the trapdoor, it took one glimpse of the ebony depths below to convince Robin that he should wait above ground with John. He reluctantly stepped away and watched as Gisborne, Tuck, and Marian descended the ladder and disappeared into the tunnel.

⚜

After a long wait, Robin heard the faint echo of voices rising from the hole in the floor.

Gisborne called up for John to lower the bucket of water that was nearby, and John complied. Hazy smoke wafted up through the trapdoor as Tuck and Guy extinguished their torches.

Gisborne emerged first. There was a shallow cut on his forehead with a smear of blood beneath it. When he climbed into the brew house, he blinked from the light. Briefly stretching his tall frame, he reached down into the hole to help Marian up, and she also squinted as she adjusted to the light.

Lastly, Tuck clambered out of the tunnel. He explained to

Guy, "By leaving the torches on the ground next to the ladder, they should be easy enough to find."

Marian pointed at Guy's injury, "I tried to warn you about that low hanging board. You've got blood on your forehead."

Grinning, Gisborne acknowledged, "Obviously, the tunnel was not designed to accommodate me."

Robin rose and impatiently asked, "Did you find the taxes?"

"Oh, Robin," exclaimed Marian, "I wish you could have seen it. I opened two chests, and the tax rolls were still lying on top. Not only can we recover the taxes, but we will know which towns paid them."

Tuck remarked, "My concern is the slant of the tunnel; it's quite steep."

Nodding, Marian added, "We can transfer the money into barrels and roll them towards the brew houses as long as the men prevent them from gathering too much speed. But I was hoping to fill the empty chests with rocks, and I fear that having the men carry rocks up the slope will be too arduous."

"My lady, your ideas are sound," declared Guy. "I think it would be worth the effort to haul rocks up to the location of the cache. It will help disguise the fact that we're emptying the chests."

Tuck recommended, "We might use wheelbarrows. The men could walk backwards as they descend, and that would give them more control. I'm just worried about fitting wheelbarrows through the trapdoor."

Robin was displeased to be excluded from their conversation, and his words were sharper than he intended. "All of you need to discuss this scheme with me first. Marian, remember our agreement: I'm the leader, and I make the final decisions."

Gisborne scoffed rudely.

Narrowing his eyes, Robin challenged, "Do you have a problem with that, Gisborne? I recall that you swore fealty to me, not my wife."

"Yes, my lord," Guy replied, scarcely disguising the disdain in his voice. "But if you're as smart as everyone thinks, then you'll listen to your wife."

Robin faced Gisborne, his fists clenched.

"Oh, please stop," groaned Marian. "I have every intention of describing my ideas to you for your approval."

"It's getting late, and we should be on our way," observed Tuck.

John suggested, "Let's go check on the horses."

Tuck agreed, and the two men left.

"I will tell Robin the news you shared with me and discuss my proposals with him," Marian informed Guy, "but can you get the items I mentioned and bring them to Locksley? If Robin likes my plan, then we'll need them."

"Of course, my lady." Turning to Robin, Guy dropped to one knee and requested, "My lord, with your permission, I will take my leave."

Robin gladly sent him on his way.

10 August 1193, On the Road to Nottingham

Guy listened patiently as Amery Fitz Giles, the Baron of Mountsorrel, prattled on about his expectations for Prince John's ascension to the throne.

Lord Amery was in his thirties, and he was short and stout; the picture of a pampered nobleman who preferred the comforts of his keep to the hardships of travel. Fortunately for him, the distance between Mountsorrel and Nottingham was not far, and they would arrive at Nottingham by sunset.

He was telling Guy how Prince John had revealed his plans to create an Earldom of Nottingham, and John had hinted that it could be within Lord Amery's reach. For a price. Therefore, Amery was determined to preserve as much of his wealth as possible in hopes of purchasing a lofty title from a newly crowned King John.

Guy glanced back at the heavily laden wagon that was carrying the entirety of Lord Amery's fortune. Prince John was encouraging his supporters to hide their money from the crown's tax collectors. After all, if they hoped to profit from King John's beneficence, then they shouldn't be funding King Richard's ransom.

Thus, Lord Amery had struck a deal with the sheriff to shelter his treasure in the fortress of Nottingham. The sheriff had offered to provide an escort, and Guy had brought ten guards with him.

"It's midday. Would you like to stop for a brief rest?" suggested Guy.

"That's an excellent idea," Amery replied. But then he hesitated. "What about bandits? I've heard many disturbing reports of ruthless thieves in Sherwood Forest. Even though Sheriff de Argentan assured me that I'm in no danger, I'm uneasy to be on the road with all of my money."

Guy casually remarked, "I thought the sheriff told you about these so-called bandits."

"What do you mean?" the other man inquired.

"Well, they're not really bandits. The sheriff is one of Prince John's staunchest supporters, and he has hired mercenaries to steal the tax payments intended for Richard's ransom. Like you, he has no desire to see Richard return."

Amery grinned. "Such a clever idea! I feel my fortune will be in good hands."

"Certainly, Lord Amery. It will be carefully secured at Nottingham. We are safeguarding the wealth of several other nobles, but I'm not at liberty to disclose their names."

"I expect similar discretion for myself," Amery sternly advised.

"Of course, my lord," Gisborne agreed.

They rounded a bend, only to find a tree lying across the road and blocking their way.

Guy raised his hand to halt everyone. Turning his horse in a tight circle, he commanded, "I want five men to move that tree.

The rest of you will take up positions next to the wagon. This could be a trap."

"A trap?" Amery's eyes darted from one side of the road to the other. The thick forest was uncomfortably close. "I thought you said we were in no danger."

"Be at ease, Lord Amery," Guy soothed. "If it is the work of forest bandits, we can easily defeat them. If it's the mercenaries, I'll tell them you are under the sheriff's protection."

Amery breathed a sigh of relief, and the men strained to push the heavy tree out of their way.

Without warning, six men with drawn bows emerged from the trees, aiming at the guards moving the tree, and six men on horseback surrounded the soldiers near the wagon. Their swords were drawn and at the ready.

A thirteenth man walked towards Guy and Amery and yelled at them to dismount. He had a cloth covering the lower half of his face.

A pale and shaken Amery questioned, "Who are these men?"

Guy answered, "This man is Sir Gaspard, the leader of the sheriff's mercenaries. I will talk to him, but first we should cooperate, or they will slaughter us all."

After he and Amery had dismounted, Guy ordered his men, "Get off your horses, and raise your hands. Don't fight them, or you'll die."

Gisborne walked up to the leader and said, "Sir Gaspard, you know that I'm the sheriff's captain. This man is under his protection. You must allow us pass."

"The sheriff has been cheating us and not paying what he promised!" the other man roared. "We're taking whatever you have in that wagon, and you can tell the sheriff to burn in hell."

"No!" exclaimed Amery. "This is all I have; please, let me give you a portion, and I will ask the sheriff to pay you more."

The leader said nothing. He signaled to two additional masked men who approached Guy and Amery with lengths of rope and scraps of cloth.

Amery continued to beg for his fortune as the men led him and Guy to a nearby tree, forcing them to sit on the ground as they tied their hands and feet.

Guy quietly recommended, "I suggest you plead for your life instead of your money. These men are ruthless."

Amery whimpered, and tears rolled down his face as one of the men blindfolded him.

Guy was also blindfolded, and the two men sat helplessly as they listened to what sounded like a battle; there were screams, shouts, and the sound of the wagon being driven away. Soon, an eerie silence descended. Guy wriggled out of the bindings on his wrists and lifted his blindfold.

Untying Amery, he urgently explained, "My lord, they've killed everyone except for us, and we must flee."

Amery and Guy rushed to their horses and hastily mounted them. When they surveyed the road behind them, they saw it was littered with the bodies of the guards who had accompanied them. The wagon was gone.

Spurring their horses around the fallen tree, they raced towards Nottingham.

✍

Marian sat on a low branch overlooking the scene of the battle. As soon as Guy and Lord Amery were out of sight, she dropped from the tree and wandered out onto the road.

"They're gone," she loudly proclaimed. "Well done!"

The men littering the roadway sat up and then stood to brush the dust from their clothes. They laughed and clapped each other on the back as they recalled their melodramatic yelling and screaming.

Marian beckoned them. When they had quieted and were attentively gazing at her, she announced, "Robin, John, and Much have taken the wagon and will put the treasure in a safe place. We will follow Tuck back to our campsite."

"What about these uniforms from the castle?" Allan asked.

Marian thought for a few moments. "For now, we'll keep them in the hunting lodge. I don't know if Gisborne will want them back."

As the men gathered their horses and prepared to return to camp, Tuck approached Marian. He had been disguised as one of Guy's soldiers, while Robin had taken the role of leader of the mercenaries.

"My lady, have I told you lately how much I enjoy your bold schemes?"

"Thank you, Brother Tuck. Having two dozen men allows for more possibilities than we had last year when there were only six of us." The two of them strolled towards their horses.

"I hope this will cause a further estrangement between the sheriff and his mercenaries," Marian remarked. "I doubt the mercenaries will convince Montlhéry of their innocence when he hears the report of their betrayal directly from his ally, Lord Amery."

Chuckling, Tuck declared, "King Richard should have kept you in the Holy Land as a general."

Marian rolled her eyes. "He would never have accepted a woman general."

"The king's mother is a courageous, clever woman who accompanied her first husband on his Crusade. Richard probably would have enjoyed the novelty of a woman general advising him."

"Perhaps, but my opinion of Queen Eleanor is greatly diminished considering her unjust treatment of Robin. These royals only care about themselves. I despise them all."

"Monarchs have responsibilities that are hard for us to fathom," Tuck thoughtfully stated. "Good kings and queens must balance many needs, and they often face conflicting demands when making decisions. I think Queen Eleanor's actions against Robin were unwise, but we must recognize that her focus is on ransoming

Richard and managing John. At her age, I can't imagine bearing such burdens."

20 August 1193, Locksley Manor

Robin, Marian, and Tuck slipped into Locksley's kitchen and were met by Elvina and a sullen Odella. The sight of Odella's rounded abdomen reminded Marian that, after all these months, she still had not been blessed with another child. Although God had restored Robin to her, she worried that He had made her barren as a punishment for her sins.

Dismissing such gloomy thoughts, she greeted Odella and inquired about her health.

"Oh, Lady Marian," she wailed as tears streamed down her face. "Can't you make him go away? This is your home, and he doesn't belong here."

Marian was taken aback. She glanced at Robin and Tuck, but the two men had matching expressions of dismay on their faces, and they hastily retreated towards the great hall.

Elvina came forward and took Odella in her arms as the younger woman sobbed on her shoulder. She gazed at Marian and explained, "She's upset that Gisborne is here. Lady Constance has asked him to stay away from Odella, and to his credit, he has. And you might remember that carrying a child makes a woman weepy."

Marian nodded, remembering how emotional she had been when she carried Robbie. She left Odella in Elvina's care and joined the men.

Constance was there, along with Gisborne, Robin, and Tuck.

Tuck told her, "I was just giving Lord Robin an update on our efforts to move the treasure out of the tunnel by packing it into barrels and loading them onto wagons. It's a slow process, and we must be careful not to attract too much attention by suddenly making that particular brew house the busiest one in Nottingham."

Guy reported, "We've worked out a schedule for when the men will retrieve the taxes. I've informed the other brew houses that this one is the sheriff's favorite, and they're not to interfere."

"Do you know how long this will take?" asked Robin.

"It depends on whether the sheriff's mercenaries will add to the cache," replied Tuck. "But I expect to finish in less than a month."

"The sheriff and his mercenaries are at odds," Guy declared. "Just as Lady Marian had hoped, the raid against Baron Mountsorrel has infuriated Montlhéry, and the mercenaries are adamant that they are innocent."

Chuckling, Tuck commented, "There is no honor amongst thieves."

Robin laughed. "Unless they are my men," he remarked.

"Many of the mercenaries are leaving. Originally, there were nearly forty men, but they have been so frustrated by their diminishing income that half of them have deserted," Guy revealed.

"That is excellent news!" Robin proclaimed. "We're evenly matched now."

"Unfortunately, there is also some bad news," Guy disclosed. "Ernehale has notified the sheriff that they are sending a tax payment in four days. This payment will replace the taxes that were stolen at the end of June."

"Do you think the mercenaries will target this shipment?" questioned Marian.

Guy responded, "I'm certain they will. The sheriff made a special effort to tell them the date. At this point, most of the towns have already paid their taxes."

Robin declared, "We can't let the people of Ernehale suffer another loss of men and money."

"Guy, do you know what the sheriff planned to do with the fortune that was in the tunnel?" Constance inquired.

"I believe he is planning to store it in the tunnel until after he has eliminated Richard and John," answered Gisborne.

Robin startled at his words. "What do you mean, 'Richard and John?' I thought he was plotting to put John on the throne."

Guy fretfully ran his fingers through his long, dark hair. "I don't think that's the real plan."

"Gisborne, you need to tell me everything. Don't keep me in the dark," admonished Robin. "Our lives and the future of England depend on your candor."

Sighing loudly, Guy explained, "Montlhéry has refused to tell me his plan except to say that he wants John on the throne. But I've overheard things, and I've seen things..." His voice drifted into silence.

"Yes?" Robin encouraged him to continue.

"Montlhéry is methodically murdering all the members of the English royal family. He poisoned Henry the Younger and King Henry. He sabotaged Prince Geoffrey's saddle at the Paris tournament, and he's made several attempts to kill Richard."

Marian and Constance gasped in horror.

Robin questioned, "Who would rule England?"

"I'm not sure," Guy admitted. "Perhaps King Philippe thinks he has a claim to the throne because his mother is a direct descendant of William the Conqueror."

"Robin," exclaimed Marian, "we must warn the Great Council. They must be told about this so they can arrest the sheriff."

"Marian, we have no proof. Gisborne's word is not enough," cautioned Robin.

"No one would believe that the sheriff could have accomplished such evil deeds," Tuck observed.

"Do you believe it?" asked Constance.

Both Robin and Tuck chorused their belief in the truth of Guy's claims.

Robin countered, "But me believing it does not constitute proof. Besides, I'm an outlaw whose properties and titles have been seized by the throne. I'm hardly in a position to convince Eleanor or the Great Council of anything."

Gisborne cleared his throat nervously. "There's more." His voice barely above a whisper, Guy divulged, "He killed our father. I was not there, but he told me he personally murdered Duncan."

After a pause, Guy somberly added, "I swear to God that I was not present in the chapel when Marian's father was killed, but I know Montlhéry murdered him as well."

23 August 1193, Ernehale

Allan pushed his way through the crowded tavern. He found his quarry and tapped him on the shoulder.

"Garin," he beckoned.

"Go away and leave me alone," the man gruffly demanded.

Allan smiled to put him at ease. "There's a pretty girl just outside the tavern, and she's looking for you."

Garin frowned. "Is she a curvy little blonde?"

Still grinning, Allan nodded and exclaimed, "She's real eager to talk to you. She's right outside the door."

"That little whore," Garin bitterly muttered. Rising to his feet, he snarled, "I'm eager to talk to her as well."

Allan trailed behind him as Garin nearly knocked several men off their feet in his rush to the door.

Marian watched as Garin stumbled out of the tavern and began scanning the street. It was late in the afternoon, and she was standing a short distance away on the opposite side of the road.

Robin and Tuck were hiding behind her, and she nervously flinched when Robin whistled loudly to get the man's attention.

She raised her hand and waved at him, smiling sweetly.

The moment he laid eyes on her, she saw his face darken into a murderous rage, and her heart thrummed in fear even though she knew she was safe.

Garin marched in her direction. "You!" he shouted as he pointed at her. "I have a few choice words for you, you lying bitch!"

He hastened across the street and reached for her, and she instinctively recoiled from him. Robin and Tuck emerged from the shadows, and six additional outlaws moved to stand behind Garin. He dropped his hands when he realized he was surrounded.

"Now, Garin," Robin scolded, "I don't appreciate the way you're speaking to my wife."

"Wife?" Garin was momentarily stunned, but he quickly recovered. "I should have known." With resignation, he asked, "Are you here to blackmail me? You've already taken all my money."

Tuck reminded him, "That money belonged to the Exchequer of Ransom, not you."

"Come with us," Robin ordered as he led everyone to an alley where they would have more privacy.

When they were out of sight, Robin said, "We're here because of tomorrow's shipment of taxes."

An alarmed Garin questioned, "How do you know about that? It's supposed to be a secret."

"It's not a secret to the mercenaries," Tuck countered. "They're already positioned along the road and waiting to attack you and your men."

"You must realize that they won't spare you a second time," advised Robin.

"They'll probably murder you first, as soon as they recognize you," Marian interjected.

"I know," Garin admitted. "I've been dreading tomorrow. That's why I was in the tavern, despite the early hour. I figure it's my last night on earth."

"It doesn't have to be that way," suggested Tuck. "We're here to help."

"If you steal the tax payments, then I'll be hanged. Either way, I'm a dead man," Garin responded.

"I don't want any man to die tomorrow," Robin emphasized. "And I want to ensure that Ernehale's taxes are sent to London." He looked at Tuck and requested, "Show him."

Tuck retrieved a rolled parchment from a pouch tied to his belt. "This is a receipt stating that Ernehale's taxes have been received. You just need to tell us the amount, and I will add it. I will sign it as a Knight Templar in service to the queen." He then pulled out an aging piece of folded parchment that was frayed and stained. "This is a letter from Queen Eleanor, affirming that I am her agent in Nottinghamshire. Can you read?"

Garin answered, "I can read numbers and dates."

Tuck showed him the queen's orders, dated May of the previous year, and her seal.

"What do you want me to do?" Garin asked.

Robin explained, "When we stop you on the road tomorrow, convince your men that their choice is to transfer the taxes to us, or face death at the hands of the mercenaries. Brother Tuck will provide this receipt, and I will give you a message for Lord Ernehale. Hopefully, I can set his mind at ease that his taxes are safe, but with the bounty on my head, I don't dare approach him directly."

After Garin had left, Marian angrily confronted Tuck. "Have you been spying for the queen all this time? No wonder you were so quick to defend her. I trusted you!"

"Marian, Tuck is the queen's agent, but that doesn't mean he is against us," said Robin.

"But the queen is against us," she cried. "Look at how unfairly she's treated you!"

Tuck tried to reassure Marian. "My lady, my first allegiance is to God. But I'm also a servant of King Richard and Queen Eleanor. That does not mean that I agree with everything they do. I gladly join you and Lord Robin in your efforts to raise the king's ransom. We are all on the same side, and we have the same goals."

CHAPTER 15
SACRIFICES

6 September 1193, Nottingham Castle

obin and six of his men rode towards the gate that separated the inner and outer baileys of the fortress of Nottingham. They were wearing the uniforms that Guy had supplied for Marian's raid of Baron Mountsorrel's fortune. Trailing them were Tuck and John, each man guiding one of the wagons that Robin had taken from the sheriff's mercenaries earlier in the summer.

The sun was barely peaking above the horizon as they rendezvoused with Gisborne at the gate. After they crossed into the inner bailey, he led them to the kitchens, and the people working there disappeared into the main keep when they spotted their approach.

They came to a stop at the pantry, and Guy hopped off his horse, taking a key that was suspended on a cord around his neck and unlocking the heavy oak door. Robin ordered his men to stay with the wagons while he and Tuck entered the pantry with Gisborne.

"What's this all about?" Robin demanded. He had been surprised when Guy had sent word for him to come at dawn to the locked pantry and bring his men.

Guy dropped to one knee and rose. "My lord, I have excellent news," he proclaimed with glee.

Robin crossed his arms and waited for him to continue.

"First, more mercenaries have deserted. I believe there are fewer than a dozen left. But more importantly, Montlhéry was called back to Paris. He will return, but he'll be gone at least a fortnight. This is the best opportunity you will have to recover the remaining taxes."

Robin maintained a neutral expression, although Tuck received the news with enthusiasm.

"What is happening in Paris?" asked Robin.

"On August 15th, King Philippe remarried. His new wife is Princess Ingeborg of Denmark. Her family is descended from Cnut, a King of England. Perhaps this is how he plans to take the English throne."

Robin frowned, "Denmark has a fleet of fine ships. Philippe could be planning to invade England."

Gisborne was still beaming, so an annoyed Robin added, "I fail to see how this is good news or why you are so pleased."

"I haven't gotten to the best part," Gisborne announced. "The story Montlhéry received was that the morning after the wedding, Philippe insisted Ingeborg return to Denmark, and that the wedding be annulled."

"On what grounds?" inquired Tuck.

"I'm not sure," admitted Guy, "but Montlhéry was furious. He complained that this is the sort of thing that always happens when he's not there to advise Philippe. But then, Montlhéry made an offhand comment that Philippe...how shall I say it? He sometimes lacks *confidence* in the bedchamber." Gisborne howled with laughter, and Robin and Tuck joined him at Philippe's expense.

Robin remarked, "I doubt that Ingeborg's father will be eager to help Philippe invade England after this debacle."

"Exactly," agreed Guy. "And with Montlhéry gone, you can come to this end of the tunnel. It will be much easier than navigating the slope between here and the brew house."

By midday, they had retrieved the remaining tax payments from the tunnel, and the wagons were departing Nottingham. Gisborne and Constance rode with them, as Constance had received a letter from Countess Isabel, and she wanted to share it with Marian, who was at Locksley Manor. Robbie had been asking for his mother, and Isabel was encouraging Marian to come for another visit.

As they passed near Locksley, Constance and Gisborne left them, and soon they reached the spot where the wagons would exit the road and turn into the forest. The rest of Robin's men were waiting for them there, and they joined the procession to the caves.

The wagons rumbled along the increasingly narrow path, and Robin maneuvered his horse to the space between the two wagons, content to allow Tuck to lead the way, since he had been in charge of the operation to transfer the treasure from the tunnel to the caves.

John's loud whistle caused Robin to halt their progress as he went to see what John wanted.

John had clambered off his wagon, so Robin dismounted and asked, "Is there a problem?"

"Tuck's a good man, but he didn't grow up in this forest," he cryptically remarked in a quiet voice.

"Tell me," Robin commanded.

John motioned for Robin to follow as he walked to the rear of the second wagon. Robin knew all eyes were on them, and he signaled for everyone to stay in place.

A short distance behind the wagon, John stopped. "I should have been more involved, but you know what it was like in that tunnel." He shivered at the memory.

"Be at ease, John. We had plenty of men to help Tuck."

"It's not that," John admitted. "Look." He pointed at the ground.

Robin looked down and saw nothing but the worn path and the wheel ruts that furrowed the ground from the heavily laden wagons as they carried the taxes of Nottinghamshire to the caves of Locksley. Just as he was about to ask John to explain, he realized the problem.

Panic briefly seized him, and he scanned the surrounding trees. His gaze flew to John. "Is there a place nearby where we could unload these wagons and conceal the barrels?"

John squinted at the trees, lost in thought. At last, he suggested, "There's creek bed about 100 yards to the north. In the spring, it's filled with water. But this time of year, it's dry. We can put the barrels there and cover them with limbs and debris."

Robin nodded in relief.

Tuck walked up to them and inquired, "My lord, what is wrong?"

Robin gestured at the ground. "Tuck, how difficult would it be for a group of trained soldiers to follow your tracks to the ridge above the caves?"

When Tuck looked down, he blanched. Lifting his eyes to Robin and John, he cried, "My lord, forgive me! I never thought… I'm so sorry."

Robin beckoned to the men. "We've got to get the silver hidden as quickly as possible, but we can't use the wagons or the horses." He surveyed the heavy barrels. "I want the twelve strongest men to work in pairs to carry the barrels. Follow John, and he'll show you where to put them. Six men will flank the men transporting the barrels, your bows at the ready. The rest of us will wait here to guard the wagons."

The wagons were promptly unloaded, and after inspecting the camouflage of the barrels in the gully, Robin instructed John to return the next day with a few men to add more concealment.

As the men were turning the wagons, thoughts of how they could obscure the obvious path that extended from the road to the caves distracted Robin. He wondered if Tuck had also left a worn trail along the slope that led to the mouths of the caves. He resolved to check on it as soon as possible.

An all too familiar whoosh passed by him, and one of his men cried out. Robin glanced over his shoulder to see an arrow protruding from the man's chest. The wounded man slumped forward in his saddle and then slid to the ground. Robin whistled an alarm as several more arrows struck a wagon and a second man.

Abandoning the wagons, the outlaws scattered into the woods. Still mounted on his horse, Robin reached over his head, grasping a limb and pulling himself into a tree. He shifted to a branch that overlooked the path, and he grabbed his bow, nocking an arrow and aiming at the men who had swarmed the wagons.

He could hear one of them shout, "The wagons are empty. Retreat!"

The mercenaries spurred their horses into a gallop back towards the main road, but not before two of them had been brought down by Robin's arrows.

When the mercenaries were out of sight, the outlaws emerged from the trees and returned to the wagons. One of the outlaws had been killed, and another injured. Robin decided to take him to Constance. They loaded him into one wagon, and the dead were put in the other wagon.

Leaving some of his men behind to watch the path to the caves, Robin and the others hastened to Locksley.

❧

They arrived at Locksley in the middle of the afternoon, and the wounded man was taken into the manor's hall where Constance treated his injuries.

Robin summoned his men, and everyone, including Guy, gathered around him near the front of the manor. "I want men stationed day and night along the trail leading to the caves until I can arrange for Earl Hamelin to collect the taxes," Robin explained. He then ordered Much to organize the men into shifts.

Gisborne pulled Robin aside. "Did you notice what direction the mercenaries took when they left you?" he asked. "I'm acting sheriff, and I'm wondering if I need to go back to Nottingham."

Robin paused in contemplation. "They recognized that the wagons were empty, which means they must have seen them when they were loaded with barrels. It's more likely they will return to the path where they attacked us and search there."

"What is your plan?"

"I left six of my best archers to guard the area. Tomorrow, I must devise a way to hide the path." Suddenly, Robin stilled and inhaled deeply.

Guy smelled it too.

Smoke.

To the east, they observed dark smoke curling above the trees.

Much and the rest of Robin's men joined them; they had seen it too.

Gisborne squinted at the sky. "What's in that direction?"

Robin and Much spoke in unison, "Lenton!"

Robin and his men rode hard towards Lenton, which was only a few miles from Locksley. When they arrived, Lenton Manor was engulfed in flames, and the people were carrying buckets of water in a futile attempt to extinguish the conflagration. Robin's men joined them while Robin sought the steward of Lenton and pulled him aside. Although Robin had been stripped of his titles, the people still considered him Baron of Lenton because of his marriage to Marian.

"What happened?" he asked.

The steward was dazed, and he needed a few moments to regain his composure. "Some men rode up to the manor, and they began releasing flaming arrows at the roof and open windows."

"They didn't demand money?" questioned Robin.

"My lord, they just attacked. I don't understand it." He shook his head in disbelief.

"How many men?"

"I think there were nine or ten. I'm not sure."

Robin commanded, "Tell everyone to focus on the chapel and nearby buildings. Use ladders to soak their roofs, especially the chapel. Move all the horses and tack from the stables to the far side of the village; we can't risk losing them if the fire spreads. Abandon the manor; it's beyond hope."

He wondered why the mercenaries would attack Lenton. It wasn't along the route to the caves. Then he realized the danger, and he yelled for his men.

᷍

Constance observed Guy gripping Marian's arm as she squirmed and swung at him with her free hand, clipping him in the jaw.

"Lady Marian, Robin specifically told me to keep you here at Locksley," he calmly stated.

"That's my home!" she shrieked at him. "Let me go; I'm ordering you!"

They were standing outside the front door of Locksley, and the smoke in the sky had ominously increased.

"My lady, as Lord Robin emphasized the other day, I am his vassal, not yours," Guy reminded her.

"Marian, just this once, please do as Robin asks," Constance implored her. "If you were there at Lenton, what could you do? Nothing. Whatever is burning, it's likely beyond saving. It's out of your hands."

"Those mercenaries who attacked Robin could still be in the area," Guy warned.

Marian slumped in defeat. She knew they were right, and she grudgingly reentered Locksley.

After Marian left, Constance stood next to Guy. She hoped to engage him in conversation, but she didn't know what to say.

He was studying the sky over Lenton when the thunder of approaching mounted men shook the ground. She initially thought that Robin was returning.

Guy stiffened, and under his breath, she heard him swear, "Merde!" Without looking at her, he insisted, "Constance, go into the manor. Now."

Before she could take a step, soldiers encircled them, their horses snorting and sweating. One man dismounted and demanded, "Hands up, Gisborne."

Guy complied, and the other man took his sword. Marveling at Guy's elaborate, high-quality weapon, he proclaimed, "I like this. I'm keeping it as part of the pay the sheriff owes me and my men."

Guy lowered his hands. "Sir Gaspard, the sheriff is away on important business. There is no need for this; give me my sword and meet me at the castle tomorrow. I will pay you from the money in the tunnel."

The man's sneering grin made Constance shiver in fear.

"I think you're stealing the treasure for yourself. I saw you and your wife riding with a group of soldiers who were guarding wagons loaded with barrels. You left Nottingham and traveled towards Locksley. I gathered my men to follow, and by the time we tracked the wagons into the forest, the barrels were gone."

Pointing, he triumphantly announced, "And there are the wagons. Now you will tell me where the silver is hidden."

Guy attempted to dissuade him. "On my honor, the taxes are not here." He tugged at the cord around his neck. "Here is the key to the pantry above the tunnel. I will give it to you as an act of good faith."

"Your honor?" Gaspard scoffed. "You and the sheriff have been lying and cheating us for months, but we're going to have the final word." He snatched the key from Guy. "First, I will search Locksley." He motioned to his men, and they dismounted, tying their horses to the post.

Dividing his nine men into groups, he sent some to the stables and the Locksley church, while the rest rifled through the manor.

A few moments later, a man escorted Elvina, Odella, and Leofric out of the manor and forced them to sit on the ground. Constance made eye contact with Elvina and mouthed, "Marian?"

The older woman shook her head.

After a short wait, the men returned from the church and the stables, saying that they had found nothing. Finally, the remaining men exited the manor, and one said, "We looked everywhere. We found this bag of coins, but that's all." He showed the others the small bag.

"Burn it to the ground," Gaspard ordered.

"No!" exclaimed Constance, who stepped forward without thinking. "There's an injured man in the hall; at least allow us to carry him out first."

When Gaspard's cruel, cold eyes focused on her, a terrified Constance shrank back.

He leveled Guy's sword at her chest and suggested, "Perhaps you know where the treasure is hidden."

Guy pounced on the man, pushing him away from Constance, but Gaspard struck him on the head with the pommel of his sword, and Guy slumped to the ground.

Unexpectedly, an arrow flew through the air, lodging in Gaspard's side, and Constance knew Marian was hiding nearby and trying to save her. She scanned the area, hunting for her friend, only to see Robin and his men galloping over the ridge above Locksley and towards them.

The mercenaries pivoted to face the outlaws, and Gaspard became enraged as he realized they were outnumbered. He pulled the arrow from his side.

Constance glanced at Guy; he was dazed and struggling to regain his feet.

Looking back at Gaspard, she saw him yelling at his men. He spun towards her, shouting obscenities as he raised Guy's sword to strike her.

She tried to scream, but no sound came out of her mouth. She wanted to run, but her feet would not move. As the blade descended, the setting sun reflected in the polished metal, as if the sword itself were aflame. Abruptly, her side exploded in pain, and she slammed into the ground with a thud that knocked her breathless.

Gazing up, she watched Guy grappling with the man. He wrestled his sword from Gaspard, slashing at the other man's throat without hesitation.

Constance scrambled to her feet, and Guy promptly grabbed her, throwing her over his shoulder, and sprinting away from the manor. But then he faltered and stumbled. He dropped his sword and fell to his knees, releasing her as he panted, "Run, Constance, run into the woods and hide." He collapsed face down in the dirt.

She knelt and put her hand on Guy's shoulder, pushing on it to rouse him. "Guy, Robin's here, and everything will be all right."

He did not stir, and her heart pounded in fear.

She labored to roll him onto his back, only to discover that the front of his tunic was soaked with blood. She gasped, but her training as a healer took over, and she searched for his injury.

He moaned, and she breathed a sigh of relief. He was alive, but she could not find the location of his wound. His tunic was not torn, and he had not been stabbed.

Odella joined them, staring down at Guy and Constance.

Constance looked up at her and asked, "Odella, are you all right?"

"Yes, my lady. I came to tell you that Lord Robin and his men have killed all the mercenaries." She moved closer and hastily crossed herself.

"What's wrong, Odella?"

"I saw him save you." She gestured towards Guy. "When that man swung his sword at you, Gisborne pushed you out of the way and blocked it with his hand."

Constance examined Guy again and realized that his hands were resting on his stomach, and one was protectively clutching the other.

When she lifted his right hand, she was horrified to see that his left hand was bleeding profusely. It had been sliced in half, and only part of his palm and his thumb remained.

Bile rose in her throat, and tears blurred her vision as she pulled off her wimple and wrapped it tightly around his mutilated hand.

7 September 1193, Locksley

The sun had not yet risen, but the sky was pink with the promise of a new day. Autumn would soon arrive, and the heat of the summer had transitioned into chilly mornings and pleasant afternoons.

Robin was with Marian and Tuck in the Locksley stables. He instructed Tuck, "Go to Conisbrough and tell Earl Hamelin to come at once with as many men and sturdy wagons as he can spare. We must take advantage of the sheriff's absence and transport these taxes from Nottinghamshire to London."

Marian's red-rimmed eyes glowered at him, full of sorrow tinged with angry defiance.

While Tuck waited in the stables, Robin took Marian's hand and led her around the back of the building, where they would have privacy.

Before he could say anything, she sobbed, "Please, don't do this. It's too dangerous, and I don't trust that woman."

He spoke softly, hoping to calm her fears. "That woman is the king's mother, and for all intents and purposes, she's ruling England."

"But the way she treated you, after all you've done for her son..." Marian's voice faded.

"I don't understand why Eleanor turned against me, but I'm going with Hamelin to London to plead my case to her. There are risks; I will not lie to you."

Marian wiped her face with her sleeve, but her tears persisted. "I don't want to lose you again," she whispered.

Robin pulled her into an embrace and held her. "I can't swear that I'll return safe and sound. I won't offer you empty promises. But we can't live as outlaws. Since Tuck is the queen's agent, I'm sending him to Hamelin on my behalf."

He leaned away to look into her eyes. "I'm insisting that you go with him for two reasons: first, Robbie needs you; I read that letter from Countess Isabel. Second, if I'm unable to convince the queen that I'm innocent, then I want to know that you and Robbie are in a safe place, where you'll be protected. I can't send you to Embelton because it's too far. I trust Hamelin whole heartedly, so I'm sending you there."

She laid her forehead on his chest and wept. The sun was now peeking above the trees, and he silently cursed it, knowing that they were out of time.

"Marian, tell Robbie that I love him, and that I'm proud of him."

When he felt her nod, he emphasized, "And never forget that I love you." He hugged her close, not wanting to let her go, yet recognizing that the time for her to leave had arrived. Pressing his lips to the top of her head, he proclaimed, "You have always been the queen of my heart."

She looked up at him, and he kissed her passionately, as if he might never taste her lips again.

Robin surveyed the dirt and debris that had been spread over the spot where the wagon ruts veered from the road and into the forest. He wasn't satisfied with his men's attempts to camouflage the area.

"Let's cut several branches and lay them on top. I'd bring down an entire tree, but Earl Hamelin's men will need to have access to this pathway when they arrive," he advised.

He was there with his original outlaws: Little John, Much, Will, and Allan. The other men had been sent back to Locksley to rest and partake of a meal.

After they had arranged a few branches across the path, Robin signaled for them to follow as he walked to the caves. As he had feared, Tuck had also left an obvious trail extending from the ridge to the mouths of the caves.

It had been an honest mistake by a man who had spent his adult life in the arid landscape of Outremer. By his own admission, Tuck had lived in various fortresses such as Acre and Jaffa during his years of service to the Templars. And, although there were forested areas in the Holy Land, no sensible Crusader would linger there.

Robin gathered his men, and they sat on the ground in a circle near the entrance to the largest cave.

"I'll never forget the times we were here before Lord Robin left for the Crusade," Will reminisced.

"Those were good times," acknowledged John.

"Do you remember how Kenric was always cheating at dice?" Allan recollected.

Everyone laughed, but it was a hollow merriment, as they mourned the men who had been cruelly poisoned by Payen.

The somber moment prompted Much to ask, "Will the sheriff and Payen ever be brought to justice?"

Robin placed his hand on Much's shoulder. "I vow to do everything in my power to seek justice for all the men murdered by Montlhéry and Payen, not only the men who were originally part of our band but also my father and Marian's father."

The men became lost in their thoughts until Robin revealed, "When Earl Hamelin arrives, I'm going with him to London. I plan to plead my case before the queen."

All the men spoke up, hoping to discourage him.

"I must do this," Robin insisted. "My future, and my family's future, depends on clearing my name." He then disclosed, "I brought you here for a reason, and I don't want anyone to know what we're about to do, especially not Tuck."

A surprised Much questioned, "Do you think Tuck might betray us?"

"No," Robin assured him. "I trust Tuck, but we must never forget that he is the queen's man, and he might not appreciate my plan."

"I don't understand," Will confessed.

"The people of Nottinghamshire have been incredibly loyal to King Richard and scrupulous in paying their taxes for the ransom," Robin declared. "I can't say the same for many nobles and high-ranking churchmen in our towns."

Little John grumbled, "Rich men like Lord Amery, who wouldn't pay his fair share, while there were men with families forced to give a quarter of what little they had."

"That's right," agreed Robin. "And that's why I've invited you here. In the cave behind us, we have Lord's Amery's wealth. According to the Great Council's own edicts, three-quarters of that money is not part of the ransom."

"What are you saying, Lord Robin?" asked Allan.

Robin rose and briefly entered the nearest cave, returning with four empty leather bags.

"Since I will leave for London soon, and I don't know whether the queen will execute me for treason, I'm announcing that John will resume leadership of the band. Winter is coming, and I'm worried about the people who've been impoverished by these burdensome taxes."

He handed each man a bag.

Robin explained, "I want you to fill these bags with money from Lord Amery's treasure. John will distribute the funds to widows, orphans, and poor families who are struggling to feed themselves. I don't care whether you use the money to buy food, or give it directly to the people. I trust John to make those decisions. But we must do this now, before Earl Hamelin arrives and Tuck returns."

As the men stood, Little John vowed, "I will tell the people that Robin Hood has taken from the rich to give them food."

"I'm not seeking praise or adoration," declared Robin. "The people have sacrificed enough for their king."

"You've sacrificed more than anyone else, because the king's mother has taken everything you own," Much observed.

Without responding, Robin led them into the cave and showed them the chests belonging to Lord Amery.

CHAPTER 16
BY THE WRATH OF GOD, QUEEN OF ENGLAND

21 September 1193, Locksley

Pausing on the ridge overlooking Locksley, Guy was astounded by the sight before him. Tents, wagons, men, and horses crowded the outskirts of the small village. He continued to the manor where he entered and discovered that Robin and Constance were conversing with Earl Hamelin. He briefly dropped to one knee upon his entrance, and he observed Constance smile warmly at him as she left on her way to the kitchen.

"What brings you here, Gisborne?" asked Robin.

"Montlhéry returned late yesterday, and he was deluged with reports of an 'invading army' encamped at Locksley. He's assuming that it's all an exaggeration, but he sent me to investigate," explained Guy. "What do you want me to tell him?"

Hamelin grinned. "Tell him I've arrived with an army to search for Robin Hood. Ask him to grant me permission to visit him at the castle. Last I heard, I'm not allowed to enter Nottingham."

"Have you ever met Montlhéry?" Robin inquired. "We think he has barred you because you would recognize his true identity."

"It's possible that I would recognize him, if I saw him," admitted Hamelin. "I have a good memory for faces, but not so much for names."

Guy hid his disfigured hand by holding it behind his hip, and he grimaced from the throbbing ache he was experiencing in fingers that were no longer there. Perhaps tightening the bandages would ease the pain. He was thankful that he still had his thumb, but he couldn't help but feel like a fool for trying to block a sword with his bare hand.

He refocused on the conversation as Robin announced, "We will leave in two days, and we hope to arrive in London before Michaelmas."

Hamelin agreed, "The heavily laden wagons will slow us down, but I believe we can make it there by the end of the month."

"How many men did you bring?" Guy asked.

"I summoned men from all my fiefs, and I've brought nearly all the men-at-arms who live at Conisbrough," Hamelin responded. "That's sixty men."

Reacting to this impressive number, Guy remarked, "You'll attract a lot of attention as you move south, but there will be no force of arms that could challenge you."

Laughing amiably, Hamelin confirmed, "That's the idea."

Then Robin and Hamelin coached Guy on what he should say to Montlhéry.

Guy was untying his horse as he prepared to return to Nottingham, and he was frustrated when the reins became entangled. He startled and pivoted at the sound of a step behind him.

"Guy, were you planning to leave without even saying hello?" a smiling Constance inquired.

"Hello," he muttered. He regretted his mocking response when her face fell with dismay. Again he fumbled with the reins, stymied because of his injured hand.

Constance took the reins from him and untied them. She handed them back and said, "I should return to the castle. After all, the sheriff ordered me to stay with you at all times, since he doesn't trust me."

Gisborne sighed in resignation. She was right, of course. Fortunately, Montlhéry had been distracted and had not realized that she wasn't there.

Before he could respond, she added, "I've gathered my things, and they're sending me a horse from the stables. May I examine your hand again?" she requested. "I'm still worried about wound fever."

Reluctantly, he offered her his bandaged hand, and she unwound the linen wrappings, studying his injury. He chastised himself for reveling in her touch as her hands cradled his.

"You are healing quickly. Are you in any pain?"

"No," he lied.

Just then, a stable boy brought her a horse, and she re-wrapped his hand.

✥

Constance trailed Guy as they entered the keep. It was late in the day, and he had invited her to share a meal with him. When they arrived in the great hall, she was surprised to see that the sheriff was also there.

Guy genuflected and Constance curtsied.

"Tell me everything," Montlhéry demanded.

"Earl Hamelin de Warenne and his men are camped at Locksley. They are here to search for Robin Hood."

The sheriff rose from the table and marched to the hearth, where a blazing fire was providing much needed heat to the hall. Staring at the flames, he responded, "I don't believe him. He's an ally of Robin Hood. Moreover, Nottinghamshire is under John's authority, and Hamelin is the queen's man. He has no right to bring men-at-arms into John's domain." Returning his gaze to Guy, he insisted, "He must leave at once."

"My lord, Earl Hamelin has sixty men with him. How do you propose I make him leave? He offered to meet with you. Would you like to invite him here for a parley?"

Constance observed the color drain from Montlhéry's face.

Guy continued, "He informed me that, regardless of whether he captures Robin Hood, he must depart for London in two days."

Montlhéry started pacing in front of the hearth. At last, he decided, "If it's only two days, then there's no need to meet with him. Perhaps the arrival of this great force of arms from the crown will persuade any remaining mercenaries to leave. I no longer require their services."

The sheriff exited the hall without even a fare-thee-well, and Constance enjoyed a delicious meal with Guy. Her heart ached to see him struggle with his bandaged hand, but she resolved to behave as if nothing was out of the ordinary.

Their conversation was relaxed, but they avoided any difficult subjects. Soon, they were trudging up the stairs that led to their separate bedchambers. To her surprise, he motioned for her to join him in his chamber, and she willingly followed.

"Constance, you should go back to Embelton. I will make excuses for you with Montlhéry."

"Why are you sending me away?" she questioned. "I don't want to go."

He frowned. "Surely, you recognize the danger that Robin will face in London. He's been convicted of treason."

"Earl Hamelin will speak to the queen on Robin's behalf."

She watched as Guy went to the hearth and stirred the smoldering ashes, adding kindling and a small log to create light and heat in the chamber. She joined him and sat in a chair near the fire.

Constance was pleased when he sat in the adjacent chair, and she worked up her courage to inquire, "Guy, why have you stayed with Montlhéry all this time?"

Her unexpected question clearly surprised him, and his gaze

returned to the crackling flames. He finally answered, "I swore fealty to him. Montlhéry paid for my education. He provided food and shelter for me and my mother." Shrugging, he asserted, "Isn't that enough?"

Constance considered his answer, but she wasn't satisfied. "I don't think so. He's consistently cruel to you—"

"That doesn't matter. Most lords treat their men that way. You don't understand because you've spent your life with Lord Edmund, an uncommonly benevolent and honorable man."

"I know that's true," she countered, "but what about the way he's ensnared you in this web of poisonings and political murders? He killed your father; he beat your mother. I don't understand how you could tolerate him after witnessing his abuse of your mother."

Despite the low light of the fire, Constance saw a flash of anger in his eyes. "Are you doubting my affection for my mother?"

"Of course not," she snapped back at him as she wondered how he could have possibly misconstrued what she had said in such a way.

They fell into silence again, until he asked, "Do you really want to know? I've never discussed this with anyone."

Constance reached out and put her hand on his forearm. "Please tell me; I'm listening."

"I will tell you only if you lie with me on the bed."

For a few moments, Constance was speechless, but her curiosity and desire to know the truth outweighed any trepidation that she might have otherwise had over such an unexpected request. She stood and walked to the bed, and he pulled off his boots before joining her.

She was lying on her back, but he insisted she roll onto her side, facing away from him as he shifted to lie close behind her. He draped his arm, the one with the injured hand, over her waist.

The tempo of her heart sped with an odd mixture of nervousness and excitement.

He quietly began, "When I was fourteen summers, Montlhéry promoted me from page to squire. For any boy who dreams of becoming a knight, it's an important time. I would live in Paris with him, furthering my education and making new friends."

Her voice equally hushed, she recalled, "Lionel was so excited when he left for his training."

"At that time, my mother became ill, and she called me to her bedside."

Constance noticed that sound of his voice had changed; it was now thick and strained.

"I was angry at her for being sick, and I assumed she was planning to ask me to stay with her instead of going to Paris. So I went to her, and I spoke rudely to her, mimicking the disdain I often heard Montlhéry use when he addressed her."

"You were young," she suggested.

He scoffed. "That's no excuse. I saw her eyes fill with tears, but she still smiled at me and told me she would always love me, that she was proud of me, and that she knew I would become a distinguished knight. I should have apologized to her, but I did not. And then…" His voice faded.

"And then what?" she persisted.

"She asked me to do one thing for her."

Constance apprehensively whispered, "What was that?"

"She asked me to remain loyal to Montlhéry. She said that even though he had often treated her harshly, she would have endured anything to ensure that I had a chance for a better life."

"Oh," Constance breathed. She didn't know what else to say.

He added, "She told me he's more than an advisor to the royal family; he's a close blood relation to them. She claimed that if I stayed with him, I would have a wonderful future and many opportunities. So, I gave her my word."

There was another pause, and Constance realized that Guy was struggling with his emotions, and that he had purposefully positioned her so that she would not see him cry.

He finished the story. "I went to Paris, and a few days later, I received word that she had died."

"I'm so sorry, Guy. My mother died from a sickness too, and I will never forget the grief I felt."

They remained in silent contemplation for a time.

"Guy?"

"Yes?" His voice had returned to its normal tone.

"Thank you for telling me this; I understand everything better now."

He did not respond, so she continued, "If your mother had lived, don't you think she would have eventually recognized that Montlhéry was poisoning your future?"

Sighing loudly, Guy acknowledged, "I believe that my mother would not have wanted this life for me, but it's too late; Montlhéry has already destroyed my future. If he doesn't kill me, then King Richard will."

Constance's heart leapt with fear, and she turned to face him. Caressing his face, she could feel the dampness that lingered on his cheek. She begged, "Please don't say that; I have faith in Robin. He will talk to the king and explain how you have helped recover the ransom. Every night, I pray for your safety and redemption."

He fell quiet, and at length, he conceded, "If you are praying on my behalf, then perhaps there is hope."

"There is always hope, Guy. Please don't despair!"

"Why do you care? Once I am gone, you will be able to marry again and have children. I'm certain you will be a good mother; you're already a good wife."

She blushed and hoped that he could not see it. "I'm not much of a wife to you."

His brow creased in confusion, he declared, "You're kindhearted and clever." He turned his head slightly and kissed her palm. "I am blessed to have you as my wife."

"I believe you mean that. I remember how my suitors would say anything to flatter me, and I knew they were lying, especially when they would wax poetically about my beauty."

"But you are beautiful."

She scoffed.

He rolled onto his back, pulling her close to his side, and she rested her head on his chest, where she could hear the steady beating of his heart.

Guy confessed, "I did not think you were beautiful when I first met you, but I was a fool. Now I can see your beauty clearly."

She closed her eyes and reveled in the warmth of his embrace. Constance considered how he had opened his heart to her by speaking about his past. She realized she could also take risks in the intimacy of this darkened room. In a small voice, she whispered, "I want to be your wife."

"You are my wife."

"I mean, I want a real marriage with you." She braced herself for the possibility that he might refuse her, or worse, laugh at her.

Instead, his lips eagerly sought hers.

30 September 1193, The Tower of London

"Your Grace, please come to the great hall and join the celebrations for the Feast of Michaelmas."

Eleanor leveled a contemptuous stare at her elderly lady-in-waiting, and she bitterly remonstrated the other woman. "Grace? It is by the wrath of God that I am queen of this miserable island populated by men who will not ransom their king."

The woman stuttered an apology and hastily exited the chamber.

Outside her window, the sky was painted in brilliant, fiery hues, but Eleanor could not appreciate the splendor of the setting sun. It was merely another reminder that her days continued their march towards the inevitable end of all things, yet each morning she awoke with the weight of a kingdom pressing down upon her. She had become grain under a millstone.

She walked to the table to read, once again, Richard's latest dispatch from Germany. This letter included the lyrics for a song that he had written, and the words pierced her heart in a way that only a mother who had also suffered the anguish of imprisonment could fathom.

The shadows in her chamber were rising, and her aging eyes were blurred with tears, but she sought the most meaningful phrases:

My much beloved mother,
I've written a song, and I hope it will please your most discerning tastes:
No man who is imprisoned sees his fate
With honesty; for all he feels is sad,
But he can still compose a hopeful song.
Friends I have many, but their gifts are slight;
They should be ashamed if, for my ransom,
I lie here one more year.

Reluctantly placing the precious letter on the table, she picked up the latest tallies from the Exchequer of Ransom. They were still far behind in raising the ransom, and her advisors had already warned her that, when the final sums for the harvest were recorded following the Feast of Michaelmas, it still would not be enough.

Any day, envoys would arrive from Germany to inspect the ransom. What would she tell them? That Richard's people had failed him?

She tossed the accursed accounting sheet to the floor.

Marching to the window, she gazed up at the darkening sky and lamented, "Why have I, the queen of two kingdoms and the mother of two kings, been forced to endure this abominable old age? Henry the Young King and Prince Geoffrey sleep in the dust, while their wretched mother is compelled to live, tortured by the memory of these beloved sons.

"In all things, the Lord has become cruel towards me. In His anger, He has set my two remaining sons to fight against each other, if indeed it can be called a fight when Richard languishes in prison while John attempts to usurp the kingdom."

Sharp knocking on the door intruded upon her gloomy pondering, and she granted the person permission to enter.

The captain of her personal guard rushed into the chamber, and he dropped to one knee before rising. He announced, "Your Grace, many men-at-arms just passed through the city gates, and they are marching in this direction."

Somehow, her aged heart found the strength to quicken in alarm. Before she could respond, a second man ran into the chamber, and in his panic, he forgot to genuflect before the queen.

He declared, "Your Grace, a man who was stationed at the gate reports that it's the Earl of Surrey, and he's leading an army of sixty men."

Eleanor's heart collapsed in despair, but from decades of practice, she arranged her features into a neutral expression and remarked, "And so it begins."

Her captain stared at her curiously, but she did not deign to clarify her meaning.

Instead, she commanded, "When Earl Hamelin arrives to arrest me, do not hinder him. We do not have enough men here at the tower to resist his army since so many are guarding the ransom under Saint Paul's Cathedral."

The distressed man countered, "But, Your Grace—"

She pointed him towards the door.

❦

Tuck accompanied Earl Hamelin up the stairs and down a corridor to the queen's chambers. They were granted entrance at once.

Both men went down to one knee and rose. Hamelin smiled fondly at Eleanor and said, "Your Grace, I've—"

"Of all the men who serve me, I would have never expected you to betray me," the queen thundered.

Hamelin frowned in confusion. "Your Grace, I haven't betrayed you."

"When you betray Richard, you are betraying me," she asserted.

Tuck glanced nervously between the two.

Hamelin was obviously bewildered by Eleanor's accusations. He admitted, "I don't understand—"

Again the queen interrupted. "I've received word of this great force of men that you have brought. I know your purpose: you intend to imprison me and put John on the throne. I'm prepared to surrender, as I lack the men needed to defend the tower. I just wonder how many of the justiciars have joined you in this treason."

Her eyes narrowed at the sight of Tuck. "And how could you condone such sedition? Can a Knight Templar be purchased like a tavern whore?"

Tuck was aghast at the queen's words.

Hamelin had heard enough. "Your Grace!" he shouted. Attempting to calm himself, he tried to explain, "You've misunderstood my intentions. Please, come with us; there is something I wish to show you."

"You've no need for such artifice to lure me away from my chambers. I will come with you; I only ask to be allowed to keep this letter from Richard."

Daring to enter the conversation, Tuck said, "You are welcome to bring the letter, but you will return to your chambers soon."

She ignored him, and when she picked up the letter, he noticed a slight trembling in her hands. Holding it against her chest, she closed her eyes and mouthed a brief prayer.

❦

Darkness rose in the streets around the Tower of London, and Hamelin's soldiers had lit torches as they awaited the arrival of the queen. Robin stood near the lead wagon wearing a hooded cloak.

After what seemed to be a long time, Hamelin, Tuck, and Eleanor finally exited the tower. Robin watched her sway slightly at the sight of Hamelin's army.

Hamelin offered her his arm, but she refused him. He then led her to the first wagon, and she did not even glance in Robin's direction.

"What is this, Hamelin?" she demanded.

The earl stepped forward and drew back the rough cloth covering the chests stacked in the wagon. He lifted the lid of one of the sturdy boxes and took a torch from one of his men to provide more light. "Your Grace, look," he entreated.

She approached the wagon and immediately recognized the shimmer of silver in the light of the torch's flames. Robin noticed she was clutching a piece of parchment in one hand, but she reached out with the other and tentatively touched the coins.

Hamelin spoke gently to the queen, in a personal manner that surprised Robin. "Eleanor, how could you doubt my loyalty? You are my sister by marriage. And how could you doubt Robin Fitzooth? I've heard Richard describe Robin as the brother of his heart."

Eleanor reluctantly tore her gaze from the chest of silver. "What are you trying to say, Hamelin?"

"This wagon, and the others behind it, do you see them?" he asked as he gestured towards the other wagons.

She nodded, and Hamelin continued, "These wagons are bringing the missing taxes from Nottinghamshire. I have the tax rolls too. And we must thank Robin Hood for this treasure."

Hamelin beckoned to him, and Robin lowered his hood, approached Eleanor, and knelt.

She paid no attention to Robin as she asked Hamelin for a tally sheet that would show just how much wealth he was delivering. After reviewing the ledger, she bade Robin to rise, and he was heartened to see that the queen's face was wet with tears.

Eleanor declared, "When added to the final accounting for the harvest, we will have enough to prove to Heinrich's emissaries that Richard's people have raised the ransom."

Hamelin implored, "Your Grace, please grant me leave. I must take these wagons to Saint Paul's at once. This force of men is not here to arrest you, but to safeguard the taxes during our journey from Nottinghamshire."

She sent him on his way as Robin remained at her side. He beseeched, "Your Grace, may I request an audience with you?"

᷼

Robin returned with Eleanor to her chamber. She put the letter she had been carrying on a table, and then she hastened to sit by the fire and warm herself, as the autumnal air had swiftly chilled following the sun's surrender in the west.

Robin stood awkwardly nearby. He cleared his throat.

"What do you want, Huntingdon?" she irritably snapped.

"You've convicted me of treason and placed a bounty on my head. You've confiscated my lands and my titles. I'm here to plead my case; I am innocent of these charges."

She observed him for a few moments, and then, to his chagrin, she laughed out loud. Recovering somewhat, she said, "Very well, I'm listening."

Robin wanted to ask her what she found so amusing about destroying his life, but instead he asserted, "I have not been stealing taxes. The Sheriff of Nottingham hired mercenaries—"

"And you've been stealing from the thieves," she finished his sentence.

He was taken aback but quickly recovered. "How did you—"

"For heaven's sake, Huntingdon. My agents keep me well informed. Even though Brother Tuck's reports have been few and far between, he has been quite useful."

Robin boldly requested, "Will you clear my name and restore my lands to me?"

She silently studied him.

"Your Grace, I protest the unfair confiscation of my property. I've always been loyal to King Richard. Forgive my impertinence, but you've misjudged me."

In the flickering light of the chamber, she smirked at him and countered, "Au contraire, young man. I've judged you correctly. I'm an excellent judge of character."

An exasperated Robin ran his fingers through his hair. He was tempted to just pull it out in frustration. He admitted, "I don't understand."

"When these reports of stolen taxes in Nottinghamshire first arrived, Archbishop Hubert sought me out and swore that you were a man of honor who loved the king. He was adamant that you would never betray Richard, and he droned on and on about your noble character and steadfast Christian faith. I asked him if he planned to recommend your canonization. Unfortunately, he does not appreciate my sense of humor."

Robin opened his mouth to speak, but she raised her hand to hush him.

"Later that night, Earl Hamelin came tapping on my door. He described how, even as a boy in training, you were principled and honest. He touted your reputation for selflessness and courageous deeds. He also insisted that you would never betray Richard. And then your uncle begged the council on your behalf. He proclaimed your bravery as well."

She grinned and asked, "Do you know what I learned from these men?"

Robin sighed. "No, Your Grace."

"I learned that you are exactly the type of earnest, self-righteous young man who would never accept the sullying of his honor and integrity. I surmised that you would do whatever it took to clear your name, and if it required you to steal, borrow, beg, or kill to recover the taxes, then you would do it. And I was right."

Robin was horrified. He could have been killed for the bounty. Even worse, Marian could have been hurt. Or killed.

Eleanor must have read the look on his face, so she reminded him, "Last February, you knelt at my feet and solemnly vowed to do anything to ensure Richard's release, up to and including sacrificing your life. When you pledged to risk everything, I took you at your word."

Robin drew a calming breath. He was angry at how the queen had treated him, but there was nothing to be done about it. "Your Grace, I'm humbly requesting that you restore my lands and my titles to me."

She stared at him, and as the time stretched, Robin suspected that she was testing his resolve. He returned her scrutiny and did not blink.

She chuckled and turned her gaze back to the fire in the hearth. "Consider it done, Earl Robin."

CHAPTER 17
GHOSTS OF THE PAST

1 November 1193, Lenton

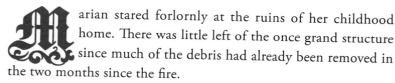arian stared forlornly at the ruins of her childhood home. There was little left of the once grand structure since much of the debris had already been removed in the two months since the fire.

"Countess Huntingdon, we have questions about the plans you gave us for rebuilding this manor." A carpenter and stonemason who had been recommended by Guillaume de Warenne approached her. The carpenter was holding a piece of paper with Marian's sketches.

Pointing to the blackened remains of a huge oak on the other side of the manor's foundation, he said, "We must cut down that oak. I examined it, and I believe it's dead from fire damage."

Marian sighed. She had so many memories of climbing out of her bedchamber and using the old oak to exit the manor without her father's knowledge. Robin had taught her how to climb that tree when they were both children.

"Are you sure?" she asked. "Can we wait until spring—"

"Mama! Mama!" Robbie ran up to her and began tugging on the sleeve of her fur-lined cloak. It was a grey, chilly day, and there was a light dusting of snow on the ground.

"Look!" he cried, as he excitedly bounced up and down while pointing at something behind her. Jack started barking.

She pivoted away from the builders and saw Robin riding towards them. Her heart overflowed with joy, and she forgot about the craftsmen as she joined Robbie in running to greet him.

When Robin drew near the Lenton chapel, he leapt off his horse, picked up Robbie, and opened his other arm to her, pulling her close as his lips greedily consumed hers. It had been eight weeks since he had sent her to Conisbrough as he made plans for his journey to London.

Robbie intruded upon their tender moment. "Mama is mad at you," he announced.

Robin loosened his tight embrace and frowned as he gazed into her eyes. "Is that right?"

The little boy admonished, "You made us wait a long time before you came home."

Marian smiled sheepishly. "I confess that I've been impatient for you to return. Brother Tuck brought me your letter with the good news that the queen had exonerated you, and I rushed back to Locksley, expecting your return any day. Where have you been all this time? I've been worried."

"When I sent that letter, I thought I would leave London at once, but the queen had other ideas."

Robbie interrupted again. "Did you bring me a gift?"

"Did you have another birthday?" Robin countered.

Robbie eyed Marian hopefully, but she shook her head, and his face fell in disappointment. Then he proclaimed, "I'm hungry."

Robin set him down and retrieved a few pieces of bread and jerky from his saddlebag. Marian watched as Robbie happily took the morsels and walked to the steps of the nearby chapel to sit and eat. Jack whined at his feet, begging for a portion.

Redirecting her attention back to Robin, Marian questioned,

"What did the queen ask of you? Haven't you already done enough for her and her son?"

"She wanted me to help Earl Hamelin prepare the first installment of the ransom for its voyage to Germany."

"They've sent the ransom? When will Richard return?"

"They've sent half of the ransom. They'll need to send the remaining ransom and the hostages before Richard is set free." He added, "From London, I traveled to Huntingdon."

"I just wish you had sent word to me that you would be delayed."

"I sent a second letter, but it must have gotten lost." Robin was pulling her into another embrace when he suddenly noticed the two men who were standing a short distance away, observing them.

"Who are those men?" Robin inquired.

"Oh, I'm so excited!" Marian exclaimed. "Hamelin's son recommended them. One is a carpenter, and the other is a master stonemason. They're going to rebuild Lenton Manor."

Marian was astounded when she saw all the color drain from Robin's face.

"I think we should wait until next summer," suggested Robin. "I doubt they will want to work during the winter."

"They assured me that the winter weather would not hinder them, especially if they can finish the walls and roof by the end of this month."

Robin cleared his throat, and Marian was stunned by the realization that he seemed nervous, which was definitely out of character for him.

He cautiously asked, "What's the hurry? We're living at Locksley, and there's no need to rebuild now."

Marian's temper flared. "This is my home; the place where I grew up. I want it rebuilt."

"But I've already made other arrangements for the household servants. Constance found work for most of them at the castle. If we rebuild, we'll have the expense of either re-hiring them or finding new staff. And if we're not living here..." His voice drifted away.

"Why would that matter?" she snapped. "I want my home rebuilt."

He turned towards his horse and fiddled with the latch on his saddlebag.

"Well?" she demanded.

He sighed and watched Robbie give Jack some jerky.

"Robin? What's the matter? I can't read your mind, and I don't understand why you wouldn't want to restore my childhood home. I'm sure we can afford—"

Robin began to study the ground as he continued to brace himself against his horse.

Marian whispered, "We can afford to rebuild it, can't we?"

The silence between them stretched to an uncomfortable span of time. Robin was still not looking her in the eye when he finally explained, "Marian, when the crown took control of Huntingdon, they essentially stripped it bare. All the furnishings in the castle, including the tapestries, were removed and sold. The steward tells me that the only funds left are the proceeds from the harvest that just ended. I need that money to feed the servants who work in the castle."

Staring at his horse instead of her, he admitted, "I'm thankful for the prosperity of Locksley and Lenton, and I'm praying for an abundant harvest next year. That is all that stands between us and bankruptcy."

At that moment, Robbie joined them. "Papa! Jack stole all my jerky. I want more."

Robin knelt and said, "I saw you giving Jack your jerky. It's good to share, but it's wrong to lie to your papa."

As Robin and Robbie talked, Marian looked back at the ruins of Lenton and the two men who were patiently waiting for her. Her gaze returned to her husband and son, and suddenly, it was all clear to her.

They were her future.

Lenton was her past.

She strolled over to the men and informed them that her husband would contact them at a later date about rebuilding the manor. She then paid them for their time and sent them on their way.

15 November 1193, Nottingham Castle

Robin rode through the gates of Nottingham Castle and entered the inner bailey. Near the wide steps that led into the keep, he saw his uncle. After handing his horse to a boy from the stables, he approached Edmund, and the two men embraced, slapping each other's back with great enthusiasm.

"It's been too long," proclaimed Robin.

"I wish we could just sit and talk, but I'm here because I need your help," Edmund confessed.

"What has happened? I will help you any way I can."

"Robin, I lack the eloquence to describe how much I appreciate you. If only your father had lived to see the man you've become."

"Thank you, but you have been a second father to me. I hope you know that."

"I have failed as a father."

"What has Lionel done now?" Robin asked with a sigh.

"He left Embelton ten days ago. I feared that he had run away to avoid going to Germany, but then I received a message from Constance that he was here visiting the sheriff. I'm worried that Montlhéry will ensnare him in another ill-conceived scheme. Perhaps if we talk to him together, we can convince him to return home."

"He should probably go to London instead. The other hostages are already gathering there."

A weary Edmund nodded. "Doesn't he realize that if he fails to serve as a hostage, the crown could confiscate my barony? You know better than anyone how capricious the queen can be. Doesn't he understand that Embelton will be *his* barony one day?"

They entered the keep and made their way to the sheriff's tower room, where Montlhéry sat behind his messy desk with Gisborne and Lionel standing on either side of his throne-like chair.

Montlhéry stood, and all three men moved to the front of the desk.

The sheriff grinned. "Lionel, your family looks worried."

Lionel growled, "They're only worried about sending me away." He defiantly crossed his arms. "I'm not going."

"Lionel, you have no choice," Edmund declared. "Any day, you'll be called to London."

Robin took this opportunity to goad Montlhéry. "Sheriff de *Argentan*, are you aware that last month, the Great Council sent half of the ransom to Germany? King Richard will return soon, and I assure you he has not forgotten what happened in Acre."

His eyes narrowing in annoyance, Montlhéry feigned nonchalance as he retorted, "You have no guarantee that Heinrich will release Richard. We all know Germans are barbarians. Besides, travel these days is so dangerous, wouldn't you agree?"

"The German court at Speyer is not a great distance, not like Outremer. I'm confident that Richard will be hale and hearty when he arrives back in England," asserted Robin. "Perhaps you should leave while you can."

Edmund redirected the conversation. "Lionel, you cannot escape this obligation."

Lionel stepped closer to his father and sneered, "Did you even try to help me? No. If you really cared about me, you would've saved me from going to Germany." Gesturing in Robin's direction, he speculated, "After I'm gone, will you name Robin as your heir?"

Edmund sputtered indignantly at Lionel's outrageous accusations.

Robin could not contain his anger. He rudely pointed at Lionel and shouted, "How dare you speak to your father in such a way! He's one of the best men I know. And you won't be in Germany forever. As soon as the remaining ransom is paid, you'll be sent home. Don't you understand that, you ungrateful fool?"

Lionel faced Robin and roared, "You insufferable, pompous arse!" He seized Robin by the front of his tunic, and Robin strove to push him away.

Gisborne and Edmund swiftly intervened to pull them apart.

Montlhéry howled with laughter, proclaiming, "I love family reunions."

Edmund held Robin while Gisborne restrained Lionel.

Lionel resumed his rant. "My own father wouldn't lift a finger to help me. He was perfectly happy to send me away. But Sheriff de Argentan cares about me; he has already arranged for someone else to go in my place."

Edmund released Robin, and they glanced at each other, stunned by this news. They stared at Lionel and the sheriff, speechless and awaiting confirmation of Lionel's assertions.

Gisborne let go of Lionel, who shoved him and jeered, "Never put your hands on me again."

The sheriff revealed, "It's true. Lionel is no longer required to go to Germany as a hostage."

Edmund frowned. "I don't understand; how were you able to change the queen's mind?"

Montlhéry leaned over his desk and retrieved an official document. He handed it to Edmund for his perusal as he explained, "Poor, unfortunate Lord Amery, the Baron of Mountsorrel. He could not pay his taxes because bandits stole his entire fortune. Sadly, I had no choice but to detain him here in the dungeons. He was not fond of life in a jail cell, and he eagerly volunteered to take Lionel's place as a hostage in Germany. After all, an actual baron is more valuable than the heir to a barony."

"This is good news," Edmund acknowledged as he gave the

document back to the sheriff. "Lionel, I didn't want you to go to Germany, but I had no way of preventing it."

Lionel scoffed. "You didn't even try."

"Come home," Edmund requested. "I want to resolve our differences. I'm going to insist that Constance come home as well. We'll be a family again."

Lionel countered, "First of all, I'm not a child—"

Robin muttered under his breath.

Ignoring Robin, Lionel announced, "I've been invited to Paris to serve and advise Prince John."

An alarmed Robin begged, "Lionel, please, don't go to Paris; Richard will return soon, and although he might forgive his brother, he will not forgive John's supporters. You are playing a lethal game of chess where you are merely a pawn."

Lionel glowered at Robin and contended, "You're one to talk. My friends at court tell me that *you* were the pawn in the queen's latest gambit."

Before Robin could respond, Edmund decreed, "Enough arguing. Lionel, I'm asking you again, please come home. We can talk about this more, and I'll listen to everything you want to say. Where is Constance?"

"Gisborne can escort you to Lady Constance," replied the sheriff. "I'm sure he knows where to find her. But Lionel has clearly stated his intention to remain here in Nottingham until I can arrange for his passage to Paris."

Robin and Edmund followed Gisborne as he led them to his chamber.

When they reached the door, Edmund paused and said, "Guy, before we go in, I wanted to thank you for saving Constance's life. Robin told me about the attack at Locksley and your injury. You have my eternal gratitude."

Robin had tried to avoid staring at Gisborne's disfigured hand, but when Edmund raised the subject, his eyes were drawn to it. Only the heel of his palm and his thumb remained, and the edge of his injury was still an angry red. Robin contemplated the bravery required to block a sword with one's hand, so he was surprised when Guy glanced away in what appeared to be embarrassment.

Entering the chamber, they found Constance sitting by the fire and working on a piece of embroidery. Her face lit up at the sight of her father, and she rushed to him, throwing her arms around him and exclaiming, "I'm so glad you came, Father! You must talk to Lionel."

A somber Edmund replied, "We were just talking to him in the sheriff's tower room. Against my wishes, he plans to go to Paris."

Constance's face fell. "He was so outraged about being selected as a hostage that when the sheriff found someone to take his place, I thought he would be pleased, but he's still fuming. He's like a—"

"Child throwing a temper tantrum," Robin interjected.

Guy nodded his agreement.

Sighing, Constance confessed, "I was hoping you could discourage him from going to Paris."

"Constance, he refuses to listen to either me or your father," stated Robin.

"The sheriff has disclosed his true identity to Lionel," Guy reported. "If Lionel goes to Paris, it will be impossible for Montlhéry to maintain the charade that he is Baron de Argentan."

Robin asked, "But what about Prince John? He's in Paris too."

"King Philippe told Prince John the truth about Montlhéry several months ago," divulged Guy.

"Montlhéry's presence in England is an attack on our sovereignty," Robin asserted. "How did Philippe convince John otherwise?"

Guy explained, "Philippe claimed that five years ago he recognized John's innate brilliance, and since it was his dearest wish for John to become king, he sent his most trusted advisor to England to protect and support him."

"Five years ago, Philippe was allied with Richard against King

Henry. What kind of fool would believe such a laughable explanation?" questioned Edmund.

"The sort of fool who desperately wants it to be true," Robin wryly suggested.

Sobering, Robin placed a hand on Edmund's shoulder and reluctantly said, "Lionel is a grown man. Even though he is placing his future and his very life at risk, you cannot stop him. I'm sorry."

Nodding in resignation, Edmund took Constance's hand and implored, "Come home, Constance."

Robin observed Constance's eyes dart to Gisborne, her lips parted in surprise.

She said, "Father, I miss you and Embelton, but I want to stay here."

"No, my dear. There's nothing for you here."

Robin then noticed the way Constance and Guy gazed tenderly at each other.

"Father, please, I want to stay here," she repeated.

His brow creased in confusion, Edmund responded, "But there's no reason for you to stay, and you might be in danger."

A tear rolled down Constance's cheek. "Please don't be cross with me, but I want to stay here with my husband. He will protect me, and...I love him."

30 November 1193, Locksley

Marian watched as Edmund rolled a ball along the floor for Robbie and Jack to chase. Robbie's high-pitched laughter echoed in the great hall of Locksley Manor, and in the distance, she heard a baby wailing.

She hushed them. "Shhh! You just woke Odella's baby."

"I'm sorry, Marian," said Edmund.

An exhausted Elvina rushed into the hall and lured Robbie to the kitchen with an offer of freshly baked biscuits, but only if he would promise to eat them quietly.

Marian proposed, "Elvina, tell Odella that I would be happy to hold little Alina for a while, if it would help her get some rest." Thoughts of the tiny infant girl made her ache for another child of her own.

Edmund wandered over to the hearth and stared intently into the flames. In the fortnight since his arrival, he had been uncharacteristically silent and unwilling to engage in conversation. Playing with Robbie was the only thing that lifted his melancholy.

Marian reminisced about the time she had lived at Embelton, and how Edmund and Constance had become a second family to her. She had never seen him so despondent, and Marian darkly mused that Lionel should be mercilessly tormented for his appalling treatment of his father.

Edmund had been lodging with them at Locksley, hoping that Lionel would either change his mind, or at least come and talk to his father. But Guy had sent word to Robin that Lionel had left for Paris two days ago. And given that Constance had chosen to stay in Nottingham, Edmund planned to go home the next day.

Robin returned from hunting in the woods with a brace of coneys, and after taking them to the kitchen, he joined Edmund and Marian. A short time later, Brother Tuck arrived, and Robin welcomed him.

"We're just about to have a meal," said Robin. "Will you join us?"

"Thank you, Lord Robin, I will gladly accept your kind invitation. But first, the queen directed me to deliver a letter to you." Tuck gave him a sealed dispatch, while Marian and Edmund crowded around, eager to hear the latest news.

Reading by the light of the fire, Robin reported, "Emperor Heinrich has announced that, upon receipt of the final installment of the ransom and the arrival of the hostages, King Richard will be released on the 17th of January."

Everyone cheered.

Robin continued, "The queen is leaving for Germany with the hostages and the remaining ransom on the 20th of December. She has ordered me to take command of the knights who are guarding the ransom during the journey. Hamelin and Archbishop Hubert will stay in England and suppress any resistance that might arise from John's supporters."

"This is a tremendous responsibility she is placing on your shoulders," Edmund observed.

"The queen has great faith in Robin," stressed Tuck.

Robin's expression shifted from enthusiastic to alarmed as he resumed reading the letter.

"What's the matter, Robin?" asked Marian.

"There's more," he replied in a tight voice. "She has declared that Marian will assume the role of her principal lady-in-waiting, as her current ladies are too old to manage such a journey in winter."

"No," Marian emphatically asserted. "I won't do it. Besides, I've never even been to court. What would I know about waiting upon the queen?"

Robin sighed deeply and lowered the message as he gazed at Marian.

"And what about Robbie?" she demanded. "I'm not leaving him again."

"Marian, Queen Eleanor is not *asking* you," Robin explained. "You don't have a choice. I've sworn fealty to Richard, and you are my wife. We have an obligation to serve the royal family, and we can't refuse."

"But, but—" Marian sputtered.

"I'm sorry, my lady," a contrite Tuck apologized. "I think this is my fault. Queen Eleanor has often inquired about your travels to the Holy Land and your adventures leading the outlaws, and she once commented that a fearless, clever girl like you would be quite valuable to her."

Marian briefly glared at Tuck before looking at Robin and requesting, "Can Robbie come with us?"

Robin shook his head. "This will be a dangerous journey, and the queen will require all of your attention. Robbie will have to stay here."

"Please, let me take him to Embelton," Edmund offered, wistfully adding, "I would enjoy spending time with Robbie; otherwise I will be all alone."

11 December 1193, The Tower of London

"All right, I'll admit that I was wrong," Marian announced.

Robin grinned. "With all the noise from the musicians and the throng of people surrounding us, I'm having trouble hearing you. It almost sounded as though you said something about being wrong. That doesn't sound like you," he teased.

She rolled her eyes playfully and laughed.

Robin took her by the hand and led her to the corner of the great hall furthest from the music and dancing that had followed the evening's grand feast. He drew her into his arms and stole a quick kiss.

"Marian, I'm sorry that we can't spend more time together. It never occurred to me we'd be sleeping apart, me in the barracks with the other knights and you with the ladies-in-waiting. Now repeat what you were saying. You're never wrong, so I must have misunderstood you."

She sighed. "I miss you. And I was wrong about something. The other ladies-in-waiting have been very nice to me. No one has made me feel stupid, even though I have a lot to learn about waiting on the queen. The other ladies are much older than me, and many are widows. I've enjoyed their company."

Robin asked, "What about the queen? Has she treated you well?"

"We've been introduced, but I haven't spent any time with her. The other ladies-in-waiting are afraid of her, but I refuse to be intimidated."

"Good for you. She'll have more respect for you if you are self-confident."

"It was good to see your friend, Baldwin de Béthune, again. I fear that my last meeting with him in Acre was under the worst of circumstances. Many of your old crusading companions are here. Are they coming with us to Germany?" Marian inquired.

"Yes," affirmed Robin. "Not only are they my friends, but they are also talented, experienced warriors. We are forming a team of knights that will be invincible against any force we might encounter on our way to Speyer."

"Do you think King Philippe will—" Marian stopped speaking as she looked over Robin's shoulder and saw three drunken men walking towards them. Robin pivoted and stood protectively in front of her.

"Huntingdon!" one of the men slurred. Another man stumbled and nearly fell, but the third man helped steady him.

Robin coolly acknowledged them. "Fithian, Rayner, Felix, you've had enough wine tonight. Go back to the barracks now. There's a training session planned at dawn; everyone's skills must be sharpened before we depart for Germany."

Rayner leered at Marian and suggested, "I know what skills you'll be sharpening tonight."

The other men laughed, and their boorishness incensed Marian.

Felix complained, "Are you planning to bed all the pretty girls here like you did in Poitiers? Don't be so selfish!"

Fithian cried, "Have pity on us poor knights without fancy titles!"

The others roared with laughter, and abruptly Felix leaned in close to Marian, asking, "What's your name, sweetheart?" The strong smell of wine on his breath made Marian's stomach lurch.

Robin roughly pushed him away and snarled, "This is my wife, you crass idiot. I told the three of you to return to the barracks. Do I need to call the guards on duty to escort you?"

Rayner squinted at Marian in confusion. "I thought your wife died. Did you get married again?"

Marian had heard enough. "I'm his wife, and I assure you I'm very much alive. Now leave us alone."

⁓

Robin observed the three men as they stumbled away. It had been a close call. Ever since their arrival in London four days ago, he had realized that Marian would be in the company of many people who knew about his indiscretions in Poitiers. And his other marriage.

"Marian, there's a chamber nearby where we will have more privacy. Come with me; there's something I need to tell you."

She gazed at him, her eyes alight with love and adoration; her expression trusting and unguarded.

Robin's heart, his very soul, was pierced with such an excruciating stab of remorse that he closed his eyes and begged God for help. He recalled Hamelin's advice: the longer he waited to confess the truth, the more difficult it would be. He knew he had already waited too long.

"Robin?"

Her sweet voice sliced through his gloomy musings, and without responding, he took a torch from its bracket on the wall and guided her to a small chamber with a desk and stool that was just off the grand hall. It was used by one of the stewards who kept accounts. He set the torch in the chamber's lone bracket, shut the door, and reluctantly turned to face her.

Her expression had darkened into trepidation. "Is there a problem? I was hoping you were luring me into this room for a kiss." She forced a hollow sounding laugh. "But from that look on your face, I can see that you're upset. Did I do something wrong?"

Robin realized he would rather go back to Jaffa and face a thousand Saracens than disappoint Marian. He replied, "No, Marian. I'm the one who's done something wrong. Please, never forget that you're the only woman I have ever loved, and the only wife I ever wanted at my side."

Robin watched as a flash of understanding lit her eyes. She asked, "Is this about those other women?" Her voice became taut with apprehension. "Are they here in London?"

"I haven't seen any of them here," he responded.

Robin chastised himself for his cowardice. After all, Marian loved him. He loved her. In a torrent of words, he revealed, "But there was one girl, she was a cousin of King Richard. After I had a liaison with her, she complained to Richard that I had stolen her innocence. Then she discovered she was with child. And I had to marry her—"

Marian grabbed the chamber's small desk as if her knees had given way.

"Marian, I swear to God, I didn't know we were married. I just wish you had told me."

In a voice breaking with emotion, she queried, "Where is she? Where is this child?"

"She and the babe both died. She was poisoned, and I believe Montlhéry was to blame because it was an attempt to kill Richard."

Marian stared at him, her eyes wide with shock, and all the color drained from her face. "Who knows about this?"

"Probably everyone here at court. Most of them attended the wedding."

"Wedding?"

He nervously cleared his throat. "Well, yes, we had a formal wedding, and everyone was there."

"By 'everyone,' do you mean—"

"The royal court and various nobility."

"And where was this wedding with all these important people?"

He glanced away, unable to endure the growing resentment in her eyes. "At the cathedral," he mumbled.

"Where?" she demanded. "I couldn't hear you."

"The Cathedral of Saint Peter in Poitiers," he confessed. "King Henry and Queen Eleanor sponsored its construction."

"What was her name?"

Robin inwardly flinched at the hard edge in Marian's voice. He answered, "Blanche de Châteauneuf."

"Robin, you need to make sure that this other marriage is officially annulled. Otherwise, Robbie's legitimacy might be questioned."

"I will try—"

"No, you *will* fix this. Our son will *not* suffer the stigma of illegitimacy."

"After Richard returns, I will ask for his help in sorting this out," promised Robin.

"I told Richard about our clandestine marriage and Robbie's birth after you were wounded in Acre. He never mentioned it to you?"

"I'm afraid not. What did he say to you?"

She grew even more pale, if that was possible. "He asked me to keep it a secret. I assumed that he planned to proclaim Robbie's legitimacy when he returned to England, but now I'm wondering if he was merely placating me."

Robin admitted, "Knowing Richard, that was likely the case."

Glaring at him, Marian insisted, "You must resolve this; not for me, but for Robbie. In the meantime, I have duties to perform for the queen, and you should return to the barracks."

He reached for her, hoping to embrace her, but she swerved around his outstretched arms and pulled open the door, exiting without another word.

Seething with self-loathing and frustration, Robin took the old stool next to the desk and smashed it against the wall again and again, until it was splintered beyond recognition.

CHAPTER 18
DIPLOMACY

6 January 1194, Cologne

Marian patiently stood a short distance behind Queen Eleanor as the grand Feast of the Epiphany was concluding. Eleanor's mood had steadily improved the closer they were to King Richard's location. The taciturn elderly woman whom Marian had met in London was now relaxed and smiling as she traded stories with the Archbishop of Cologne.

Richard's release was only eleven days away, and the huge entourage that accompanied the king's ransom was slowly progressing up the Rhine River, making its way to the imperial court at Speyer.

The more time that Marian spent with the queen, the more she found herself bonding with the often prickly Eleanor. The queen's steadfast devotion to Richard, and her unwavering belief that he was the most talented ruler, the most fearsome warrior, and the most accomplished troubadour in the world, made Marian smile indulgently as she recognized that, even at four years old, Robbie was equally brilliant in her opinion.

But beyond their maternal attachments, there was also a certain fortitude that the two women shared: a resolve to mold events to their own purpose and the stamina to persevere against obstacles.

In those rare moments when she was alone, Marian still resented Eleanor's treatment of Robin and the crown's ransacking of Huntingdon, but the rest of the time, she could put it all behind her and focus on her responsibilities. She took great pride in performing her duties well; she didn't want to give the queen a reason to regret selecting her as a lady-in-waiting.

In the end, Marian was glad that she had been included in the vast retinue of nobles, servants, knights, and soldiers going to Germany, despite the discomforts of traveling in wintry weather and the seasickness that had dogged her since their departure from London. It was truly a once in a lifetime event, and even though they were rarely together, she was heartened by the knowledge that Robin was there too.

Except that she was furious with him, she reminded herself.

Six months ago, he had confessed his indiscretions to her, and although it had been heartbreaking to learn of his exploits, Marian had been pragmatic about it, believing that these past improprieties would not impact their future. But to discover that he hadn't trusted her with the entire story and the complete truth was very dispiriting to Marian.

More significantly, this particular transgression placed Robbie in a precarious position. His future hung in the balance. As a mother, there was nothing more important to her than her son's future, and like Eleanor, she would do anything to protect her dear son.

During the journey from London, she had met many people who had known this other woman and had been at this grand wedding. To them, Marian was just Robin's second wife. Only Eleanor and Robin knew of Robbie's existence.

Scanning the crowd, her heart leapt when she saw Robin approaching the queen, his handsome face smiling warmly at her. She lamented that they couldn't be together because they had other obligations.

Again, she reminded herself that she was mad at him, and she tried to convince herself that they needed this time apart; it would help him appreciate just how angry and hurt she felt.

"Your Grace," Robin briefly knelt. "With your permission, may I borrow my wife from you?"

Marian watched as Eleanor shifted in her chair to glance back at her. Returning her gaze to Robin, Eleanor responded pointedly, "With all the beautiful women here, you want to take my principal lady-in-waiting from me? How terribly inconvenient. Besides, I believe she is unhappy with you."

"My wife is the most beautiful woman here, and if she is unhappy, I beg you to allow me a few moments with her," implored Robin

"Another time," decreed Eleanor. "I'm tired and ready to retire for the evening. Perhaps you can speak to her tomorrow as we travel to Mainz." The queen stood, and Marian offered Robin a wan smile before she pivoted and followed Eleanor out of the grand hall.

❧

Marian built up the fire in Eleanor's chamber and then helped the queen change from her elaborately embroidered silk bliaut into a warm gown and matching robe. As she brushed the queen's long white hair, Marian's mind drifted to thoughts of Robin and how much she missed him.

A question occurred to her, and since Eleanor seemed to be in a good mood, Marian asked, "Your Grace, why did you want me to accompany you?"

"My ladies-in-waiting have grown old. And most of them are as timid as field mice."

The queen's expression grew wistful, and she elaborated, "Many years ago, I had a lady-in-waiting who was witty and intrepid. We had great fun together, but she passed away during the time of my imprisonment. She had willingly remained at my side, but like a caged bird, confinement crushed her spirit and then stole her life."

She shrugged, and Marian knew from the watery shine in Eleanor's eyes that her nonchalance was feigned.

The queen explained, "When Brother Tuck told me stories about you, I was reminded of her."

"Your Grace, at first, I didn't want to come, but now I'm glad to be here with you." Marian set the brush down and prepared to retire to her small cot. When she felt the weight of Eleanor's stare, she turned and gazed expectantly at her.

Grinning, Eleanor demanded, "Why are you angry with your husband? Don't deny it; even after our short acquaintance, I will recognize deceit on your part."

Marian's good humor faded. "I don't want to bother you with such matters, Your Grace."

The gleam in the queen's eyes signaled that there would be no avoiding her question, so Marian sighed and confessed, "Shortly after we arrived in London, he told me about this other woman whom he married when he was already married to me."

"Did he know he was already married to you?"

"No, he didn't realize that canon law—"

"Although clandestine marriages are allowed under canon law," Eleanor acknowledged, "they are not appropriate for the nobility. There is too much at stake in terms of political and dynastic alliances."

"But—"

"The Earldom of Huntingdon is too important to be sullied with this type of dubious union. Therefore, your clandestine marriage will never be deemed valid. Instead, your true wedding will be the ceremony that Richard performed in Acre."

Marian grew increasingly alarmed at Eleanor's adamant condemnation of her first wedding to Robin. Once more, she tried to explain, "But Robin—"

"Your anger at Earl Robin is justified: he's an adulterer and a bigamist. He doesn't deserve your trust or respect," Eleanor stated matter-of-factly.

Marian was horrified, and her temper exploded. "How can you say that about Robin after all he did to secure your son's ransom?" she exclaimed. "If you can believe such things about Robin, then you're a poor judge of character!"

Eleanor replied, "He bedded many women and married another girl, even though he was already married to you. His conduct clearly indicates that my assessment of his character is correct."

"No!" Marian shouted. Then she forced herself to lower her voice for fear that the soldiers outside the door might rush into the chamber. "Robin is the most courageous, honest, self-sacrificing person I've ever known. He cares about other people, regardless of their rank. He deserves nothing but respect. Besides, he didn't know about our clandestine marriage."

"Has he been faithful to you since his return?" Eleanor asked.

"Of course, he has. He's a loving husband and a wonderful father."

To Marian's consternation, Eleanor laughed at her.

When the older woman regained her composure, she observed, "You say he's faithful to you. You trust and respect him. I must conclude that you are upset because your pride is injured. That's *your* problem, not his."

Marian froze in shock. On this day, the Feast of the Epiphany, Marian experienced her own sudden enlightenment. Of course, the queen was right.

Not ready to surrender, Marian countered, "What about my son? His legitimacy will be questioned unless this other marriage is annulled."

"That is a problem," Eleanor conceded. "I doubt he will ever be considered legitimate."

"Robin and this other girl were only married a few months,"

Marian declared. "What harm would there be in annulling a marriage that wasn't lawful to begin with?"

"There is much you do not understand. First, Richard's alliance with the de Châteauneuf family will be crucial during the coming war with Philippe. And even though I thought Blanche was an insipid girl, her family cherished her and rejoiced in her fortuitous marriage to an earl of the realm. The inscription on her crypt in the family's mausoleum reads *la Comtesse de Huntingdon*."

Marian's heart sank to hear of the political ramifications of Robin's marriage, but then her conscience was pierced by the recognition that Blanche had been a real person, and her family must have been devastated by the sudden death of both her and the babe she had been carrying. For the first time, Marian realized that Robin must have also mourned the loss of his child.

Surprisingly, Eleanor addressed her in a personal manner. "Marian, you can't solve this problem. It's a bitter pill to swallow, but as a woman, you have no standing in this dilemma. Do you trust Robin to petition Richard fervently on Robbie's behalf?"

"I do."

"Then let it go. It's out of your hands. Over the years, I have lost many loved ones, including two sons who died unexpectedly as young men in the prime of their lives. Don't waste precious time by punishing your husband with petty grievances, especially now. Have you told him yet?"

Marian's brow creased in confusion. "Your Grace, I don't understand. To what are you referring?"

Eleanor gestured at Marian's midsection. "That you're expecting another child."

At Marian's open-mouthed surprise, Eleanor asked, "You didn't know? Considering your previous travels to the Holy Land and back, I would have thought that you knew all about seasickness. It doesn't persist after you leave the ship for dry ground." The queen chuckled at her own wit.

17 January 1194, The Imperial Court at Speyer

Robin stood with Eleanor, Archbishop Walter de Coutances, and a handful of men who were the highest ranking members of the queen's retinue. His role was to wait until Richard appeared, and the moment the king was released into his mother's custody, Robin would exit the hall and make the final arrangements for the hostages and the chests of silver to be transferred to agents of Emperor Heinrich.

He glanced over his shoulder, searching for Marian. When their eyes met, he grinned at her and winked. He was heartened to see her smile back at him with genuine affection; the iciness he had endured since his confession to her in London was thawing, and he was immensely relieved.

It was made all the better by the news that, by late summer, there would be a new addition to their family.

A group of men entered the hall, and Robin focused on a stately older man, guessing that he was Heinrich. To his surprise, everyone in the entourage genuflected to Queen Eleanor except for a man who was Robin's age. He bowed.

Realizing that this young man was the Holy Roman Emperor, Robin joined the rest of the queen's men as they respectfully dropped to one knee and rose.

King Richard was not with the emperor.

Robin observed that Heinrich was nervous, even agitated, and his eyes kept shifting around, as if he could not look Eleanor in the eye.

Eleanor's voice was strong, but a distinct quaver of uncertainty could be heard as she demanded, "Where is my son? I will not release the ransom or hostages unless Richard is brought to me."

"Ransom?" questioned Heinrich. "You mean the dowry for your granddaughter to marry Duke Leopold's son?" He chuckled feebly, as though he were attempting to engage in light-hearted banter with an old friend.

Eleanor was having none of it. She glared at him, and the other man squirmed under the intensity of her scrutiny.

Heinrich cleared his throat. "Something unexpected has happened—"

"Bring Richard to me at once." A strong shading of panic colored Eleanor's heated response, and Robin despaired that Richard might be ill, or worse.

Holding his hand out to an attendant, Heinrich was given a rolled parchment. He still could not meet Eleanor's steely gaze as he passed it to her.

She snatched it from him and read silently.

An alarmed Robin watched as the queen blanched. She then handed it to Archbishop Walter, who had a similar reaction.

Heinrich announced, "King Philippe and Prince John have made intriguing counter-offers for custody of King Richard." Heinrich's eyes continued to dart from person to person while avoiding Eleanor. He explained, "I must evaluate these other offers. I have a duty to my people to make wise decisions. I'm sure you understand such responsibilities."

Eleanor frostily replied, "You have a duty to keep your word. My son negotiated with you in good faith to set the terms of his release. His people have met those terms. Would you auction a Crusader-King to the highest bidder?"

"I need time to review the situation and discuss it with my fellow German princes," Heinrich declared. "I'm preparing to move my court to Mainz, and we will resolve the matter there as we celebrate Candlemas in sixteen days."

Heinrich bowed again, and then he pivoted and abruptly departed.

Archbishop Walter gave Robin the parchment, and he scanned it, his heart sinking when he realized the quandary they were facing.

King Philippe and Prince John had offered to match the 100,000 marks raised by Richard's subjects if Heinrich would transfer custody of Richard to Philippe. They also outlined two alternatives:

80,000 marks to keep Richard in prison until the 30th of September, or 1,000 marks for each month that Heinrich kept him captive.

Robin pondered John's treachery, and under his breath, he muttered, "See how much John loves him; he has carefully calculated Richard's value."

4 February 1194, The Imperial Court at Mainz

It was early in the morning, and a queasy Marian listened as Robin and his friend, Baldwin de Béthune, lamented the news from Paris. Prince John had signed a treaty with Philippe that gave the French king huge swaths of territory and dozens of fortresses.

"But is this treaty legal?" questioned Baldwin. "John is not Duke of Normandy, so how can he forfeit all of Normandy east of the Seine River to Philippe?"

"John has also surrendered all the key castles in the County of Touraine," Robin added. "This treaty is not only illegal, it's treasonous."

They were outside the entrance to the imperial keep, awaiting Richard's release, and Marian reflected on the preceding two days. The emotional ups and downs had been difficult for Eleanor, and Marian had striven to offer whatever support she could, whether it was insisting that the queen eat a meal to sustain her strength or listening attentively as Eleanor ranted about the injustice of it all.

After their arrival in Mainz for the Feast of Candlemas, Eleanor had finally been reunited with her beloved son. Their tearful meeting had been brief, and then Richard had been compelled to testify before the court of the emperor and the German princes.

Standing behind Eleanor, Marian had not understood what was happening, because the proceedings were conducted in a language foreign to her. But when everyone paused for a short respite, Robin had described how Richard was defending himself, just as he had been forced to do the previous Easter. The difference was that, over the past ten months, Richard had shrewdly established alliances with many of the German princes.

During a recess in the middle of the second day, she had asked Robin if Heinrich's dour expression was a good sign. Grinning, Robin praised her astute assessment. He explained how the bishops and princes of the empire had rebuked Heinrich for attempting to renege on his earlier agreement with Richard. To Marian's relief, Robin had disclosed that, despite Heinrich's desire to sell Richard to the highest bidder, he would not be allowed to do it.

Instead, the emperor decided to use Philippe's proposal to extort additional concessions from Richard. And so it was that, at the end of the second day, Heinrich had demanded that Richard surrender England to him. Richard would become Heinrich's vassal, and for an annual tribute of 5,000 pounds, England would be returned to Richard as a fief of the Holy Roman Empire.

At that point, Richard's supporters had stormed out of the negotiations and gathered in a separate chamber to discuss their options. Robin and the other men were enraged, and some called for a declaration of war against the Holy Roman Empire. But Marian would never forget Eleanor's cool-headed response. She had calmed the men, telling them that this was an illegal and immoral demand, and it should be treated with the all the respect such a ludicrous ultimatum deserved.

The queen reminded everyone that nothing was more important than liberating her son and leaving as soon as possible. She sent a message to Richard, instructing him to accept Heinrich's terms. Eleanor then ordered everyone to suppress the news of this latest indignity from the people of England.

Richard's release was scheduled for mid-morning, and Marian realized he would appear at any moment. It was also time for Baldwin to join the other hostages. He briefly embraced Robin and bowed to Marian as he bid them farewell. As one of Richard's most loyal men, he had not only donated generously to the Exchequer of Ransom, but he had also volunteered to be a hostage.

Marian asked, "How long will you have to stay here?"

Baldwin replied, "I don't know. But I have faith that God will provide the means for Richard to redeem us soon. Tell the king that I wish him Godspeed."

❧

Marian was waiting with Robin at the foot of a wide stairway that rose to the massive double doors of the imperial keep. It seemed to her that the world was holding its breath; all sounds died away, and a hush descended.

Then the doors began to move as two servants pushed them open. From the shadowed interior, King Richard stepped forward, his euphoric mother at his side.

After the royals completed their descent from the keep's grand entrance, all the men went down on one knee while Marian curtsied.

When Robin rose, Richard smiled fondly at him and said, "Robin, it's good to see you again."

His gaze swung to her. Marian had forgotten just how tall the king was; he towered over everyone else. "Countess Marian! This is an unexpected pleasure."

Marian mumbled a polite reply, but Richard had already shifted his attention back to Robin.

"We must leave at once," the king proclaimed.

The four of them mounted their horses, and a small retinue of guards surrounded them. They hurriedly exited the castle's bailey and rode towards the English encampment on the banks of the Rhine where their ships were anchored.

Upon their return, Eleanor retired to her cabin while Richard took Robin aside. Marian paused to observe Robin's interactions with the king. They were clearly at ease with each other, and Robin was listening raptly as he nodded.

As she turned to walk away, Robin jogged over to her. "Marian, the king has a plan. I need you to pack warm, comfortable clothing for the queen and yourself. Only bring what will fit into your saddlebags. Do it quickly."

"Where are we going? What is happening?" Marian inquired.

"We're going to travel fast and light to Cologne, while the rest of the queen's entourage follows. From Cologne, the three of us will accompany Richard as he conducts reconnaissance along the Flemish coast, hoping to determine Philippe's naval strength."

"I'm confused; why are we traveling separately to Cologne?"

"Richard is convinced that Heinrich will change his mind and send his men-at-arms to recapture him. We've no time to lose. Hurry."

Marian nodded, but then she questioned, "Does he expect his elderly mother to join him on this mission?"

Robin chuckled. "I asked him about that. He said he's already discussed it with her, and there is no force on earth that could keep her from his side after all the time they've been apart. I think it will be challenging for her, but with your help, she'll be all right."

Marian beamed at the compliment, and then she hurried to Eleanor's cabin, where she found that the queen was packed and ready to go.

23 March 1194, Nottingham Castle

Edmund impatiently observed Earl Hamelin as the other man squinted at the latest message from King Richard.

Shouting in the distance distracted him, and he surveyed the large force of men-at-arms that surrounded the fortress of Nottingham on three sides. The fourth side was a precipice where a row of brew houses sat nestled between the foot of the cliffs and the castle's moat.

It was the fifth week of the siege of Nottingham, led by Earl

Hamelin, along with the Earls of Chester and Derby. The previous day, they had received word that Tickhill Castle had surrendered to Hugh de Puiset, Bishop of Durham, and Edmund was anxious to hear the news from the king.

Hamelin revealed, "King Richard has left London and is traveling north. According to the itinerary in this dispatch, he expects to be in Huntingdon by the 23rd—"

"That's today," Edmund interrupted. "When will he arrive here? And does it say whether Robin and Marian are still with the king and his mother?"

A shadow of irritation darkened Hamelin's face, and Edmund apologized. "Forgive me, my lord. I'm sick with worry about my daughter. She's been trapped in the castle for the entire siege."

His expression softening with understanding, Hamelin explained, "The letter says that Robin and Marian are still with Richard and Eleanor. They should arrive here in two days."

Edmund asked, "Does it say anything else?"

"Richard is eager to take Montlhéry prisoner. He's heard the accusations from Robin that Montlhéry murdered two of his brothers and his father."

"Have you considered my offer?" inquired Edmund hopefully.

"I've discussed it with the other earls. We think it would be beneficial to get someone inside the castle under the pretext of negotiating a possible surrender. You could evaluate their current strength. Perhaps you can convince Montlhéry to release your daughter as a gesture of good will."

"Thank you," replied a relieved Edmund. "At Christmastide, she sent word to me that she is expecting a babe. I must rescue her and get her to a safe place."

Hamelin gazed intently at him, declaring, "There's no guarantee of your safety. You might be killed, or Montlhéry might take you hostage. Do you understand the risks you're facing?"

"I would take any risk to save my daughter and future grand-child," vowed Edmund.

Nodding, Hamelin responded, "I've four daughters myself. I would do the same. I've already notified the sentries at the gate, and Montlhéry has agreed to allow you into the fortress. However, you must go unarmed."

"Is there anything you want me to say to Montlhéry?"

"If he's guilty of these crimes against the royal family, then we're under no obligation to treat him fairly. Feel free to mislead him. Offer him safe passage to France. You're not representing the crown or speaking for Richard. I just wish I could go in there and get my hands on him for killing my brother and nephews."

Edmund paused at the stairs leading to the keep's main entrance. One of the double doors opened, and he saw Gisborne. Hurriedly mounting the stairs, he was breathless when he reached him. "Constance?" he panted. "Where is she? Is she all right?"

"Montlhéry requested that I escort you to his tower room; Constance is there waiting for you. She claims to be all right, but we must get her out of the fortress."

"That's my intention. Do you have any suggestions for me? How can I convince him to release her?"

Sighing deeply, Guy admitted, "I fear Montlhéry is descending into madness. You will see. Is there any word of the king?"

"He will be here in two days. Robin and Marian are with him."

"Montlhéry is telling everyone that it's John who is marching to Nottingham, and that the forces outside the gates will surrender to him because Richard is dead."

"And the men believe this?" asked an incredulous Edmund.

"Some do, and others are desperately hoping it's true."

As they walked towards the stairs to the sheriff's tower, Guy lowered his voice and said, "We won't be able to talk like this again, but you must tell Earl Hamelin to post men at the foot of the cliffs, near the brew houses."

"I don't understand."

"I don't have time to explain; just tell him to post men on that side of the fortress too."

When they arrived at the winding staircase, Edmund observed that Guy's left hand was gloved. He pointed at it and remarked, "I've never seen such a glove."

Gisborne disclosed, "I recently celebrated the anniversary of my birth, and Constance sewed this glove for me as a gift. Inside there is a wooden insert shaped like the part of my hand and fingers that are missing. Of course, I can't move them, but it gives my hand a more natural appearance. Your daughter has a kind heart; she noticed that I was unhappy when people gawked at my hand."

"Is she still expecting a babe? Is she in good health?"

"She tells me that the babe will be born in July. Edmund, I know that King Richard will prevail, and then I will be executed alongside Montlhéry. Promise me that you will be a father to my child."

Edmund swallowed in an attempt to contain his emotions. He put his hand on Guy's shoulder and solemnly gave his word.

Upon reaching Montlhéry's tower room, the first thing that Edmund saw was the desk. It was bare, and the stacks of papers and parchments that had been strewn across it were gone. Montlhéry sat in his throne-like chair and sullenly stared at him. He made no effort to greet his guest properly.

Constance sprinted to him, throwing her arms around his neck and weeping with joy. Edmund could feel her rounded abdomen, and his protective instincts rose. He silently vowed to do anything to rescue her and his grandchild.

"Baron Embelton, to what do we owe the pleasure of your visit?" Montlhéry calmly inquired.

Edmund hugged Constance, and then he encouraged her

to stand with Gisborne. He declared, "Count de Montlhéry, we meet again."

Montlhéry's brow arched in surprise, but he said nothing in response.

Edmund continued, "We have learned your true identity. You are no longer Sheriff of Nottingham, and the Barony of Argentan has been seized by the crown as well."

Pointedly ignoring Edmund's pronouncements, Montlhéry asked, "Tell me, Lord Edmund, is Hamelin commanding the siege of my castle? Has he brought a great force of men from Conisbrough? Is his son also here?"

Taken aback by these unexpected questions, Edmund answered honestly. "Yes, Earl Hamelin is directing the siege, and his son is with him along with the full might of Conisbrough. I recommend you surrender now."

"And what is he offering me if I surrender? A quick trial? A painless death?"

"King Richard is planning to take you hostage and give King Philippe the opportunity to ransom you," Edmund lied.

"My lord," interjected Guy, "that is a generous offer. I'm certain that King Philippe will pay a ransom for you."

Montlhéry scoffed darkly.

Edmund suggested, "If you release my daughter, it will be seen as a gesture of good will. I'm begging you, please, let her go."

"Are you willing to take her place?" proposed Montlhéry.

"Yes," Edmund replied at once.

"No!" cried Constance.

"Constance, please, let me handle this," admonished Edmund.

Montlhéry rose from his throne and walked around his desk. He announced, "I will give your offer all the careful consideration that it deserves. First, you will hand over that bag of coins tied to your belt. Give it to Gisborne."

A surprised Edmund obeyed.

"Guards!" Montlhéry shouted, and two men-at-arms entered from the antechamber.

"Take Baron Embelton to our most comfortable cell in the dungeons—"

"No!" chorused Guy and Constance.

"Quiet!" ordered Montlhéry. "Nothing will happen to him there. I merely want time to consider the generous offer he has brought me from my dear old friend, Hamelin."

"How do you know Earl Hamelin?" inquired Edmund.

"Oh, we've known each other for many years," Montlhéry enigmatically alleged.

Edmund gazed at Constance and said, "It's all right; I can spend the night in a cell." Turning once more to Montlhéry, he implored, "Do you promise to decide by tomorrow morning?"

Montlhéry nodded, and then the two guards led Edmund away.

After Edmund had been escorted down the tower's stairway, Montlhéry stated, "Well, Gisborne, it's time."

"Time for what, my lord?"

"Time to leave Nottingham. It's a new moon, and as soon as darkness has blanketed the land, we will go through the tunnel and make our escape."

"And will you allow Constance to stay here with her father?" asked a hopeful Guy.

"Heavens, no. I would miss her terribly," Montlhéry sarcastically professed. "I insist that she join us for the little adventure I have planned."

⁂

With every twig snap and equine grunt, Guy's heart stuttered in alarm. He was creeping away from the camp of the soldiers besieging Nottingham Castle with three stolen horses. It was a new moon, and the only lights were the campfires behind him and the distant stars above the mostly bare trees.

He had methodically taken one horse at a time and tied it to a nearby tree. After he had secured three horses, he located the piles of tack and pilfered several saddles and bridles. To his relief, no one was guarding the horses; the men-at-arms from Conisbrough apparently did not consider the possibility of someone approaching their camp from the forest. Or the possibility that someone might steal a few of their horses. With so many men and horses, Guy was convinced that they would not even notice they were missing for several days.

When he could no longer see light from the camp, and it became too dark to continue, he took his flint from the pouch attached to his belt and lit a small torch. He guessed it was at least midnight, and he said a silent prayer that any guards on duty were facing the castle and not the forest.

Soon he was back in the clearing where Montlhéry was waiting with Constance. He was both incensed and terrified by what he saw: Montlhéry had bound Constance's hands in front of her. He had a noose around her neck, and his dagger was aimed at the child inside of Constance's belly. Guy's eyes narrowed. This was *his* wife, *his* child, and he had to protect them from Montlhéry.

As usual, Montlhéry had an uncanny way of reading his mind. "Settle yourself, Gisborne. As long as you do exactly as I tell you, no one will get hurt."

"Why not release her now? I will do whatever you want, but only if you let her go," he proposed.

Montlhéry laughed at him. "You will put your sword and your dagger on the ground. Help her get onto a horse and then hold your hands in front of you."

Constance struggled to mount her horse; it was taller than the palfreys she was accustomed to riding, so Guy boosted her into the saddle. He reached up to pull the noose off of her neck, but feeling the point of the other man's dagger in his back, he sighed and turned, offering his wrists to be secured. Next, Montlhéry instructed Guy to mount his horse.

After picking up Guy's sword and dagger, Montlhéry slid them into a scabbard hanging from Constance's saddle, and then mounted the third horse, drawing alongside Constance and grabbing the end of the rope. It was about ten feet long, and it looked like a deadly leash around his wife's neck. He burned in anger, but he was also profoundly frustrated as he was bound, unarmed, and too far from Montlhéry to attack him without endangering Constance.

"How are we going to avoid the soldiers surrounding the castle?" questioned Guy. "How will we cross the Channel? Which port?"

"So many questions," lamented Montlhéry. "We are heading north, so the soldiers are irrelevant to us. You will ride in front, and I will follow, helping your dear wife."

To Guy's horror, Montlhéry leaned towards Constance and tightened the noose. She whimpered, either in fear or discomfort.

"If you do anything to thwart my plan, I will have to gallop away while dragging your wife by her neck. Just pulling her off her horse would probably kill her. Wouldn't you agree, Gisborne?"

CHAPTER 19
THE RETURN OF THE KING

25 March 1194, Nottingham Castle

obin stood with King Richard outside the gates of Nottingham Castle as Earl Hamelin apprised them of the state of the siege.

"We arrived here nearly six weeks ago. Two days ago, Baron Embelton entered the fortress to negotiate his daughter's freedom. I'm sorry to report he's still in there, and we can only assume he has either been detained as a hostage or killed."

Robin grimly accepted the difficult news. "Have you received any word from inside the castle?" he inquired.

"We've had no contact with Montlhéry. That's one reason we allowed Edmund to venture inside the fortress. There are rumors that Montlhéry has convinced his men that Richard is dead, and that John will be crowned soon."

The king barked a short laugh and ordered the trumpeters to herald his arrival, stipulating, "Tell them to blow their horns so loud that Montlhéry will hear them in his tower."

The noise of the trumpets was deafening, and when they quieted, Hamelin invited Richard and Robin to his tent, where he showed them a sketch of the fortress and the positions of his soldiers.

Staring at the rough drawing, Robin's heart dropped. He looked a second time.

Hamelin reported, "I've brought my entire force of arms from Conisbrough—"

"How many men are stationed opposite the cliffs?" Robin urgently interrupted.

Gazing at him curiously, Hamelin replied, "Strategically, we can't mount an assault from the base of the cliffs, and the defenders cannot descend the precipice at night, so I have a few men posted where we can watch that area during the day."

"Are you saying that no one is watching this side of the castle at night?" a dismayed Robin questioned.

"Tell me, Robin," insisted the king. "What's wrong?"

"Sire, I hate to tell you this, but it's likely that Montlhéry has already escaped the siege. Uncle Edmund wasn't here during the summer; he wouldn't have known."

"Known what?" Richard demanded.

"About the tunnel. Montlhéry dug a tunnel extending from the keep's kitchens to a brew house at the base of the cliff."

"Merde!" exclaimed Hamelin.

Richard strode out of the tent to a location that afforded a better view of the brew houses in the distance. He asked, "Can we use the tunnel to mount a surprise attack?"

"The other end of the tunnel is inside a locked pantry. I doubt our men could break through a sturdy locked door without losing the element of surprise," Robin explained.

Richard paused to think. With resolve, he commanded, "We don't need to use the tunnel; it's unnecessarily dangerous. I can take this castle without such measures. But I don't want anyone escaping through this tunnel—especially not Montlhéry. Robin, burn the brew houses. Hamelin, post men opposite the cliffs day and night."

Just as Richard pivoted to return to Hamelin's tent, arrows

fatally struck two soldiers standing near him, and the king's anger exploded. "Hamelin, we're attacking, *now*."

"But Richard," sputtered Hamelin, "there's only a few hours of daylight remaining."

The king marched away, calling for his armor.

Robin remarked, "There's plenty of time for Richard to let the men inside the fortress know that the king has returned." He then summoned several of the king's finest archers, and grabbing a torch, he led them to a spot where they could release flaming arrows at the brew houses.

∽

The sun had set, but the fires in the outer bailey of Nottingham Castle were still blazing.

Richard's late afternoon assault had been so unexpected and ferocious that he had promptly taken the outer bailey and its barbican. The castle's garrison had retreated into the inner bailey, and they had released flaming arrows into the buildings of the outer bailey in a desperate ploy to slow Richard's advance.

The king had halted the attack for the night, and he had sent additional men to monitor the smoldering remains of the brew houses. The alcohol soaked buildings had ignited with mighty whooshes that quickly consumed the simple structures. It would be at least a day before anyone could exit the tunnel through the hot ash.

Although he was heartened by the king's initial success in attacking Nottingham, Robin could not help but fret that it was too late. The siege had begun in the middle of February, and Montlhéry could have left through the tunnel at any time; after all, that had been its purpose. His mind continued to dwell on Edmund and Constance. Were they prisoners in the castle? Were they still alive? And what of Gisborne?

Filled with nervous energy, sleep eluded Robin that night.

26 March 1194, South of Conisbrough

It was early morning, and Constance held her hands out in front of her as Montlhéry untied the rope looped around her wrists and tethered to a low branch extending from the tree behind her. He instructed her to attend to her needs quickly.

She stood and stretched, hoping to ease the ache in her back from sleeping on the ground. When she took a step, she grimaced from the sore muscles in her legs. Montlhéry had forced her to ride for almost two days as they traveled north from Nottingham.

When she returned, she surveyed the clearing where they had made camp the previous afternoon. On one side, it was bordered by a swollen, swiftly moving stream, and on the other side, there was a copse of trees separating it from the road.

Cold, hungry, and sick with worry about her father, she walked to their dying campfire and extended her arms, holding her palms towards the glowing embers. Suddenly, her baby kicked, and she placed her hands protectively on her rounded abdomen. She turned to look at Guy, wishing to share the moment with him, but he was staring off into the distance, lost in his thoughts. She hoped he was formulating a plan to escape, but Montlhéry had confiscated Guy's sword, and whenever they were not riding, Guy was bound at his wrists and ankles.

Montlhéry approached and insisted that she return to the tree near the stream. Again, he tied her wrists. She wanted to weep, but she didn't want to give him the satisfaction of seeing that she was distraught. She silently observed as the former sheriff took his saddlebag and strolled into the forest.

In a low voice, Guy asked, "Are you all right?"

Constance whispered, "Yes; do you know where we are going?"

In an equally hushed voice, he responded, "I think we're going to Conisbrough. We're only a few miles from there; this is the northern edge of Sherwood Forest."

"Guy, what will you do if he opens one of those bags from the tunnel? Didn't Brother Tuck replace all the silver in those bags with small stones?" She eyed the two leather pouches resting on the ground near Montlhéry's saddle.

"It's a miracle that he hasn't bothered to look into those bags. Fortunately, he's been spending the silver that he took from your father. But once that's gone…"

Constance shivered in fear as she finished his sentence. "Then he'll realize that you betrayed him. What is he planning to do with the silver that he thinks is in the tunnel?"

Guy divulged, "He said something about returning for the rest of the silver later."

At that moment, Montlhéry entered the clearing, and his voice interrupted their quiet conversation. "Gisborne, it's time for you to carry out the next part of my plan."

Constance gaped at Montlhéry in disbelief. In all the time she had known him, he had always worn somber, black clothing. But now he was dressed in an expensive red silk bliaut with gold embroidery. She glanced at Guy, who also seemed to be stunned by the change in the other man's appearance.

Montlhéry untied Guy and, pressing a sword against his chest, he commanded, "Gisborne, come with me, and I'll explain what will happen next. If you have not returned by sunset, then I'll kill your wife. Do you understand?"

This threat did not surprise Constance. She bravely met Guy's concerned gaze and nodded encouragingly at him.

The two men walked over to the horses, and she could see them talking, although she couldn't hear what they were saying.

She watched as Guy readied all their horses, and he hung the rock-filled bags on either side of Montlhéry's saddle. A short time later, Guy mounted his horse and left.

Constance startled awake. Exhausted by their frantic flight from Nottingham, she had fallen asleep while waiting for Guy to return. Striving to sit up, she moved closer to the tree behind her, hoping to lean against it. The trees were mostly bare as spring had only just arrived, and she glanced up at the sky, guessing that it was nearly noon.

Montlhéry was standing a short distance away, intently watching the path that led to the road.

She was growing drowsy again when she heard voices. As Montlhéry retreated into the shadows of the trees, she saw Guy and Countess Isabel walking into the clearing and leading their horses.

The moment Isabel spotted Constance, she dropped the reins of her horse and ran to her, crying, "What has happened? Where is Hamelin?" Isabel fell to her knees and tried to untie the rope encircling Constance's wrists.

A perplexed Constance replied, "My lady, Earl Hamelin isn't here."

"But Sir Guy told me he was injured, and that you were attending to him."

Before Constance could respond, Guy approached Isabel and apologetically insisted, "Please, my lady, you must do as I ask, or Constance will be killed."

She stood and faced Guy, her brow creased in confusion. "What?"

"Hold out your hands," he instructed.

Increasingly alarmed, Isabel obeyed, and he gently bound her wrists. He implored, "Forgive me, but I must do this."

"Why?" she asked in a whisper of despair.

Guy removed her wimple and used it as a blindfold.

He then sat next to Constance, and she recognized that he was following a series of carefully orchestrated steps.

Montlhéry reappeared, and he hastily tied Guy's hands behind his back and knotted a rope around his ankles.

Isabel demanded, "Sir Guy, what is happening? You said my husband was here waiting for me, and that he needed me. Are you kidnapping me for ransom?"

Guy replied, "No, my lady—"

"Quiet," growled Montlhéry.

Isabel stilled. "Is someone else here?"

Montlhéry drew near to Isabel and untied her. With trembling hands, she pulled off her blindfold and let it fall to the ground. Staring at Montlhéry, all the color drained from her face.

"No, it can't be you," she breathed.

"Yes, my dear," he answered. "Tell Gisborne and his wife who I am."

"I don't understand," she admitted.

To Constance's amazement, Isabel reached out and tenderly caressed the side of Montlhéry's face.

Montlhéry grinned and announced, "Just like Robin Hood, I'm back from the dead. But you haven't told them my real name."

Isabel seemed unable to tear her gaze away from him. Still staring into his eyes, she revealed, "You are my husband, William of Blois."

Guy and Constance glanced at each other in shock.

William proclaimed, "I am the true King of England, and I've returned to claim my throne. You are my queen, and together we will rule. I want you at my side again."

Isabel's gaze fell, and her hand slid from his face to cradle his hand. She marveled, "You still have the ring that belonged to William the Conqueror."

Constance craned her neck to get a better look.

William remarked, "My father always told me that this ring was the key to the kingdom, the talisman of the Conqueror. Only the rightful King of England and Duke of Normandy would possess it. So, of course, I've kept it all these years."

"But, William, why didn't you tell me you were alive?"

He frowned. "Duncan Fitzooth foiled my plan to take the throne during the siege of Toulouse, and I had to go into hiding. I had neither the money nor the means to send you a message. When my cousin Adele was crowned Queen of France, I became her advisor. And then I received word that you had betrayed me by marrying the brother of my worst enemy. I'm very disappointed in you, Isabel."

"Oh!" she exclaimed. "This means that my marriage is unlawful and my children are—"

"Bastards," suggested William. "As king, I will not punish your children for the sins of their father, and I'm willing to forgive you, if you disavow them. As for Hamelin, I promise that he will suffer before I execute him for the crime of putting his hands on you."

If possible, Isabel became even more pale. "William, no!" Tears rolled down her cheeks, "Please, don't hurt Hamelin. If you spare him, I will do whatever you ask. Please," she begged, "we've been together for thirty years, and...and I love him!"

At that moment, Constance noticed that Guy was frantically pulling against his bindings.

In a low voice, he muttered, "If she doesn't stop talking like that, he'll kill her."

Constance looked back at the other two, and she could tell that whatever warmth Montlhéry, or rather, William had been exhibiting towards Isabel was rapidly turning to ice.

He grabbed Isabel by her shoulders and shook her. "You belong to me. You will only love me. Do you understand?"

Isabel was weeping and shaking her head.

Returning her attention to Guy, Constance watched him struggling to free himself. It was then that she realized something. "Guy!" she urgently hissed. "Take off your glove."

To her relief, he must have heard her because she could see his intact hand tugging at the ties that secured the glove she had fashioned for him.

Her gaze shifted to Isabel, and to her horror, William was choking her and snarling, "I thought you were different—that you had been forced to marry that bastard! You don't deserve to be my queen."

Isabel was clawing at his forearms, trying to pull his hands away from her neck, but her movements were growing feeble.

Constance tried to distract him by shouting, "Montlhéry! I mean, King William! The people will never forgive you if you kill their queen!"

Again she looked back at Guy to see that he had removed his glove. Since his disfigured hand was much smaller than the other, he was able to slip his hands out of his bindings. He quickly started pulling on the rope around his ankles, but he was hindered by his missing fingers.

"Take off your boots!" Constance ordered, and he complied, freeing his feet.

Guy rushed forward and trapped William's neck in the crook of one arm while wrapping his other arm around the older man's waist. He roared, "Let her go!"

William released his grip on Isabel, and she slumped to the ground. He then thrust his elbow into Guy's stomach and stomped on his bare foot, causing Gisborne to lose his grip and stumble backwards. William pivoted, and he shoved Guy with all his strength.

Guy was unarmed, and William drew his sword and advanced towards him. Backing away, Guy misjudged the distance to the stream behind him, and his bare feet slipped on the muddy embankment. He teetered on the edge for a moment, his arms flailing in an attempt to regain his balance, but in the end, he tumbled into the swiftly moving water.

To Constance's horror, William returned to Isabel and raised his sword over her unconscious form. But then his face softened, and he hesitated. Sheathing his weapon, William picked her up, carried her to the stream, and tossed her into it.

Guy had just crawled out of the water, and he yelled, "No!" when he saw what the other man had done.

William sneered, "Gisborne, come with me now, and I will give you a lofty title, power, and wealth. Or stay here and face Richard's wrath."

Without hesitating, Guy dove back into the water to rescue Isabel.

Constance's heart was beating so hard in her chest that it was painful; she felt dizzy and feared she would faint. William sauntered over to her, cut the rope that tethered her to the limb above her, and dragged her to the edge of the stream as she writhed and twisted in his grasp. She remembered what he had done to Guy, and she mimicked the move by driving her elbow into his stomach. He merely grunted before throwing her into the frigid water.

It was so cold that she gasped, and her mouth was flooded. Lifting her face from the surface, she spit out the water and gulped for air. The stream's relentless current pushed against her. She managed to stand briefly until the force of the water knocked her off her feet. With her hands bound in front of her, she couldn't find her balance, and she tried to swim to the embankment before she was swept downstream.

Just then, she felt someone lifting her from the water and carrying her to the shore. Sputtering and coughing, she recognized the strength of Guy's arms. He placed her next to Isabel, who was as white as death and as still as a corpse as she lay on the ground.

Constance searched her mind, desperate to help Isabel, and she remembered something that her mother had told her many years ago.

Panting and wheezing, she said, "Turn her on her side, and thump her on her back between her shoulders."

Guy promptly followed her instructions. Nothing happened. He struck her again. Suddenly, Isabel began to retch and water spewed from her mouth, as some color returned to her face.

❧

Guy had built up the fire to provide warmth and dry their clothes.

Montlhéry, or rather, William, had left, taking all their supplies and the bags that he thought contained silver coins.

Guy suggested, "My lady, I will take you back to Conisbrough. I'm sorry for lying to you, but he threatened to murder Constance if I didn't bring you to him."

"I want to go to Nottingham," Isabel grimly insisted. "Take me to Hamelin, now."

"But it's past noon, and Nottingham is at least a day and a half ride," Constance interjected.

"I don't care," Isabel declared. "I want Hamelin. The moon is waxing, and the sky is clear. We will ride as far as we can today, and then we will stop for the night."

Constance observed Guy, and his expression was full of dread at the thought of returning to Nottingham and the likelihood that he would have to face King Richard.

Endeavoring to hide his distress, he responded, "Of course, my lady. We will do as you wish."

28 March 1194, Nottingham Castle

Following the unconditional surrender of the garrison in Nottingham Castle, Robin had conducted a thorough search of the fortress, and he had also sent a group of men through the tunnel.

He had been overjoyed to find an exhausted and hungry Edmund in the dungeons. However, it was apparent that Montlhéry had fled, and evidently, he had taken Guy and Constance with him.

When he and Edmund entered the great hall, they found it

crowded with luminaries including Eleanor, Hamelin, the Earls of Chester and Derby, Archbishop Hubert, and even the elderly Hugh de Puiset.

But the only person he really wanted to see was standing behind the queen; he winked at Marian, and she beamed at him.

Robin and Edmund genuflected before the king, and they reported that Montlhéry had likely escaped through the tunnel sometime between Edmund's incarceration in the dungeon and the king's arrival at the siege.

A commotion drew everyone's attention, and Robin was stunned to see a disheveled Countess Isabel burst into the hall and run to her husband. She flung herself at him, sobbing loudly.

Constance was trailing Isabel, and she hurried to where Robin was standing with Edmund.

Hamelin unwound his wife's tight embrace and held her at arm's length, confused by her sudden appearance. When he looked at her, he exploded in anger. "Who has done this to you!" he roared.

She cried even harder, and he pulled her back into his arms. Their son, Guillaume, hurried over to them.

Robin moved closer, and he saw dark, mottled bruising on her neck. She was now whispering into Hamelin's ear.

Another disturbance at the double doors heralded the arrival of a contingent of soldiers escorting a bound Guy of Gisborne.

Constance tugged on Robin's sleeve and implored, "You must do something! They've arrested Guy!"

King Richard stood, and the entire hall hushed except for the sound of Isabel's muffled sobs as she clung to Hamelin.

His voice booming, Richard proclaimed, "We meet again, Guy of Gisborne. I condemn you to death for your many crimes. Take him to the dungeons; he will hang tomorrow after giving a full confession to Earl Robin and Brother Tuck."

The soldiers escorted Guy from the hall.

With a shrill cry, Constance threw herself at Richard's feet and begged, "Sire, no! Please spare my husband. He—" Her words were drowned by her sobs, and Edmund went to her, insisting that she stand before he led her away.

At that moment, a shaken Hamelin said, "Richard, we need to speak privately."

The king gestured for everyone to leave, except for the de Warennes and Eleanor.

As Marian walked past him, Robin joined her. To his surprise, Hamelin beckoned and bade him to stay. Robin suggested to Marian that she go to Constance and comfort the other woman, and then he returned to the de Warenne family.

After the guards shut the heavy doors, the hall descended into an ominous silence.

Hamelin and Guillaume stood on either side of Isabel, supporting her, as she could barely stand on her own. Everyone gathered around them.

"Tell him," urged Hamelin. "Everything will be all right. We must place our trust in God."

Robin worriedly observed Isabel. Not only was her neck bruised, but her hair and clothing were in a disarray. In all the time he had known her, she had always maintained a dignified, genteel appearance.

Isabel wiped the dampness from her face with her sleeve as she took a calming breath. She gazed at Hamelin, and he nodded in encouragement.

"Prince William—" She paused and frowned, concentrating her thoughts.

"Who?" demanded Richard.

Her words tumbled forth. "The man who calls himself 'Montl-héry' is my husband, William of Blois, King Stephen's son. He didn't die at the siege of Toulouse, and he's here in England to claim the throne."

༄

At the sound of someone approaching, Guy stood and moved to the bars of his cell. He assumed it was Robin and Tuck, so the sight of Constance's tear-stained face startled him.

She rushed forward and reached for him through the bars, and he wrapped his arms around her. Gazing over her shoulder, he saw Edmund was there as well, and he nodded at his father by marriage.

Edmund dipped his head in return, and then he retreated to the corridor to give them privacy.

They stood together, clinging to each other for some time.

Guy was at a loss for words. There seemed to be so much that he needed to say, yet he didn't know where to start. He finally admitted, "I'm sorry, Constance. You deserved a better husband and a happy life."

Crying against his chest, she lamented, "I can't bear the thought of losing you. I don't want any other husband; I want to spend my life with you. Only you."

"I'm a selfish man," Guy acknowledged. "I should have never taken you to my bed." He placed his hand on her swollen abdomen. "All the same, I'm glad that a part of me will live on, and that you and Edmund will raise our babe. If only I could have grown up with such a father."

"I don't think you're selfish, and I'm also glad that I will have a part of you…" her voice faded, and she began to sob again.

He held her as tightly as he could through the bars, and he suddenly realized something. He was a fool, and only now did he understand everything clearly. Now that it was too late. Now that he was bidding her adieu. But perhaps there was time for one more confession.

"Constance, there is something that I've never told you, and my time is short," he declared.

She leaned away to look at him, her brow creased with worry.

He continued, "I should have told you this a long time ago, but I've been a coward, unable to speak the truth to you because of my own foolish pride."

He smiled wistfully at her and caressed her cheek with his good hand.

Constance paled. In a hushed tone she asked, "What is it, Guy? You can tell me anything."

"I love you."

She gasped in surprise.

His voice cracking with emotion, he fervently requested, "When you tell our child about me, this is what I want you to say: that I loved you unreservedly."

CHAPTER 20
THE PRICE OF TREASON

29 March 1194, Nottingham Castle

Robin and Tuck descended the stairs that led to the dungeons under Nottingham Castle. It was just past dawn, and they had been sent to escort Guy to the gallows after spending much of the prior evening with him. He had told Robin everything he knew about Montlhéry and the French court, while Tuck had listened to his confession.

Guy was standing near the door of his cell, waiting for them.

Robin swallowed, surprised by the rush of emotion he felt at the imminent death of his half-brother, a man who had tried to kill him on several occasions, had nearly succeeded, and had attempted to take Marian from him. Yet they shared a unique connection that could not be denied.

Four guards stepped forward, but Robin waved them away. He decided to allow Guy the dignity of walking unbound to the gallows, something that the other man had not done for him all those years ago.

Without speaking a word, Guy left his cell and trailed Robin. Tuck followed, softly reciting prayers for Guy's soul. They reached the main corridor of the keep, and a guard approached Robin, dropping to one knee and announcing, "My lord, the king has requested that you bring the prisoner to the tower room before he is taken to the gallows."

They followed the guard, and Robin wondered how Guy felt about climbing the winding stairs to the sheriff's lair one last time.

Entering the tower room, Robin saw Edmund and Hamelin flanking Richard, who was seated on Montlhéry's throne. He joined Guy and Tuck as they genuflected before the king. Robin observed that the king was scowling angrily.

Richard sternly proclaimed, "To attempt regicide, whether it is your own liege lord or the king of another land, is an offense against God, and it must be punished; there is no possibility of mercy for this crime. Therefore, I condemn Guy FitzCurzon of Gisborne to death. It will be announced throughout the land that this man was executed on the 29th of March, in the year of our Lord, 1194."

Robin watched Richard curiously. What was the point of condemning Guy to death a second time?

"Since your arrest yesterday," Richard continued, "I've been besieged with pleas for your life. Baron Embelton and his daughter claim that you have changed much in the past two years. They begged me to grant you mercy. Then Earl Robin approached me and described your invaluable help in recovering the stolen ransom. He insisted that you have been loyal to him, and by extension, to me." Again, the king paused.

Robin recalled his effort to persuade Richard to spare Guy; the king had irritably ordered him out of the room. He glanced at Guy, who appeared utterly defeated.

Richard sighed loudly; there was no mistaking his aggravation. "All of you must understand that, if one man is allowed to escape punishment for attempted regicide, then my God-given authority will be undermined."

The king gazed at Hamelin. "Nevertheless, I am inclined to listen when someone in my immediate family, a man whom I respect and love, petitions me for mercy. Uncle Hamelin tells me that Gisborne twice saved his wife from death, first by fighting off her attacker, and then by rescuing her from a watery grave. Hamelin has offered a solution to the conundrum I face."

Richard stood and announced, "Guy of Gisborne must die. However, Guy de Toury of Embelton will be allowed to live if he agrees to certain stipulations."

Edmund walked to Guy and stood next to him. "Sire, I will take full responsibility for this man, and I welcome him into my family as my son by marriage." Edmund tugged on Guy's sleeve, encouraging him to kneel.

Guy fell to his knees before the king and hastily rubbed his hand over his face, trying to hide the tears that were leaking from his eyes.

Richard nodded approvingly. "Here are my terms: he is exiled to Embelton. He cannot leave the barony without permission from Earl Robin or a royal summons.

"Because Lionel de Toury will be arrested and executed for treason if he ever sets foot in my domains, he cannot inherit the barony. Likewise, Guy de Toury can never become baron by right of wife. Instead, the eldest surviving son of Guy and Constance de Toury will become Baron of Embelton. Finally, Guy de Toury will remain a vassal of Earl Robin."

Richard looked at Robin. "Are you willing to become your brother's keeper?"

A relieved Robin smiled and answered, "Yes, Sire."

Richard stared unflinchingly at Guy. "Do you accept these terms, Guy de Toury?"

Again, Guy wiped at his face, struggling to control his emotions. His voice cracked as he declared, "I accept. I know I don't deserve your mercy. But I would like to spend the rest of my life at Embelton, hoping to become worthy of the de Toury name."

Richard snarled, "You're damn right you don't deserve this.

After today, if I ever see you again, I'll personally execute you on the spot, and I'll take great pleasure in doing so."

The king tried to settle his rising indignation as he continued, "I have published a royal proclamation declaring that Guy of Gisborne has been executed. But before you begin your new life, there is a service you will perform for your king."

"Anything, Sire," promised a contrite Guy.

"I am sending you to France with Earl Robin. You are to help him track this pretender to the throne, this vile man who murdered my father and two of my brothers."

Robin was pleased to hear this; he was eager to hunt Montlhéry, and Guy's connections at the Paris court would be invaluable.

Richard concluded their meeting by announcing, "Lastly, no one is permitted to reveal the truth about Montlhéry. There is nothing more important than keeping his true identity a secret. England has suffered enough; another usurper claiming the throne would be untenable. Everyone will refer to this man as Count de Montlhéry."

Richard marched towards the door and gestured to Robin. "It's still early in the morning. My mother and I are eager to visit Sherwood Forest. You will be our guide."

29 March 1194, Sherwood Forest

Robin and King Richard led the procession into the forest mounted on impressive destriers as Marian and Queen Eleanor trailed them on a pair of sedate palfreys. The king's entourage followed them, including his guards and a chronicler. Once again, Robbie was riding with Robin, and Marian was thankful that he was on his best behavior.

She was also pleased that Robin had brought their son on this impromptu visit to the forest. It was vital that Richard and Eleanor meet Robbie; it would emphasize to them that he is a flesh and blood little boy and not just a point of debate involving the challenges of declaring his legitimacy. Marian still wondered how the king would resolve their dilemma, but she was hopeful that he would be more inclined to help Robbie now that he had met him.

They entered the clearing and approached Duncan's hunting lodge. Robin had sent word to the outlaws, and they had all gathered there to meet the king. Odella was there with Allan, and she was holding their baby daughter.

"Look, Richard," exclaimed Eleanor as she spurred her horse forward until she was next to her son. "It's one of your father's hunting lodges. I commend Earl Robin for taking such good care of it all these years."

A perplexed Robin cleared his throat. "Well, um, my father built this many years ago. I don't believe King Henry ever visited here or ordered it built."

"Nonsense," the queen chided. "Henry commissioned a number of these hunting lodges to be constructed in the royal forests. Your father would have had no legal right to build a structure in Sherwood Forest without the king's permission. This is a royal hunting lodge, and it belongs to the crown. You are merely a caretaker."

"Mother is correct, Robin," Richard declared. "My father mentioned these lodges to me. I am grateful that you have maintained it so well. Sherwood Forest pleases me greatly, and I look forward to visiting it often after I have defeated Philippe."

"Of course, Sire. I will continue to ensure that your lodge is ready for you whenever you wish to visit," Robin judiciously answered, and Marian recognized the amused quirk of his lips.

Everyone dismounted, and Marian took Robbie's hand as Robin encouraged his men to come closer.

"Sire, I would like to introduce you to my men. Some of these men were originally pardoned when we left for the Crusade, but the sheriff ignored your exoneration of them. These men risked their lives to help me recover your ransom after the sheriff had stolen it."

The men knelt before the king, and he instructed them to rise.

"I commend all of you for your service to me," proclaimed Richard. "I have ordered my scribe to prepare written pardons for each of you, and I promise to appoint a new sheriff who will be just and fair. But first, I insist that Earl Robin introduce me to each of you by name."

Marian was impressed as Richard and Eleanor went down the line of awestruck men, all of them peasants who had likely never imagined that they would meet the king, or that the king would greet them in such a personal manner, using their names.

In keeping with his disdain for nobles, Little John did not seem particularly impressed by the royals, but he was respectful, and to Marian's relief, he didn't spit on the ground at Richard's feet.

Richard spoke to Allan at length. He must have remembered meeting Allan in Acre, when the minstrel had accompanied Marian on her journey to the Holy Land. Richard and Eleanor both complimented little Alina's beauty, and the queen tenderly caressed the baby's cheek. Although the five-month-old infant would never remember the moment, Marian knew that Allan and Odella would often tell her the story.

Following the introductions, Richard requested that Allan perform one of his ballads, and the king praised him as a talented minstrel.

Richard and Eleanor briefly entered the lodge to inspect it, and then Robin and Little John took the king on a hunt in the nearby woods while the outlaws waited in line to give their names to the scribe who would later prepare their written pardons.

It was decided that Eleanor and her guards would return to Locksley, as the queen was growing weary and wished to rest. Taking care to follow a path that would avoid the hunting party, Marian, Robbie, and the former outlaws made their way back to Locksley.

As they were riding, Marian asked, "Your Grace, do you know when the king plans to send Robin to search for Montlhéry?"

Eleanor replied, "There will be a four-day meeting of the Great

Council, to be held in Nottingham, and I'm certain Richard will require Earl Robin's presence as many important issues will be addressed. Then we must travel to London for the crown wearing."

Frowning in confusion, Marian inquired, "What is a crown wearing?"

"It's an affirmation of Richard's right to rule. I'm going to suggest that it be held on Easter Sunday in Winchester Cathedral. You will find it to be an inspirational ceremony."

As the meaning of the queen's words dawned on her, Marian dared to respond, "But now that you're back in England, uh, wouldn't you prefer your other ladies-in-waiting?"

Eleanor eyed her slyly. "You will serve me a little while longer. After the crown wearing, we are going to Normandy. As soon as I've returned to my palace in Poitiers, I will grant you leave." Gesturing at Marian's expanding waist, she continued, "You will be home well before your time."

Marian's heart sank at the prospect of another separation from Robin and Robbie. Her little boy was seated in front of her as they rode back to Locksley, and she instinctively hugged him tightly.

9 May 1194, The Royal Palace, Paris, France

Robin followed Guy as they navigated the corridors of the royal palace, and he reflected on the tortuous odyssey of the previous six weeks. First, there had been the interminable Great Council meeting in Nottingham with four days of mind-numbing administrative sessions.

Then, he had been ordered to help with the preparations for Richard's crown wearing and to participate in the elaborate ceremony. Certainly, it was an honor to have been one of four earls carrying the royal canopy during Richard's procession, but Robin could hardly relax and enjoy the festivities while the trail of his quarry was growing colder by the day.

The day after the crown wearing, Richard had finally released him to begin his search for Montlhéry, and Robin had sped to Portsmouth where Guy was waiting for him. They immediately crossed to Barfleur, but spring storms, swollen rivers, and washed out roadways had hindered their progress.

After traveling to Argentan, they had journeyed to the town of Montlhéry where they visited the grave of their father, and Robin renewed his vow to seek justice for Duncan's murder. In the town, they learned that, although Montlhéry had arrived in early April, he had been summoned to Paris a fortnight ago.

During their travels, Guy's close connection to Montlhéry had provided a crucial advantage. Everyone they met, from the commander of the garrison in the town of Montlhéry to the guards at the royal palace, had shown deference to Guy as the count's most senior knight. They had easily passed through every gate. Robin knew he could not have breached King Philippe's formidable security on his own.

When they entered the royal palace, Robin was concerned that someone might recognize him. During the Crusade, Robin had met King Philippe and his senior military advisors several times. A few of these men had died in the Holy Land, but others could potentially be at court. The only other men who could identify him were Montlhéry and the poisoner, Tancred de Payen.

Guy had ascertained that all the military advisors were stationed at various Norman castles that Philippe had taken during the previous year, and also that Philippe and Montlhéry had left Paris five days ago. However, their destination was a closely guarded secret, and no one would reveal it to Guy.

Since Payen had been instructed to stay with Prince John, who was at Évreux, that left only one man who would recognize Robin, and they were on their way to find him, hoping that he knew Montlhéry's whereabouts.

As they moved along the hall, Guy carried the torch that lit their way, and Robin found himself in the shadows behind Guy. *How fitting*, he thought as he recalled Montlhéry's riddles about shadows. Robin was convinced that the riddles referred to Prince William of Blois hiding in plain sight after faking his death. And now he intended to bring this man out of the shadows and into the light of justice.

They stopped in front of a door at the end of a long corridor, and Guy rapped sharply on the aging wood as Robin drew his sword and stood to the side, out of sight.

In the distance, Robin heard a voice yell at them to go away until morning.

"It's Gisborne, and I have a message for you," growled Guy.

The hinges squealed in protest as the door was flung open, and an anxious Lionel appeared, dressed in a long shirt. His hair was tousled, and he had apparently been sleeping. "Is Constance all right? My father?"

Guy and Robin hastily pushed Lionel back into his chamber before he could sound an alarm.

Robin pointed his sword at Lionel and declared, "You've broken their hearts, but otherwise Constance and Edmund are well."

Lionel raised his hands in surrender as Guy closed the door.

Blanching in fear, Lionel asked, "Are you planning to take me back to England by force? I won't go quietly, and there are many guards between my chamber and the streets of Paris."

"I'm not here to abduct you. It's true that the king has ordered your execution, but I would never cause your father and sister to suffer the heartbreak of seeing you hanged. Gisborne and I need information, and we're hoping you will honor our familial ties by helping us," explained Robin.

Lionel lowered his hands and countered, "Will you deliver a message to my father?"

"Of course," Robin responded as he sheathed his sword.

Deciding that they needed privacy, he requested, "Guy, can you stand watch while I speak to Lionel?"

Guy nodded and slipped out of the chamber while Lionel pulled on a pair of chausses. Nervously running his fingers through his hair, he said, "Tell my father that I'm sorry. He was right, and I should have listened to him. And to you."

"Are you in danger here at the French court?" inquired a concerned Robin.

"No," Lionel answered. "I've enjoyed living in Paris. But father was right about Prince John. He's a weak, duplicitous man, and he should never be allowed to take the throne."

"What opened your eyes?"

"When I met King Philippe, I found him to be a truly impressive leader. It's obvious to anyone observing Philippe and John that one man is a king, and the other is a pretender. I am fortunate that King Philippe took an interest in me. I think he was pleased to learn that my mother was distantly related to his mother. He was also impressed with my language skills."

"Has the king treated you well?"

"Yes. I know that returning to England is out of the question, so I've sworn fealty to Philippe, and he's invited me to become one of his advisors, especially since I can provide intelligence about England and the royal court."

Robin sputtered, "That's treason! How could you turn your back on your homeland?"

"I don't have a choice. Richard will never forgive me. If I return to England, I'll be hanged as a traitor. I have to find a new home, and the French court is a very pleasant place. I'm actually quite content, except that I miss my father and sister."

"Do you really think that you have a future here?"

"I'm certain of it. Philippe has arranged an advantageous marriage for me, which will give me a title and entrée into the ranks of the French nobility. Tell Father that I'm happy, and I'm sorry that we parted in anger. Maybe someday, after the war between Richard and Philippe has ended, he can visit me," suggested Lionel.

"I will tell him."

"And Constance? Is she all right? Will she remain with Gisborne? What about his death sentence?"

Robin described Guy's pardon and Richard's proclamations about the Barony of Embelton. He was relieved when Lionel calmly accepted the news, and he wondered what had happened over the past six months that had led to this new maturity in his cousin.

"What do you need from me?" inquired Lionel. "I will help you if I can, but I won't betray any confidences of King Philippe."

"We need to find Montlhéry. King Richard wants him returned to his jurisdiction."

Lionel paced a few moments. "You are asking a lot from me. Montlhéry is Philippe's favorite advisor. I've been told that they are close blood relations, although I don't know the details."

Robin withheld from Lionel the truth about Montlhéry and his conspiracy against the English royal family. Regardless of the fondness that Philippe felt for him, if Lionel knew the full extent of the plot to take the throne of England, his life would be forfeited.

Instead, Robin revealed, "Montlhéry has made several attempts on Richard's life. But he also murdered my father and Marian's father too."

"God in heaven!" exclaimed Lionel.

"All we want is Montlhéry's location. I won't pretend that there is no danger in helping us, but consider how your assistance will improve your father's standing with Richard."

"The location of Montlhéry and Philippe was a secret because they were moving into position for their next battle. By tomorrow, it will be widely known that they are laying siege to Verneuil, hoping to capture it before Richard's arrival."

"Lionel, I assure you that the Lionheart will retake all the stolen Norman castles with a ferocity that will crush Philippe and his forces. I recommend you stay at court, because if you are apprehended by Richard's men, you will be swiftly executed for treason."

"Perhaps you are right, but I caution you: do not underestimate Philippe. He sees the world around him as an elaborate game of strategy, and he is bold and brilliant. I don't know Richard, but he has a reputation for recklessness that might hinder his ability to secure the borderlands between Normandy and Philippe's domains."

Lionel then disclosed, "There is something you should know. Richard has not yet landed in Normandy. Yesterday, spies from Barfleur reported that the weather has been dreadful. He is trapped at Portsmouth until the storms clear."

Robin briefly pondered this. Richard had planned to sail from Portsmouth on April 26th, a fortnight ago. He could only imagine the king's frustration at such a delay. Considering that Marian was traveling with Richard and Eleanor, he prayed they would not take any chances in stormy seas. The shipwreck at Aquileia was still fresh in his mind, and he shivered in dread at the memory of his brush with a watery death.

"Thank you for telling me this," Robin replied. "I wish you happiness in your new life. As you said, someday this war will end, and we will meet again."

"In the meantime, please look after my father and sister," requested Lionel.

The cousins embraced, and Lionel pledged, "I promise I will not betray you as you leave the royal keep. Go in peace and Godspeed, Robin."

13 May 1194, The Gates of Verneuil, Normandy

Guy lingered at the edge of the French camp. He wiped the sweat from his brow and swallowed the bile that kept rising in his throat. If only he could calm the frenetic beating of his heart. He contemplated his miraculous escape from execution at the hands of one monarch, but now he was expected to risk his new life by facing King Philippe.

They had arrived at the siege of Verneuil the previous day, only to discover that Montlhéry had left two days ago. Guy had mistakenly assumed that Robin would be satisfied with this news, but to his dismay, he learned that Robin expected him to find out where Montlhéry had gone. This would require that he approach the French king himself, as no one else seemed to know.

But he didn't know whether Philippe was aware of his betrayal of Montlhéry. Or if word of his supposed execution had reached anyone at the Paris court. So far, the other French knights hadn't been surprised to see him, so he hoped that his alleged death hadn't been considered important enough to be communicated across the Channel.

He adjusted the glove that concealed his disfigured hand and squinted at the late afternoon sun. To settle his nerves, he tried to focus on the task at hand. Robin had spent the day helping him practice what he would say to Philippe, and they had also rehearsed several scenarios that might arise during the audience. Guy was irked that his clever brother found all this subterfuge so easy, and he envied Robin's glib tongue and fearless nature.

Guy's mind drifted, and he wondered if Embelton was as bucolic as Locksley. The thought of a quiet life managing his new family's estate lifted his spirits. And in two months, he would be a father. His entire life was taking a turn that offered security, peace, and joy.

If he survived this audience with King Philippe.

"Guy," a hushed voice beckoned from the trees behind him. "What are you waiting for? Don't just stand there. You can do this."

Guy closed his eyes in exasperation. He would go when he was ready, and Robin needed to leave him the hell alone. Sighing loudly, he stepped into the camp.

❧

"Montlhéry has been gone two days, and he is already sending word of his progress?" King Philippe's brow rose in surprise at the sight of Gisborne as he entered the royal tent and knelt at the king's feet.

Still battling his nerves, Guy stood and replied, "Sire, I recently escaped from England. I thought my master was with you, and that's why I'm here."

Suspicion shadowed Philippe's expression. "The weather has prevented all crossings for the past fortnight. How were you able to cross?"

Guy froze in fear, but the memory of his reunion with Constance after Richard had spared his life flitted through his mind. The joy and love shining in her eyes was an image that would stay with him for the rest of his life. She had faith in him, and she was counting on him to return. His resolve strengthened, and for the first time, he believed he could succeed.

"Sire, forgive my lack of precision. I sailed from Dover in April, just before the storms. After traveling to several locations looking for Count de Montlhéry, I learned he was here. I hope to reunite with him as soon as possible." To Guy's profound relief, Philippe relaxed and accepted his explanation.

"Gisborne, you have always been a loyal man. I know Ambroise values you highly. He is on his way to Barfleur to welcome King Richard to Normandy. You will join him, and he will apprise you of the latest plan." Philippe waved to someone on the other side of the large tent, and the man, a courier, stepped forward.

"Before Ambroise left, he asked that I send a message to his other knight, the one with white hair." Philippe seemed to be searching for a name.

Guy suggested, "Do you mean Payen?" Irritation flashed in Philippe's eyes, and Guy recalled that the king did not like to be addressed. His stomach lurched in apprehension, but no rebuke from the king was forthcoming.

Philippe motioned for the courier to give a sealed dispatch to Guy. "Tomorrow, you will take this to Payen. He's at Évreux guarding John. From there, you will journey to Barfleur and assist Ambroise. This time, I demand success. The failures of the past will not be tolerated again."

"Yes, Sire," Guy dutifully responded.

Philippe walked to a nearby table and scribbled something on a piece of parchment. He then placed his seal on it. The wax was still warm when an attendant handed it to Guy.

Initially confused, Guy glanced at the document and smiled. It was a royal pass, allowing him to move freely within Philippe's domains. Robin would be pleased.

∽

Guy silently watched as Robin held the blade of his dagger over their small campfire. He then carefully slid the heated blade under the seal of the dispatch intended for Payen, loosening it without damaging it.

Robin read the message and frowned.

"What does it say?" Guy asked.

"It doesn't make any sense."

Guy waited, his impatience growing. "Well?"

Robin explained, "It just says, '*Serve my favorite wine.*' Is this a code?"

The moment Robin mentioned a code, Guy remembered a conversation that he had overheard a year ago.

"Merde!" he exclaimed. "It's the signal for Payen to kill John by poisoning him with tainted wine."

CHAPTER 21
VENGEANCE

16 May 1194, Évreux Castle, Normandy

Robin wore a helmet with a face guard that had been stolen from one of Philippe's soldiers at Verneuil as he entered the great hall of the castle in Évreux with Guy. Prince John was there with several French nobles awaiting the meal that would soon be served as afternoon transitioned into evening.

They genuflected before John, and Robin was pleased when no one seemed to notice or care that his identity was obscured. His plan required him to talk to John in person, and there was no way to avoid the risk of discovery.

Payen was standing a short distance away, and he was visibly dismayed to see Guy.

John was familiar with Guy as Montlhéry's captain, and his arrival surprised the prince. He inquired, "Gisborne? Has Montlhéry sent you?"

Guy gestured at Robin and announced, "King Philippe sent us to deliver an urgent dispatch, and I beg you to grant us a private audience." He offered John the royal pass Philippe had given him. They hoped it would convince John that they were there on official business.

John scanned the document and frowned. Just as Robin feared that their gambit had failed, the prince gave it back to Guy and pivoted. They followed him up a flight of stairs to his lavishly furnished chambers.

After they entered, Robin closed the door and slid the latch to lock it while John stared expectantly at Guy.

Guy pointed at Robin and said, "This man—"

The moment John turned to look at Robin, Guy grabbed the diminutive prince and covered his mouth with his good hand, while he wrapped his other arm around his waist. John began to twist and thrash, his cries sufficiently muffled so that no one could hear him.

Robin removed his helmet, and all the color drained from John's face.

Dropping his helmet to the floor and holding his hands up in a nonthreatening manner, Robin declared, "My lord, please be at ease. I'm not here to hurt you or abduct you. Grant me time to explain, and if you are not satisfied, then you can call your men to arrest us. Will you allow me to deliver the messages I carry?"

John had settled some, and he nodded. Gisborne gradually removed his hand from the prince's mouth, and when he remained quiet, Guy released him.

John promptly slapped Guy across the face and hissed, "Don't you ever put your hands on me again."

Guy dropped to one knee and implored, "Forgive me, my lord."

Ignoring Gisborne, John faced Robin and demanded, "What do you want, Huntingdon? Speak quickly, because I'm in no mood to suffer your company for long."

Robin disclosed, "My lord, I have brought two messages. The first is from the queen mother." He pulled a dispatch from the pouch tied to his belt and handed it to John.

The prince scrutinized the seal to make sure it was intact. After opening it, he read silently.

Richard and Eleanor had hoped that Robin might encounter

John during his quest to locate Montlhéry, so they had given him a letter and revealed its contents. He watched as John closely studied it.

Eventually, John refolded it and placed it on a nearby table. "Mother insists that I trust you," he divulged, "and she is promising to protect me from Richard. Give me the second message."

Robin nodded at Guy, who retrieved the dispatch intended for Payen from a pouch attached to his belt and gave it to the prince.

John's brow rose in alarm. "This seal had been loosened!"

"My lord, I can explain," Robin stated evenly. "Look at the name on the front. This letter was sent from Montlhéry to Payen. Please, read it."

Flipping over the dispatch, John verified Robin's assertion, and then he unfolded it and read aloud, "Serve my favorite wine." His voice rising in confusion, he asked, "What is the meaning of this?"

"Tell him, Gisborne," instructed Robin.

"My lord, I have been Count de Montlhéry's captain for many years. But now I am Lord Huntingdon's vassal, and I must tell you the truth: Montlhéry has been planning to kill both you and your brother—"

"Nonsense," John interrupted. "I will admit that Ambroise has been...overzealous in his enthusiasm to promote me as king, but you are wrong; he wouldn't hurt me. He has been diligent in his efforts to keep me safe. That's why Payen is here."

Guy gravely countered, "Forgive me for my impertinence in disagreeing, but I know with certainty that this is a coded message to Payen, instructing him to poison you. I heard Montlhéry say it himself."

John's face darkened in anger, and when he opened his mouth to argue, Robin interjected, "My lord, let us prove it to you. If we are wrong, then you can arrest us. But if we are right, then you will know that we are here to protect you, as the queen mother herself wrote to you. I have a plan."

⟡

After re-sealing the dispatch for Payen, Robin had donned his helmet and backed away to the far corner of the chamber. *Into the shadows*, he mused. Prince John had summoned Payen, and a soft tapping at the door prompted Guy to open it.

The pallid poisoner slithered into the chamber, and Robin recalled the first time he had met Payen, when the oddly pale man had alleged that Robin had murdered Baron Alfred, Marian's father.

Payen curiously swung his gaze between Guy and Prince John. He genuflected to John, and asked, "My lord, you summoned me?"

"Gisborne, give him the letter," John commanded.

Guy gave Payen the dispatch and said, "This is from Montlhéry."

Robin watched as Payen opened it without inspecting the seal and grinned at the lethal message.

"What does it say?" John casually inquired, his face carefully arranged in an expression of bored nonchalance.

Smiling broadly, Payen replied, "My lord, this is wonderful news! A calamity has befallen your brother, and you will soon be crowned king. This is a coded dispatch from Count de Montlhéry." He offered the note to John so that he could read it for himself.

Feigning surprise and confusion, John demanded, "What is the meaning of this? I don't see anything about Richard dying."

Payen explained, "Count de Montlhéry cannot divulge such things in a letter that might be intercepted. He told me that if I ever received this message, then Richard is dead, and you must celebrate. For this purpose, he has provided a bottle of excellent wine for you. Let me fetch it."

"Very well," agreed John. "Bring me this wine."

Payen sketched a short bow and hurriedly exited.

John glared at Robin and growled, "Are you certain that my brother is alive and well? And that Payen is lying to me?"

"My lord, I'm not aware of any 'calamity' suffered by your

brother. He will arrive in Normandy any day now after enduring delays due to poor weather," answered Robin.

After a brief wait, Payen returned carrying a tray with a bottle of wine and a single goblet. As soon as he entered the chamber, Guy closed the door, setting the latch and leaning against it.

After filling the goblet, Payen proclaimed, "To my future king, I'm honored to present this wine to you." He bowed low as he handed it to John.

The prince raised it to his lips, but then he lowered it without drinking and declared, "Payen, you have served me well for many months. I insist you join me in this toast."

John retrieved an earthenware cup from the table and passed it to Payen, who hesitated before taking the cup. Even from his hiding place on the other side of the chamber, Robin recognized the naked fear shining in Payen's grey eyes.

"My lord, it's a small bottle, uh, I'm not worthy to drink with you...and besides, Montlhéry would be angry..." Payen's voice trailed off as he searched for an excuse that would placate John. In desperation, he looked at Guy. "Gisborne, don't you agree that I shouldn't drink this wine when Montlhéry wants it given to our new king?"

Guy stared at him stonily.

John scowled at Payen and repeated, "I ordered you to join me in a toast to my future."

Payen's hand trembled as he poured wine into his cup, spilling some on the table.

John lifted his goblet and announced, "Payen, we will drink to my future as King of England."

Payen raised his cup and echoed, "To your future as King of England."

The two men slowly brought their cups to their lips, staring into each other's eyes, but not drinking.

It was a combat of wills, and Robin never doubted who would prevail.

Payen abruptly dropped his cup and ran to the door, only to have Guy block the way. He spun around, and his normally placid expression was filled with terror.

"I find it curious that you would not join me for a toast," observed John. "What exactly makes this wine so special?"

"My lord, it's just what I've already said: I'm unworthy to share this drink with you, uh, I'm nothing, and you're the King of England," Payen stuttered.

Robin emerged from the shadows, removed his helmet, and advanced towards the poisoner.

"What is he doing here?" Payen shrieked before Guy grabbed him and covered his mouth.

Robin questioned, "Why won't you share a toast with the King of England? Most knights would consider that quite an honor."

"You were right, Huntingdon," conceded John. "He wouldn't drink it. As a prince of the realm and next in line for the throne, I require a taste-tester. Gisborne, hold him."

A triumphant Guy held Payen while John emptied the goblet into his mouth. Payen choked and sputtered as he tried to break free from Guy's iron grasp and avoid the poisoned wine in a doomed struggle to escape his fate.

When Gisborne released Payen, he fell to the floor, where he convulsed and foamed at the mouth. A stunned Robin was reminded of the agonizing deaths of Blanche and her sister, Clothilde.

After intense suffering, Payen finally stilled.

"What a horrible death," John calmly remarked. He then looked at Robin and admitted, "I acknowledge that everything happened just as you predicted."

A sharp rapping on the door startled them, and at John's nod, Guy opened it as Robin retreated into the shadows.

A man entered and genuflected to John. "My lord, we've

received word that King Richard, accompanied by his army, landed at Barfleur three days ago. He is marching towards King Philippe's siege of Verneuil." The man noticed Payen's body and blanched.

John's composed façade faltered for a moment, but then he recovered and demanded that the man remove Payen from his chambers.

After the other man had dragged the body away, Guy shut the door, and Robin approached John. "My lord, have you considered the queen mother's proposal? I hope you will now believe me when I say that I'm here to protect you."

When John hesitated, Robin suggested, "Would Montlhéry have ordered your death without King Philippe's knowledge and consent?"

John was thoughtful for a few moments. "We will leave tomorrow morning."

19 May 1194, Villa of Archdeacon John de Alençon, Lisieux, Normandy

"The people will be disappointed if you are not there, Maman." Richard spoke tenderly to his mother.

Eleanor smiled wanly at her favorite son and confessed, "My bones cry out for rest; I have nothing left to offer the people today. Besides, it's you they want. They must see you to know that the Lionheart has returned to protect them and set things right."

Marian observed the king and his mother as they sat at the table, breaking their fast. She could plainly see the lines of exhaustion etched upon Eleanor's face, and she knew the elderly queen simply could not continue the pace that Richard had established over the past sennight.

After spending eighteen days trapped at Portsmouth because of bad weather, they had disembarked at Barfleur the previous week. Since then, Richard had triumphantly marched across Normandy, visiting important towns such as Bayeux and Caen. Yesterday, they had arrived in Lisieux, where the archdeacon, John de Alençon, had invited them to stay at his impressive villa.

Richard was eager to go to Verneuil, which was under attack by King Philippe. In order to speed his travels, he had left the main body of his army behind, and he was traveling with only a small, elite force.

However, their progress had been hindered by the huge crowds that had gathered in every town and along every thoroughfare as the people cheered and waved at their long absent ruler and his beloved mother.

Marian was also fatigued, as she was now at the midpoint of her pregnancy and could no longer hide her condition under loose clothing. She was relieved when Richard relented and allowed them to rest at the villa while he left with John de Alençon and his guards to greet the people of Lisieux in the town square.

As soon as they were alone, Marian suggested, "Your Grace, would you like to return to your chamber and lie down?"

Eleanor nodded, and Marian helped her up the stairs to the room set aside for them. After Eleanor was settled into bed, Marian sat in a chair next to the hearth and promptly fell asleep.

In the distance, Marian heard a voice calling to her in an oddly familiar sing-song cadence.

"Maid Marian, Maid Marian…"

Her body felt heavy and lethargic, and exhaustion fogged her mind, so she labored to rouse herself. At last, she opened her eyes and startled at the sight of her nemesis staring at her, the point of his sword nearly touching her chest. She wrapped her arms around her swollen abdomen, protecting her unborn child.

In a hushed voice, Montlhéry warned, "If you sound an alarm, I will happily kill you where you sit. As a matter of fact, I'm tempted to kill you now and be done with you. But you might be useful to me."

Marian glared at him and whispered, "What do you want?"

Still speaking quietly, he replied, "I want Richard, of course, but he has been quite elusive. However, today he has made his first mistake since his arrival in Normandy by leaving the two of you here in this villa with only three guards at the front door. I will take his mother prisoner and deliver her to King Philippe. If you manage the old woman for me, I'll let you live."

"Do you expect us to just obediently leave with you?" Marian hissed.

Montlhéry grinned. "Truthfully, I hope you give me a reason to kill you. Nevertheless, I have a wagon waiting at the back door with my men. You and the old witch will dutifully climb into it, or my men will kill every servant in this house, and I will kill the two of you."

Marian countered, "How would you explain killing a valuable hostage to Philippe?"

"I've successfully managed Philippe all his life, and although it would please me to deliver Eleanor to him, the thought of Richard returning to find his dear maman with a dagger through her heart would be just as satisfying."

He angled his sword away from her and commanded, "Now go wake up the queen. It's time to for us to leave."

Just as Marian awkwardly shifted in her chair, endeavoring to stand, she heard a crash. She looked up and saw that Eleanor had hit Montlhéry on the head with an old ewer. It broke in half, and water rained down on his shoulders.

He spun around and raised his sword to strike the queen, and Marian lunged at him, grabbing his wrist in an attempt to wrest the sword from his hand.

Still clutching part of the broken ewer, Eleanor swung it at his face, and its sharp edge sliced into his cheek.

Montlhéry roared furiously as he shook off Marian's grip and shoved her to the floor. She landed with a heavy thud that briefly stole her breath.

He pointed his sword at Eleanor and sneered, "If you want to live, follow my orders and stop resisting. I'm sure King Philippe will arrange a comfortable captivity for you."

Eleanor dropped the ewer and lifted her chin defiantly. "I refuse to return to prison. I've already lived a long life, and I'm ready to die. But tell me, is it true that you killed two of my sons?"

A smug Montlhéry acknowledged, "Although I enjoyed ending the lives of Geoffrey and Henry the Younger, my greatest achievement was executing that usurper to the throne, your late husband."

"Are you William of Blois? Do you really believe you have a claim to the throne of England?" Eleanor interrogated. She then slid her gaze to Marian, who had regained her feet.

Marian realized the queen was stalling for time. They could not allow him to transport them to a secret location.

Montlhéry was evidently savoring the moment, and he responded, "I am the rightful King of England. On his deathbed, my father, King Stephen, named me his heir. But Duncan Fitzooth and Alfred Fitzwalter betrayed me, and their treachery prevented me from taking the throne."

"I know you killed my father," Marian bitterly contended. "He was a kind, decent man, who served Duncan as an obedient vassal. He didn't deserve to be murdered for something Duncan did."

Ignoring Marian's outburst, Montlhéry rotated his wrist as he held his sword. "See my ring, Eleanor? It belonged to William the Conqueror. Only the true King of England and Duke of Normandy would possess this ring."

Eleanor scoffed. "That means nothing. Without the power of an army and the support of the nobility, you will never be king. You must face the truth: you are the past, and my descendants are the future."

Marian searched for a weapon. Near the hearth was an iron poker, and she slowly backed away, hoping to grab it.

Unfortunately, her movement caught his notice, and he pivoted towards her, angling his sword in her direction and chiding, "My dear Maid Marian, are you planning to run away? I have men stationed at all the doors to this villa. There is no escape."

With his attention diverted, Eleanor hit him in the back with a small wooden stool. He swayed slightly, but the queen had little strength, and he took the stool from her and tossed it across the chamber. He then clutched her wrist and twisted her arm as she cried out in pain.

Marian seized the iron poker and swung it with all her might against Montlhéry's shoulder. He released Eleanor, and she whimpered as she cradled her arm.

Turning again to face Marian, Montlhéry raised his sword, and as it descended towards her, she held the poker over her head with both hands to block his strike. When the sword struck the poker, the force was so jarring that she could feel it all the way to her shoulders. She hastily retreated, only to find herself trapped against the stone wall behind her. She tried to hit him with the poker again, but he snatched it from her and dropped it on the floor.

He transferred his sword to his left hand so that he could grip her neck with his right. His eyes were blazing with fury, and blood was still trickling down his cheek from the cut inflicted by the jagged edge of the ewer. He growled, "For so many years, I've dreamt of this moment, and now I will finally have the satisfaction of watching the light in your eyes dim for eternity as I take your life."

His hand tightened around her throat, and Marian felt her lungs painfully constrict as they begged for air. She clawed at his forearm in a futile attempt to pull his hand away, and she recalled the day of Robin's hanging many years ago, when he had choked her in the same manner. The edge of her vision darkened, and thoughts of Robin and Robbie rose in her mind.

Just then, she saw Montlhéry's eyes widen in surprise. He released her, and she doubled over, coughing and struggling to catch her breath as he turned away from her. Although her eyes were blurred with tears, she looked up and saw a dagger lodged in the center of his back. He stumbled towards Eleanor, who was backing away from him. Once more he raised his sword.

The poker was on the floor at her feet, and Marian grabbed it again. Rushing forward, she used all her strength to hit him on the side of his head. Dazed by the blow, he dropped his sword and pressed his hands against his forehead, swaying on his feet and bleeding profusely from a cut on his temple.

Eleanor picked up his sword and stepped back, but even though she held the hilt with both hands, she was not strong enough to point it at his chest. As a befuddled Montlhéry staggered towards her to recover his sword, Marian pulled the dagger out of his back, thankful to have a weapon at last. He yelped from the sudden pain, his back arching in response.

Then Eleanor slashed his thigh with the sword, and he howled in agony. His chausses swiftly turned dark with blood, and he fell to his knees. As he knelt in front of her, Eleanor promptly stabbed him in the stomach.

Montlhéry collapsed backwards, lying on the floor and staring up at them. He gasped, "No! You can't defeat me…my destiny… I'm…rightful king…"

A triumphant Eleanor cried, "That was for Geoffrey!" She plunged the sword into him a second time, exclaiming, "This is for my son, Henry!" She then pulled the sword from his stomach and dropped it next to his leg.

Montlhéry groaned, and the queen leaned over and grasped his hand, sliding the Conqueror's ring from his finger and proclaiming, "This belongs to my son, the true King of England."

For a few moments, Marian contemplated the dagger in her trembling hand. A sudden resolve settled upon her, and she knelt next to him and stabbed him in the middle of his chest, crying, "And this is for my father!"

His entire body convulsed from her blow, and he moaned in

pain. His hands reached for the dagger embedded in his chest, but he no longer had the strength to grasp the hilt, and his arms dropped to his side. Montlhéry turned his head, and his eyes met hers. He tried to speak, but the only sounds he made were incoherent wheezing and mumbling. He continued to stare into her eyes as his face grew ashen, and the light in his eyes faded into a vacant, unseeing gaze.

A clamor of shouting alerted them that something was happening in the villa. Marian remembered that Montlhéry had a force of men with him, and she was certain that they were attacking.

With Eleanor's help, she labored to pull a chair over to the door. They tilted the chair against the latch, hoping it would prevent the men from forcing the door open. The queen returned to Montlhéry's body and retrieved his sword.

At the sound of men running up the stairs that led to their chamber, Marian focused on protecting the queen. She demanded, "Your Grace, give me that sword and go hide on the far side of the bed." Without waiting for Eleanor to respond, Marian took the sword from her, and holding the hilt with both hands, she found the strength to lift it in preparation for the expected onslaught.

The banging against the door was an echo of the pounding in her chest. With a loud crash, the press of men shoved the aged door into the room, ripping it from its hinges and snapping the chair in two.

At first, Marian could only see the shimmering of swords coming into the chamber. She raised her sword higher and braced for the attack.

"Mother!" Richard's voice boomed above the cacophony as he led the men streaming into the chamber.

Marian choked out a cry of relief and lowered her sword.

Eleanor approached Richard and drolly announced, "You are late to the battle, my son. Fortunately, Countess Marian has the heart of a warrior."

∽

The sun had set, and darkness was rising throughout the town of Lisieux, as Robin guided Prince John towards the villa of John de Alençon. They had just parted ways with Guy, who would wait for Robin at a nearby inn since he wanted to avoid a potentially fatal meeting with King Richard.

John, wearing a hooded cloak to conceal his identity, was in a highly agitated state, and he had often wavered between reconciling with Richard and returning to Philippe. Every time he dithered, Robin had implored, cajoled, and then demanded that the prince continue their journey to find Richard.

When they arrived, the archdeacon escorted John and Robin to the dining hall where Richard and Eleanor were sitting next to the hearth. They rose and silently observed John.

In a sudden rush, John ran to Richard and fell to his knees in front of his brother. With tears streaming down his face, he begged for mercy.

Robin found his loud sobbing and lamentations quite theatrical, and he noticed that Eleanor and Richard regarded him dispassionately.

Richard encouraged the distraught John to stand. He declared, "Don't be afraid, John. You are but a child led astray by evil counselors. I promise they will be punished for what they have done to you."

Richard and Eleanor had told Robin that their plan was to forgive John in order to regain control of him, and Robin was amused by Richard's condescending, dismissive words.

The king then addressed John de Alençon. "Earlier, the people of Lisieux presented me with a large salmon. I insist that it be prepared at once and served to my dear brother."

The archdeacon left to inform the kitchen.

As Eleanor drew near to John and began conversing with him, Richard led Robin to the corridor beyond the great hall.

Robin informed him, "Sire, I discovered that Montlhéry planned to poison John. It's fortunate that Gisborne was assisting me. He identified the threat, and his familiarity at the French court enabled us to move freely and thus, rescue Prince John from danger."

"Thank you, Robin. Despite John's betrayals, he's the only brother I have left. We cannot allow him to remain under Philippe's influence."

Robin understood, and he requested, "With your permission, I would like to see Marian before I leave in the morning to resume my search for Montlhéry. Philippe told Gisborne that Montlhéry had traveled to Barfleur. I suspect he is following you, looking for an opportunity to strike. With all due respect, Sire, are you taking precautions? Do you have enough men to protect you?"

"Come with me." Richard retrieved a torch, and handing it to Robin, the two men exited the villa and entered a nearby building. It was the wheelwright's shop, and in the center of the space, where the craftsmen would repair and fashion tack for the horses, was a long table. A body, covered by a length of fabric, was lying on it.

Robin walked to the table and lifted the cloth from the body's head. Holding his torch aloft, he recognized Montlhéry. There was a dark bruise on his temple and dried blood on his face. As Robin continued to pull back the cloth, he saw that the former sheriff's tunic and shirt had been removed, and he noted a bruise on his shoulder and multiple stab wounds in his stomach and chest. Deep scratches marked his forearm.

Robin remarked, "It looks as though he fought to the end, but I'm surprised that he put himself in harm's way. It's not in keeping with his usual methods. After all, poisoners are cowards. Did he and his men attack you directly?"

Richard barked a short laugh. "Montlhéry breached my security with a small force of men. But I cannot take credit for his defeat. I wasn't here when he attacked."

A perplexed Robin asked, "John de Alençon's men did this?"

Chuckling wryly, Richard explained, "My mother and your wife defeated Montlhéry without any help from the men who were supposed to be protecting them. I've always known that my mother was a warrior, but I'm very impressed with Countess Marian's bravery. I'm tempted to knight her myself."

20 May 1194, Villa of Archdeacon John de Alençon, Lisieux, Normandy

Robin watched as Marian finally stirred. It was morning, and he had spent most of the night sitting in a chair next to her bed, allowing her the rest that she needed after the events of the previous day.

He observed dark bruising around her neck, and it reminded him of Countess Isabel's injuries after Montlhéry had nearly choked her to death. He was in awe of Marian's fighting spirit, especially after Eleanor had told him all the details of what had happened.

"Robin?" Marian's dulcet voice snapped him out of his reverie.

He moved to the bed, and when she sat up, he gathered her in his arms and hugged her tightly. He was distressed when she began to sob, but he gently rocked her and waited until she settled.

"Are you all right?" he asked.

She nodded, and he helped her to stand. She briefly left him while she attended to her needs and dressed.

When she returned, she inquired, "Did they tell you what happened? That Eleanor and I killed Montlhéry?"

"Yes, I spoke to the queen last night. Marian, I'm so thankful that you are all right." He led her to a comfortable chair next to the hearth and encouraged her to sit as he knelt at her feet and cradled her hands in his.

She contemplated the glowing embers in the hearth for a few

moments. Refocusing on him, she revealed, "When he was dying, I was the last person he saw, and it occurred to me that Montlhéry was the last person my dear father saw on this side of heaven."

Robin considered her words as he silently wished he could have been the one to end Montlhéry's life.

"I keep telling myself that I should feel guilty. And that I should go to the nearest priest and confess. I know that vengeance belongs to the Lord, but I..." She glanced away.

"What is it? Marian, you can tell me anything."

After a pause, she looked at him and admitted, "I'm glad I helped kill him. Do you think I'll be damned to hell for that?"

Robin smiled tenderly and said, "Considering the bruises on your neck, and based on what the queen told me, I believe he intended to kill you."

"Yes, that's true."

"Then, you had no choice. God allows you to defend yourself." He placed his hand on her swollen belly. "And you were protecting our child, too."

Marian's face brightened. "You're right, of course." Then she sobered and declared, "Robin, I want to go home to Locksley. I miss Robbie."

He reached up and caressed her cheek. "I have good news. At my request, Eleanor and Richard have released us from our current obligations, and we'll begin our journey home today. We just need to retrieve Guy from the local inn, and we'll be on our way."

"But the queen wanted me to go with her to Poitiers."

"Richard made other arrangements for her travels. In fact, she has already left. Richard has departed for Verneuil, and John is returning to Évreux, where he hopes to retake the town for Richard."

Once more, Marian began to cry. "I can't seem to manage my emotions. I promise that these are tears of joy."

"I know," Robin replied. "Soon we will be back home with Robbie. And then we can welcome this child into our family." He swept his thumb across her cheek, wiping her tears away as he gazed at her lovingly. "The shadows that Montlhéry cast over our lives have retreated. We can now live in peace knowing that our future begins today. And whatever the future brings, we will face it together."

EPILOGUE

22 September 1197, Sherwood Forest, The Meadow near Locksley

obin relaxed as he sat in the shade with his back against the great oak that dominated one side of the meadow. Marian was sitting next to him, cradling Edith. In a few weeks, his daughter would celebrate the first anniversary of her birth.

Several yards away, eight-year-old Robbie and his three-year-old brother, Alfred, were throwing small stones at a tree. Every time little Alfred hit the tree, big brother Robbie would cheer him loudly.

"Boys, Edith is sleepy; please be quiet," admonished Marian.

Robbie countered, "But, Mama, the castle is ready to surrender."

Robin had wondered about the purpose of pelting a tree with rocks. Now it made more sense. The boys moved further away to mount a siege against a different tree, while Marian gently wrapped Edith in a length of warm fabric and laid her on a blanket.

Although the sun shone brightly, the autumn air was cool.

Marian sat facing him and asked, "When are you going to tell me about your journey? The longer you make me wait, the more worried I become that you are bearing bad news."

The previous day, Robin had returned from a trip to Rouen, and he had hoped that Marian would be more receptive to his news if she heard it while spending time in their favorite meadow.

Wishing to delay delivering the news from King Richard, Robin inquired, "I heard from Odella that you received a letter from Embelton while I was away. How is Uncle Edmund?"

"Edmund's gout has been bothering him, so he is resting and enjoying his grandchildren."

"How are the children? Is Lucienne still jealous of baby Edmund?"

Marian grinned. "Constance says that Lucienne is no longer jealous. Instead, she has become very possessive of her baby brother, and she wants to be his mother."

They chuckled in amusement for a few moments, and then she continued, "She also wrote that Guy has assumed all the duties of managing Embelton, and Edmund is very pleased by how well he is doing."

Robin announced, "Queen Eleanor asked about you, and I told her you've been busy handling the accounts for all my estates. I boasted that no one can manage a budget as well as you."

"Oh, no!" cried Marian in mock distress. "You should never tell her such stories about me, or she will force me into her service again. Besides, it's her fault our finances were so depleted. I'm merely working to restore what the crown took."

"Be at ease. Eleanor is living in an abbey, and she's not involved with any aspect of governing."

"But she was there, at the ceremony?"

"Yes," answered Robin. "Richard has formally recognized John as his heir. I was there as a witness, along with Earl Hamelin, Guillaume, and many other nobles. Oh, and Baldwin was there. It was good to see him again. He's leading Richard's army."

"I can't believe that the war with Philippe has continued for so long," Marian commented.

"Philippe is a wily opponent. When Richard meets him directly on the battlefield, the French are routinely defeated. However, Philippe creates distractions that require Richard and his army to fight on multiple fronts. I fear that Richard's men are stretched thin and lack the focus needed to win the war decisively."

She pondered this, and her gaze drifted to their sons, who were now roaming the meadow, collecting additional rocks. "Has the king given up on having a son of his own? Is that why he named John as his heir?"

"Baldwin told me that Richard has spent more time with Berengaria in the past year, but he fears that she is barren," explained Robin.

"I feel so sad for her. Do you think Richard might cast her aside for another queen?"

"That would be impossible. Although there are kings who have annulled a childless marriage on some pretext, Berengaria's brother is now King of Navarre, and he's a powerful ally in the war against Philippe. And with Richard's nephew, Arthur, living at the French court under Philippe's influence, John is really the only option as heir to the throne."

Marian hummed thoughtfully. She then said, "Speaking of heirs, I'm waiting to hear how Richard will resolve the issue of Robbie's legitimacy."

Watching his sons, Robin contemplated how the king's ruling would shape the rest of their lives. He returned his attention to Marian and admitted, "I did what I could. I fought for Robbie. Perhaps, if the war had ended quickly, Richard's decision would have been different."

Marian sighed. "Are you saying there is nothing more to be done?"

"Richard has decreed that Alfred is the heir to the Earldom of Huntingdon. But, it's not all bad news. With my consent, the king has granted Robbie the Barony of Lenton. I will administer the barony until he comes of age. Although Richard did not officially declare Robbie's legitimacy, he feels that, by bestowing this title on him, issues of his legitimacy will be obscured over time."

Tears of disappointment pooled in Marian's eyes, and she hastily wiped them away when they spilled down her cheeks. "But that's not fair."

"You're right; it's not fair, but I agree with something Richard said: Robbie will be a baron with a prosperous estate far from the court in London. We are free to proclaim his legitimacy locally. But in Richard's domains on the continent, Blanche's family would strenuously object. An earl has more responsibilities to the crown and duties at court. That's why Richard wants Alfred to be the next earl."

Marian speculated, "Perhaps over time, Blanche's family will become less important, or they might forget."

"I suppose that her family's objections might fade over time, but by accepting Richard's decision now, I can guarantee that Robbie will have a title and an estate with a steady income. I didn't want to reject a good solution in hopes of eventually securing a perfect one."

Marian frowned in disappointment, but in an effort to remain upbeat, she observed, "Robbie is so smart and charming. I believe he will win over anyone who questions his circumstances."

Robin reached out and took hold of her hand. Smiling affectionately, he declared, "With your good stewardship of our money, we will rebuild Lenton Manor in a grand style well before he is old enough to marry. In the end, Baron Robbie will make his own future, just as we all have to make our own future, regardless of the legacy we received from our parents."

The two fell into a thoughtful silence until Marian gazed intently into his eyes and asked, "Are you thinking about your legacy from Duncan?"

"I've often reflected on how my father's actions affected the course of my life. Or rather, our lives."

"You mean his duplicity in his dealings with King Stephen and William of Blois?"

"I'm thankful for the written confession that your father left hidden in the altar of the Lenton chapel, because we finally learned what happened at the time of King Stephen's death and at the siege of Toulouse," Robin remarked.

"I wish my father had not suffered such guilt over Duncan's actions," lamented Marian, "and you shouldn't accept any responsibility for what Duncan did all those years ago either."

"I agree. Likewise, Robbie is not to blame for my marriage to Blanche. Nevertheless, it has profoundly affected his future."

"I must accept some fault as well," Marian acknowledged. "I should have told you about his birth before you left for the Crusade."

"What's done is done. I'm just sorry that Robbie will pay a price for my sins." After another thoughtful pause, Robin concluded, "I suppose all parents are guilty of committing sins that cast shadows over the lives of their children. Each of us must accept that legacy while shaping our own future. We will help Robbie as much as we can, but ultimately, he will have to become master of his own fate. Considering his fearless and inquisitive nature, I'm certain that he will make us proud and lead a consequential life."

With those words, Robin drew Marian into his arms, and they sat together in quiet contentment, leaning against the trunk of the huge oak that still bore the faint carving of their initials. Around them, the great forest was beginning its annual transition from summer to autumn. Traces of red and gold were spreading along the edges of the leaves, but they would not fully change color or begin to fall for another month.

Robin closed his eyes and cherished the moment, thankful to God for his wife, his children, and the splendor of Sherwood Forest.

The End

❧

Visit our website to learn more about the Robin Hood Trilogy. You will find bonus materials relating to this book and articles about this fascinating, exciting time in history.

AngevinWorld.com

Glossary

Angevin

Originating from or belonging to the County of Anjou in France. Henry II's father had been Count of Anjou, and Henry ruled both England and vast continental territories, including Anjou. For this reason, Henry II, Richard the Lionheart, and John are referred to as the Angevin Kings of England, and their holdings are called the Angevin Empire. John lost control of these continental lands; thus, he is considered the last Angevin King of England. These three rulers are also referred to as the first Plantagenet kings.

antechamber

A chamber that serves as a waiting room and entrance to a larger room.

apothecary

A person with specialized knowledge of herbs, spices, and medicines. An apothecary would also be knowledgeable about poisons.

bailey

The courtyard of a castle. It's an open area enclosed by the castle wall.

barbican

An outer defensive area that protects the main gate of a castle.

berm

The area between the castle wall and the moat.

bliaut

A long outer tunic worn by both men and women. The bliaut had a full skirt, a fitted bodice, and sleeves which were fitted along the upper arm while flaring between the elbow and wrist. The lower part of the sleeve sometimes flared into a trumpet shape. The length of the men's version varied, but the women's bliaut would have been full-length. Women's tunics were also called gowns or kirtles.

bow *(bōh)*

A weapon that propels projectiles (arrows).

bow *(rhymes with how)*

1) Bending at the waist towards another person as a formal greeting. Typically performed between men of equal rank.

2) The front of a ship.

brace

In addition to the usual architectural meanings, a brace also refers to a pair. The phrase, "a brace of coneys," refers to two wild rabbits.

bracer

A bracer is wrapped around the forearm of an archer in order to protect the arm from the bowstring. Bracers were made from leather or horn.

braies

An undergarment that was made of linen and worn by men. Although underwear as we know it today was not worn, these would have been similar in that they were worn under other clothing.

brooch

A clasp or ornament with a hinged pin and a catch to secure the point of the pin on the back. In the 12th century, there were no buttons or zippers, so a brooch was an indispensable piece of jewelry for securing clothing, especially cloaks. Elaborate, jeweled brooches were a sign of wealth and status. Brooches were popular gifts.

by right of wife (jure uxoris)

During this time, a man could assume a title of nobility when he married a woman who held the title in her own right. He would also become the legal possessor of her lands.

camp ball

A popular game from the Middle Ages where opposing teams attempted to move a ball into a goal while fighting off their opponents. Also called football, although it is not the same as today's sports by that name.

Carentune

A town east of Nottingham which was mentioned in the Domesday Book of 1086. Today, the town is a suburb of Nottingham, and it is called Carlton.

castellan

A keeper or governor of a castle.

causeway

A road or path that is raised in order to cross a moat, marshland, sand, or similar impediments to travel.

chausses

Leggings or stockings. They could be made of either cloth or chain mail.

clandestine marriages

Before 1215, a couple could declare their intention to marry in front of witnesses, and if these vows were followed by consummation, canon law considered the couple to be legally wed.

coney

An older term referring to wild rabbits or hares.

courtier

An attendant at court, especially a person who spends a great deal of time attending the court of a king or other royal personage.

cross guard

For swords and daggers, this is positioned crosswise to the blade and between the grip and the blade. It protects the user's hand. See also: hilt, pommel, and grip.

curtain

Another name for the castle's outer wall surrounding the bailey.

curtsy

A formal gesture of greeting and respect made by women and girls consisting of bending the knees to lower the body while slightly bowing the head.

destrier

A large, strong war horse. Only wealthy lords and knights could afford them.

dowager

A widow whose title was obtained from her deceased husband.

Adding this modifier to a title distinguishes the widow from the wife of the man who currently holds the title.

dowry

Money or land given by the bride's family at the time of her marriage. If the girl entered a convent instead of marrying, the dowry would be given to the convent.

drawbridge

A bridge that can be raised to prevent access or lowered to allow passage of vehicles or pedestrians.

Ernehale

A town northeast of Nottingham which was mentioned in the Domesday Book of 1086. Today, the town is a suburb of Nottingham, and it is called Arnold.

ewer

A large earthenware jug or pitcher with a wide mouth.

fealty

Loyalty that a vassal owes to his lord. This often refers to the actual loyalty oath, as in "an oath of fealty."

Feudal System

This land-based economic and social system determined the rights and obligations of men. See also: fief, vassal, lord, liege, homage, and fealty.

fief

Land granted to a vassal for his use. In return, the vassal provided loyalty and service to the owner of the land. A fief could also be a payment instead of land.

fiefdom

Land owned by a noble or knight.

field

In heraldry, the background color of a coat of arms is called the field.

forthwith

An old word that actually dates to the 13th century. It means immediately, at once, without delay.

fortnight

A period of two weeks, or fourteen days.

gatehouse

A complex system of gates and towers which protected the entrance to a castle. See also: causeway, drawbridge, and portcullis.

genuflect

Briefly dropping to the right knee before rising. This was a formal greeting performed when in the presence of a man who is of superior rank. It is also performed towards the altar when in church.

great hall

Known as the heart of the living space in a castle, it was the location of feasts, and it was often the area where business was conducted. In earlier times, it was also where people slept.

grip

The part of sword or dagger that is gripped by the hand. See also: hilt, cross guard, and pommel.

hauberk

A chain mail shirt or tunic that protected the upper body, especially the neck and chest.

high table

An elevated table in the great hall where the lord, his family, and important guests were seated during feasts.

hilt

The handle of a sword or dagger. It is comprised of the cross guard, grip, and pommel (see the entries for these words for additional information). Hilt is often used interchangeably with grip.

homage

A declaration of loyalty from one man to another. The man declaring his loyalty would typically receive a fief in return. The first step in becoming a vassal is to pay homage to the lord.

homily

A sermon, usually on a Biblical topic.

infidel

For Christians, a person who is not a Christian. For Muslims, a person who is not a Muslim.

interdict

In the Roman Catholic Church, a decree by the Pope to exclude either a specific person or a group of people with something in common (for example, their location) from certain sacraments and other benefits, although not from communion.

justiciar

In medieval England, from the reign of William the Conqueror to Henry III, a justiciar was an important political and judicial officer who presided over the king's courts and performed consequential functions during the king's absence.

keep

The living area inside of a castle complex. It was a heavily guarded and fortified building or tower. The great hall would be located in the keep.

Knight Templar

A member of the "Poor Fellow-Soldiers of Christ and of the Temple of Solomon" (simplified to "The Order of the Temple of Solomon" in this book). A religious military order founded by Crusaders in Jerusalem around 1118 to defend the Holy Sepulcher and Christian pilgrims. Plural is Knights Templar.

Lent

A Christian season of fasting and penitence in preparation for Easter, beginning on Ash Wednesday and lasting 40 weekdays to Easter, observed annually.

liege lord

A feudal lord who is entitled to allegiance and service from his vassals.

lord

A landholder, typically a noble or the king, who granted fiefs (the use of land) to vassals (who were often knights, or even other nobles).

lute

A stringed musical instrument that is plucked to produce sound. It has a long, fretted neck and a hollow, pear-shaped body.

Maman

French word that translates to momma, mommy, mum, and similar informal versions of mother.

mantle

A long, loose cloak or cape usually worn over other clothing, similar in function to a modern overcoat.

Mass

A Catholic Church service which includes Holy Communion.

mêlée

A fight or brawl that is noisy, riotous, and disorganized.

men-at-arms

A general term for trained soldiers. Typically, they were trained like knights, but not all men-at-arms were knights.

Mère

French word that translates to mother. More formal than Maman.

Michaelmas

The Feast of Saint Michael was celebrated on September 29th. It also marked the end of the harvest season. It was considered a major feast that was observed as a holiday and required fasting on the previous day.

Midsummer

Also known as the Feast of Saint John the Baptist; it was celebrated on June 24th. It was considered a major feast that was observed as a holiday and required fasting on the previous day.

millstone

A heavy disc-shaped stone. Grain was placed between two millstones, and they were rotated against one another in order to grind the grain into flour.

minstrel

An entertainer. Minstrels were primarily performers. Although some wrote their own songs, they often sang songs composed by others, notably the troubadours. Minstrels also performed acrobatics, juggled, told jokes, and recited poems.

motte

An earthen mound, usually artificial. These mounds were often created in order to build a defensive structure, such as a castle, on higher ground for strategic purposes.

Nine Men's Morris

A popular strategy board game for two players that dates back to Ancient Rome, perhaps even earlier.

obeisance

Giving proper respect and deference to someone of superior rank. Typically this would require kneeling (see genuflect), bowing, or curtsying.

Outremer

A French word meaning, "overseas." Used as a name for the Crusader States, especially the Kingdom of Jerusalem, after the First Crusade.

page

A boy in training to become a knight. He would progress from page to squire to knight.

palfrey

A horse used for everyday riding. These smaller horses were often ridden by women.

paper

A word originating from the Latin *papyrus*. It was composed of varying fibers which had been pounded into a pulp and then spread out and dried flat. It was not long-lasting, so it was used for documents without much importance.

parchment

Animal skin that has been processed to use as a writing surface. It was typically sheepskin, and it was also used to cover windows before the widespread use of glass. It was reserved for important or official documents. Less expensive forms of paper were also available. See: **paper**.

physician

A university educated doctor.

pilgrimage

A religious journey to a holy place.

Plantagenet

This became the family name of Geoffrey V, Count of Anjou. Reputedly this name was given to him due to his habit of wearing a sprig of yellow broom blossoms (in Latin: *planta genista*) in his hair. Geoffrey's descendants would rule England from 1154 to 1485 as the Plantagenet dynasty.

Poitevin

Originating from or belonging to the County of Poitou in France.

pommel

1) A knob attached to the end of the grip in swords and daggers. It provided a counter balance to the blade, and it helped the user maintain a better hold on the weapon because it prevented the hand from sliding off the grip. See also: hilt, cross guard, and grip.

2) A knob at the front of a saddle.

portcullis

A heavy gate that was raised and lowered to control entry into the grounds of a castle. It was part of the gatehouse. A portcullis was composed of crossed bars, forming a grate or grille. The bottom edge consisted of spikes.

postern gate

A small door hidden in the castle wall that allowed soldiers to enter and exit the castle grounds without using the main gate. This was useful during sieges. Typically, a postern gate was only large enough to allow the passage of one man at a time.

Saracen

During this time period, Muslims, particularly Arab Muslims, were called Saracens.

scabbard

A rigid sheath made of wood, metal, or hardened leather. It is used to enclose and carry the blade of sword or dagger, both to protect the wearer and to keep the blade clean and sound.

sennight

A period of one week, or seven days.

shire

A county in England, typically combined with the name of the shire to form a single word: Nottinghamshire.

Shrove Tuesday

An important movable feast that always falls on the day before Ash Wednesday (which is the first day of Lent). Although repentance of sins is considered an integral part of Shrove Tuesday observations, it was frequently seen as the last opportunity to engage in merriment before the start of the somber Lenten season. In the Middle Ages, feasting and games were popular activities on Shrove Tuesday.

Sire

The form of direct address used for royalty prior to the 16th century. "Your Grace" was also used for royalty and high-ranking clergy.

solar

Inside a castle tower, this room (or suite of rooms) was the primary living area for a lord and his family, and it provided them with some measure of privacy.

squire

A boy in training to be a knight. He would progress from page to squire to knight.

staff

A traditional pole-shaped weapon popular in England during the Middle Ages. It was made of hardwood and was typically 6 to 9 feet (1.8 to 2.7 m) long. It was also called a quarterstaff or a short staff.

surcoat

This sleeveless cloth tunic was worn over chain mail. Heraldry symbols were often sewn onto the chest of the surcoat. For example, Crusaders often wore white surcoats with a red cross emblazoned on the chest.

tack

Saddles, stirrups, bridles, halters, reins, bits, harnesses, and so forth. The equipment and accessories needed for horseback riding and for hitching horses to wagons and carts.

Templar

See: Knight Templar.

tournament

A sporting event that allowed knights to demonstrate and hone their skills. Tournaments also provided an opportunity for knights to build wealth from winnings.

trebuchet

A powerful type of catapult that throws a projectile using a sling attached to a swinging arm. A counterweight is used to swing the arm, giving greater force and speed to the projectiles that are hurled towards the enemy.

trestle table

A table composed of a removable top supported by trestles (A-frame supports with horizontal beams at the top). This type of table could be easily moved around or stored when not needed.

troubadour

A poet and songwriter. Troubadours sometimes performed, but they were primarily seen as composers. They were sometimes from noble families.

Truce of God

Originally a papal edict that was intended to discourage fighting amongst Christians, it also protected Crusaders from attack and allowed them to travel in peace within Christian domains as they made their way to and from the Holy Land.

vassal

When a man swore loyalty to a noble landowner in return for use of that land (a fief), he became a vassal of the lord. A vassal was expected to provide services to the lord whenever needed. A vassal might be required to go to war and fight for his lord. If the vassal could not go to war, he would have to provide a substitute to fulfill his vassalage. Although it is often thought of in terms of lower ranking men, such as knights, anyone could be a vassal. Henry II was King of England, but he was also Duke of Normandy (and many other noble titles). As Duke of Normandy, Henry paid homage to King Louis VII of France; thus, he was also Louis' vassal. The same was true for King Richard; as Duke of Normandy, he was King Philippe's vassal.

vestry

A small room in a church used for storage of items such as vestments, sacred vessels, and other worship-related supplies and accessories.

waning

When the illumination of the moon is decreasing; the time between a full moon and a new moon.

ward

A person who has been placed under the control and protection of a guardian. In 12th century England, if the child of a noble family became an orphan, the child automatically became a ward of the king. This would include unmarried daughters, regardless of their age.

waxing

When the illumination of the moon is increasing; the time between a new moon and a full moon.

wheelwright

A craftsman who builds and repairs wooden wheels.

wimple

A medieval headdress worn by women, typically married women. It covered the top of the head and wrapped around the neck and chin.

wound fever

An infection.

Printed in Great Britain
by Amazon

66655725R00215